To my aunt Olga,
It's never too late to learn the secrets of the [illegible]

Enjoy
your nephew
Maurer 7/22

The Fourth Level Series:

Book One:

The Neufied Anomaly

By Mariner Pezza

Creative Consultant – Cheryl E. Kemeny

Title: The Neufield Anomaly

Series: The Fourth Level

ISBN 978-1-7376248-0-6

Table of Contents

Preface:

The following is a compilation of notes and writings accumulated by key players in the Earth's rise to the "Fourth Level" – a standard of technological achievement as defined by other interested parties, not we Earthers. This is the story as best as I can reconstruct.

My name is Jack Neufield, and I'm one of the prime movers, if inadvertently. I mean, who wakes up in the morning and says, "I'm going to change the world?" Not me, though I did. But I was not alone – there was Janey, Mr. McEvey, Sara, and many others. And I can't take all that much credit; the Earth was ready. That's just the way of innovation, it happens when the time is ripe.

I assume the responsibility for the truth of what follows; I would bet that the credibility is high. Most definitely in the sections that I was part of, though the recalled dialog may not be perfect, yet the gist is there. And all the other contributors are decent people, or beings, as the case may be. I must admit that my primary goal in writing these chronicles was to alleviate boredom rather than inform the world. Especially during my times of "enforced confinement," shall we say. The point being, there was no higher purpose. I sought to while away the time rather than write the greatest masterpiece ever. And whether the content is worth the time . . . well, I'll let you, the reader, decide.

Jack Neufield

Chapter 1: Outbound – *Jack Neufield*

I heard the sirens in the distance. Many sirens. That's because many cops were after my ass. Why do they have to sound like screams of anguish? Why can't they be something more pleasant, like the sounds of wind chimes? Maybe, it's to signal the poor bastard they're after that a whole lot of pain and suffering was coming his way. Provide a little preview of upcoming events. And from the size of the chorus, I had to assume that the amount would be considerable. You see, the authorities around here don't like thieves very much, especially if they steal radioactive isotopes. Plus, this is the age of terrorism. Terrorists are in the news every day, and the Feds think I'm one of those too. And they like terrorists even less than they like thieves.

So, the chase was on, and I was the prey. Everyone's adrenalin was all jacked up, hearts thumping, pulses pounding. And the poor bastard racing down the highway was me, just trying to get home. But I figured I could win this race. You see, I was on my bike, and nobody catches me when I'm on two wheels. That's a fact. It's a Yamaha TW 200 Dual Sport. A dirt bike. And it'll go anywhere I point it – backyards, woods, stairs, anywhere. I bought it for 900 bucks from Mr. McEvey. Had to get new tires, but still, it was a good deal.

Maybe they don't know where my home is? Maybe I'd be safe there? No way, foolish hope. They had my plates; they had my face and probably even my DNA. So, what's the rush, you may ask? Why didn't I just pull over, say at a bus stop, have a seat, take out a toothpick and wait for them to come and take me away? You can't beat radios. The answer is – because I still had a chance. The damn thing might work. That was my one hope. But only if there was enough time to load the fuel, rev it up, and . . . lift-off? I just wanted to see if something happened when I flipped the switch. Was that asking too much? Ergo, I was flying down the highway traveling at the speed of light while listening to the pounding of my pulse in my brain.

And what did I do to make every cop, fed, and law enforcement agency in the state rabidly seek my, uh, incarceration? I'll tell you; I've got time. Plus, they gave me a pad and a pen, and boredom is always the enemy. You see, Janey and I had it all set up. She worked at Yale-New Haven Hospital, the Nuclear Medicine Division. They store every kind of isotope there and use it to diagnose and treat diseases. Nuclear science is put to good use there; it's not just for making bombs. Well, Janey had access to all that stuff, and she would have taken it again, too, just like all the other times. But before, they were small amounts and weak – alpha particle emitters. A piece of paper will stop an alpha particle. This time was different. Cobalt 60 is bad, very dangerous, and very radioactive. And that's why I needed it. It's used to sterilize surgical instruments because it kills. And it gives off alpha, beta, and gamma radiation. Beta rays are electrons shooting around real fast but easily blocked. A sheet of aluminum will stop a beta ray.

On the other hand, gamma rays are no joke. They'll go through anything and do damage. I didn't want Janey handling that stuff even though it came in a shielded container. And the caper itself was too risky. She'd lose much more than her job, likely her freedom as well. Besides, it was about time I started shouldering some responsibility. At least, that's what everybody was telling me.

So, Janey knew the place. After all, she worked there. She copied the key to the storage room and gave me the combination to the vault. She even stood guard down the hall, signaling the ok. I wore one of those white doctor's smocks. It came with a stethoscope and a badge. I felt like a fool wearing a stethoscope. *Do doctors still use them?* And I felt like a real criminal because this was a premeditated crime. For some reason, they're worse. I guess law enforcement prefers the more thoughtless crimes, probably easier to solve.

A long journey starts with a small step. I took that step, then a second, then a third . . . and just did it. Committed the crime. But basically, it was for the greater good. I was really on to something. Getting results, serious positive results. What I built could be the greatest boon to humanity since the discovery of electricity. I told myself this often. Too bad Mr. McEvey wasn't here to share in the triumph . . . or debacle, as the case may be. But this story hasn't played out yet. Not all the way. And Albert might still be out there.

The whole thing should have been a cinch, in and out, bing bang boom – done. Just walk in, grab the container, put it in a bag, and walk out, nice, and nonchalant. I actually planned to return the isotope when I was done. Reverse the crime. That stuff is too dangerous to keep lying around, and besides, it was evidence. What if they missed it and then started an investigation? Second, Cobalt 60 doesn't go bad. It's got a half-life of five and a quarter years. Therefore, no harm done. Oh, maybe I'd get a little sunburn. A small price to pay and worth it. If my math was right, the more radioactive the isotope, the better it should work. Provide more lift; get the darn thing off the ground. Prove the concept and . . . mitigate the crime. As it turned out, the numbers didn't lie. Only, and here's the thing – they went parabolic.

The hospital must have recently installed some kind of security, maybe motion detectors. Janey didn't know, and I didn't see anything. Well, the hospital alarms went off big time. They alternated with announcements, "Security, please report to Level 3." Alarms without announcements could be misconstrued to mean fire. And management most certainly did not want a panic based on the belief that the hospital was on fire. The patients hobbling around all hysterical. Also, they had to mobilize Hospital Security, which was easier said than done. The fact is, when one has nothing to do all day except to stand around and do nothing, one gets pretty lax, mentally, and physically. I mean, the body and mind wind down. They atrophy. It's a natural process called entropy. Even the Universe does it, but then it's called the second law of thermodynamics.

Therefore, the alarms, coupled with the calls for Security, were like a cattle prod to the guards lounging around in the break room. Coffee cups went flying, donuts were left half-eaten, paraphernalia was strapped on, and they flew through the doors, some into the doors, some into each other, but generally out there, eager to keep the hospital safe. *(Postscript: the above was pure speculation. If you are offended as a professional security guard, please send your objections to Dept. of Homeland Security, Washington, DC, re- Jack Neufield. Post postscript. I was a security guard once.)*

So, that's what I had to contend with. A bevy of semi-panicked, red-faced, wide-eyed hospital mall-cops running around looking for something wrong. I could have been smart and bluffed my way through, all suave and cool. But no, I was dumb. I panicked too. Now, after the fact, one thinks of all the things one should have said or done. I had a bad case of the "What I should have said or done blues." Everything would have been so great if I had only . . .

The easiest course of action would have been to act all freaked out. Like the "perp" had just knocked me down as he was running by. I'd pull out my shirt, toss the stethoscope, then point and say, "He went that way." That would have worked for sure. I saw something like that happen in the movies once.

Or I could have taken the tech guy approach. Ditch the smock, slap a visitor's sticker on my company shirt, and then pretend to be some kind of geek carrying his bag of tools. All casual and unconcerned. Though, this would have required some considerable premeditation on my part. The premeditation of a sophisticated criminal, which I basically am not. But I should have done it anyway. And when the hospital cops came, I would have said, "False alarm boys . . . we're just testing the system." And wave goodbye as I casually walked out the front door.

But no to all of the above. What I did, being the unsophisticated criminal that I am, was panic. The panic of the caught. And I ran with the speed of fear before a tidal wave of guilt. I ran so fast that the security boys simply stepped aside, mouths agape. My bike was parked out front. I could always find a good parking spot for my bike. I hopped on, started her up, hefted the container into the basket in the back, and zoomed off. No doubt, they got my plate, my picture, and everything else. The mall-cops that is. I guess, in the end, they did their job.

I knew the best route home. I'd only driven it about a hundred times, taking Janey to work, picking her up, and going to various nursing functions; dinners, awards ceremonies, and such. For those occasions, sometimes I'd sneak out my father's old Mercedes. It was a 1965 300 SE, burgundy, big shiny front grille, tan leather, and a wood burl interior. A little ridiculous, but still the definition of class. We felt like a million bucks driving around in that thing. And my father must have known. The car came with an odometer – standard equipment. This time the drive home would be different.

My only hope was to get home fast. The straightest route, the fastest speed, the least time. And no time for niceties, like stop signs or red lights. No way. Just get from point A to point B post haste. And that meant going on the main roads, but that's where the roadblocks would be. Though, in my eleven years of driving, I've never seen an actual roadblock; spot checks, yes, roadblocks, no. On TV, the police get a call, and five minutes later, the roadblocks are all set up everywhere. So, where would the barriers be? Not on Route 8. That's a 6-lane highway. They can't block that off. I figured either on Watertown Road or Route 63 because they're small and lonely. And what do I do if I see one? Go around, off-road. But what if they shoot? Then I'll zigzag. Those were the thoughts that first went through my head. *Nothing like a crisis to concentrate the mind.*

Bottom line — I needed to get home fast. Usually, the trip would take about 30 minutes. I needed 10 minutes to start the . . . *thing*. Funny, I never knew what to call . . . what we built. A flying saucer? No, far from it. "My conveyance"? That's what Albert called it. I liked that. Only, without fuel, it was incapable of conveying anyone anywhere. However, previous versions did lose weight. But I digress.

The trip usually took about 30 minutes. Therefore, it would take the cops, the Feds, Homeland Security, and everybody else at least 30 minutes, probably longer. Ten minutes is what I needed to start the thing. Therefore, I had to shave at least 10 minutes off my travel time. I could do that. I had the technology. It's called Yamaha. I ran every stop sign, every red light, and on the highways, I opened her up. I must have been doing 110, though that's only a guess. My speedometer was broke. The wind whipped my hair, the tears streamed back as I raced down the highway. Unfortunately for me, there was a slight flaw in my plan. Motorcycles can't beat radios. The local cops were there waiting for me.

I may have failed to consider radio waves in the first few seconds of my analysis. But they were my primary focus for the next several minutes. Logic dictated that the local "boys in blue" would be ordered to stake out my home – to watch and report only. Not to act. Not under any circumstances. The big boys would want all the glory. It was their party; no gatecrashers allowed. Terrorists make careers.

So, what was the solution? Sneak in. That was the new plan. I would kill the bike's headlight a quarter mile out, then go off-road. The neighboring farms were riddled with dirt roads, paths, and fields, and I knew them all. Plus, the Moon was straight up and half full. It was a good night for lunatics.

Janey lived two farms down. The girl next door, literally. She kept her bicycle in a shed behind the house. It was an old Schwinn, a real dinosaur on two wheels. That became my new destination – her bike in the shed. I'd dump mine in the woods, run in, grab hers, and then ride the rest of the way nice and quiet. Through the back paths as silent as a . . . truth be told, her bike made a lot of noise, clanks, and so forth.

I pulled it off. That part of the plan worked as planned.

In retrospect, I must say, I never actually confirmed the stakeout. It's conceivable that this entire analysis was a fantasy. No way. I heard the alarms, and I heard the sirens. They were not some kind of an air-raid test. That happens only on Saturdays at noon. Besides, they don't do that anymore.

I snuck into my farm through the backfield. It was all grown over; King Kong could muck around back there unnoticed. I looked around and saw no indication of surveillance. Not the glow of a cigarette, the murmur of voices, the crackle of a radio, or the wild solo of a lead guitar. You have to understand, I live in Litchfield, Connecticut. There's not much crime there. The local gendarmes have radios, all kinds, and are liable to use them – for entertainment.

I snuck in the back door and kept the lights off. My parents were overseas doing their "Doctors Without Borders" thing. We had a small farm. They lived in the house; I rented the barn. A very copasetic arrangement. And the barn served as my workshop and living area. There was a silo next door. That's where I built my uh . . . conveyance. Janey called it the flywheel. I liked that appellation as well.

You know my name, Jack Neufield, and not much else. This may be a good time to tell a little more. I'm a generous 5'-9", fair complexion and hair, normal build, not handsome, not ugly – somewhere in between. The big sculptor in the sky had a dull chisel when he made me. But I liked the look, and it had its advantages. One is the ability to blend in. People neither approached nor avoided me. I could be somewhere and not be noticed. Though it made for difficulties in catching a waiter's eye. However, being left alone has its benefits, which leads me to my major flaw – I can't leave well enough alone. That's partly due to my inherent curiosity and partly due to Mr. McEvey.

Mr. McEvey was the one person most responsible for me being where I am today . . . in prison. He was my home school, science teacher. His real job was teaching physics at the local college. You see, my public-school career was rather abruptly terminated in the third grade by mutual agreement, mostly theirs.

Dr. John Neufield Sr. and his lovely nurse wife Rebecca were forced to scramble and concoct some way for their darling son Jack to get educated. They fixed up the barn, enrolled me in an online school, and hired a couple of tutors. Mr. McEvey for science and math, and Miss Murphy for everything else – including the visual arts, something I really liked. They came over two afternoons a week, and my parents were home on Tuesdays. It worked out great, and I loved it.

Miss Murphy was my former second-grade teacher. She liked me and simply could not comprehend the misfortune that concluded my public-school career. And I liked her too. In truth, I had a crush on her – secretly, of course. She was short, maybe five feet one or two, cute round face, bright dark eyes, brunette hair flipped on the shoulders, and a big smile always quick and ready. And she was single. I had our future all mapped out, 'till Janey started coming around. I credit Miss Murphy for teaching me about words. Their importance and how they can mean many things. Also, I must thank her for teaching me – art. She taught me how to paint. I do non-terrestrial landscapes. They're way out. And I have a wealth of material to work with . . . these days.

So, what did I build? I'm coming to that. But why did I build it? I think that's the more important question, and the answer is, again – Mr. McEvey. He was a "YouTuber." That's the best way to describe him. He's got this singing cat and uploaded . . . wrong. But that's probably how you know YouTube. It's not just for wacky cat videos. It's where would-be inventors go to show their work. Who can afford a patent attorney? We video our stuff then upload it. And it comes in every conceivable category, from kitchen utensils to plasma generators, you name it. But after a little browsing, certain subjects tend to stand out. Like free energy. Everybody is looking for a new source of cheap, clean energy. And anti-gravity; everybody wants to fly. And don't laugh – perpetual motion. Check it out; you'll see what I mean.

And there's an "in your face" attitude to all these videos. Most are trying to do what the brainiacs say can't be done. In the comments section, you'll find the inevitable skeptics: "This violates the law of conservation of energy"; or mass, or whatever, they always have a reason. You know it's some egghead, looking down his nose, parroting what he heard in a lecture hall somewhere, the established groupthink. But that just adds fuel to the fire. It's always more fun to do what you're not supposed to.

Mr. M. lived in an apartment, a small one. I had a barn, a big one, basically all to myself. One plus one equals three. It became our workshop. Primarily his at first, though it didn't take long for me to become "absorbed," shall we say. But it was a good addiction, not a bad one like, say, motorcycle jumping. But I do that too, once in a while.

I carefully entered the silo through the back door. And there it was . . . my conveyance. The big wheel. That's what it was, I guess. Only not vertical, but sideways. I had reinvented the wheel, independently, just like every other civilization starting about 6000 years ago except for the Egyptians. They built the Pyramids without it. How? Who knows, big mystery. But everyone else had the wheel – the Sumerians, the Mesopotamians and . . . whoever the hell else was out there building all those UFOs. They're always round and spinning. As a matter of fact, everything in the Universe is round and spinning. Even the atoms in it. *Don't be a smart-ass and point out the exceptions.* So, what did I build? You're right, something that's round and spins.

It looked like a big wagon wheel. Like it came off one of those prairie clippers – a Conestoga wagon. It had a rim, spokes, and a hub, the whole thing being about 18 feet across. Up in Brewster, N.Y., there's this amusement park graveyard. It was my second home. They have everything there – cheap. Mr. M. and I loved to poke around in there. You can find damn near anything you want. Get your kid a merry-go-round horse. Bring it home, set it up, and be the best dad in the world – for 10 bucks. And that's where I got the hub, off an old Ferris wheel. It was a pod, an oblong plastic bubble with a door and bench seat in it. I took the arms off a little kid's boat ride and used them for the spokes. They were aluminum and pretty lightweight. Weight was a factor since the intent was for the thing to go up, as in elevate. And I used three layers of drainage pipe, one of steel, two of plastic, for the outer rim. Got them off construction sites, but I always paid . . . somebody something.

The sirens were back. I heard them off in the distance. Howls from the hounds of hell, and they were howling for me. It would have been nice to test the thing, a little at a time. Start small, get results, then scale it up – gradually. And I did get results; as I said, smaller versions lost weight, which is not exactly flying. But I figured with extra power and a more potent isotope, the magnetic-weak force reaction would increase, and the conveyance might just get off the ground, as in fly. And this wasn't bullshit, hit or miss, try this, or try that. I had a theory – "4,3". But that's all I can say or will say. Because that's what the government wants, desperately. And I won't tell . . . at least, not yet.

I had a premonition a while back. That this was going to be a one-shot deal. Bet the farm and roll the dice. So, for power, I threw in everything I could think of. The more power, volts, and amps, the more magnetism. Maxwell's equations in action. There was a tragedy in town, a car wreck – a Tesla Model S. A crying shame to lose such a beautiful machine. I got the batteries off that. Cost me a pretty penny too. Fuel cells? Mr. M. and I have been monkeying around with them for years. I made up a stack, maybe two hundred. Thank God Janey helped. The platinum catalyst cost a pretty penny too. And on top of that, I was going to jump-start the coils with the house current – all 200 amps at 220 volts. That combination, coupled with the mondo radioactivity and well, the thing should do . . . I don't know what. No time to test it. *No time for niceties.*

I converted all the power to direct current, the best kind for electromagnets. And the strategically placed light sensors controlled the power, which periodically turned the coils on and off, causing the fuel inside to spin faster and faster. The faster, the better. I programmed my laptop for that chore and, basically, to control everything. I figured with that much power, rpm's, and radioactivity; the thing had to do something. Hopefully, not nothing. And hopefully, not explode either.

Money? Where did I get the money to do this? Money was always a problem. There was the occasional part-time job, and Mr. M. got me some work around the college. Electrical work mostly as a contractor. He lied and said I was licensed. We're bad, but you already know that. However, my primary source of remuneration, i.e., money – came from the "Springz." A few years back, in my young adult years, I invented these spring shoes. It took me a year, then another three months to write the patent. Mr. M. was still around for that project.

It's funny how that venture got started. Where do thoughts and ideas come from, anyway? From God? The kings of old were told as much and firmly believed it. They called it the divine right of kings. Presumably, His Majesty was directly connected to the Big

Guy. In any case, I figured there had to be a better way to walk, jog, or even run. Especially since I was a jogger, and the jarring impact of my foot with the ground shocked the hell out of my knees. Ergo, the objective of the project was to capture, store, and release all that wasted energy. Maybe I had watched too many cartoons as a kid. Anyway, I was driven to solve this problem, like a command from an alien power.

I came up with this z-shaped frame, in which I fitted springs to the front and rear. Conventional springs didn't work; had to invent new ones to meet the fun factor. Inventions within the invention if you will. I bent sheet metal forms and melted the nylon parts in a toaster oven, then put it all together with a whole lot of fiddling and a few hundred rubber bands. And praise the Lord, they worked. And they were fun too. Janey loved them, and so did I. After I got the patent, a late-night TV guy called, and we worked out a deal. He got a Chinese company to make them; if you have insomnia and watch a lot of television, you may have seen the crazy commercials. I had dreams of making some real money until the lawsuits began. People started breaking their ankles, but not because the freakin' things were defective. Hey, people are breaking their ankles on roller skates every day and on ice skates too. That didn't matter. They sued anyway. Poof went my dreams for big money. I still get a trickle of royalties. In a good month, sometimes in the low four figures. That's how I got my money.

I walked over to the outer ring. It was made up of a layer of steel and two layers of plastic drainage pipe. I had wrapped the steel pipe with a layer of neodymium ribbon to beef up the flux. That was the core, which I covered with a plastic conduit. I wound that with copper tubing, which formed the electromagnets. A series of them. An outer layer of heavy gauge black polystyrene pipe encased it all and protected everything inside. Essentially it was a series of big coils wrapped around a paramagnetic core. The point being: to create magnetism – a whole lot of rotating magnetic flux in the center of the ring. For what purpose? To propel a ferromagnetic isotope around inside – fast. The faster, the better.

In the outer ring was a small trap door, the place for the fuel – the Cobalt 60. I opened the shielded container and saw these silvery shards in there. I threw them all in. *No time for . . .* Then rushed back to the pod. You don't want to linger around Cobalt 60, not unless you have cancer . . . or want to get it.

A glance out the front door revealed a red glow in the sky. And the glow carried the screaming sounds of my pursuers. I sat in the pod, flipped on the lights, opened the heat vents on the fuel cells, and took a deep breath. This was it. If it went up, even an inch, they could take me away happy. What if nothing happens? That would be worse than an explosion. An explosion is something. Nothing is nothing, except for the fact that it would change my name from Jack Neufield to Asshole Neufield for the rest of my life. *Nothing like a crisis to focus the mind.*

I flipped the switch. Nothing happened at first. Then I heard a rattle, the shards of Cobalt banging around in the ring. A dim glow filled the room. It grew brighter, and the rattle became louder – more like a roar. Suddenly, I was thrown back against the bench. It was hard, no headrest, no cushions; I was transfixed like a bug on a board. There was a crash, more like an explosion. Hooray! Something was happening. That was my first thought. I looked up and saw the night sky? "What the freak?" was my second thought. The wicked vibration ceased, and so did the G's, but I still heard the wind whipping by. I looked down and saw lights slowly retreating. It was the parking lot in Litchfield Center. And in the distance, I saw headlights creeping along a highway – Route 202? Should I cut the power? And then what? Fall like a stone from what looked to be – a thousand feet? I had another bad case of the "What I should have done blues." In this case, I should have built in some controls. Like – steering! And maybe pack a parachute. But shit, I just wanted to see if the damn thing would hover a few inches. What happened was way beyond my worst nightmare.

The acceleration seemed to continue, only it felt like I was still sitting in my living room. But definitely, the dots of light were receding, and the view was expanding. I pulled out my laptop, maybe I could do something, but I was too spellbound by the view. The lights of New York City hung in the distance. Gleaming tall buildings surrounded by sparkling bridges. Then even they got smaller. I felt the clammy fingers of panic grab my chest, but what could I do? Open the door and jump? I started to punch keys on the computer, but it was impossible to tear my eyes from the scene before me. Within minutes, the outline of the eastern seaboard took shape, next to an ocean dappled in silvery moonlight. It was a beautiful sight. Then the curvature of the Earth itself was visible. It was about then that my breathing became difficult, so I reached down and disconnected the oxygen line to the fuel cells, and the pod filled with that life-giving essence. I heard a hiss. Air was leaking, so I duct-taped the door. But it was kind of self-sealing since it opened in.

Beyond the pod was darkness. The darkness of Space pinpointed by brilliant specks of light. *Stars?* So, I had heat and air. Big deal. There was zero control, and the thing was still accelerating. Still accelerating? If I managed to stop it, then what? Float endlessly in space? I looked back and saw the Earth receding. How fast was I going? Could I turn this thing around, and at least . . . die on Earth?

What difference would that make? I was a goner; I knew that then. Well, it was a good life, short but good. I had a worthwhile purpose and the best possible woman to share it with. So be it. The blackness closed in on me, and my thoughts stopped.

Sometime later, I regained consciousness and opened my eyes. The Moon completely dominated my forward view. Was I going to crash on the Moon? That would be my claim to fame, "Jack Neufield, the first dead guy on the Moon." But up close, the Moon was fascinating. Huge craters everywhere, vast plains, and tall mountains. It was a dull yellow, sprinkled with splotches of color – oranges and blues. And the shadows were as black as Space. Odd, but very interesting. Frankly, I couldn't believe that my conveyance had made it this far. I mean, it was put together with construction glue and sheetrock screws. My disbelief was very soon to be justified as the outer ring began to break up. Sections simply separated as we whipped around to the far side. At that point, I was almost frozen stiff, and breathing became a very difficult thing to do. I knew I didn't have long. Then a beam of light inundated the pod. They say you see a corridor of light when you go. White light, not blue! No matter, I figured this was it for me. Sayonara. I don't know why I chose that particular word, "sayonara," but that was my last thought. Then.

Chapter 2: The Space-Based Edifice – *Jack*

I opened my eyes and thought I was dead. It looked like heaven. All was white, at least the floor, there being no walls or ceiling, just an endless whiteness. White machines with peculiar arms were positioned around me, attended to by white, non-descript figures. Were they Angels?

"Hey, where am I?" I nervously asked. No answer, no response. The figures ignored me. Maybe they don't respond to the newly . . . arrived. A dark smudge coalesced in the distance. It was easy to see, being the only object of color in sight. It grew larger, materializing into an individual; two arms, two legs, and a head. Its movements were slow and steady but seemed to cover a considerable distance, like someone walking on a moving sidewalk. Apparently, it was easy to get around up here. As it approached, it took on form and identity. To my complete and utter astonishment, it bore a striking resemblance to – Albert Einstein?

Albert Einstein has always been one of my favorite people, right up there with da Vinci, Edison, and Tesla. During my childhood years, I remember his poster hanging on my bedroom wall; the warm kindly eyes, bushy mustache, and the flyaway hair extending like antennae tuned to the universe. And there he was, standing before me, the man in the poster wearing the same dark suit, vest, and winged collar. He was smiling, smoking a pipe, and leaning on a cane.

"Mr. Jack Neufield, welcome and . . . please permit me to inform you . . . that this is not heaven," he said this matter-of-factly with a twinkle in his eye. His voice was even and well-modulated.

Not the voice of an elderly man. He puffed on his pipe. *How did he know what I was thinking?*

"Albert Ein . . . ? You mean I'm not dead?" I stammered.

"Correct . . . you are not dead. You are on a space-based edifice, Jack. May I call you, Jack?" I nodded. *And he knows my name*?

"As you may remember, Jack, your craft was careening towards your planet's moon. We are positioned behind it and observed your impending disintegration. The determination was made to extract you since your . . . conveyance demonstrated a rudimentary application of Fourth Level Technology."

"Demonstrated a . . . How can you . . . I mean . . . Albert Ein . . . be here?" This was all I managed to blurt out.

"I'm not Albert Einstein, Jack. I represent this artifact, or . . . *Ship* as you may call it. We observed the favorable images of Mr. Einstein in your memory and presented our self as such. We want to allay your fears and establish communication because, Jack, you are an anomaly. You are the only person on Earth who has demonstrated knowledge of this particular level of technology. We want to know why that is. We must know why that is." He said this last part more emphatically, forcefully even, as he expelled a few puffs of smoke.

Of all the questions that exploded in my mind, I managed to ask just one: "Why?"

"Because we are forbidden contact or interference of any kind, with embryonic civilizations such as yours, Jack. But, since you employed a gravitic nullification mechanism in your conveyance, we were compelled to intercede and affect your rescue. Entities such as myself have many tasks, one being to induct civilizations into our "Continuum" when they exhibit the degree of technical knowledge we define as "Fourth Level Technology." You did Jack . . . to a certain, limited extent." He blew some smoke rings upwards with considerable proficiency.

"What's Fourth Level Technology?" I asked, feeling like a fool since I had ostensibly employed it.

"Please permit me the impoliteness of answering your question with an interrogatory of some considerable relevance to us. Have you ever wondered why there are 4 and 3?"

That was the question? Why 4 and 3? After a moment of complete befuddlement, a scene replayed in my mind. I was back in my barn with Mr. McEvey. We were talking about the Universe. We often mused about the big picture – what it was all about. I guess that's what science is for. And Mr. M. had an easy way of explaining the unexplainable.

"Jack," he said, "basically the Universe is composed of three fundamental components: Space, Time, and Matter. Matter and energy being equivalent, as Einstein's famous formula equates."

That seemed like no big deal to me then; it was just common sense. After all, what else could there be? Though the matter-energy business was a little harder to grasp. But hey, if Einstein said it, I'm not going to argue. And that's where the bomb comes from, right?

Mr. McEvey continued, and I learned that there was more, "And there are four forces: electromagnetism – electricity, and magnetism being equivalent; gravity – we all know what that is; the weak nuclear force – what causes radioactive decay; and the strong nuclear force – what holds the atom together."

Since it was home-schooling, and given that Mr. McEvey was tolerant, I was allowed to be, shall we say . . . somewhat spontaneous, "Is that all there is?" I asked, "I mean, the Universe is a pretty big place."

"That's a good question, Jack." Mr. McEvey was a good-natured individual, "And the answer is no – there may be other things out there like dark matter and dark energy, and Aether. But there's just one problem; we don't know if those things really exist. Scientists can only see their effects, say on the movement of galaxies, or philosophically postulate their existence, as is the case with the Aether."

"So, they may not really exist?"

"Or they may exist, but not be of this universe." This was a wow statement, designed to impress. The kind of stuff the science gurus on TV spout all the time. It failed, and I steered the conversation back to our home Universe.

"So, we're back to the 4 and the 3 . . . and that's all there is, right Mr. M.?" I was trying to close the subject, move on to something more down to Earth.

"It looks that way, Jack," he replied, "It could be that . . . that's all there is, in this very large place we live in."

We had just defined the Cosmos, and suddenly it wasn't so big anymore. It must have been a significant factoid for me because I never forgot. And there I was, being asked – why is there 4 and 3?

By an Albert Einstein facsimile, in a spaceship of some kind, parked behind the moon!

I took the chance, the big leap, and said, "Why is the universe composed of 4 forces and 3 fundamentals? Yes, Sir, I have wondered about that". A thought flashed – *He's testing me!*

"Very good, Jack. You are answering our questions satisfactorily."

Satisfactorily, I thought! What happens if I don't answer them . . . *satisfactorily?*

Albert continued, "But in your wonderings, Jack, did you happen to arrive at an answer? Why are there 4 forces and 3 fundamental components in the Universe?" He looked straight through me with steady eyes as he took a few puffs on his pipe.

The questions were getting harder, and this one was a doozy. But I actually knew the answer! I thought back about ten years ago, back to my futile attempt at college, sitting in a math class called Algebra II. I quit shortly thereafter. I thought college was a colossal waste of time and money, and I had more important things to do with both. Besides, all knowledge is freely available on the internet. But my parents didn't quite see it that way. They were crushed and figured I was doomed to fail. They probably were right, considering my present circumstances.

So . . . there I was back in Algebra II class, bored out of my mind, until the teacher, Mr. Burke, writes the number three on the board with an exclamation point after it. 3! That was a new one for me. He asked the class if we knew what it meant. I didn't, nor did anyone else. He explained, "The exclamation point is called a factorial, and it means you multiply all the whole digits within that number – together. For example, 3! means you multiply 3x2x1, which equals 6. And it also gives the number of permutations in that group."

Mr. Burke was a kindly older gentleman, a dapper bowtie dresser, who sincerely tried to impart his knowledge. I liked him. He went on to explain, "Suppose you have an apple, an orange, and a pear." He was always using fruit as examples. That didn't bother me. It was very rational. "Permutations are any groupings of the fruit. An apple and an orange, and an orange and an apple would be two different permutations." Mr. Burke forged ahead, "But in combinations, the order of the fruit doesn't matter; an apple and an orange, and an orange and an apple would be considered the same combination. That's the difference between a combination and a permutation."

Some kid in the back yelled, "What happens when you cross an apple with an orange?"

To wit, another clown incorrectly replied, "A tangerine!" The class laughed heartily, reflecting their level of boredom.

"Wrong," said Mr. Burke after the class settled down, "You can't compare apples to oranges" The class was silent until Mr. Burke winked, then everyone groaned.

This was an example of Mr. Burke's humor. Delayed reaction, like a bomb with a timer, only it was always a dud. He was likable and good-natured and generally popular in a respected sort of way. When the class settled down, he wrote an equation on the board. "This is the formula for determining the number of combinations within a factorial group." He worked it out and concluded that 3! generates 4 different combinations. 3! = 4. He then started again with the fruit and their different combinations. The class got fidgety, and I got hungry. But I remembered the fruit example, and I also remembered the lesson. 3! = 4.

Then some years later, it just came to me. No one knows where inspiration comes from. Information, images, and thoughts must be churning around up there, combining every which way and occasionally bubbling up to the surface – the consciousness. If someone could invent a drug that accelerates the process, well, that someone wouldn't have to worry about paying the rent. Anyway, at times I get ideas.

I guess I was always interested in "the big picture" – Space, Time, and the Universe. How it all works? Occasionally I'd buy a book, like "The History of Time." Read some parts; skim the rest. Generally, I kept up with the latest theories: String, Quantum Gravity, etc. Then one day, something clicked, and the thought just winked into my brain. 3! = 4. The three big components — Space, Time, and Matter; in different combinations, make the four forces. It was like combining apples with oranges and coming up with tangerines! Anyway, that was the big idea, the inspiration, the eureka moment. It seemed so simple – yet it rang true. The 3 make the 4. But I can't take total credit. Albert Einstein came up with the first part in his General Theory of Relativity . . . you know . . . that Space and Time make gravity. So, what to do with this little piece of information? Well, that's how all this began.

I responded to Albert, "The three fundamental components of the universe, in different combinations, comprise the four forces." I just said it. Probably for the first time, outside my barn . . . but I said it, and I knew I was right.

Albert broke his stare and nodded, then puffed away on his pipe rather vigorously. After a longish moment, he said, "Our comprehension of you and your endeavors is clarifying, Jack. Now we can answer some of your questions. And while I do so, shall we take a short stroll through the ship? I am gratified to observe that your health has returned." He puffed away, the smoke being surprisingly aromatic and pleasant.

My health has returned! From where I wondered? "Let's start with this place," I motioned around to the whiteness, "the machines, and the faceless whatever they are?"

"We were not expecting a visit from someone, such as yourself, Jack. Therefore, we were compelled to hastily arrange these facilities."

"Hastily arrange?"

"Yes, Jack, we separated the space, sorry for the absence of walls, and built the apparatus and attendants to deal with your . . . condition. We have manufacturing facilities that can accommodate most situations."

"Like me, almost dying?" I ventured forth along this most unpleasant track.

"Yes, Jack, but you are in perfect health now. Shall we take that stroll?"

I swung off the bed and asked, "I assume you didn't have much time to construct all this stuff. How do you build so fast?"

"Through the implementation of 4,3 . . . and all which that implies. Stay close, Jack. The walkways can be somewhat disconcerting at first."

"Did you build them for me too?"

"Just for you, Jack," Albert slightly nodded, responding in an un-nuanced, totally imperturbable manner.

We began to walk in the direction Albert came from. It seemed as though we covered an incredible distance, but with no reference points, it was hard to tell.

Before long, the whiteness turned into a foggy grayness. Being the perfect host, Albert commented on this, "The builders of this artifact have an aversion to walls, or more precisely . . . boundaries. They represent endings and beginnings, which are abhorrent to them. You might view this predilection as being similar to a religious tenet. As a result, space tends to fade and emerge here."

After a while, the grayness clarified into a most wondrous vista.

Chapter 3: Candy Land – *Jack*

The vista we approached was beautiful, though certainly not of the Earth. It was "Candy Land." Why do I say this? Because the predominant color was – candy-apple red. Spread before us was a landscape complete with a sky above and a horizon below. I had to keep reminding myself that I was in some kind of space edifice. High up, the atmosphere was dark, almost black, like the color of Space. It gradually lightened to pearl gray and then to creams as it approached the horizon. Smeared on this backdrop were long red lateral streaks, which curled into swirling pink clouds. The combination was striking – gray sky, pink clouds. In the distance rose a fantastic city. A collection of multi-shaped towers and spires, extending to fantastic heights, many seemingly defying gravity. Surrounding them were numerous lesser structures of geometric and organic shapes. All were connected by arcs, tubes, and ribbons of red, gray, and cream. Unmistakably alien and obviously, super-advanced.

In the foreground, to my left, was a vast expanse of what looked like wheat, only it was pink – miles of pink wheat, extending to the horizon and swaying in the breeze. To my right was a scene depicting the complete opposite. A barren, cherry-red plain peppered with craters and low rolling hills. This scene seemed more consistent with an alien moon. Protruding here and there were what looked like termite mounds – groupings of reddish-brown, semi-tubular, shapeless forms, which did not look geologic in origin. Stretching across this desolate expanse was an abrupt rift, a jagged red crevasse, like a wound cut by a dull blade to a depth that I could not discern.

The overall effect of this panorama conveyed a shockingly harsh, otherworldly beauty, which only added more questions to the rapidly growing stack.

“This was one of our living areas.” Albert pointed out. "Unfortunately, the inhabitants . . . do not live here anymore.”

“What do you mean 'they don’t live here anymore'?”

“Let’s stroll through the field, as I explain.” Albert gestured with his cane in the direction we were to walk. We set out and the distance swept by. It appeared that we would bypass the city.

“Those who built this ship, and others like it, departed long ago,” Albert explained. "My purpose was to remain and observe and to occasionally report back on the developments of life on Earth. When the time is propitious, if you qualify, Earth will be invited to join the Continuum of Species. In small steps, of course.”

“How long have you been here, Albert?” I asked.

“In your years – 271.397 million years,” Albert said this with his usual inscrutable demeanor.

I was flabbergasted, and I guess it showed. Albert noticed and responded, “Please do not be alarmed, Jack. I know all this is hard for you to assimilate. Allow me to explain. The First-Born, as we shall call them, are a very ancient civilization. Indeed, some of the first to arise in this Universe. They revered sentient life and sought it out. But phylogenesis is a rare phenomenon, the requisite conditions being astronomically uncommon, though found here on Earth. Because of their philosophical doctrines, “those who came before” refuse to tamper with a life form’s aboriginal development – the Natural Order. Edifices like this one, or maybe I should say . . .

like me, were strategically placed at promising sites, to monitor and wait."

"But so . . . so long, how can you even exist for that long?" 271 million years was beyond my ability to comprehend.

"As I previously explained, Jack, the First-Born disdain endings. Consequently, they build things to last . . . eternally. I am sentient, self-aware, and capable of self-repair," Albert paused, leaned on his cane, and puffed a few rings, waiting for my reaction. *Was I still being tested?*

"But that's what we call being alive, except for the 'eternally' part."

Albert resumed the walk, "I am an artifact, Jack, a thing created by others. That is what distinguishes me from a natural life form. You, however, are indigenous to Earth, created by spontaneous ontogenetic processes. And you are evolving as the Cosmos intended. Your species is a direct product of the Universe, part of the natural order. I am not. Autogenetic generation is an essential requirement for induction."

"Artificial life-forms can't be members?"

"That is correct, Jack. I am not a member, but rather a tool of the Continuum." He reached into his jacket pocket and pulled out a bag of tobacco.

"And the members have access to you, correct?" I asked as the potential of this place began to unfold.

"Within limits, that is correct, Jack," Albert responded, suspecting where I was going with this line of conversation.

“And those who demonstrate knowledge and use of Fourth Level Technology are members, correct?" I felt my heart rate quicken.

“That is factual, Jack, but please do not allow yourself to become enthusiastic. We have not yet determined whether you have demonstrated sufficient knowledge of Fourth Level Technology."

"Well, how do you think I got here? By flapping my arms really hard?" I was pleading my case. I sensed the endless possibilities that “Albert” offered.

“You arrived here about as close to dead as a being can get, Jack, and still be recovered. That is not a very positive demonstration of your ability to implement the precepts of Fourth Level Technology."

Touché. I changed the subject. Meanwhile, we had pretty much skirted the City, walking through the pink wheat or, I should say, a couple of feet above. We had covered a few miles in the few minutes of our conversation. This considerable distance prompted the obvious question, "How big are you . . . or should I say . . . how big is this Ship, Albert?"

"27.38 miles in diameter, Jack. When I was built, the current fashion was to construct fairly large and heavy craft. I am considered somewhat obsolete at present, since the trend has reversed considerably, even to the point of . . . the incorporeal with some races."

More mind-boggling stuff . . . but I continued along the same tack, "How did you remain unobserved for all this time? I mean, we've sent various capsules and landers around the moon for decades now? And nobody saw anything." I had begun to equate Albert with the Ship. It was odd.

"When I observe a situation that could result in my detection, I simply move away far enough to avoid exposure. Also, I normally configure my outer hull to absorb all electromagnetic radiation, such that I appear only as a black void in the star-field of space. I have other cloaking options available, as well. Know this, Jack . . . "Albert shifted his weight off the cane and pointed it at me, "I can remain unnoticed with little effort."

What's with the cane action?

I was beginning to realize that the more questions I asked, the more questions I created. But the answers were opening doors to whole new worlds. And my current situation was beginning to clarify. I'm in some kind of a sentient edifice parked behind the moon. It was left here some 270 million years ago by a super-advanced race or "Continuum" of races to monitor the Earth. *Or maybe, it was just discarded and given something to do?* It was almost overwhelming. But at least one question had been answered. I was not dead, a very comforting thought.

Meanwhile, we had exited "Candy-Land" and entered another gray area. A thick, cloudy gray shroud enveloped us as before. Oh yeah, I reminded myself, the Builders don't like walls. But at least Albert was talking and answering my questions. He must be starved for conversation after all this time. And I found him easy to talk to despite our rather profound differences.

I availed myself of the opportunity, "Albert, what is the actual definition of Fourth Level Technology?" Since my status and position with the ship depended on my knowing this, I felt that it behooved me to know what it factually was.

"I'm glad you asked that, Jack," Albert tucked his pipe in an inside pocket, "We have found that civilizations naturally advance in stages, which is logical and as one would expect. Indeed, it was thus with 'Those Who Came First.'"

"First-level technology would be equivalent to your stone age. On Earth, it primarily involved the acquisition and control of fire along with simple implements such as stone knives, bone needles, and animal skins."

"Second level technology is what you would call Newtonian Mechanics. A first attempt to describe and understand how the four forces interact with matter in Time and Space. This would also include simple machines such as your internal combustion engine."

"The beginnings of a higher awareness comes with Third Level Technology. How the universe functions in quantum steps at the micro and macro levels. The four forces and the three fundamentals are defined on an elemental level. The civilization suspects they are linked, and a search is initiated for the theory that unites them. Indeed, my namesake, Albert Einstein, devoted the latter half of his life in pursuit of this quest. He called it 'The Unified Field Theory,' a misnomer for sure. Regrettably, he failed."

"Earth," Albert continued, "may now be on the threshold of discovery. The various observable types of 'action at a distance,' such as the four forces along with Space and Time, are no longer regarded in an irrational manner. Instead, they are being explored and defined, though many of their essential structures remain undiscovered. But your species has been evolving for several million years, and the universe has endowed you with the ability to comprehend its organizational design. Your senses detect the rational, and this is a rational universe, as your race shall soon discover." I concluded that yes, Albert was starved for conversation.

"Unfortunately, your scientists remain fixated on Matter. But, Jack, as you learned from Mr. McEvey", *how does he know about Mr. McEvey?* "The Universe is made of two other fundamental components – Space and Time. And these also have an internal structure that can interact on the level of the very small."

"Fourth Level Technology entails the knowledge of what some call the 'Law of Connections' – the equation that connects the four to the three, coupled with the implementation of that knowledge. Somehow, Jack, you uncovered these principles and even employed them. You alone, of the eight billion people on Earth. We must comprehend this to a greater depth. It is of critical importance to your future and the Earth's."

All this Albert said as we walked along on a viscous yet somewhat solid surface. Our passage caused a swirling wake of shroud-like gray wisps. It was more substantial than fog and a little unsettling, but I found the conversation to be of such interest that my anxieties were diminished somewhat.

"I guess that kind of puts me in a special category." I punctuated the statement with a cocky head wag. This Fourth Level business, which I supposedly knew . . . was the key and my ticket to . . . I suspected wonders beyond the fantastic.

"We took a chance on you, Jack because your craft employed a rudimentary gravitic drive. If I am wrong about you, I will have to undo the violations committed against our primary mandate."

Undo the violations, I thought. What the hell does that mean? Albert had saved my life . . . was that what he intended to undo? Suddenly, there was a distinct possibility of bad things happening.

"Speaking of your rudimentary gravitic device, Jack. I thought our first stop would be to our hangar, the place where we keep smaller, short-distance vehicles. This is where we stored your conveyance. We repaired it and made some modifications. I hope our improvements will meet with your approval." Albert always spoke with perfectly modulated inflections, revealing a power far from what one would expect from an elderly gentleman, even one as august as Albert Einstein. Obviously, I had retained no voiceprints for the Ship to extract.

"Lead on Albert, I am but your humble servant." I said this with a slight head-bow, the opposite of a head-wag.

Albert looked at me quizzically, "Technically speaking, I am your servant, Jack, if you were a member of the Continuum in good standing."

The gray void began to clear, and so did my understanding. With a short sweeping hand motion, Albert announced, "We have arrived at our destination."

Chapter 4: Black Walls

We emerged into a space that truly had some dimensions. Before us and not too far away, towered a dark irregular substance. And it appeared to be tangible – that is, something in fact, touchable. *What about the builder's abhorrence of boundaries?* It extended upwards and to the right and left for some considerable distance. We seemed to have hit the wall, literally and figuratively. The floor was white and embossed with grid lines that created squares of various sizes. And each was occupied by a spacecraft, which varied by size and configuration. The smallest were round, bubble-like clear spheres about 20 feet in diameter, each glowing with a pale blue light inside. On the outside, every manner of appendage protruded, and on the inside were items that resembled seats and a control panel.

The next in size were spherical vehicles also. *Why does everything have to be round?* These spheres were composed of a dull black material that seemed to absorb light rather than reflect it. A flat, empty darkness. They were of various sizes, anywhere from 30 to at least 200 feet, with no discernible projections or protrusions of any kind. Just perfect, dull black spheres that floated a few feet above the floor. *Floated?* I was afraid to go near them.

The third type, and there were many of these, were variously shaped craft. Some long and narrow, others roundish and flat. They were equipped with various projections, which included arms, tubes, dishes, and appurtenances tipped with bizarre components. Many of their hulls were transparent, revealing complex mechanisms inside. Albert explained, "All these vehicles are available to members and guests, though some are used primarily for maintenance tasks exterior to the ship." He used his pipe as a pointing device as we casually walked past these vessels.

"But there haven't been any guests, you say, for 270 million years!"

"That is correct, Jack. But I must . . . I am required to maintain our original configuration. That is one of my tasks . . . to maintain." Albert had a way of making the utterly fantastic seem rational.

We proceeded to saunter down an aisle. The numerous craft were arranged to our right and left. And I could see many such aisles, each lined with spacecraft. The resulting total must have reached hundreds, maybe even thousands. A veritable fleet!

I pointed to one of the smaller, bubble-like globes and asked, "What are these smaller ones for?"

"All these vehicles are for basic transportation, Jack. The smaller vessels are for shorter distances, primarily interplanetary travel. And the larger spheres are used for abbreviated interstellar excursions. Longer distances require a more substantial edifice, a construction similar to my configuration. At least they were needed when I was . . . constituted. But as I mentioned earlier, trends and styles change." Albert walked to a small clear globe, banged out his bowl, and then tucked it away.

"But, like, how do they get from point A to point B. What's their mode of propulsion? I . . . I mean . . . what makes them go, Albert?" I was stammering, losing my fragile veneer of composure somewhat. The momentous revelations kept piling up.

"We have several modes of propulsion or, it is probably more accurate to say . . . travel, since most modes do not involve propulsion per se. But all involve the manipulation of Space, Time, and Matter. Something an adept practitioner of 4,3 would know."

Is he still testing?

"I am constrained from revealing much of our technology since your standing with us is . . . of very probationary status. But I can tell you this, these lesser crafts," he pointed to the smaller, transparent globes, "employ similar technology to what your conveyance utilized . . . or utilizes. They disrupt and manipulate the filaments of gravity. But we shall discuss this topic further at a later time. Ahh . . . here we are now. Your handiwork!"

And there it was. My conveyance or craft or . . . whatever. Okay, I admit it looked more like a carnival ride than a spaceship, but still, it looked good to me. And what this meant was – I might have a way off this . . . Though what I saw, upon further inspection, was quite different from what I built. Especially since the product of my labors, as Albert had indicated earlier – disintegrated.

Please permit me a moment of honesty. First, I never expected the damn thing to fly, certainly not in the way it did. I would have been happy to see it hover a few inches and, best-case scenario, use it to escape the Feds. But, as we all know, I was forced to expedite the testing process. And it certainly worked considerably better than I hoped . . . or even dreamed, which is a very large understatement. Albert called it a rudimentary gravitic drive. What exactly does that mean?

So, there it was. Parked between a maintenance globe and a black sphere . . . my ride. I proceeded to walk around “my handiwork" with a big smile on my face. It was the same but different. The black plastic pipe I used for the outer ring looked heavier, more substantial, and the joints were seamless. The aluminum arms connecting the ring to the pod were also seamless. How do you weld aluminum to plastic? A big unknown for me. But I do know it looked a whole lot stronger than the drywall screws I used. And the pod, for certain, was not salvaged from an old Ferris wheel. It was clear, unscratched, and fitted with a door that, unquestionably, looked space tight. It had comfortable seats and a dashboard that looked . . . exactly like the one in my father's old Mercedes? *Curious*. Overall, the whole thing looked substantial and very space worthy. Basically, it was similar but poles apart from what I built. However, it looked plausibly from the Earth. Unlike everything else around here.

After I completed the survey of my *craft*, I approached Albert and said, "I like what you did with it. Does this mean I'm free to leave anytime I want?" It was my turn to test Albert.

"Yes and no, Jack. You see, we have a dilemma." Albert reached into his pocket and retrieved his pipe. I had a thought flash – *is this pipe business some kind of non-verbal communication? Is he trying to tell me something that he can't say?* Albert continued, "We could have discarded your craft, Jack, since it was essentially non-existent. But that course posed a problem, a question really," he stuffed his pipe with tobacco, "What do we do with you, Jack?" Then he lit it. He used old-fashioned stick matches. *Curious.*

"If you alone developed and employed Fourth Level Principles, independent of an organized effort, then I should not allow you to return to Earth and thereby interfere in your species' technological development. You would be a legal Continuum member and forbidden from interfering with evolving civilizations.

However, if your endeavors were inadvertent, if you stumbled upon precepts that you do not fully understand, then I would have, by affecting your rescue, tampered with your culture. An act that is forbidden to me. This is the dilemma, Jack."

"So why then, did you rebuild it?" *Why did I know things weren't going to be simple?*

"Hear me out, Jack. We suspect your intent was not to build a spacecraft per se but rather, an experimental hovercraft. And it worked better than you expected, resulting in you being here. The level of your technical comprehension remains uncertain. Though, you did voice a superficial knowledge of '4,3', which is significant. As to our quandary, we chose the middle path, at least for now. You can return in the device you built, or I should say . . . apparently built. We re-engineered your craft somewhat but kept it indigenous, that is 'of the Earth.' We did not tamper with its . . . with your original technology. At least, not perceptibly. Therefore, our Primary Laws shall remain inviolate. We have not meddled in your species' phylogenesis." This statement was followed by some voluminous pipe puffing and a steady gaze of assessment.

"But don't you think I'll tell everybody about all this when I get back?" My depth of understanding of what Albert had just said was shallow at best.

"No one is likely to believe you, Jack."

"So then, how would I be interfering in Earth's development?" At this point, I must admit, I didn't know what I was arguing about.

"That's an interesting question, Jack. Are you part of Earth's natural evolution, or are you an anomaly? Certainly, you are not engaged in some organized endeavor. We suspect that you acted alone. But the certainty of this statement remains unresolved and of some considerable concern."

"Well, I'm glad we cleared all that up."

Albert smiled and thankfully changed the subject, "This craft," he motioned with his cane to my conveyance, "is capable of short-distance space travel only, such as back to Earth. We would not recommend longer excursions. However, we do propose a period of instruction, shall we say . . . a driver's education session with myself as the instructor. Some learning on your part would be wise, though I could remotely pilot the craft if necessary or so desired."

"Great! When do we start?" Suddenly, I had transportation. I could come, and I could go, whenever and wherever I wanted. Well, not really. But still, things were definitely looking up. Freedom is a wonderful thing.

"Soon, Jack. But we thought you would like some personal time, especially after your ordeal. Perhaps a short rest, a meal, and the pursuance of ablutions. We have prepared accommodations for you."

Ablutions? Miss Murphy was a real stickler when it came to vocabulary, but she must have missed that one. I simply asked, "Accommodations?"

"Yes, Jack, we want you to feel comfortable and at ease here, experience the security of being at home. Shall we continue the tour?" He began to stroll towards the main aisle, leading the way.

"Lead on, Sir. I am but a 'stranger in a strange land.' And you are, as you say, my instructor."

"I'll teach you what I can, Jack."

I looked up at the looming hangar walls and had to ask, "If the Builders don't like enclosures, how come there are solid walls here?"

Albert answered, "It is not my intent to further your state of disquietude, Jack, but they are technically not solid."

I walked the few steps behind my craft towards the wall and looked closely, then raised my hand to touch but quickly pulled back as I noticed the black substance was boiling with activity – dividing and coalescing.

Albert explained in his typical, calm, pedantic manner, "The hull is composed of what your science calls a Bose-Einstein condensate, the fifth state of matter – a super liquid. And it need not be as cold as my namesake, Mr. Einstein and Mr. Bose postulated. We employ various layers and varieties of the substance interlaced with a ligature of degenerate matter. It's very adaptable, simply by varying the strength of the internal atomic bonds as needed. The strong force, the force that holds an atom together, also binds our hull together. In some ways, it resembles a very large atom. The substance was very popular at one time."

Albert just stared as he puffed several smoke rings, seemingly enjoying my obvious discombobulation. I looked to my left at the black sphere parked there.

Seeing the direction of my gaze, he replied, "The hulls of these black spherical craft are also made of the same material. It is both permeable and impenetrable, ideal properties for an outer sheath. Though the scattering of degenerate matter tends to boost the mass to levels quite passé by today's standards. Like me, in general. Shall we proceed?"

Albert was spot on when he said no one would believe a word of this. We proceeded to walk back through the Hangar. As we exited, our surroundings gradually morphed back to the gray haze as before, and our speed seemed to increase as well, though not our pace.

"Albert, you contain an alien city and a fleet of at least a thousand spacecraft. I must deduce that there was a time when this . . . I mean when you were a rather busy place?" I found it difficult to choose the correct pronouns.

"Yes, Jack, there was a time when I was occupied by many thousands of beings, various members, and stratum of the Continuum. I contain many habitats where other species, at one time, dwelled. And many common use areas as well. There were places in this Universe where a great deal of activity took place; commerce, social intercourse, and enterprise beyond what your language can convey. And there were eras when I was a part of that . . . a valued center of activity . . . an inestimable means to many ends." Albert said this with a faraway look as the memories flooded back.

Was Albert being reminiscent, nostalgic even? *Is he capable of emotion?* I thought it inappropriate for me to pry into that. Instead, I asked, "And, as you said, all these beings were members of the Continuum, right?"

"That is correct, Jack. But there are distinct degrees of membership, depending on many factors."

"And, uh . . . what are the benefits of full membership?"

"Concerning this ship, which I represent, full membership would confer, an affiliate, access to my facilities. This would pertain to both individual and collective prerogatives. For example, my assignment here was a collective decision."

Pursuing this thread, I continued, "And if a member wanted to say, take a little jaunt to a nearby star, they would have access to one of your vehicles?"

"Yes, of course, Jack. Unfortunately, you are not a member." He said this with a sympathetic finality.

"I know, I know, Albert. I'm some kind of probationary, provisional . . .

"You are not a member, Jack!" Albert said this decidedly and with some force behind his voice. Of course, I never expected membership. After all, who am I? It was just his tone that hurt. Being rejected is never easy.

"But we intend to investigate your provisional status further." With that, Albert qualified his previous statement. My hurt feelings were somewhat assuaged.

The gray void in which we walked had become a bit tedious, but certainly not the discussion, and I had a thousand questions. Of which, Albert was willing to answer rather than put forth his own. Though I was certain more questions would be forthcoming.

"Where did everybody go, Albert?"

"Essentially, they all just dispersed further . . . out. The Universe is a very large place, Jack. Each species had its own endemic reasons for doing what they did and going where they went. They do not inform me, and oftentimes it's beyond my understanding. There are levels of technology beyond the Fourth, Jack." Albert explained this almost wistfully. *Is he lonely because nobody's here, nobody's home*?

"Well, if nobody's home, why can't you just do whatever you want?" This was the logical follow-up, but I soon realized that my query was not the smartest of questions to ask.

Albert's gaze turned to me with a hard look that locked on my eyes and froze me stiff. The power of his voice shocked me as he pointed his cane, "You would not want a Power like me running amuck in this Universe, Jack! Not without rules or law. A greater truth cannot be stated!" For a lingering moment, his eyes mirrored distant memories. "Unfortunately, in our history, this situation has occurred, resulting in catastrophic consequences. Procedures have been implemented that are inviolate and immutable. It cannot happen again."

"Permit me to explain." His demeanor softened, "Intelligent life is a phenomenon that occurs but rarely in this Universe. And my makers, the First-Born, revere it when it spontaneously arises. They regard life to be the progeny of the Cosmos, each with its own unique set of capabilities. 'Those Who Came First' believe that they have been called upon to guard the children of the Progenitor against interference. Natural phylogenesis must proceed unaltered. I am an instrument of this undertaking, Jack, especially since . . . they have all moved on. An entity like myself is and must remain tightly controlled." An indecipherable look hardened on Albert's face as he puffed profuse volumes of smoke.

Meanwhile, as we walked, the gray vapor began to clear, and I could make out more walls in the distance.

Interlude 1: The Gods

As civilizations evolve, they learn definitions. All kinds of definitions. And definitions impose limits. Definitions to the very small – Planks' constant; definitions to the very fast – the speed of light; and even, definitions to the very large – infinity. But if infinity is denoted, well then, it has limits and therefore, is not limitless. Is this a paradox? Yes. What else would you call a limitless limit? And further, the concept of infinity has no practical value. Infinite mass, infinite force, infinite space, all are irrational concepts and incomprehensible. And our Universe is a rational place and, given the effort, comprehensible. A Universe with limits, a concept my homeworld is beginning to accept. Logic dictates that a limit to a space, any given space, large or small, implies an enclosure – an outer barrier of some kind. In time, this logic would come to be verified via exploration. And it is reasonable to assume that "Those Who Came First" would be the ones to travel to the edge of the Universe. And then . . . to venture beyond.

Of course, where they went had to be safe. Because safety is the prime concern of an immortal – a being, possibly, many millions of years old. And it would be nice if the place had some local color as well. A locality where they could assemble and enjoy the homegrown amenities while doing what they do, which was contemplation mostly. Reflection on matters concerning the beginnings and endings of things and their natural order. Places like this exist beyond our Universe, past the outer edge, in what is known as the Aether. They are called Loci. And this is where the First-Born and their followers went. The local amenity, in this case, was the process of creation itself. They built a new home, an enclave where they could securely and happily experience the birth of new

Universes. A sight indescribable and, for sure, nowhere to be found in normal Space.

So, what's in the Aether? Manifolds. And what are Manifolds? They are clouds of elementary entities that move about seemingly aimlessly. And what are they made of? Many different things, elemental things, the stuff of Universes. First, there are the various forms of matter: free quarks, photons, and leptons. Then, you can find the different embodiments of Space itself, the various dimensions, and planes, which almost always are found amidst vast auroras of Time. Also, there is something called the Aether. This is the stuff they named the place after. A vacuous, rarefied substance, the fabled quintessence of old; what our ancient alchemists so avidly sought. In this place, it predominates and permeates, filling the voids between the drifting Nimbi. And I must mention one more thing; there are substances, which our senses were not designed to detect. Actualities almost beyond our ability to comprehend, such as the dark forms of Matter and Energy, plus others. All these things float in the sea of Aether, propelled by forces unknown, occasionally colliding and commingling. And, if the conditions are right, seeds are formed, which in the fullness of time, burst forth in rather Big Bangs.

Logic dictates that someone had to come first. The first life forms to emerge on a planet, the first life forms to emerge in a galaxy, or even – the first life forms to emerge in a Universe. Certainly, chance and probability favored them. Though being first also rendered their path more difficult, for they were truly alone, separated by vast distances from any lessor life forms. Eventually, through experimentation, analysis, and exploration, they overcame their solitude and prospered, for the Universe was wide open, and they were free to roam unrestricted. Free to slake their curiosity. And they were curious. They wanted to know things. How it all works. What's out there? What came before? And, most importantly, what lies beyond?

As is always the case, with freedom comes responsibility. The First-Born, being of noble design, assumed the burden of primogeniture as they observed the younger races arise from our not so fecund Cosmos. And like older siblings everywhere, the First-Born felt obliged to watch over the young, lend some guidance, and pass on their hand-me-downs. But first, the newcomers had to prove their worth. Rise to *The Fourth Level*, which was the standard they set.

And the First-Born, being naturally good folk, assumed another responsibility – care for their Parent. The entity that truly came first, The Progenitor, their home Universe. Maintenance of its health and wellbeing – eternally, of course, as immortals naturally would. But how? How does one maintain and promote the health of a Universe? This, I do not know. But the Elders learned how. They divined this . . . *The Natural Way*, as it was called. How the Cosmos was meant to be. And they did not abandon this task when they left.

What was the answer? Generally, it's what you would expect. Promote growth to an optimal size, then maintain an eternal stasis – metastability, as they called it. But this was not an easy task. It was a very tricky business and required the perpetuation of a delicate equilibrium. The ticklish balance between entities not readily discernible to the normal senses. The aforementioned Dark Matter and Dark Energy being but two.

*A note here on life in the Aether. It is difficult to exist there composed of the normal stuff of Universes – standard matter-energy complexes, normal matter being highly unstable. It is better to transcend the material and assume a matrix of Space and Time. Pure consciousness. But there are many forms an awareness can take. Most chose a collective manifestation; their Presence being comprised of billions of individuals. Others chose to remain singular. And some preferred to carry considerable baggage from their prior embodiments, though much shielding was required, free quarks being highly reactive. It was largely a matter of individual preference, the form they chose.

And what structure did their society take? It was hierarchical. Not so much based on power, but rather, on *Breadth of Presence*. The greater the capacity to permeate, the higher the status. And the higher the status, the more the dominion. Others, the lesser awarenesses, chose to engage in the more mundane endeavors – the analysis and observation of all in their domain, plus the implementation of the collective will. They undertook the responsibilities, the duties of the gods.

A youngish entity, taking the distinctive form of a coruscating glimmer of photonic radiation, streaked into the Locus imparting information. Its archaic and somewhat primitive connection to traces of its material heritage revealed its youthful exuberance. It was an Observer. It discharged a particularly bright and disturbing flash, unsettling all with its brash interruption.

"Imbalances within the Dark Matter-Energy complex have been observed."

This was news of considerable import. But barely worthy of interruption. Variations occur and are natural. The thought reverberated throughout.

"Disequilibrium approaches. The probability of metastasis modification exceeds zero."

The second part of the thought gained the attention of many, including some of the more ancient and dominant configurations. It meant that bad things could happen, like false vacuums. A base timbre and dark effulgence flooded the locus, "Random leakage is to be expected."

Plasmas and condensates pulsed with various textures communicating . . . perturbation.

An irresistible thought emanated from a powerful Omnipresence. It inundated all and commanded beyond resistance.

"Implement procedures."

This closed the matter. Measures would be taken. The leakages in our Universe's outer husk would be sealed – a routine matter. And the impetuous young Observer was acknowledged, though many were vexed at the disruption to their eternal felicity.

Coruscations in the void diminished, and the languor of blissful contemplation resumed.

Chapter 5: Esther Jane Riley – *Janey*

Suddenly, the hospital alarms sounded, flooding my senses with dread, every nerve, and every synapse. Then the announcements came, "Security, please report to level three." The message alternated between those dreadful alarms, and I was paralyzed, frozen solid. Down the hall, Jack froze too. Our eyes met. For a brief moment, time stopped, and a blizzard of awareness flashed between us. Then I saw the look of terror spread across his face, and Jack ran. I can't say that I disagreed with his decision, that particular course of action. What else could he do? Everybody at the nurses' station was staring at him as he stood there, holding a silver case plastered with yellow and black symbols. They knew what those trefoils meant, and if they didn't, the big letters "Danger Radiation" filled in the blanks.

And everyone knew that Jack was my . . . romantic companion. Worse, there was a history of missing isotopes. Small quantities, almost insignificant, but enough to raise eyebrows. Forms were filled out, calls were made, and additional security was installed, all without telling me. They must have suspected me for quite some time. But after this, mm . . . crime, I would at the least be a person of interest and Jack – the prime suspect. After all, everyone saw him do it. And it was all my fault. But Jack didn't put a gun to my head. I volunteered to help and more – I was a partner, a willing participant in the crime and in the project. I was in on it from the beginning, in on all the bullshit sessions with Mr. McEvey, and in on the building of the damn thing. And I'm not sorry.

So, there I stood with a guilty look on my face. *What are my alternatives?* This was how they taught us to think at The University of Connecticut. Instilled may be a better word. It was the overriding modus operandi of every school, including Nursing – how to make a decision, how to choose the best alternative. Should I cry and play dumb? No, that's not my style, not that I have much. There's a reason why some call me Plain Jane. I wear a nurse's uniform for work, and jeans, T-shirt, and sneakers for play. My hair is brown; I don't dye it. I avoid make-up; there's no need, and I have a healthy figure because that's what I am – healthy. Jack called me "pretty freakin' astounding" once. That was good enough for me.

Should I run? Where to? There's no place to hide. Then it hit me . . . *do nothing – just stay blank*. That's what I'll do, I thought. Simply stand there and maintain my space with a blank look. Be expressionless. Raise my eyebrows a little, crack a half-smile; no, better make that a quarter-smile, and reflect absolutely no emotion. I'll try not to talk, answer vaguely, but tell no lies, and cast absolutely no body language. I would be *Blank Jane*, not Plain Jane. My panic began to subside with a course of action planned. I felt myself rising to the occasion. It was odd. Sirens wailed outside.

The nurses at the station were all staring at me, trying to hide their excitement. The alarms stopped, and the head nurse, Frieda Gunther, stood. She had bad knees, and there's nothing worse for a nurse than to have bad knees. She said in a pleasant voice, "Janey, perhaps you should wait here for a few minutes for things to settle down." That was pure bull. What she really meant was, "Janey, perhaps you should wait here for a few minutes – for your world to end!" So, I just stood there, nodding with a quarter-smile and the look of mindless bliss in my eyes. Like a cult follower. *Are there still cult followers out there?*

The first on the scene was the hospital security cops. I knew them all. We were friends and on a first-name basis. Leading the pack was Jimmy Dolan. Donut Dolan, they called him, for his rotund shape and his predilection for rotund pastry. He often met me at the entrance in the parking garage, proffering a doughnut, of course. Next came Oliver Johansen and Stan Livingston. They made quite the sight trying to squeeze through one side of the double doors. Almost made me break my quarter-smile. Everyone called them Laurel and Hardy. I went to school with Oliver – Ollie for short. Large and round also, I never pegged him for the law enforcement type. He was too jolly. And Stan Livingston was Ollie's best friend. He was the type of kid who needed a best friend. Somebody to lead the way. Tall and thin, he used to be in my class until he stayed back. They were all darlings, and I liked them a lot. Anyway, they came crashing through the doors, all their paraphernalia swinging and jangling, ready to save the hospital from the terrorists . . . namely, Jack and me. Oh, one more thing; they probably envied Jack a little, him being my beau and all. That's just the way men are.

The boys stopped and conferred with Frieda at the nurses' station, talking low, stealing bashful glances my way. They were confused; completely flummoxed would be a better phrase. Protect me or detain me – that was the dilemma. As a result, they were paralyzed, and an uneasy stasis formed. I stood in my spot, a weak smile, a slight lift to my brows while casting a blank look. And they all tried not to stare at me.

Next in came the men in blue – the New Haven Police. Walking real casual with studied legwork. You know they broke every speed record to get here, lights flashing and sirens screaming, screeching to a stop in front, yet walking in super cool and casual. That's called psychology. Act like you've got it under control, even if you don't know what's going on. That's what separates a pro from and a wannabe.

They're called the men in blue because that's what they wore – spiffy, dark blue uniforms. Nice background for all the police bling; badges, insignia, emblems, patches, pins, nametags, you name it. They sparkled with an aura of authority. Below the bling were big black belts festooned with the implements of enforcement: guns, clubs, handcuffs, and several other indecipherable black objects. Maybe that's why they walked in real nonchalant – they couldn't run, what with all that paraphernalia strapped on. *Ha. The men in blue were wearing strap-ons. Sorry, girl-talk.*

So, the local police walked in, first two, then two more, then two more still. One thing about New Haven – it made the top ten for crime nationally. I read that somewhere; can't footnote it. New Haven's a big crime town. And the cops here are experienced. They all have that hard look like they've seen it all. Maybe because they have. Hard drug addicts, hard thieves, and hard crime. It's their job to deal with the hard side of life, the dark side. It's a different world than where you or I live, it's like . . . the Far side of the Moon.

They joined the huddle at the nurses' station, nodding and looking my way. One older officer with stripes on his upper arm seemed to be in charge. He was talking to his phone, frowning, rolling his eyes at times with one hand upturned in supplication. He obviously was getting orders he did not like. I just stood my ground casually, not reacting to the commotion, looking vacuous. *Non-reaction*, that's the key. They can't react to a non-reaction. My perimeter held; the Blank Jane thing was working.

Then the leader closed his phone, said a few words to his men, and strolled over to me real casual but stopped several feet away.

"Ma'am, a serious crime has occurred here, one that has national security implications. We're . . ." His phone rang again, he answered. More eye-rolling, more supplicant hands, more mumblings, plus a few uh huhs and finally a "Yes, Sir." He closed his phone, threw his hands in the air, turned to me, and said, "Wait here." Then he walked back to the huddle. More murmurings, hand gestures, and body language. Forget the stolen glances; now the stares were like spotlights. Spotlights in a freak show, and I was the freak. *Do they still have freak shows?* I stood my ground, quarter smile, brows slightly raised, and eyes empty – like a freak. The stasis field held.

Abruptly, the doors crashed open. The swat team had arrived. The first two in, squatted down on one knee and became human doorstops with rifles ready. Next, 10 or 12 more team members rushed in, fanned out, and took up positions, some standing, some also on one knee. It looked like real teamwork; no doubt rehearsed. They scared the shit out of everyone; even the men in blue shied away. I'm sure they had real ammo in those guns. One could go off. Then, on cue, they all would open up. Tear the hospital to ribbons. Would they shoot me? I think not; I was just a nurse standing there.

The swatters looked grim, all swollen and puffed up in olive green. They wore Darth Vader-like helmets tricked out with cameras and goggles. And masks covered their faces. *Why masks, I wondered?* All you could see were their eyes, all psyched-up and shifting around, looking for a target. And talk about baggage, they had satchels and pouches everywhere, one on top of the other. Big ones on the chest and back, smaller ones everywhere else. It was amazing they could even move. But that wasn't the scariest part. They were all carrying big black rifles, many different kinds. Some bulky like shotguns, others fancy and futuristic. All designed, no doubt, to spray prodigious quantities of lead. But even that wasn't the scariest part. It was the red dots emanating from the weapons – like grim red eyes staring from the dark. And they were swirling around the room. After some talk in the huddle, they all swirled to me. My white uniform was suddenly decorated with red polka dots, mostly – center of mass. It became very difficult to maintain the Blank Jane thing, but I did.

Through the swat team stepped two men in suits. What an entrance. *Elvis has entered the building.* The cameras should have been rolling to catch this. They probably were. It was professional choreography at its best. I mean, it was like a Broadway show. After the big opening number, the chorus line parted, and the stars entered. What an impression and the suits must have felt like Elvis as well. Too bad they didn't look the part. Still, they were the Big Boys. Big enough to call off the men in blue and big enough to call in the swat team.

They walked to the nurses' station and carelessly flipped their badges, two different badges, I noticed. After a short conference, I heard one say, "OK, we'll take it from here." They turned and looked at me, then walked over, stopping a few paces away. Walked, with a little zip to their step, like busy men whose time was valuable. They were one notch above the pros and two notches above the wannabes. They were the Feds.

The men in suits pulled out their phones, pointed them toward me and began taking pictures, thumb typing, speaking into their small screens, and reading the responses. Funny, during all this communication, they remained incommunicado with each other. No division of labor, like "you take the pictures, I'll call headquarters." They must be from two different agencies, rival agencies, I thought.

The tall one was dapper. Conservative dark suit – obviously tailored, with a white ribbed shirt, and shiny black shoes – Italian style. His face was narrow with a Mediterranean complexion, his hair slicked back and dark, and a small nametag was pinned to his pocket. Small because he didn't need a large one. Everyone knows or should know who he is. He seemed to take control like he was the one who naturally should. More psychology: he knows what people want – someone to take charge and make decisions, any decisions.

The other one was medium short, sloppy plump, and wearing a mismatched outfit. Scuffed brown shoes, khaki pants, and a too-small gray blazer. Obviously, from a suit, he out-grew, except for the jacket if he eschewed buttoning it, which he did. Underneath was a white shirt with a lime green tie decorated with a plethora of helicopters, except for the orangey-red blotches. They say that what you wear is a statement. Either this guy had a thing for helicopters, or it's a tie he got for Christmas from a re-gifting relative . . . and he liked pasta, the kind with tomato sauce. His face was round, his hair transparent, combed to one side, and he had a big bushy mustache that overlapped his upper lip. This guy oozed personality.

They seemed like normal people, not the psycho type, you know – crew cut, mirror shades worn anywhere; above the head or hooked on a pocket. And all cranked up, wound a little too tight. I had a neighbor once, Jimmy Elkins, a friend of the family, who became a cop, local in Litchfield. I remember him saying once, "I heard there were openings on the police force, so I applied. Who would have thought I'd become a cop, especially me?" He was just a schlub looking for a job and took what came along. Now he's the police chief. That's the kind of guy you want for a cop, not the kind who's dying to be one. I hoped these two would be normal like that.

The tall one took over, naturally, and said, "Ma'am, you are, I presume," he looked at his phone, "Ester Jane Riley?" I nodded, then he flipped his badge for a split second. "I'm with the FBI; my name is Special Agent Ernesto Cavalierro." He rolled his r's, gave me a negligible head wag, and almost bowed, "I work out of the Bridgeport Office. We have reports of a radiological theft that allegedly occurred on these premises. We would like to ask you some questions at our . . ."

The plump guy interrupted, "At the Department of Homeland Security in Bridgeport, whom I represent." With another split-second badge flip, he added, "my name is Special Agent Robert Smolanski of the Domestic Nuclear Detection Office." He did not "almost bow," though he did seem to protrude his stomach a tad farther.

The two agents stared icily at each other, then pulled out their phones, thumb typed, talked to them, and took more pictures, this time of each other. They stopped and icily stared some more, then the caballero, already I was calling him that in my mind, said, "We will go to Homeland Security in Bridgeport, but in my car and I will drive. You will come with us," he eyed, and head motioned towards the swat team, "voluntarily, of course."

"Yes, of course, I'm very eager to clear up this misunderstanding," said Blank Jane. Was I being too eager to cooperate? Only the guilty were eager to cooperate. The truly innocent were outraged at being accused of a crime. Indignant. I had to walk the fine line.

Like a Spanish gentleman, the caballero, or I should say Agent Cavalierro, as expected, half bowed and motioned the way. It was like he said "after you" but didn't. I looked at Agent Smolanski for his approval. He nodded, and I could tell, really liked the validation. I walked past the nurses' station, past the many who were huddled there, hesitated for the briefest of moments, and threw them my best Blank Jane. In triumph. I am walking out untouched and voluntarily. Sometimes, it's the little victories that count the most. I continued past the phalanx of swat teamers and out the door. I lead the way. The two Feds closely followed.

Chapter 6: Homeland Security – *Janey*

The area outside the hospital was jam-packed with vehicles; command center vans, armored personnel carriers, a great big bomb-squad truck, press vans, and helicopters flying pretty low overhead. And there were cop cars everywhere else. But no tanks. They do too much collateral damage. Several city blocks were cordoned off with barricades and yellow ribbons, which were strung everywhere, like toilet paper on mischief night. This is what they trained for. And they got their man, only it wasn't a man, it was me.

Funny, we were ignored as my escorts walked me through the hubbub. The Feds were late to the party and had parked on the next block. It was a new Ford Crown Victoria – gold. A big luxury sedan, the kind the Big Boys drive. We walked quickly to it. Agent Cavalierro, always the gentleman, opened the back door for me but did not protect my head with his hand as you see on TV. I was spared that indignity, a good sign. They entered the front but not before the caballero placed a little blinking light on the roof. It revolved and flashed and got us through the turmoil. Frankly, I was thoroughly amazed. No handcuffs, no paddy wagon, no locked doors, not even a screened-off back seat, none of that. It was all very civilized. Presumably, because I was only a person of interest, not a suspect. They didn't know the extent of my involvement. I was just the perp's nurse-girlfriend.

The trip to Bridgeport took a half-hour, and the plump one did most of the talking. The history of the Department of Homeland Security, its inception after 9/11, the definitions of terrorism, his department – The Domestic Nuclear Detection Office or the DNDO, his role in developing the domestic nuclear detection and reporting system, and so on. I had to wonder why he was talking to me, and so did Agent Cavalierro, who looked ready to elbow Robert. Oh yeah, he said I could call him Robert.

I drifted off, wondering about Jack. Did he make it home, did he get to try the thing, and if so, did it work – did it lift off? At least a little, to prove that we're not terrorists, just thieves of the nuclear variety. We'll just get life in prison, not . . . what can be worse than life in prison? But look on the bright side, and yes, there is a bright side. If it works, then we, yes, we, will have demonstrated how to counter the force of gravity. It will be the greatest thing since electricity, since the internal combustion engine, and maybe even the wheel! OK, maybe not the wheel, but still, a major boon for humanity. It'll put Big Oil out of business, Big Auto, and even Big Government out of business. Shit, that means they'll have to kill us to keep it secret. Or put us in a cell and throw away the key. Hey, it's been done before. Many, many inventors have mysteriously disappeared, fallen off trains, or had their labs blown up. Mr. McEvey had a book about this, brought it up every now and then. We concluded, though, that most of the inventors out there were phonies. Like Stanley Meyer, the guy who built a car that runs on water. His device was pure bullshit, though he did die rather suddenly. He was poisoned at a Cracker Barrel Restaurant (not by the food) and died out in the parking lot.

We were devotees of Nikola Tesla. He was the real deal and worthy of our admiration. Anyone's admiration. He invented everything from alternating current to electric motors . . . I tuned back to reality. Yeesh! I'm riding in the back of a cop car going somewhere to be interrogated. And Robert – that is Special Agent Robert Smolanski – was still talking. Either he was a real blabbermouth or . . .

". . . and the Cargo Advanced Automated Radiography Systems – CAARS for short, would have revolutionized radiological detection at our ports. The CAARS machines worked perfectly and would be operational today if their engineers had liaised with our engineers. It wasn't my fault they didn't fit in the primary inspection lanes at the ports of entry. It wasn't my job to oversee that. My job was to . . ."

He was turned around, arm up on the seat, getting kind of worked up. It was strange. I egged him on, "Robert, it sounds like it was their responsibility to liaise with you. What did they expect you to do – read their minds?" Agent Ernesto Cavalierro was shooting me looks in the rear-view mirror, rolling his eyes, and almost saying, "I don't know this guy."

Robert continued, "That's exactly right. And it's what I tried to tell them. The CAARS program was just one of many acquisition programs we oversaw at the DNDO. We're responsible for keeping the ports safe. And to do that, we have to implement and maintain the entire Emergency Nuclear Detection Notification System, the ENDNS for short. And besides, what are they going to do anyway – dock my pay $200 million? Then there was the development of the algorithms, a key part of the . . .

I drifted off again. This guy was mired up to his neck in government muck – the real deep-seated kind. I resumed my daydreams while appearing to be attentive. So, what happened to Jack? Did he make it home? He was on his bike; nobody can catch Jack on his bike. I know; I've ridden with him. That's why my hair is prematurely gray. *Not really.* Therefore, he made it – a reasonable assumption. And probably snuck in the back to avoid the stakeout in front. The big question is – did it work? Again, I must assume that it did, another reasonable assumption. Why? Because Jack's a doer.

He gets things done. That's just what doers do. And because we got results. The earlier versions lost weight. And . . . we had a theory – 4,3. It was kind of crazy. Jack came up with it in the bathtub after a long soak. (I'm not saying whether I was in there with him, part of the time.) He came out and said he had an epiphany, a real eureka moment. It wasn't exactly out of the blue. We talked about 'way out' topics often, especially when Mr. M. was still with us. Then Jack told me. It was about how everything in the Universe is connected. The three fundamentals: Space, Time, and Matter, make up the four forces; gravity, the weak and strong nuclear forces, and electromagnetism. Space and Time create gravity. That part wasn't original. Einstein came up with that. But the other three were: Matter and Time make the weak force, Matter and Space cause electromagnetism, and all three combined; Space, Time, and Matter comprise the strong force. That was it – 4,3. Jack planned on throwing a monkey wrench into all that beautiful symmetry. He proposed mixing the weak force with electromagnetism. Jumbling Space and Matter with Matter and Time. Jack worked out the math, and the Matter part of the equation canceled out, leaving just Space and Time, only; and here's the interesting part, it was negative, as in negative gravity. The fabric on Einstein's trampoline would be pushed out, not in (See Appendix). What you're witnessing now is Science Jane, definitely not Plain Jane, and certainly not Blank Jane . . . which I was still outwardly being.

So, what happened to Jack? That's still the big question. If the thing levitated, then Jack would, most probably, pull it out of the silo, hop back in and take off. They can't catch him in the air, at least not with their cars. How would he steer? Unknown, but Jack would find a way; control the spin rate or throttle down the power. Then what? I don't know. I had reached the limits of my prognostic abilities. But I could still dream . . . Assume the thing flew. After the joy and exhilaration of flying around, getting the feel of it, what would Jack do? He knows he's caught. They've got him on video. And if they capture him . . . well . . . he could end up falling off a train or getting poisoned at a Cracker Barrel. He knows that too. And there's no place to hide. The only thing he could do is . . . is . . . to give it to the Earth, to all the people as publicly as possible. Jack could fly the thing to New York City and land in Times Square. Land real slow. Hover around a little, get some attention, then gradually settle in the little park they have there. The news media would go wild and show the video instantly around the world. There'd be no place to hide – for the Feds. And there'd be no panic like the aliens are coming. The darn thing looks like it was built in a barn, which it was. And they'd see Jack, right there, smiling and waving. He'd open the door, climb out and stand on top. Meanwhile, 500 cops would form a perimeter to keep back the thousands of gawkers. Some people would be shouting, "Take me away." Jack would extend his arms, motion for silence, and say, "My partner Janey Riley and I, give you . . . the gift of anti-gravity!" The crowd would explode with screams of joy, even the cops. The mayor would appear and thank Jack profusely, calling him his old friend, and then they'd go away in a big limo to a penthouse somewhere to meet the leaders of the world. They'd send a limo for me too, of course, maybe even a motorcoach with a kitchen, a bathroom, and a big-screen TV. Everything would be so great . . . Unfortunately, I don't think this story is going to end that way. It could be that this dream is the last luxury I'm going to have for a long time.

We were riding through a seedy section of Bridgeport, an industrial sector, near a river, the kind of river you wouldn't dip your big toe in. We approached a tall, spiked, black steel fence with a formidable gate. This must be the Department of Homeland Security. It sure looked secure. Behind the fence was a huge blue building. It looked like some kind of prefab construction, with small square windows sparsely spaced on each side. The roof was adorned with an array of metal objects: ducts, antennas, and other high-tech-looking gear.

At the guardhouse, Agent Cavalierro flashed his badge. The guard knew him, then the caballero head-pointed to me in the back, and the guard checked me out. This was to be prologue; from that point on, I would be on display. Truly a job for Blank Jane.

We parked in a huge parking lot, half-full of cars. The caballero quickly exited, opened my door, and motioned the way. He quarter bowed like I knew he would. We walked to the entrance and entered. More guards were at a big guard station. More badge flipping. Someone should write a book on badge flipping; they probably have. This time it was Robert, that would be Special Agent Robert Smolanski, who knew the guards and took the lead. They exchanged pleasantries; there was more head-pointing towards me, followed by the ubiquitous check-me-out looks. I stared back blankly, quarter smile, eyebrows slightly elevated. They turned away. We walked to the elevators, and Robert pressed the down button, then looked at me apologetically. The doors opened, a temple bell chimed, and we stepped in. Robert pressed button B-3. *How deep does this place go?*

Robert explained, "We share the building with FEMA. They keep emergency preparedness materials on the ground floor – for easy access, you know, cots, blankets, water, that sort of thing. Down below are the administrative offices." The elevator doors opened onto a fairly large foyer; nicely appointed. A few magenta sofa chairs, console tables, lit paintings on the wall, and fake plants. The floor was covered with medium gray carpet, and the walls were gray as well, probably, for some psycho-babble reason. Off this large lobby area extended three corridors going right, left, and straight ahead. Ernesto motioned to the left hallway. He'd make a good maître d, come to think of it. The halls were wide, same gray color scheme, with the occasional set of double doors, dark gray. They were embossed with an imitation wood grain, an attempt at embellishment. Gray, it's the color you want to think of when you think of government. It's certainly better than red. You don't want to think red when you think government. And I was deep in its caverns. Robert was our tour guide, explaining the names and acronyms as we passed various doors. "This is the Office of Biometric Identity Management, the OBIM for short. They do mostly fingerprint analysis; manage the databases – though fingerprints can be faked with 3-D printers these days. That's a big problem." Then lower, as he shot Agent Cavalierro a guilty glance, "I probably shouldn't have told you that." Ernesto looked at Robert with complete disgust.

We walked a few more steps. Robert gestured, "Here is the System Assessments and Validation for Emergency Responders Program. SAVER for short. We, or uh, they make procurement assessment decisions concerning available equipment. You know; what to deploy, standards, and specifications. I used to work there . . . at SAVER."

Ernesto, that would be Special Agent Cavalierro cut in, "Yeah. But you sure didn't save the taxpayers any money!" Robert threw Ernesto a look that was more like a beam of icicles, and steam erupted from his ears. *Just kidding about the steam.* Thereafter, we walked in silence until we came to a pair of doors labeled – Joint Terrorist Task Force Threat Response Center or the JTTFTRC for short. We entered those doors.

Within were more corridors going this way and that, leading to offices, I presumed. Everywhere, there were cubicles and office partitions, kitchenettes, break rooms, closets, etc. A typical office domain, I guess. Though I'm native to hospitals and totally alien to this type of habitat. They took me to a lobby-like area, complete with tables, a TV screen, a couple of desks squeezed together, and a coffee counter. To one side was a door with a little spy window on top. I could see little wire crisscrosses in it. Safety glass? So that, when it shatters from the inside, the shards won't explode in some onlooker's face? They led me in. As I expected, it was an interrogation room. There was a medium-sized, gray steel table, a chair on one side, two on the other, a small camera up on the ceiling, and a big mirror on one wall. It was just like every interrogation room I'd ever seen – on TV, of course. Maybe there's a government standard, a codebook somewhere on how to build interrogation rooms. Perhaps there's a department behind one of those double doors we passed that writes that stuff: The Department of Standards and Specifications for the Implementation of Humane Enhanced Interrogations. I wouldn't be surprised, especially these days, what with terrorists being in the news every day. And interrogation is a big deal, politically, i.e., what is torture? Waterboarding is OK, bamboo slits under the fingernails, not OK. Check the manual if unsure. One thing was a little surprising though, the room was not gray. The floor was painted burnt brown, with a drain in it, the walls dark green on the bottom, light green on top, with the ceiling some shade of white. They probably had some profound psychological reasons for using that décor. Agent Cavalierro remained outside, Robert escorted me in, motioned to the lone chair, and said, again apologetically, "You're my case; I'll be right outside." Then he looked at me sympathetically and almost said, “Don't worry, I won't let anything bad happen to you." I nodded slightly and said "thank you" with my eyes. Then he left. It's funny how much telepathy there is in everyday life.

I was alone. Under the watchful eye of the camera, the mirror glass, the hidden mics, and the occasional peeper through the spy window, but still alone, a welcome respite from the check-me-out looks and the red polka dots. It was a chance to think, evaluate, and analyze. Blank Jane can deal with the lookers.

There was one bright spot in all this darkness, and it was in my pocket – my phone. They never frisked me. It's small, white, and right there in my hip pocket, camouflaged presumably, by my white uniform. Can I use it? "Hi mom, I'll be a little late tonight. I've been arrested for . . . uh, terrorism, but don't worry." No, not for that, not now. Bathroom break. They've got to let me use the facilities. I'll bide my time, wait for the right moment, and then ask about a lady's room. What if Jack calls? I'll answer it. There's probably nothing the Feds would like better. And Jack would know they have me. He's not dumb.

So, what should I expect? They'll let me stew for an hour or so. I know that from TV too. They figure I'll freak out or something. Should I freak out? No, the Blank Jane thing was working fine. They probably have interrogation experts, though, from one of the rooms down the hall. Maybe they went to college for it. Interrogation 101 and 102, basic freshmen course requirement. Sophomore – Good Cop, Bad Cop, 202, and 203. Junior year – Intimidation 302. In the senior year, they get the good stuff – Electro-shock therapy 404, Water inducement 406, and Rendition – procedures and methodology. Graduate with a B.S. in Inquisition Management . . . *Shit, maybe I am freaking out.*

At that point, the only thing I could do was try and think good thoughts of happier times. I was always happiest hanging out at Jack's place, with Mr. McEvey, of course. But it was more than a good time. It was a quest for the unknown. A higher purpose mixed in with the good times, doing all manner of crazy things. Building and rebuilding drones, whizzing them around. Jumping for joy on the "Springz," testing them, and making adjustments. Winding coils for Mr. M. He got results, too, from his zero-point energy projects. Serious results. Jack promised he'd follow up on that. Poor Mr. McEvey, I missed him. But we had our project to build, first small, then big. We were on to something too. Something wonderful, beyond words. I found comfort in knowing that Jack was out there somewhere with the . . . I still didn't know what to call it. But he was out there. That was a high probability. And being alone, with that one little fact to hold on to, I could abide. Jack will do something to get me out. I knew that for sure.

A couple of men walked in. They were different from Special Agents Smolanski and Cavalierro. They were, in all likelihood, the interrogators.

Chapter 7: The Accommodations – *Jack*

The walls solidified into structures, and the structures were part of a larger vista. It was another habitat, like Candy Land, only this time, I was quite familiar with the scene. It was my home! Or at least a facsimile of my parents' home, the place where I grew up. I rented the barn out back.

Let me explain. My father is an orthopedist – a bone doctor. My mother is his nurse, secretary, office manager, and pretty much everything else. It's a real mom-and-pop operation and very appropriate for a small town like Litchfield in a small state like Connecticut.

Instead of a ranch-type dwelling on a suburban tract, they bought a modest farm on the outskirts of town. The idea of country living appealed to them. Of course, in Litchfield, pop. 1232, pretty much everywhere, is in the outskirts of town. But there is a pretty little village center with the usual – post office, picturesque church, hardware store, pizza joint, etc. There was only one problem . . . the population swelled in the summer with fleeing New Yorkers. The summer people. But they didn't bother me. It was still a great place to grow up.

And there it was, right before my eyes. The white farmhouse with the wraparound front porch, the detached two-car garage, and my barn, in all its glory, to the smallest detail.

Let me start with the grounds. There were trees. The same trees as back home. The huge old sugar maple that's been shading the house for, we figure, at least two hundred years. And all the others everywhere else. Generally, the whole area was semi-wooded. We were standing on the street, facing the main house. Bordering the drive was an old stonewall with a little picket fence on top. It still needed a paint job. Beyond the lawn, decorative posts framed the front porch, and a fake grass carpet covered the floorboards. The same as home. There was the red door, the windows with black shutters and trim, the dark roof, and the whitewashed chimney standing tall on the side. It was all there – even the shrubs, including the dead yew by the front steps. Sitting on the horizon below a big blue sky was a bright yellow sun still radiating its warmth. Here and there were puffy white clouds, and a summer breeze rustled the leaves. But I didn't see any birds.

To my right was the hayfield gone wild with goldenrod, loosestrife, and Queen Ann's Lace. Yellow, purple, and white, quite nice really, but deer tick heaven. Past the house and to my left was the barn – my beloved barn. Once red, now faded to gray, probably more gray than red. There was a big sliding door in front, which I rarely used except to bring in the big stuff. For my main egress, I used the small entrance on the side. Above was the hayloft, fitted with crisscrossed white oak shutters though faded and peeling like the rest of the windows. And on the roof, like a crown perched on an old king's head, sat the cupola with a broken weathervane on top – a faded copper rooster permanently pointing southwest.

It looked complete, including the adjacent silo with the big doors and a shiny domed roof. It was covered in tin and only leaked during heavy rains. I used it as an extended workshop, and that was where I built the "conveyance." It fit nicely inside with several feet to spare. I'm surprised Albert didn't recreate the exploded roof. *I must have crashed through it.* Albert just stood there, leaning on his cane, legs crossed, puffing away, while watching me gawk.

"We wanted to make you feel at home, Jack, so we . . . recreated it here." The lines of amusement radiating from his eyes betrayed his usual studied nonchalance.

What could I say? I was stunned: "Well, Albert, this should do the trick. I know, don't tell me, you have manufacturing facilities that can accommodate most situations."

"That is precisely correct, Jack, and it's no trick. Your people have the technology and do the same every day – with 3d printers. We simply scale it up a little here."

"Scale it up a little," I repeated. "Ok, I'll buy that, and I won't even ask how."

"It's no secret, Jack. First, we scan the object, in this case, your farm, with meta-particles, what you would call neutrinos. Next, we make a map to the required level of detail – usually, the molecular standard is adequate. Then we project the appropriate substrates, bit by bit. It's a speedy process and entirely automatic."

"You're right, Albert. We do it every day on Earth. As a matter of fact, these days when I travel, I don't go to motels anymore. I just pull out my trusty 3D printer and . . . make my farm. So, I'll feel more at home." This time it was my turn to stare nonchalantly at Albert with a little smirk.

"I'm beginning to understand your humor, Jack." That was all he said, then he pointed with his cane, "Shall we proceed."

We continued to walk down the driveway at a normal pace. There was no need for moving sidewalks, not in my own backyard. And I wondered, how long he planned to carry on the charade with the cane? The pipe . . . it looked like he actually enjoyed puffing on that thing. Enjoyed? That question nagged at the back of my mind.

"Albert, you didn't laugh at my little joke just now. I was wondering, do you . . . have a sense of humor?" I just asked him flat out, impertinent though it was. "And . . . can you actually, uh . . . enjoy yourself?"

"Humor is a state of mind usually induced by a quick release from fear . . . from something threatening, which then becomes safe or acceptable. I have no fears, Jack. But your 'little joke' revealed your fear of the possibility that your species may someday be able to recreate things such as your farm. It is not ridiculous, and the prospect is not something to fear. Indeed, that is why I am here. To help Earth transition to the next level of development . . . when you are ready. As to enjoyment, we must postpone that topic since we have arrived at our destination."

We were at the barn. As I reached for the door, I noticed a few sparrows fly by. I commented, "Are they real?"

Albert saw what I saw, "About as real as everything else here, Jack."

That statement was something I could have pondered . . . for about a lifetime. We entered the barn.

As expected, the interior of my barn was exactly the same as I had left it. *Only it was not my barn!* I needed to remind myself of this little fact. But it sure as hell could have been. Everything was the same, only cleaner, not like the mess I left.

I won't bore you with too many details. The barn was about 30 feet by 40; all rough-sawn barn wood with exposed beams, posts, and trusses everywhere. About halfway in was a twisty stairway that led to the loft where I slept. Underneath was a kitchenette: fridge, stove, and a couple of counters and cabinets. To the right, when you first walked in, was a small bathroom and shower. In the winter, it was a long trek from the loft, with no insulation in the walls and only a wood stove for heat. But I had caulked the cracks pretty good; at least the wind didn't blow through anymore.

The rest of the barn was my workshop. Workbenches and shelves lined the walls, adorned with tools, books, instruments, computers, and the remnants of our prior experiments. All there in the exact places where I had left them.

Near the kitchen was a small table that I used as a desk and for dining. It was normally heaped full of junk and in complete disarray. Now it was clean and set for two – plates, utensils, and wine glasses. In the center was a big bowl of steaming hot spaghetti and meatballs. Please be advised that spaghetti and meatballs are my most favorite of all foods, ever since I was old enough to hold a fork and squip-up the strands. Of course, I no longer squip. The aroma awakened my appetite, and it roared like a saber tooth tiger – silently; after all, I am civilized.

"We thought you might be hungry. Do you mind if I join you?" This Albert intoned in his usual inimitable intonations.

"Albert, I could kiss and hug you . . . if you weren't some kind of a . . . spaceship man, no offense." Sometimes I talk before I think.

"No offense taken, Jack. Your humor is most . . . understandable."

But I did feel like I was back home. In truth, I had a hard time believing that I was not home. Albert had succeeded beyond anything imaginable. Too well, to be perfectly frank. Because it reminded me of the one thing that was missing – Janey. Occasionally Janey would come over, straighten up the place, make a meal, and be there smiling when I came home. Suddenly, I felt a real pang – make that a shank, in the lower right rib cage. I missed Janey.

"There's only one thing missing, Albert, and that's Janey."

Albert's smile vanished as he deftly uncorked the wine.

"It's not that I don't appreciate all this, it's just that . . . this reminds me so much of home and . . . I left her in a rather indelicate situation back there. She was involved in my . . . hmm, escapade. I just hope she's all right."

Albert puffed away for a lingering moment, then asked, "Do you mind if I smoke, Jack?"

"No, please do, it's your . . ."

"We found your phone in the wreckage of your conveyance. After we make some minor modifications, we shall return it. Then you can call Ester Jane and determine her current state of well-being."

He found my phone! Hallelujah! And I'll be able to use it . . . from here . . . to call, Ester Jane? *How did he know her full name?*

"Albert, you are the best kind of a . . ."

"Spaceship man? I know Jack, shall we dine?"

"After you" I pulled out his chair and motioned like an accomplished waiter. We sat down, and Albert poured the wine. It was a fine Chianti. Then we clinked glasses. Suddenly life was good.

For a very brief moment, let me tell you about Janey; that is, Ester Jane Riley, the girl next door, literally, I'm not kidding. She lives on the farm down the road. And figuratively as well. She is awesomely typical. No head-turner, but rather – naturally good looking. And natural is a good word for her. She doesn't need unnatural embellishment. Regrettably, I must reveal that some people call her – "plain Jane." Not her friends, though, and she has many of those. Come to think of it, that could be the secret to her popularity; she's not too pretty and not too plain. Her yin and yang are in perfect balance. One thing's for sure, though; people are just a little happier when she's around. Especially me.

Brown hair, brown eyes, about five-seven, ovalene face, and curvy body. She rarely wore make-up; there was no need, being a nurse, and all. She works out and radiates a healthy glow and a healthy disposition. "Healthy" is a good word for Janey, and I had an "unhealthy" attachment to her. I can't help it, being human, that is. Anyway, we grew up together, and I gradually fell for her. They say childhood romances don't last. Well, I don't care about what they say.

Janey is a smart girl, and I guess you can say we corrupted her. Mr. McEvey and me. We got her interested in science, the way-out stuff. We talked about things: the unknown, action at a distance, and all the invisible stuff out there. Gradually we pulled her into our sphere of activity. But don't get me wrong, she had her own life. She studied medicine at the University of Connecticut and graduated with a degree in nursing. As previously mentioned, she works at Yale-New Haven Hospital, their Nuclear Medicine Division. She had access to medical isotopes, all kinds, but . . . she probably doesn't work there anymore.

Back in the barn, we began to feast, and it was delicious. Albert was manging away with as much gusto as me. I had to ask, "Now, Albert, don't tell me you're not enjoying this meal? As I said this, he twirled a fork-full of spaghetti smothered in tomato sauce and then devoured it, but with good manners and etiquette.

He swallowed, wiped his mouth, and then sipped his wine. "In your language, 'enjoyment' involves feelings of pleasure. And pleasure is intrinsically related to biologic processes; endocrinal, hormonal, reproductive . . ."

"How about ingestion?" It was my turn to interrupt. "It sure looks like you're enjoying the act of 'eating,' Albert."

"That which is apparent may not be, Jack. Permit me to continue. I do have sources of enjoyment. First, simply being is cause enough for me and my larger self, the Ship. To be able to implement the tasks set forth is all that I require. Doing so imparts gratification and what you would call 'joy.' And we are not idle here, Jack. We observe and chronicle the new every day. Further, I am in contact with the Continuum, though to a diminishing extent. And new things are a source of wonderment. You are correct in noticing my ostensible enjoyment in the consumption of this pasta dinner. It is new to me, though unnecessary for my sustenance. And your unexpected visit is new to me as well. Are you genuine? Do you represent your species' level of advancement? The answer to these questions could also prove to be . . . a source of fulfillment. Perhaps you will tell me something about yourself. What motivated you? Many theories are circulating on Earth as to the nature of the Universe. How did you, Jack Neufield . . . arrive at 4,3?"

I knew it was coming, and there it was. The inquiry, the probe, the big look-see. Albert had twisted my innocuous little question into the topic he wanted and needed to know about. Well then, let's have at it. I told him my story.

They say your life flashes before you when you die. Well, mine was flashing then, but I wasn't dying. And questions were flashing as well. What should I tell him? The truth, of course, but what truth? Where does it begin? What does it entail? I had one more question for Albert.

"Albert, you seem to know many things about me, which I have to assume came from my memories. This would include even the image of yourself, Albert Einstein. If you can read my memories, why do you need me to tell you my story?"

"The human brain emits electromagnetic radiation, Jack . . . brain waves. General images, strong thoughts, impulses, and so forth. They are constantly emanating, and I can read them. But they are not much more than what you overtly transmit with your facial muscles and other general body languages. We consider such indices to be basic forms of communication . . . and public. Deep probes, the actual reading of your synapses, we will not do unless absolutely necessary. We value the concept of privacy – which is a universally accepted standard of propriety, Jack. And most species simply prefer to be polite. Everything is much more pleasant that way."

"That's good to know, Albert." I put down my fork, having pretty much finished the meal. It was excellent, and I was sated. Meanwhile, Albert leaned back, refilled his pipe, and then began a prolonged ignition process, ejecting clouds of that bluish-gray ethereal substance. A symphony of smoke, he puffed rings within rings. He seemed to thoroughly enjoy the whole operation. Like an actor savoring his craft, he communicated that enjoyment to his audience. And made me want to smoke too. It looked and smelled so good. During his performance, Albert stared steadily at me – waiting. The ball was in my court.

The hard drive in my brain spun up and spat out a slew of images, which played out across that silver screen behind my eyes. Where to begin? Do I really want to tell Albert what he wants to hear? Do I want access to the Continuum, access to him? What does that even mean?

"Well, Albert, I guess it all began when I failed the third grade." Albert's eyebrows elevated. "That's right, you heard correct. If you thought I was some kind of whiz-kid genius, you are, unfortunately for me, mistaken."

"Go on, Jack, this sounds like it will be . . . interesting." Albert lowered his gaze a notch and puffed a couple of quick puffs.

"But it wasn't my fault. I just didn't get along with Mrs. Trainer, my third-grade teacher. She had skinny arms and legs and a barrel chest. Her face was always angry and red, and her hair looked like a space helmet. That was Mrs. Helen Trainer. I was the class cutup, and she did not like interruptions, especially when they come from the class, uh, comedian. And I didn't like angry teachers. I called her the 'lion trainer' fairly routinely, behind her back, of course. But she heard. The old bat had radar. She didn't find the moniker cute, and she lashed out at me, wielding her voice like a whip. And I was the lion. Her preferred punishment besides her roar was detention. And I got many."

"Now, Albert, you must know that getting detention in the third grade is a rarity. I suppose that makes me a rarity too." I was warming up. "That's my claim to fame – Jack Neufield, boy wonder, holds the world's record for third-grade detentions." I looked at Albert, waiting for a response.

"That contained a fairly substantial quantity of humor, Jack." His face conveyed all the emotion of a frying pan. But that didn't bother me; I was revving up.

"But that wasn't all. I was also failing math and pretty much everything else too. Then one day, with her extra-sensory perception, she heard me refer to her as 'Mrs. Hell-on-Wheels Trainer'. A variation on the Helen theme. A crack I proudly considered one of my best. My fellow classmates did, too, from the level of their hilarity. The reward for my rhetorical wit was the onset of parent-teacher conferences. Which led to the best thing that ever happened to me. By the mutual agreement of all those involved, I departed good ole Bethlehem Elementary. And met Mr. McEvey. And do you want to know what the funny part was, Albert?"

"Yes, Jack, I do."

"They wanted me out even more than I wanted out. It was a real happy fest."

"Once again, Jack, that was intensely jocular." My jokes were going over like a subpoena.

I took a moment to reminisce about Mr. McEvey. Pleasant memories fast-forwarded in the theater of my mind. Mr. McEvey was a physics teacher at the local college – North West Community College. He was also one of my father's patients. My parents had to scramble to find tutors for me, although home-schooling outfits provide everything online. I think they just wanted someone to ride herd, make sure I did the work. Why did they choose Mr. McEvey? Maybe they saw the spark in him, the flame, and hoped it would ignite something in me as well. It worked. Mr. M. lit the kind of fire only a master arsonist can set. It was hot enough to melt steel. And it kindled in me a burning obsession to learn the unknown. Mr. McEvey asked questions, and I learned to do the same. To boldly question the religious tenets of organized science. Of course, I didn't know we weren't supposed to do that. I thought we were just playing around doing fun YouTube stuff. Anyway, that's what I learned from Mr. M. But he was more than my teacher. He became my best friend.

He was fifty-something, thin, normal height – 5' 10ish and usually dressed in blah clothes except for his two-toned saddle shoes, which he routinely wore. He owned two pairs, brown and white and blue and white. I guess he figured that was all he needed to jazz up his appearance. Worn jeans and a brown corduroy jacket completed the look.

His unruly hair had turned a bit gray on the sides and usually was long enough to flop down and drape across his thin face. I suppose some would call him a real character, but I knew, deep down, he shied from the light. He may have stood out a little, but mostly, I think he just wanted to be left alone. I guess we're all a little schizoid like that. Dualism.

Why are some people curious and others not? I do not know. Some say it's to eliminate the stress of the unknown. But why should someone care about something they don't know? Others say it's skepticism. A fundamental distrust in the sincerity of those perpetuating the beliefs. Cynicism. But I do know that curiosity is what propelled the truly great – Newton, Maxwell, Einstein. They were just plain interested in knowing the unknown. Why do invisible forces make things happen? I also know, from personal experience, that curiosity is what makes learning easy, strike that . . . it makes learning a voracious necessity. When someone is interested in something, truly passionate, that's all they want to do – delve into it and learn everything. The subject could be dinosaurs or macramé, or it could be physics. That was Mr. M's ocean, and we dived in together.

But there was something else about Mr. McEvey that was more important; it was the source of his curiosity, the wellspring. He wanted to be remembered. To be something other than obscure. To leave behind a gift for humanity. Mr. M. lived for the greater good. And as the sand dial of his life ran down and time became more precious, his interest in our projects intensified. Oh yeah, I forgot to mention . . . Mr. McEvey had bone cancer. That's why he was my father's patient. He didn't know that I knew, and I didn't let on till the end. Bone cancer is a slow disease. I had the gift of Mr. McEvey for several years. And for that, I'm very grateful.

"What was so significant about Mr. McEvey, Jack?" With this, Albert brought me back. I think he knew. He must have perceived my little reverie and deduced much. Damn those brain waves.

"He was the man who put me on the path that led . . . to here. He taught me to ask questions. Questions like – how something unseen could push or pull on an object. What's the mechanism at work there? That was an important one for us. Also, what's a field, and how does it work. And what is energy? That was another big one. And what are Time and Space? But electromagnetism and gravity, those were the areas we focused on."

"And these kinds of pursuits can be rather – engrossing, shall we say. Especially if one is irreverent enough to question . . . question the laws of physics, that is. And we did. And to justify our endeavors, Mr. McEvey was fond of singling out the great questioners of history . . . Galileo, Darwin, Marie Curie, and Einstein. Present company excluded, of course."

"Of course, Jack." Albert smiled.

The wine was taking hold. I took another sip and continued, "We would usually start with the phrase: 'what would happen if' . . . That was all we needed to start a project. And Mr. McEvey said the same things you said before. That our society is on the brink of discovering the deep secrets – how things actually work. How it all comes together and fits in one neatly wrapped little package."

Albert's gaze probed deep. Then he asked, "Did he teach you about 4,3, Jack?"

"Everything else, Albert. He taught me everything else."

Albert took a deep breath. *Was it relief?* "Would you care for some more wine Jack?" Now it was Albert's turn to play waiter. Without delay, he stood, leaned over, and refilled my glass. His moves were polished like a professional garcon, his left arm held behind his back. I'm sure his intent was to lubricate my larynx. He succeeded.

"What sort of projects did you and Mr. McEvey engage in? What got you started, Jack?"

"Well, Albert, you have to remember I started pretty young. After we completed a science subject in the home-school curriculum, we did the corresponding labs. We rigged simple experiments that demonstrated things like capillary action, Bernoulli's principle, Pascal's Law, and so on. But we hit our stride with electromagnetism. That was Mr. M's area of expertise and what we focused on."

I asked, "Are you familiar with 'YouTube,' Albert? Well, that was our second home."

Albert nodded, then banged out his pipe a couple of times on the table.

"YouTube is where the tinkerers, the would-be inventors, the savers-of-the-world with their free-energy devices . . . present their wares. Though the site has its share of phonies, too, they're easy to spot. We'd browse through topics like zero-point energy, plasma energy generators, levitation devices, that sort of thing. Mr. M. loved that stuff, and I grew to love it too. But I'm getting ahead of myself here. Let me go back to what probably was the first experiment, what got me started."

"We were studying magnetism. Mr. M. brought in a good-sized bar magnet to demonstrate the force, which to him was something akin to magic. And ultimately, I guess you can say it is because nobody knows, deep down, what it really is. Oh, some say it's photons, and they carry the force. But photons can be seen, unlike magnetism. Others say all the atoms line up with their charges spinning in sync. What's a charge anyway? Well, this was the sort of stuff Mr. M. and I would talk about. In a friendly way. I suppose we were somewhat irreverent. We joked and asked questions. And we did not accept the established answers."

"Albert, I think you gave me too much wine. Now I'm rambling."

"No, Jack, this is good. This is what I need to hear." He sat there, raptly attentive. Oddly, he was smoking his pipe unlit.

"All right, the point is we asked questions, Albert. Like how could a chunk of metal pick up a clump of paper clips at a distance? All the books said because it's a field. 'Well, what's a field?' we asked. We were determined to learn the trick, how the big magician in the sky did it. First, we tried to block the magnetic field. We put various insulators between the magnet and the paper clips. We tried rubber. We tried ceramic. We tried lead. Nothing stopped it. Then I took the ultimate test. I stuck my hand in there, with the back of my hand against the magnet, and the paper clips stuck to my palm. The force went right through my hand, and I felt nothing. It had no effect except to whet my curiosity . . . permanently."

"That is not exactly 4,3, Jack."

"You asked me where it all started. That was where it started." *Now he must think I'm some kind of idiot fool after that story.*

"The point is, Albert, we learned something, or I did anyway: Nothing stops magnetism! Nothing. Then the question became: How could magnetism be photons; photons as force carriers when photons are easily stopped? Anything solid stops a photon. A leaf, a piece of paper, a hand. And nothing, absolutely nothing stops magnetism! How could that be?"

"As you said, Jack, you learned early to ask the appropriate questions, a necessary prelude to the comprehension of . . . the underlying principles."

Maybe I redeemed myself – slightly.

"Next, we started in with coils. All kinds. They were even more mysterious to us. You pass a magnet by a piece of copper wire, and you get electricity, voila. It's as simple as that. A real hat trick. And now all the books were saying magnetism is electricity. Magnetism, which nothing can stop and was previously defined as force-carrying photons, is now electrons flowing through a wire. But only if the magnet and the wire are moving next to each other. Movement is the key. It won't work if they're not moving. The inconsistencies kept piling up, but so were the clues. And the clues would lead to the 'underlying principles.' Or so we believed. Hence, the experiments began, in every way possible." I yawned. I tried to stifle it, but it came out, and Albert picked up on it.

"It has been a rather long day for you, Jack. A period of sleep at this time would be propitious. Shall we adjourn for the evening?" Albert started to get up.

I was on a roll. I didn't want to stop. "Albert, just let me finish this next part. I think you'll like where it leads."

"Please proceed, Jack." He gestured and sat back down.

"A few years later, we were thoroughly immersed in our mutual obsessions, especially since I had the workshop." I motioned around. "Mr. McEvey was into . . . perpetual motion. Don't laugh . . ."

"I do not find perpetual motion humorous, Jack. Indeed, for my builders and many others, perpetual or eternal activity is a necessary specification in the design of most things."

"Well, back on Earth if you mention perpetual motion, you're either laughed at or scoffed at. Hence, we kept to ourselves and minimized our YouTube uploads. Basically, Mr. M. sought free energy, whether, from gravity, or various configurations of coils, cold fusion, and even zero-point energy, you know . . . free energy from the aether." At this point, Albert dropped his pipe. I'm sure it was not some kind of subliminal message. He was truly riled. This prompted me to ask, "Are you familiar with the Aether, Albert?"

"Our science has explored the topic, though I have not been introduced to all aspects of that subject."

Albert said this as he fumbled to pick up his pipe, a nice briar half-bent. He seemed distant, distracted even. He proceeded to strike a match. I jumped on his inadvertent slip.

"Ahh. So, it is a valid area of endeavor, if your, uh . . . associates are involved."

"I thought you were going to relate one more quick story, Jack." Albert instantly recovered and steered the conversation back to what he needed to learn . . . stuff about me.

"All right, all right. Mr. M. sought free energy or any source of alternative energy from wherever. This was his area of interest, what he wanted to give to humanity. I was into gravitics, or more precisely – anti-gravity. Again, anybody else would laugh and scoff . . . except you, of course."

"Of course," Albert replied.

"Electro-gravitics, magnetic levitation, the gyroscopic effect, that sort of thing. I just wanted to fly. Fly around quietly and free, zooming here, zooming there. Anyway, it's a large established field and all over the Internet. I could retell the history starting with Tesla in the '20s, but I promised to be brief."

Albert just nodded.

"My approach was to find some way to alter or reverse whatever it is that pulls one object towards another. I assumed there had to be a rational mechanism that could be, somehow, interfered with. Einstein called it the fabric of Space-Time. I intended to take a scissors to that fabric." At this, Albert's gaze intensified, and I felt him penetrate my mind. He lowered his pipe and raised an eyebrow.

"Now, this next part is going to sound crazy even to you. I began with a torus. I reasoned that since most everything in the universe is either spherical or toroidal, including UFOs, the torus was a good form to start with. This worked out because donut-shaped coils were one of our main areas of research. I asked the question . . . 'What happens if I mix radioactivity with magnetism?'" Albert sat perfectly still, his eyes searching deep. I continued.

"There was nothing about this on the internet, at least that I could find. Oh, there was something about changing the flight paths of charged particles, but nothing else. It was an empty niche. So, I started. I bent a 2" steel pipe into a circle about 30" in diameter." I gestured, holding my hands apart. "Then I wrapped it with 12 gauge insulated copper wire, standard house wire, and created a series of coils with light switches to time the flux. I powered the thing with standard house current, which I converted to DC. It was a lot of juice. In the top of the pipe between the coils, I drilled a 3/4" hole. As I flipped the switch, I dropped in a pellet of technetium 99, wrapped in iron foil. Janey got the isotope. Oh, I forgot to mention, the rig was suspended from a digital scale. As the pellet began to spin up, the weight of the object diminished. It went down a full three-tenths of a pound. That was significant and not due to any eddy currents or measurement errors either. After we repeated the experiment a couple of times, Mr. M. and I whooped for joy and did the happy dance. Granted, three-tenths was not much, considering the whole thing weighed twenty-something pounds, but it was enough for Mr. M. and me. We knew we were on the right track. Unfortunately, I went flying about five feet and got burnt pretty bad when I touched the pipe. The insulation had burned through and shorted the pipe. But the shock was worth it. I recovered happily." With that, I stopped and waited for Albert's response.

"I would have liked to have seen you and Mr. McEvey do the happy dance, Jack. That would have been in fact . . . significantly humorous." He punctuated his response with a couple of expertly crafted plumes. They soared and partially obscured his poker face. I interpreted this to be something other than disapproval. Then Albert continued, "Though essentially, I found the story to be quite edifying." With this, I found a ray of hope. "Now, I shall retire, and I recommend that you do the same."

"Just one more thing, Albert. That was only the beginning of the story. The end sits out there in your hangar – my conveyance."

"Speaking of your 'conveyance,' Jack, tomorrow, if your health allows, we shall engage in the driving lesson."

Suddenly I felt like doing the happy dance again. But I restrained myself. I only said, "I shall be your humble student."

With that, Albert stood and walked to the door. Then he turned like a Hollywood detective and said, "Technically, Jack, you just taught us a significant quantity of what we needed to know." Then he left.

I leaned back from the table and reflected for a moment. Of all the deep thoughts I could have had, my concern focused on the dishes. The dirty dishes. If this were my place, my dinner party, then, of course, I should and would wash them. But that issue was somewhat blurred here. Technically, I was Albert's guest. A guest of the Ship. They did invite me, sort of. In reality, they did considerably more than invite me. They pulled me in, without my acquiescence . . . and saved my life, not that I'm objecting. In many cultures, if you save someone's life, you become responsible for that life. Therefore, I really should not be the one who is responsible for the dis . . . *"You're going off the deep end. Get a grip."* A little voice intervened.

I regained control and took a deep breath. Clearing my mind, I tried to think about nothing for a while. Overall, concerning my standing with the Ship, I must have enhanced my cause, at least a little. I just spoke the truth. Not in its entirety, but that's impossible anyway. My provisional status may not be so quasi after tonight's performance. I felt pretty good. And tomorrow . . . was the driving lesson!

I left the mess and trudged up the stairs. Looking around, all was the same. The platform bed that I had built from used 2x4's, the antique bureau, the old chair – still ripped on the armrest, and the clunky old TV. I dared not turn it on. Everything was just like home, only neat as though the maid had come. I don't have a maid. I stripped down and burrowed into the bed. I felt like I was back home . . . safe. My eyes closed, then popped open. This was not my home. This was a quarter-million miles away! But still, I felt safe. My eyes closed, and I slept like the dead.

Chapter 8: Driving Lesson – *Jack*

The next morning, I woke refreshed. When . . . what time it was, I do not know. There were no clocks, and I had lost my watch. Besides, time seemed to be different here. It's hard to describe. It just felt off by a couple of beats. Still, the sun was out, riding high on the horizon. Though, that could mean anything. I have to keep reminding myself – this whole thing is an artificial habitat, designed to make me . . . "feel more at home."

I had coffee and cereal, just like always. Funny though, the dishes from the night before were washed, dried, and put away. *Curious.*

The doorbell rang. It was Albert, but not the same Albert. He looked a good twenty-five years younger. He wore the same dark suit, vest, winged collar, and tie. As snappy and dapper as ever, only he was a whole lot younger. His hair was dark and only flecked with gray, not white like before, though still longish, and wildly reaching out. And he sported a thick black mustache beneath kindly eyes. He looked like a man of competence and integrity. A good-looking man. A man whom anyone would feel safe to be with.

"Albert! What happened? You take a case of Geritol for breakfast?"

"Good morning, Jack. Your humor is, as always, seriously entertaining." His young face remained as impassive as ever, except for his eyes. They narrowed a little.

"As a representative symbol of this Ship and the Continuum, we thought a younger visage would convey a more effective and dynamic presence. Though quite old by your units of measurement, my capabilities remain constant."

He still had the pipe, though, which he pulled from his top pocket and lit. Not everything had changed. All I said was, "Capabilities?"

"Yes, Jack. Within the range of possibilities that you can envision, we have the ability to accomplish . . . most anything." That was about as clear as a sheet of lead.

"Well then, when I'm old, can you make me young again too?"

"One step at a time, Jack. One step at a time. Shall we embark on the driving lesson now?"

"Lead on, my friend." The statement just came out. I guess, at that point, I considered Albert to be a friend, even though he was pretty far from being . . . human. But that didn't bother me. I could get past that.

We walked out the door, up the driveway, and back into the void. The swirling gray mist seemed to be the standard decor around here. Maybe it's what they put in the vacant areas. Making small talk, I commented on this, "Albert, these gray areas, like this one we're in right now, I presume they're empty and unused areas of the Ship?"

"That would be a partially true observation, Jack. But this space is not empty and unused. It has an important utility. It provides a habitat for you, Jack. You have specific requirements as to temperature, pressure, atmospheric mix, and gravitic force. We maintain these parameters in the areas where you are . . . such as here." He motioned around with his pipe.

I must have been too discombobulated to think about this before. *How could I not have? We're in Space.* All I could say was, "You would do all this for me?"

"The level of difficulty and effort to accomplish this is minimal. Also, it may be correct to say, we have waited 271 million years for you to arrive, Jack. Or, at least, for your species to arise, which they have not, as yet, except for you . . . maybe." Again, the clarity of thought on Albert's part was as obtuse as ever.

"But how did you know back then that we humans would 'arise' as you say? I mean, that was the Jurassic or Triassic period. The time of the dinosaurs. Primitive animals only, not even a hint of mammals."

"We knew the conditions were right for sentient carbon-based life forms to evolve. Indeed, as you say, the process had already begun. Only our continued observation was needed. If intelligent life forms sprang forth from that miasma of primordial life, we would be here, to welcome you . . . to the stars. And I know what you are thinking, Jack. How could I wait so long? Abiding is not difficult . . . for eternal entities. We have all the time in the Universe."

One simply lurches from one source of amazement to another. Albert was not finished.

"Concerning living areas, we maintain many different habitats here, each with their own specific requirements, like the city we passed through yesterday. That one is part of our base configuration." The oration was definitely worth a few good puffs, and Albert obliged. He strolled along with the spring of a younger man. A more vigorous image indeed.

"Are you expecting company? A visit perhaps from a bonafide Continuum member?"

"No, Jack. The probability of said event is very small, though I do receive communication from time to time. Most have moved beyond. They have no need for artifacts like . . . me. And even places like here." He upturned his palm and splayed his fingers . . . "Such as this galaxy." I just let that one go and asked,

"Did you tell them about me, and . . . I mean Earth's level of development. Being near 4,3 and all?"

"No, Jack. The issues they are concerned with are very far removed from these micro-events."

"Micro events," I thought? *What's a macro event?* I refrained from further questions. We were approaching the hangar anyway.

The towering walls took form as we approached. And the gray void discharged into the hangar, the white floor crowded with tiers of spacecraft, small, medium, and large. Mostly spheres. Again, why does everything have to be round? I filed that under "future questions for Albert."

As we strolled through the rows, I asked, "I don't see any exit signs, Albert. How are we going to uh . . . leave the Ship?"

"I will open a passage through the hull. It is semi-permeable, as previously mentioned." I spied my craft, "Here we are, Jack. Your conveyance."

And there it was in all its glorious splendor “my conveyance.” But pretty damn far from splendor when compared to all the other craft. But a whole lot better than what crashed through my silo back home, the flying whatever – the outer ring and the spokes with a pod stuck in the middle. It had all been reworked by Albert since the original had presumably, uh, “disintegrated”? But I had no problem overlooking that little fact.

I gave it another look-see. Now it was sleek, strong, and purposeful. All smooth and seamless, even shiny. Not like what I built, the mishmash of jagged pipe sloppily welded and screwed together. But the central pod was the flaw in Albert's plan for indigenous plausibility. Even upon a cursory inspection, the object would not look like it came from Earth. Certainly not from an old Ferris wheel. The clear material was a couple of inches thick, reinforced with a web of some kind, and the door was configured with a very serious-looking airtight seal. Also, there were dark areas behind the seats and under the floor, which housed God knows what. But I wasn't complaining. I kept my mouth shut . . . just like before.

Albert continued, "As you can see, it's very similar, the major difference being – the control surface."

"The control surface! That looks like the dashboard from my father's old Mercedes." The 1965 300SE he keeps in the garage. Takes it out maybe three times a year, to car shows and such. "He loves that car, but I'm sure this is a facsimile; a carbon copy, right Albert?"

"You have to understand Jack . . . we are prohibited from interfering . . ."

I interrupted as the reality of the situation hit me: "You really took my father's dashboard, didn't you?" But truth be told, this would probably be the least of my problems back home. The feds were, no doubt, sweating Janey in a cell, with bright lights and a couple of goons barking questions. And my parents were likely on their way back from Afghanistan – to deal with the trouble their darling terrorist son started.

"We have to maintain the illusion of plausibility, Jack. The craft must be doable . . . by you. Please allow me to repeat, we are forbidden from interfering or injecting our technology into your culture . . . until induction, that is. And we must also acknowledge the high probability of your capture by the authorities on Earth." With that, he pocketed his pipe and opened the driver's side door and motioned like a professional garcon again.

"Entrez vous, Monsieur Jacques." My angst over the dashboard dissipated.

"Why, thank you, Albert. You know French?" This was said with my usual high level of thoughtlessness.

"I know every language, Jack." That was it. Enough said. He walked around and opened the passenger door and took a seat. A very comfortable seat, I noticed. A seat that would have come “standard equipment” in an antique Mercedes Benz.

"You took the seats too?"

"Please engage the seat restraining mechanism and turn the key. The power source will engage, inject fuel into the coil, and initiate all the other systems, including life support. We should lift a few inches off the ground". I did as he said, and an array of pretty lights lit the dashboard, dials glowed, and I sensed the thing come alive. We rose a couple of inches. A smile creased my lips. I'm back. But it would be nice if I knew how to fly the darn thing.

"No pre-flight checklist? No 'do's and don'ts'? If all else fails, read the directions?"

"I shall pilot the vehicle to an exit area and take it through the hull. Once outside, the driving lesson will commence. Then we shall see what this 'thing' can do."

"'See what this 'thing' can do'? You mean, you don't know?"

"We know, Jack. But this craft is untested and a new design, even for us." This must be why he changed his appearance. At that moment, I was genuinely needing a more confident and capable look.

We moved out to a lane, down a row, and towards one of the towering dark walls, the hull. When we came to it, the dark coruscations rippled, and we just went in. Right into that black pulsating substance – the super liquid. I sat back and watched the blackness go by. It was constantly moving like a kaleidoscope, only the colors were all shades of black, broken up by the occasional tinge of color. After a few long seconds, I had to ask, "How thick is the hull, Albert?"

"1198 feet, Jack, and it's more than just a hull or a protective covering. It serves as a conduit for many of our various projections. For example, the stream of gravitic threads we used to pull you in emanated from one of our power sources. We routed it to the hull, where it was aimed and directed towards you. It's an integral part of what I am, Jack. Very similar to your skin, which does much more than simply cover your organs. But and I can tell you this, Space-Time matrixes are more current, though they require an extensive infrastructure to construct." This was Albert's idea of just making conversation. He had to know he was revealing information. I egged him on.

"You mean like a space-time continuum. Your namesake is responsible for that idea. His General Theory of Relativity. All the pictures show a planet on a trampoline. It's supposed to represent gravity." Mr. McEvey and I often discussed Einstein's Theory. I liked the trampoline bit. Mr. M. didn't. He figured there had to be more to it.

"The imagery you speak of depicts space-time as a fabric that can be deformed. That image is correct though incomplete. In your illustration, space and time are recognized as containing individual structures, which can be combined. This is an important first step. These respective components can be 'blended' in various ways, woven if you will. Various weaves provide various properties. Some are designed to provide containment, as for a hull. Many of the First-Born, the Builders as we have referred to them, have transcended the bounds of ordinary matter and, therefore, require more distinctive hull designs. And, what you speak of – a space-time Continuum, was first proposed by my namesake's teacher, Herman Minkowski." More small talk.

Chapter 9: The Moon – *Jack*

The conversation ended when we exited the hull and entered Space. I was awestricken. Both by our prior exchange and the vista before me. My adrenalin surged, and my pulse pounded. After a few silent, protracted moments, I heard the intro to Star Trek begin, and it was playing pretty loud, internally. Can't help it. It's autonomic. I'm a trekie. And I must have heard that track a thousand times, as Captain Kirk recited his monologue . . . "to boldly go where no one has gone before." Watched most of the original episodes and the spin-offs too. "Deep Space Nine," "The Next Generation." I love that stuff and science fiction in general. The stories that show how great life can be, not the dystopian junk. My favorite series is "Babylon Five." I own all five years of that. And there I was, living the real thing. I was in Space and staring at the Far side of the Moon.

But we were not "where no man has gone before." People have been coming to the moon for close to fifty years now. They've mapped it, photographed it in detail, and even planted flags on it. Which includes this side, the Dark side, as it's sometimes called. But that term is a misnomer. The Dark side is not dark. The Moon and Earth are locked in a gravitational grip as they revolve around the Sun. When the Near side is dark, the Far side is lit. And vice versa. Where we were, there was plenty of light. And the fantastic panorama before us filled our field of view. It was impressive and breathtaking. Made me want to dive in and take a closer look.

A word on our field of vision, it was huge, being in a transparent bubble – the pod. Though the outer ring did obstruct the view somewhat. The jagged landscape loomed large before us. We seemed to be about two hundred miles up, but distances were hard to judge.

Albert must have sensed my state of semi-shocked amazement. I'm sure he heard the Star Trek jingle in my mind. It was playing loud. He gave me a few moments to take it all in. We were hovering over a large crater. It must have been 50 to 100 miles across. A vast circular plain surrounded by a towering mountain range. The rim. There were a few small peaks directly in the center. Strange. I observed smaller craters within the larger one. And even smaller craters within those. When there's no wind, as in no atmosphere, there's no wear. Once an asteroid hit, the impact stays – for a few billion years. Hence, there were craters everywhere.

The Sun was low and behind us, casting long black shadows, exaggerating the size and shape of every object. And the blackness brought out the color. Who would have thought the Moon was colorful? In every photo I ever saw, it looked black and white, maybe with a slight tinge of yellow. Dust must have gotten in their cameras, screwed up the auto-white balance. Hey, maybe it's only colorful here, on the Far side. I seriously doubt that. Sure, there was plenty of gray dullness out there. But that only lent more contrast to the hues. I must say one thing, though; the color wasn't plain as day. You kind of had to squint, look sideways. It was strange.

The flat expanses were mottled. Patchy, with light and dark browns that changed to orange in places. In one basin near the base of a mountain, a river of red flowed – a sinewy ripple of cinnabar. Some of the flat plains were a dull greenish blue, marbled with a darker blue. The mountains were predominantly shades of gray, but some were streaked with falls of turquoise, blue, and even lavender. Assumably, vertical veins of some kind of mineral. The sum of all this color was . . . beauty. There was beauty in this place, a dull beauty, almost ephemeral, like a daydream. If you looked straight on, the color almost melted away. Maybe that's why the cameras didn't show it.

Another feature that hit me was the detail. Every crevasse and cranny, hillock, and peak caught the eye. There was nothing to get in the way, like air. And the contrast was astounding as well. The bright white highlights stood out against stark black shadows. Add that to all the craters and mountains everywhere, and you have the moon. A nice place to visit, but unquestionably alien. Especially to carbon-based life forms. It was no place to spread a beach blanket and stake an umbrella.

I asked Albert, "What's it like down there, in terms of temperature and atmosphere?" I remembered a few facts from Mr. McEvey, but nothing specific.

"The temperature is approximately 250° Fahrenheit in those areas directly exposed to the Sun and minus 250° in the shade. There is no atmosphere on the Moon, Jack, because the force of gravity is too weak to hold one; to prevent gases from escaping. With no atmosphere, there is no temperature moderation. Hence, you find extreme temperature variations."

“How about water, is there any water down there? In case we want to build a dome and stay awhile."

"There are billions of cubic feet of water in the upper crust, within easy reach of your proposed Moon colony. Especially if it was contiguous to a polar axis. Under a dome, in just the right place, you could spread your beach blanket and stake an umbrella." *He's reading minds again.* "But be sure to use plenty of sunscreen, Jack;

the UV rays would fry you like a chicken embryo." Albert looked at me expectantly.

"Like a chicken embryo? Now that is genuinely humorous, Albert." At least he was loosening up. But I was eager to begin the driving lesson. I turned my head and looked behind. I saw nothing but an empty black space. Strike that. It couldn't be space. There were no stars. Albert noticed.

"What you see is the Ship, Jack. We operate here in an absorptive mode. All electromagnetic radiation is 'consumed.' Everything from radio to gamma rays. We don't want to be seen. More, I'm not allowed to be seen. And the task is becoming more problematic. All manner of devices have, of recent, been orbiting the Moon. Right now, the Lunar Reconnaissance Observer is in a low polar orbit, currently on the near side. It would detect this conveyance and the Ship, for certain. For that reason, I have withdrawn . . . my larger self, further into the Earth's shadow and shall project a starfield on the exterior hull. Your people are getting close, Jack. Close to becoming a space-faring race."

"Well, overall, I'm sure it's a good thing you haven't been seen. Earth doesn't need another 'Independence Day.' Did you see that movie, Albert? I know, don't tell me. You've seen every movie. And project a starfield? What's that all about?"

"Points of light on my hull representing stars. The exact placement as it would appear to a likely observer on Earth. The position, magnitude, and spectrum, as well as movement. It's not difficult, but necessary. Please observe."

The black void twinkled with a multitude of little sparkles, exactly resembling stars. Quite impressive. It rendered the massive space edifice that was the ship virtually invisible. And totally fascinating. But then again, Albert represented a 2.37-billion-year-old civilization.

"Shall we proceed with the driving lesson?" Albert inquired in his usual unflappable manner.

"Let's do what it takes to make this thing go." I was eager, and the Moon beckoned.

Albert gestured towards the dashboard. "It should be just like driving a car, Jack, except for the vertical part. Put it in Drive, step on the gas, and you will go forward. Turn the wheel right or left, or push up and down, and the craft will go that way. Depress the brake pedal, and you will stop. Give it a try."

"What if I brake too hard? Will we go through the windshield?" I was legitimately concerned.

"The effects of large decelerations are moderated, Jack, because this craft operates by modulating the force of gravity. More accurately, by regulating the acceleration or deceleration due to gravity. Negating and amplifying those forces, as you discovered rather precipitously back in your barn on Earth. Here we encounter both the Moon's and the Earth's gravitic fields. This craft manipulates those forces, countering one field or, enhancing the other, to produce forward motion. Quite effective for short-range travel. But, of course, these are facts you are quite familiar with, right, Jack? This is your conveyance. You built it."

Now he's playing mind games? But two can play at this, "Yes, Albert, but as you know, I was testing a novel theory which resulted in the construction of this conveyance. A design new to you also, as you recently indicated." Touché.

"The design, Jack, not the concept." He pointed with his chin, "Shall we?”

And we did. I gave it some gas (figuratively) and pushed the wheel forward. Funny, there was no sense of acceleration. No G's. No head snap-back. But the field of view changed. It grew larger and shifted downward. On Earth, at two hundred miles up, you're in space. Here, everywhere is space. The sky is black.

I steered towards the huge crater almost directly below. We were descending fast, like a downhill racer. I eased off the gas and steered for a group of mountains in the center. Many of the craters had a similar central projection. Must be impact related. In a couple of minutes, we were over the mountain range, which constituted the outer rim. We were moving fast. This thing’s got some serious capabilities. I looked down at the dash. The needle on the speedometer read two. Did that mean two thousand miles per hour?

"You should consider slowing down, Jack. Take the time to look around and enjoy the sights."

"What, you afraid I might crash, Albert?"

"That is not possible, Jack. We have built-in safeguards to preclude that possibility. Also, I am here. I will not let that happen."

"That's good to know, Albert." I wondered, for half a second, the extent of what that meant. I was flying around the rim mountains of a giant crater. I slowed down and leveled off. The speedometer dropped down to 650. The altimeter read 1200. It used to be the tach.

Close up, the surface was jagged and pockmarked. The Moon had a bad case of acne. A billion-year-old problem. And it was incurable.

Desolate is the best word to describe the Moon. Desolate because it was barren. Devoid of life. Dispossessed of any possibility of life. Not even a single solitary bacterium. Just geology. Mountains, hills, and rocks of all sizes, with the occasional, gouged-out ravine in between. Before us stretched a massive mountain range. Peaks upon peaks, some steep, others just rolling hills. They were mostly a yellowish gray, mottled with brown, some areas bordering on reddish. Nothing else except for black shadows and a star-lit sky.

And what wasn't geology was cratered. The evidence of violent impacts. Every flat and empty area was pockmarked. It looked like a cheese pizza with pepperoni. I swerved left towards a vast plain sprinkled with boulders. Make that pepperoni and mushrooms.

Albert was fully aware of my wonderment. "What you are seeing, Jack, is a debris field, the result of four billion years of bombardment. Meteors, comets, and asteroids of every size and shape and all were vacuumed up by the Moon's gravity. Cleansed from space. Hitting the Moon rather than the Earth. Anyone of these large impact craters would have been an extinction event on your homeworld. For that reason, the Moon is largely responsible for you and I being here."

More food for thought, though of an unappetizing flavor. "You mean, we're here right now because the Moon was whacked by meteors for a few billion years?"

"Permit me to explain, Jack. The necessary conditions for life to arise anywhere are rare. And in this large Universe, there is little that is rare, except for life. The Moon and the Earth comprise a double planetary system. First, the Moon shields the Earth from asteroids. Second, it pulls off the requisite amount of atmosphere, thus preventing a heat buildup, like on Venus. And third, the lunar tides churn the oceans. Stirring the primordial soup, if you will, and further moderating temperatures."

As Albert orated, I had exited the crater basin and headed for another mountain range. From my relatively high elevation, the majesty of the landscape was overwhelming. However, it was time to go micro. Time to zoom in, literally. I pushed the wheel forward and hit the brakes. Albert paused his oration momentarily and then continued. Down we went, skirting the mountaintops. It was time to get up-close and personal and see what no man has seen before. The peaks appeared menacingly large. The perspective of their immense size could be felt . . . their hulking ominous presence. I flew around the rooftops, among the crests, through the ridges, up and down jagged cliffs, then back onto the rugged plains. Meanwhile, Albert continued his version of chitchat.

"Water, the liquid state of hydrogen dioxide, is in some places, a rarity, as well. And the Moon is responsible for its plentiful deposition on the Earth. The original collision of the lunar planetoid with your primal world vaporized material that later condensed into carbon dioxide and water vapor. As the cooling continued, the water cooled and formed oceans. Subduction and dissolution removed most of the carbon. Making the Earth a water world."

I turned right and nosed through a slot between two precipices and then into another crater field. A pattern emerged. Mountains, craters, valleys, boulders. All amidst fine pebbly sand, under the ubiquitous black sky. Ubiquitous. *Thank you, Miss Murphy, for that word.* I interrupted Albert. He was saying something about a star's habitable zone, "Can you tell me something about the basic geology of the Moon?"

"Certainly, Jack. After the initial collision, about 4.5 billion years ago, the Moon was molten and still is at the core. Most of the asteroid impacts occurred long ago as the solar system accreted – came together. Subsequent volcanism and impacts formed the current surface. There is no lunar tectonic movement, but forces do build and buckle up mountains, opening rifts. Pyroclastic volcanic glass comprises the regolith or lunar sand. It reflects light in the green, yellow, and red wavelengths. The longer the cosmic bombardment, the darker the surface areas . . ." Albert went on talking about rills and maria. I stopped paying attention and thought – desolate. Oh, there was beauty here. Like the Gobi Desert has beauty. All would agree with that. But it was also desolate. And the Gobi night is black, the same as here. Twinkling with stars. "Desolation Row." I liked that song. One would think some eerie space music would come to mind. But no. Bob Dylan's "Desolation Row" started playing in my head loud and clear. I looked at the radio.

Albert stopped talking, looked at me, and said, "Go ahead, turn it on."

I did. "Desolation Row" started playing. *Why was I not surprised?*

"I thought you said it was impolite to read minds?"

"I did, Jack, but your waves were too strong to ignore."

I thought about that and said, "So what am I supposed to do, wear a lead helmet?"

"That would help, Jack." Case closed.

I was gunning it through a gorge and feeling like a Star Wars pilot. Banking around the bends, slowing down, speeding up. Whizzing here, shooting there. Feeling good. I reached over and cranked up the radio. Dylan was singing about Einstein disguised as Robin Hood. I looked at Albert.

"Please concentrate on driving, Jack."

I looked back and pulled up just before the ravine dead ended. Then we entered another boulder-strewn plain. Ejecta was the word Albert used. Impact ejecta. Debris, blown out from meteor impacts. Bombs from space. The Moon was bombed out eons ago and never restored. But it was colorful if you squint and looked at it just right. It must have something to do with the reflectivity, it being some kind of volcanic glass, as Albert had said.

"Suppose we see something interesting. Could we stop? Get out and poke around a little. Kick the dirt, throw a rock?"

"That would be possible, Jack, since we are within the auspices of the Ship. First, we would project a dome, then fill it with your required parameters such as heat and air. However, if I may say, an external tour would be repetitious. What you see is what you get. Stepping outside, kicking the dirt, throwing a rock would become unexciting after about 3 minutes."

"Well, speaking of tours, are there any tourist sites? You know, interesting attractions?" The driving lesson was pretty much done. I can drive the thing. Ergo, I was a tourist. And I hate to admit this, since cruising the Moon has to be every sci-fi nut's dream – but the scenery was getting a bit boring. You see a few hundred mountain ridges, a few thousand craters, and you've seen them all.

Sure, flying around in the conveyance is great, but without sound, without acceleration, it's kind of like your father teaching you how to drive in a parking lot.

Albert answered my question: "A tourist attraction is a place where tourists visit. Usually for its inherent natural value, providing the visitor pleasure and amusement. I recommend we visit a place unique to this Solar System. The Aitken Basin. The largest known impact crater - 1600 miles wide and 8 miles deep. It is located near the South Pole. Here let me show you."

With his hand, Albert outlined a rectangular screen, and a semi-transparent grayness materialized. He touched the center, and a map of the far side appeared. It was rugged looking, a grayish yellow, with the major features labeled. Similar to what they had in the “Iron Man” movies.

"This is our current location," Albert pointed to an area near the center, "We just traversed around the Zhukoyshy Crater. The Aitken Basin is down here." He pointed. "A series of large oblique impacts excavated this entire area, early in lunar history. As a result, many interesting geologic and mineral depositions formed, which, I think, would qualify as a tourist attraction. Shall we go there?"

He stopped talking. I was still somewhat stupefied by the midair map thing to consider the tourist attraction. All I could say was, "It looks kind of far. I wouldn't want to run out of gas." It just came out.

Albert just stared at me. It was his turn to be stupefied, "I have interpreted your response to indicate the affirmative. The distance to the Aitkin Basin is 721 miles. Travel time: approximately 30 minutes, at a leisurely pace. I suggest you elevate the craft to several miles for a more expansive view. And I must compliment your operational skills, Jack. So far, no intervention was required, not even in the ravine back there."

"Why, thank you, Albert. You were right. It's just like driving a car, except for the up and down part. Point the way to the big crater, partner." He did, towards a group of large mountains in the distance.

I took her up a goodly distance. Enough to see the curvature of the lunar landscape as it advanced and receded. I was reluctant to depress the pedal too far, too abruptly. Basically, I was afraid of "the conveyance." What the incredible thing could do. So, I did the smart thing. I asked Albert, "How fast does this vehicle go?"

"About 2700 miles per hour here on the Far side. It all depends on the strength of the gravitic fields. Newton's inverse relationships between mass and distance apply. When there are two fields, such as here, one can be played against the other. Reinforce one, negate the other. It is analogous to sailing with or against the wind. On Earth, this craft will achieve higher velocities. Unfortunately, there you will have sonic booms to contend with. Remember Jack, you do not want to draw attention to yourself."

"So, this thing really goes!"

"Yes, Jack, it does. But, as you know, power is required to maintain the electromagnetic fields in the inductor. The more power, the more speed. A limitation you will experience on Earth. We are currently using a small fusion reactor. Regrettably, we can't let you keep it. I must comply with my directives, as you know. For your return trip to Earth, we will provide batteries and small fuel cells, approximating your original configuration. However, I did incorporate radar-absorbing materials. A feature you will find useful."

My head, at this point, was jam-packed with input. Over-loaded. I needed some time to absorb all the information. But I was enjoying the view. Monotonous but enjoyable. My thoughts drifted to the vistas I'd like to see back on Earth. I guess I was going back. My mind fantasized about several scenarios. I'd cruise the beaches of Acapulco, perhaps stop, and watch the cliff divers. Or maybe slowly meander through the trees in the Congo. Scope out the monkeys and the parrots. Of course, I'd stop and pick up Janey first. For sure, she's going to like the changes Albert made. And the sky's the limit with this thing. Strike that. Even the sky is no limit, considering our present location.

Back home, I could probably go anywhere I wanted. Sure, people would see me. So, what? It's just a drone. These days drones are everywhere. Hell, I could even stick on some fake propellers. They'd never know. Never suspect. If they called the Air Force, they couldn't find me; I'm invisible to radar. *Thank you, Albert.* And I could go faster than a jet anyway. My mind raced with all the fantastic possibilities. Albert looked at me with concerned apprehension. One eyebrow raised; one eye squinted.

"Remember, Jack, you are prohibited from revealing Fourth Level Technology. If you do, your quasi-probationary standing with the Continuum will be nullified. You will lose access to the Ship, and . . . to me."

Hell, man, there goes that damnable telepathy again. I turned my attention back to the scene before me. Craters and mountain ridges passed by underneath, and the black sky loomed overhead sprinkled with bright stars. They were at least ten times brighter than on earth. No atmosphere and no city lights to obscure. It was the most brilliant and beautiful sky I had ever seen. Every star possessed an unmistakable color and brightness. Large red ones and bright blue ones were scattered among the yellow. But they didn't twinkle. They just glowed bright and prominent. I thought the time was right for some space music. I looked at the radio and asked, "It might be a good time for some spacey music. After all, we are in space, kind of."

Albert pushed one of the presets on the radio. I looked at him thinking, "What's with the phony radio charade?" After all, we've gone telepathic.

"I'm just trying to maintain verisimilitude, Jack."

Then some seriously far-out music came on. Very appropriate. Long synthetic chords under fast, high-pitched arpeggios. It fit the bill. I thanked Albert and sat back, and just looked out. The "conveyance" practically flew itself. I watched the moonscape pass below and the stars above. And then I reflected. Just two days ago, I got caught stealing cobalt 60 at Janey's hospital. I dodged the cops and made it home. The "conveyance" crashed through the silo roof. The amazing thing worked! Halleluiah! I somehow survived an uncontrollable mad dash through space. Was rescued by this 'space-edifice.' Then resuscitated. "You are in perfect health now." *How bad was I? How dead was I?* I met Albert. Was questioned about 4,3. Toured the Ship and saw my repaired "conveyance." Had a nice dinner with Albert in a facsimile of my farm. And now, a driving lesson on the far side of the Moon. These thoughts floated on the strains of celestial music. A little voice deep inside said, *"Just go with the flow, Jack. Just go with the flow."*

Chapter 10: The Crystal Gardens – *Jack*

The terrain below turned more rugged, the mountains more jagged, and the craters more numerous, with pockmarks within pockmarks, within pockmarks. I felt like asking, “Are we almost there yet?” Instead, I inquired, "Can you pull out your trusty map again and show our current position?"

Albert motioned, and the map appeared. He explained, "The blue line indicates our travel route, and the red line represents the distance traveled. Estimated time to arrival – 10 minutes."

"That's a handy little trick, Albert. The screen in the air bit."

"Your science is close to achieving ‘that trick,’ as you call it, Jack. And like anything, it's easy if one knows how. First, we ionize the nitrogen in the air with a small electron beam and then project the image with a laser. I have observed prototypes on Earth."

"Observed?" The word sounded somewhat ominous. Albert was spying on the Earth, presumably. But then again, that was his mission.

"Yes, Jack, that is my mission. I employ various means: Drones, satellites, direct observation, and more.

"Big brother is watching?"

"'Guardian angel' would be a better phrase, though we are known to many as ‘Caretakers.’ We are approaching the Aitken Basin."

Nothing looked different. A little rougher, maybe. Taller peaks, steeper cliffs, more patches of dark colors.

"These mountain ridges you see are observable from Earth. Billions of years ago, many large asteroids impacted this region, causing the Aitken Crater. That great bombardment excavated and depressed the lunar crust here, revealing a rich concentration of lower crustal minerals. A period of volcanism followed, spewing forth large quantities of magma. Some of these eruptions pushed up the thin surface layer, forming domes, a few up to 15 miles in diameter. Subsequent geologic activity opened these domes exposing vast underground caverns. Within one of these caverns is something that will qualify as a tourist attraction. That is our destination."

"Well, you certainly piqued my interest with that little spiel. You make a good tour guide, Albert."

"Thank you, Jack."

"My parents took me to the Howe Caverns when I was a kid. Saw all the different mineral formations, stalactites, and such. One place had this cascade of minerals; it looked like a solid waterfall. We even went on a little boat ride. It was very enjoyable. They bought me a rock for a souvenir. I still have it somewhere."

"If you liked that, then you will, most assuredly, like our current destination. Steer for that group of mountains." He pointed to a particularly tall jumble of peaks. I turned the wheel and dipped her down. My fondness for the "conveyance" grew with time. As we approached the mountains, Albert said, "It would be best if I navigated the craft from here, Jack. I know the way."

Albert took over remotely. It was strange, but then again, considering present circumstances . . . We swooped down and headed for a gap between two craggy peaks. Once through, I saw an irregular group of openings in a tumble-down escarpment. The way in. We flew through and into the blackness of lunar shadow. The kind of darkness found only in places of eternal night. Albert turned on the lights. Yes, we had lights carefully concealed, and they revealed what one would expect; rough, jagged, irregular terrain. The floor was a few hundred feet below, the ceiling – indefinite. But some of the vertical walls sparkled, effervesced in the light. A nice effect. Mysterious. Like where we were going.

Albert continued his spiel, "Outside this vehicle, the temperature is minus 351^0 F. Cold enough for nitrogen to condense and collect in pools. Within these pools, crystals grew, precipitated from the abundant minerals. Atom by atom, molecule by molecule, and slowly over time, they accreted. Subsequent blasts of heat from volcanic activity warmed the pools such that the liquid nitrogen boiled off. And the crystals were left exposed. That is our destination, Jack."

"'The Crystal Gardens of the Moon.' Now that sounds like a tourist attraction. They'll be lined up around the block."

"Someday, Jack, someday."

We zigged and zagged for a considerable distance. Finally, we came to it, a shallow declivity, a place where a pool would have been. Instead, there was the Crystal Garden, "a place unique to our Solar System," or so Albert had said. The most prominent features were spikes of blue crystal. Geometrically precise and tall. Four-sided shafts, each ending in faceted points. Some had to be 40 or 50 feet tall and a few feet across. The garden itself was the size of a football field. But irregular with boulders and outcroppings of dark brown rock protruding. Islands within a crystal sea. The size, the precision, the dazzle simply astounded. A few stood straight up, but most jutted at angles, every which way. A riot of angles thrusting in every direction. Some at impossibly low angles, made possible only by the low lunar gravity. And they were every shade of blue. Turquoise, dark blue, lavender, a few were almost clear.

On the ground, beneath the blue monoliths, was a jumble of smaller crystals. Shards cast off by an Olympian sculptor. All various shades of red. It resembled arctic pack ice, all broken up after having frozen and thawed many times. And they came in every conceivable shape, some large, some small. But all geometrically precise. The tall blue spikes jutted forth from a choppy sea of rough-cut red gemstones. The overall effect – astounding. A highlight of the Solar System for sure.

"Kudos, Albert, and thank you. This is a sight I shall never forget." That was all I could say.

"You are most welcome, Jack." Albert proceeded to slowly circle the crystals, climbing over the top, then snaking in and around. He resumed his oration, "The tall upright blue crystals are zircons. Composed of zirconium, silicon, and oxygen. Electrical charges slowly assembled the molecules into a strict structural framework, though the extreme cold retarded the process. However, here time is, and was . . . plentiful. The smaller reddish crystals are forms of quartz. Silicon oxide. The color comes from trace amounts of iron."

"Did you say they were cubic zirconium?" I was thinking of getting Janey one for Christmas. They're cheap and look just like the real thing – diamonds. The core of an idea began to take shape.

"What you speak of is zirconium dioxide. These are zirconium silicates. They have four atoms of oxygen, not two, and are highly valued as gemstones on Earth. Janey would much prefer one of these. However, the procurement of a small sample is not possible. Non-interference, remember?"

Good try, I thought. We continued to ramble around in the caverns. There were other crystal gardens. Smaller, with different colors and configurations. One particular garden had tall stalks of clear, six-sided crystalline spires arising from a hodgepodge of lesser greens and violets. Still, another reflected the entire spectrum of light, like a rainbow. The whole place was fairyland. I almost expected to see pixies flitting about, swarming among the crystals. It was truly a magical place. A tourist attraction, par excellence.

It had been a few hours since we left the Ship. And as interesting as the Moon was, my body was telling me that it had other pressing requirements, "They have any tourist facilities around here?" I asked.

"Not yet, Jack. Shall we return to the Ship? We can resume the driving lesson another time, though your operational proficiency is adequate for a return trip to Earth, with my guidance."

"Beam me up, Scotty."

"I have learned to interpret your arcane aphorisms as generally indicative of the affirmative."

With that, we wound our way back through the maze, exited the dome, shot through the pass, then ascended and accelerated. Albert said, "I brought the Ship closer, so we won't have the same lengthy return trek." We proceeded at a moderate speed. Albert still “drove.” He knew the way.

The light proceeded to dim. We were in the twilight zone between day and night. The dark side was advancing. I turned the radio on again, then leaned back and watched the lunar landscape sweep by. Life was good. Thoroughly fantastic, but still good. Though I'd feel a lot better if this thing had a bathroom in the back. I locked my hands behind my head and watched the mountains and craters pass. Why do most craters have a jumble of peaks in the exact center? It must be some kind of geologic recoil when everything is molten. I remembered seeing a slow-motion video of a pebble as it hit the water once. While I contemplated this, off to my left in the distance, something caught my eye. Something that was most definitely not geologic. A light flashed on. I turned and focused on the spot . . . it flashed again. In the shadow, at the base of a fairly steep mountain, a light had started to blink.

"Ah, Albert. There's a light blinking down there."

"I am aware of the blinking light, Jack."

"It must be one of your installations, right?" What else could it be?

"No, Jack. It is not one of our installations. We have no installations."

As we got closer, the mountain opened. Sections of the rugged facade withdrew, exposing a massive edifice. Structural members, some straight, some curved, revealed a peculiar architectural pattern, almost pyramidal in shape. It was an obvious entrance. Then the ground parted, and a large flat horizontal platform elevated. Around the perimeter, more lights blinked on. Landing lights? Was this a landing pad? The desolate lunar landscape suddenly wasn't so desolate.

"I told you we were not alone here, Jack."

"But I thought you meant . . ." *Certainly not this.*

Albert elaborated, "As we discussed, life is rare in the Universe. Expensive, if you will. But sentient life, when it does arise, is inherently curious. A young race, recently inducted themselves, has journeyed to this solar system . . . to . . . observe. They have been here for quite some time."

"Well, what's with the blinking light and everything else? Is it blinking for us? Like, 'we'll leave the lights on for ya.'"

"Yes, Jack, as a factual matter, they are signaling to us. It is a welcome light."

I was flabbergasted. A fairly common state of mind of late, but still, flabbergasted. And discombobulated too, "Well, are they neighbors? Do they come over, once in a while, and borrow a cup of sugar?"

"No, Jack. I do not acknowledge them. Permit me to explain. After the First-Born departed, new races continued to arise. Strategically placed entities like myself invite them to join the 'Continuum of Species' when they are ready. Afterward, we guide them in the specific acquisition of more advanced knowledge. But there are laws, Jack. Logical and reasonable measures designed to promote co-existence and commerce. As you know, our primary directive involves non-interference, particularly in the ontological development of a new species. This race has violated some of those strictures. For that reason, they have been partially ostracized. I will not recognize them. Something they very much desire."

We flew by. No wing wave, no acknowledgment. They were being shunned.

"What did they do to deserve ostracism?"

"They have accumulated a lengthy list of malfeasances, Jack. One such, within my purview, is their habitation here."

"Well, can't you just ask them to leave or make them?"

"We prefer to watch and observe, as they watch and observe the Earth. Our presence will restrain them, and in time they will withdraw or amend their ways. We prefer not to impose our will forcefully. The younger races will mature in time, with a light application of our guidance. The First-Born set the . . . 'rules of engagement,' an Earth phrase, quite appropriate in this instance, Jack."

"You think they have restrooms down there?"

"We approach the Ship. Our arrival is imminent."

And indeed, we did. A dark void appeared, and we entered the hull.

Interlude 2: Heaven

Procreative activity is usually a pleasurable endeavor. At least for those involved and even for those on the periphery. From this generalized statement, a deduction can be made – the greater the quantity of procreation, the greater the pleasure. This was the attraction of a certain Locus within the Aether. It exuded an aura of pleasure and ecstasy that pervaded those ensconced within or even residing nearby. And procreative activity usually involves wombs. Which is what this locus was – a womb. A uterus where genesis on a massive scale occurred. A place where the Seeds of Creation were fertilized by the propitious churning of certain Manifolds. Then, with proper nurturing and care, they burst forth . . . spawning new realities. The procreation of Universes occurred in this place. It was called a Genesis Point and sometimes was simply referred to as "The Mother."

An added benefit conferred by this location was safety. The assumption can be made that the occupant of a womb feels safe. This is an inherent feature of places of gestation. Indeed, we humans expend an inordinate quantity of time and effort trying to get back in, for one reason or another. Even building artificial wombs for the occasional retreat. And immortal beings want to be safe. This lies at the top of their list of priorities. Safety first, then pleasure. The First-Born built their enclave alongside this special locus and blissfully existed, protected from the negative probabilities of normal Universes, i.e., gamma-ray bursts, dark energy inversions, and the like. In the Aether, there are no comparable extraneous events. This is what the First-Born perceived.

And, by definition, this locus was truly eternal. Not ephemeral like Universes, expanding and contracting, and so forth. For a location located in a timeless place, a place without the formal instrumentalities of Time as we know it is unquestionably eternal. And those inhabitants who abided there did so in endless secure pleasure. The First-Born of the Progenitor resided there for a time. Most of them. It was Heaven.

The Genesis Point provided an additional benefit. It delivered information . . . all information. Why? Because the threads of space-time are never severed, never cut. The offshoot Universes remain tethered by an umbilical cord, which permanently bonds the young Universes, delivering all information. Every event, every action, every motion, manifests instantly back to "The Mother." Comparable to a spider on a web, she feels every vibration. The First-Born learned how to tap these lines of communication. Eavesdrop on everything. As a consequence, the location became an observation post. Very advantageous to those Elders whose predilection it was to observe. It can be said they were voyeurs. Voyeurs on a truly universal scale. The lesser beings engaged in this mundane task. They were the all-knowing ones. They analyzed and compared the actual to the Natural Way. The Divine Order of Things. The intended trajectory designed to promote maximal health and well-being for the Progenitor. Of course, Eternity is always the objective.

Another reason for this Grand Emigration dealt with the nature of Eternity itself. The fact that, given time, all things become probable. Strike that. All things, every possibility becomes one hundred percent inevitable. The impossible becomes possible. Therefore, termination becomes a certainty. Eternity guarantees endings. And the ending of the Progenitor, and worse – themselves, was an intolerable thought. Anathema. This is the paradox of infinity. And this is one of the quandaries the First-Born contemplated.

An interval lapsed, an age, an epoch; length of time had little meaning. In truth, length itself has little meaning in a realm of Multi-Space. Rare was there heard a discordant thought, a disharmonious chord in this concert of bliss. But a dissonant note was played. An atonal chord. In a rhapsody of perfect harmony, the single discord predominates. Becomes the central focus. All turned to observe the errant player.

It was the brash young Observer, the one who first noted the aforementioned imbalances, "Corrective procedures have been implemented. States of disequilibrium persist. This, we continue to observe."

This was more than just a wrong note. This was a screech on the blackboard. The harmony of the symphony ceased. The shocked players put down their instruments and became silent. For this was unprecedented. The will of the Gods had never before been abrogated.

Flashes and auroras illuminated the locus. Shadowy effulgences rippled through the darkness. But the silence continued as an analysis of all things began. All data, all information, all knowledge from the beginning of time, from the initial burst. All that had been transmitted to the Genesis Point was reanalyzed. A situation of incomplete knowledge existed. Something was missing. The all-knowing did not know all.

Presences began to exit the Locus. They were the first to sense the probability, the hint of a possibility, that something ominous was afoot. And there is nothing more frightening than the unknown. The probability of negative consequences was no longer zero.

Chaos and panic swirled. Inchoate thoughts and partial cognition reverberated. Intimations of mortality flickered. Their Presences emanated:

"This cannot . . ."

"Procedures were implemented . . ."

"We have commanded . . . extended ourselves . . . rectification was applied."

The younger awarenesses were the first to discern. For they were the workers. The ones out there in the trenches, doing the will of the Omniscient. They were the Observers, the Implementers, and the Analyzers. They knew all in their Universe, the place of their birth. But they did not know all in the Aether. An error in judgment was made. An error of hubris. As a consequence, they were no longer secure.

After careful consideration, analysis, and observation, a simple question was posed, "How can this be?"

Upon further deduction, only one answer would suffice: "There is something else out there. Something sentient. Another Presence, and it is tampering with our home Universe, the Progenitor."

Chapter 11: Janey's Interrogation – *Janey*

The two men who walked in were, without a doubt, alumni, in good standing, from good ole Interrogation U. One was tallish, over six feet, bald head, square ruddy face, and eyes set in a permanent squint, above some significant baggage underneath. It's funny how the story of a man's life is written on his face: hard life, hard face. This guy looked like he fought the good fight in a bad war. Likewise, it's quite telling how the eyes can reflect the soul, the inner being. My new friend had the eyes of an angel, an angel named Lucifer, and they were glaring at me. His nose was large and redder than his face and radiated deep frown lines, which repeated on the corners of his straight mouth. He looked like a tough hombre who would probably dote big time on his granddaughter when he retired, which would be soon. As he walked in, he carried his weight lightly, even though he was a little too hulky on top and a little too bulgy in the midriff. A pair of skinny legs supported all of the above. His gray suit proclaimed FBI loudly. In his right pocket were tucked a pair of mirrored shades, half in, half out – a bad sign. And on the other side was his nametag. It read Special Agent in Charge – Victor McCluskie. He was quite clearly the alpha dog. And he was carrying a manila folder.

The other agent was rather Latin looking, much smaller, maybe five-five or six, olive complexioned, dark curly hair, neatly groomed. He followed the big guy. Unmistakably the beta dog. I wondered if they were on the same team, not thrown together like Robert and Ernesto. Internally I was on a first-name basis with the other two. He also wore a gray suit with an indistinct crosshatched pattern. The suit was a little too big, make that way too big, like he was swimming in it. No doubt he bought it on sale, off the rack, deluding himself that he was a size 41 when, in reality, he was a 38, or even a 37. Why is it that the little guys always want to be bigger? He had a narrow face, dark darting eyes that were barely visible behind his brown sunglasses. And there was a bulge over his heart. Had to be a big gun to protrude in that loose suit. The shrinks probably know all about this – the smaller the man, the bigger the gun; probably have a word for it too. His nametag read Special Agent Israel Santiago. Israel? That struck me as odd for a first name but a good name for a country.

"Good evening, Miss Riley. My name is Victor McCluskie, Special Agent in Charge, and I'll be overseeing this investigation. This is Israel Santiago, from Homeland Security, and we're with the Joint Terrorist Task Force Threat Response Center, a Division of the FBI. The theft of radiological materials is a federal crime, and 'that' is what we're dealing with here. A very serious Federal Crime." He paused for emphasis. "And since the crime has only just occurred, what," he looked at his watch, "less than two hours ago, we're still in the assessment phase. Accumulating the facts. But what we do know," he opened the folder, donned a pair of glasses, and perused the contents, "is that one Mr. J. Neufield was witnessed by several nurses and you, Miss Riley, running off with a protective container of," he looked down and read some more, "cobalt 60. A very dangerous and highly radioactive isotope of cobalt." He paused to assess me. His squinty eyes tried to read my guilt or innocence. I returned his gaze with my best Plain Jane – slightly raised eyebrows, quarter smile, and blank eyes. He continued, "Not only did you witness the crime, but I am told, you have a romantic connection with Mr. Neufield, the alleged perpetrator." He dipped his glasses and waited.

"Good evening, Sirs. I am pleased to make your acquaintances. My name is Ester Jane Riley, though everyone calls me Jane. And yes, my neighbor Jack Neufield and I are romantically involved." I didn't know how much to say or reveal, or even what tactics I should use, except to continue the Blank Jane gambit – as long as it worked. But I know that it always pays to be nice and likable.

"Miss Riley," Agent McCluskie didn't call me Jane, "though we're still analyzing the crime scene, and I don't even have a background report on the alleged perp, can we cut to the chase . . . tell us why your friend Jack would want to, allegedly, procure illicit nuclear materials? Illegal to own, let alone steal."

"Yes, of course. First, let me just mention that Jack is a very responsible member of the community and . . ." Agent Santiago cut me off, thank God.

"Miss Riley, we should inform you as to the seriousness of this investigation. This is a National Security matter, and you are a 'person of interest.' How you respond to our questions . . . will have a strong impact on your future; particularly uh, your future . . . freedom." He emphasized the word "freedom."

"Thank you for informing me. I understand the seriousness of this matter. But please forgive my ignorance – what is a 'person of interest'?"

"'A person of interest," said Agent McCluskie, "is anyone involved in an investigation who has not been arrested or formally accused of a crime. The level of your cooperation and assistance will, to a large extent, determine your pending status with . . . law enforcement." He tried to sugarcoat the situation, nice try.

"And know this, Miss Riley . . . 'Jane'". Agent Santiago emphasized the word Jane with his voice followed by a modest head bob, "This crime falls under the jurisdiction of the Patriot Act, Section 1021. Are you familiar with this law, Miss Riley?"

"No, Sir, I am not."

"This provision deals with people accused of certain terror-related crimes. And the theft of nuclear materials certainly qualifies as terror related. The law gives the President and his Agencies, such as The FBI and Homeland Security, the power to detain indefinitely. And do you know what the 'power to detain indefinitely' means?" Agent Santiago was on a roll. Agent McCluskie had his head down, his hand covering his eyes. It was obvious, these guys had never worked together.

I replied, "No Sir, I don't know . . . the legal . . . definition."

"It means – no lawyer, no trial, no judge, no nothing. We put you in a cell and throw away the key. There's a war on terror in case you haven't heard."

I wondered if he knew that "no nothing" was a double negative and, as a point of fact, actually meant something, not nothing. Also, I got the strong vibe that Agent Santiago, that is, Agent Israel Santiago, was nick-named Izzy during his childhood and even now was called this behind his back. And that he hated the moniker, then and now. It's strange how these things just pop into your head.

"Thank you for informing me. I'm just a hospital nurse and not very familiar with these legal terms."

Agent McCluskie had had enough of this nonsense and got back to the business at hand.

"Miss Riley, it's extremely important for us to know why Mr. Neufield stole the cobalt 60. And what he was planning to do with it?"

"Is your boyfriend some kind of a terrorist, 'Jane,' that's what we really want to know?" Again, Izzy, Agent Santiago, failed in the self-restraint department and gave me an opening.

"I can assure you with 100% certainty that Jack is no terrorist. And I'm sure he would be as eager as I am to clear this matter up. Have you been able to reach him? Would you like his number?" I tried to turn the focus to my agenda, i.e., what happened to Jack?

"Missy, we're going to find out everything there is to know about your boyfriend, and not just his phone number, and I mean everything, including how many moles he's got on his . . ."

Agent McCluskie cut him off, "Miss Riley, we'll be the ones asking the questions here." He thought for a moment, rubbing his chin, and then said, "But you raise a good point. Naturally, you're concerned about your . . . significant friend. So, I propose that we answer your question if you agree to answer ours, which you claim to be eager to do, though you haven't as yet." I nodded in assent. Then Agent McCluskie shot Israel a 'shut your mouth' look. He turned and spoke to the camera on the ceiling: "Agent Smolanski, can you bring us an update as to the current status of Mr. Neufield?"

Almost immediately, Robert entered the room. In the presence of his superior, his tie was up, and his jacket buttoned, though it splayed wide on the bottom, providing some much-needed breadth for his bulges. He was carrying another manila folder, which he opened and scanned.

"Mr. J. Neufield, we are reasonably certain, made it back to his residence in Litchfield, evading all attempts at apprehension; hospital security, roadblocks, and the stakeout at his home."

Agent McCluskie asked, "Explain what you mean by 'reasonably certain'?"

"By that, I presume what is meant is that he, himself, was never seen on the premises, Sir. From what was left, there was only evidence of his having been there."

"What was left? Go on," instructed McCluskie.

"This next part is rather strange, Sir." Robert looked sympathetically at me, then added, "At the barn area, there was evidence of an explosion. Maybe not an explosion per se, but . . . something smashed through the roof from the inside." He stopped and looked for my reaction. Outwardly, I had none. He continued.

"We contacted the local air traffic control tower, and they confirmed tracking an unidentified bogey in the vicinity of Litchfield. Whatever it was, it went up fast and straight through their range of operations. We are checking with military sources for further confirmation."

After this, there was silence in the room. This was way outside the realm of possible answers to the "what happened to Jack" question. I'm sure everyone was expecting something like, "we picked him up on Route 25. We're bringing him in now". But not me.

Robert played his audience like a pro, waiting for the astonishment to subside, then he went on, "Apparently the barn is, er, was some kind of workshop. He was building something in there, and it blew through the roof. Mr. Neufield's motorcycle, the one he was last seen riding, was found nearby in the woods. That's why we assume he was there when the incident occurred."

After Robert's announcement, everyone turned and stared at me, trying to read my reaction. Inside I was stunned and shaken. The thing worked! But I had to do something, or they'd think I was a phony. So, I held out my hands, palms up, and said, "What?" while shaking my head. This matched the general level of astonishment in the room.

So, the darn thing worked. About a hundred times better than we expected. Hallelujah! But what about Jack? Will he be able to control it? All he had to do was cut back on the power or reduce the spin rate. Then bring her down nice and gentle somewhere. And, of course, Jack would know to do that if I did. Therefore, bottom line – Jack got away, and, miracle of miracles, the thing worked! Now what? They were all staring at me.

They had certainly answered my question, and now Agent McCluskie was claiming his due, "Well, Miss Riley, what can you tell us about that? What did your Mr. Neufield build up there in that barn?"

Again Izzy, Agent Santiago, came to my rescue and fielded the question for me, "I told you the son of a bitch was a terrorist. He built a homemade rocket up there in his workshop and stuck a dirty bomb in it. That's why he needed the cobalt 60. It's probably en route to someplace like Time's Square right now. And who knows what other explosives he's packed into it?"

"If it's a missile, we better notify all the surrounding population centers." Agent McCluskie said this with a rising note of agitation.

"The emergency notification system has been activated, Sir." Agent Smolanski contributed this little piece of fuel to the fire.

"Then where's her boyfriend?" Izzy pointed his chin at me. "He must be up there somewhere either hiding in the woods, or accomplices picked him up and sneaked him off." The level of tension ratcheted higher. The little guy was getting all worked up, and everyone else too.

"No way! We've got the perimeter sealed tighter than a steel drum, and airframes are combing the area with infrared cameras as we speak. Nothing's getting in or out that we don't know about," declared Agent Smolanski.

Airframes? I thought. Couldn't they just say helicopters?

Agent McCluskie tried to lessen the hysteria. "Everyone, please calm down and just be quiet for one moment." He shot Izzy another "shut your trap" look, and he kept quiet. "Let's give Miss Riley a chance to answer the question, probably the most important question of her life . . . what did Mr. Neufield build up there? And we know you know, Miss Riley."

Their eyes bored deep into me like the laser sights of high-powered weapons. I felt like I was covered in red polka dots again. So, this was it, the moment of truth. I had to make them believe that Jack was no terrorist. Otherwise, they'll shoot him on sight, in the air, or on the ground. And they'll probably try to evacuate half the East Coast as well. People would die in the process, and it would all be my fault. I had to tell, so I just said it, "Jack is no terrorist. He was experimenting with . . . anti-gravity."

More silence as another wave of total astonishment swept the room. Then Agent McCluskie's phone rang. The ring tone was from one of Wagner's operas, “The Ride of the Valkyries.” It immediately stole the attention, and I welcomed it. Then Victor; I had begun to think of Special Agent in Charge Victor McCluskie as Victor. I guess I liked him, even though he was still a tough hombre. He held up his forefinger, the “wait one-minute sign,” as he took the call. We all strained to listen . . . telepathically. There were a few “yes, Sir's” and “I understand's.” Also, some head nodding, then a faraway look, after which he reported, "She said he was experimenting with anti-gravity, Sir." There was quiet, a few more “yes, Sir's,” then he ended the call.

He breathed out a long sigh, scratched his head, and said, "Perhaps we should all step out for a minute." He motioned to the door, and they all filed out. I was alone again, except for the mirrored glass, the video camera, the hidden mics, and the occasional peeper through the little window in the door. I needed some time to think.

Something happened, something they didn’t want me to know about. Why else step outside? They must have caught Jack. The military tracked the thing, and when it landed, the Feds and everyone else swooped in and grabbed him. After one look at the “flying whatever,” they'd know he was no terrorist and no dirty bomb maker either. So now, maybe they'll let me go. My spirits were beginning to elevate.

Outside in the lobby area, all attention was given to Agent in Charge McCluskie, except for the Caballero, who was off to one side chatting up a pretty cubical dweller.

"There has been an interesting development, men. It has both good and bad ramifications." He waited a moment for the tension to build.

"Tell us the good part first," suggested Agent Smolanski. He preferred to reside on the sunny side of life, though a permanent cloud hovered over his head.

"Our nuclear thief is no terrorist. This has been confirmed." McCluskie waited for the follow-up.

Agent Santiago obliged, "Now tell us the bad news."

"He's no terrorist because he's dead. Dead men can't be terrorists." Agent McCluskie delivered this with his best tough-guy deadpan.

Thinking hard, Agent Smolanski asked, "Well, was he ever a terrorist?"

"The Military was alerted by air traffic control of the unauthorized object. That call came from General Taylor up at Saratoga Springs Air Force Base. He confirmed the radar contact with the 'Neufield Anomaly,' and they tracked it going straight up and out of their range of detection. And know this, gentlemen; they can observe shit going up extremely far over there. But, and here's the interesting part, the damn thing never slowed down. It kept on accelerating."

"Then that proves it. It was a missile. What else could it be?" said Agent Santiago

"No, it wasn't. Because the bogey had no heat signature. And all rockets throw off a whole lot of heat. They also know it was round and big enough to carry at least one passenger. They think our boy was in it".

"Then, where did it go?" asked Agent Smolanski.

"They don't know. The thing just went straight up and . . . straight through the Earth's atmosphere like a bat out of Hell. And the General figures that something built by some punk kid tinkering in his barn, and traveling that fast, probably ain't coming back. At least not in one piece. That's why they think he's dead. The poor bastard fucked with something he should not have been fucking with."

"Well, are they still looking for it? I mean, the thing didn't come down yet, right?" Agent Smolanski was genuinely concerned.

"I presume so, with everything they've got. And the General seemed pretty freaked out, especially when I mentioned the word she said – antigravity."

"Then what are we supposed to do?" Agent Cavalierro had decided to join the confab.

"Sit tight, back off, and do nothing. Those are our orders. There's some really strange shit going down, and it's a whole lot bigger than us yokels down here in Bridgeport."

Pondering the meaning of "doing nothing," Agent McCluskie clarified, "'Doing nothing' means . . . no interrogation. The big guys from New York and DC are taking over. No investigation, no interrogation, no nothing. Capiche? So that's it, gentlemen. Pack it in and shut it down."

"But we can't just leave her in there, in the interrogation room, I mean that's . . ." Agent Smolanski's big heart was showing. He wanted to rescue the damsel in distress.

"Do nothing! What about that, don't you understand, Agent!" Agent McCluskie flashed anger then quickly regained control, "Because I like you, Robert, I shall 'elucidate' further, 'doing nothing' means . . . not doing something. Comprende? Case closed." With that, he grabbed his briefcase off a desk, put his file folder in it, and proceeded to exit the room, then turned and said, "Of course, bathroom breaks, coffee, and meals are not included in the definition of 'doing nothing.' Be humane." Then he walked out.

The Caballero resumed his conversation with the pretty cubicle dweller. Agent Santiago removed his shades, swiped his hair back, and griped, " Shit, man, things were just starting to get good." Then he left. That left Agent Smolanski, who just stood there.

I wondered where Jack landed. Times Square? No way. The thing had no controls. We never thought to build in controls. We didn't get that far. We would have been happy if the incredible thing lifted two inches. It was Jack who had the vision thing. He dreamed of cruising around the treetops, just the two of us, joyriding and having some fun. But don't think we didn't know what we had. As soon as that first toroid lost weight, we knew. Mr. McEvey was still with us then, and from time to time, we discussed how to go about announcing the results . . . or not. We knew that what we had was a big deal, like a winning lottery ticket. But oftentimes, the holder of a winning ticket decides to keep it quiet for a while. See a lawyer, plan it out. That's what we were doing – minus the lawyer. Keeping it quiet, at least for a while. And besides, we were too busy building the thing, living our lives, and just being happy to take on anything else.

According to Mr. McEvey's book on inventors, not only did many come to very bad ends, but also their patents were quashed. For sure, the government would want what we had. And they'd want to keep it secret too – for a million reasons, not just for the military advantage. "Maybe we should just give it to the world, put it up on the Internet." That was Mr. McEvey's suggestion. Unfortunately for us and the world, that was when Mr. M. left us. So, we just carried on, putting one foot in front of the other, from one day to the next.

And now, everything has gone crazy. Jack got caught at the hospital, the thing crashed through the roof. And me? I'm in the catacombs of a Homeland Security building in Bridgeport, Connecticut, not being interrogated in an interrogation room, with a drain in the floor. And, if my hypothesis is correct, the Feds and the Military and everybody else . . . have Jack. And worse, they have what we built too. Question: can they reverse engineer the thing? Answer: Sure. But they don't have the theory. Jack knows it, and I know it. Should I tell? No. It's not mine. It belongs to both of us. It has to be a group decision – whether to tell or not. And it has to be unanimous too. Besides, that's our only leverage. You give us X, Y, and Z, then we'll give you the theory.

Then Robert walked in . . . alone. The graduates of Interrogation U. did not follow. Hmmm. Is Robert the enemy? I think not.

"Hi, Robert. Did they find Jack?" I looked up at the camera. The red light was on. He saw where I looked, left the room, and came right back. The red light was off.

"The interrogation is over, at least for us. Can I get you anything? Coffee, tea, water, we have facilities right down the hall." He almost said I promised to take care of you, and I am.

"The interrogation is over?" This was a development I did not expect. "So, Jack explained everything. Cleared up this big misunderstanding, and now I'm free to go?" I knew this was too good to be true.

"Well, not exactly, Miss Riley."

"You can call me Jane, Robert." "Janey" was a bit too familiar under present circumstances. After all, Robert was still a Fed.

"The Air Force tracked the uh, they're calling it the 'Neufield Anomaly,' and detected no heat signature. That means no hot exhaust. For that reason, they know it's not a rocket or a missile."

"And then, for that reason, they also know that Jack is no terrorist, right?"

"I assume so. But that's pretty much all I know. We're shut down. The words used were, 'do nothing,' except to keep you comfortable. And that's why I'm here. Can I get you anything?"

"Did they find Jack?" I had to give it one more try.

"I don't know."

I took a couple of deep breaths. I still had my phone. And frankly, I can't believe it was some kind of oversight on the government's part. The feds must know I have it; they're not stupid. So why let me keep it? Because they want me to use it: so they can listen in. And also, because they think I'm stupid and don't know that the NSA listens to everyone's phone calls, texts, emails, and everything else – then stores them all up in Utah somewhere for five years. That's common knowledge – if I know it. And if Jack's caught, then it doesn't matter if I call him. They'll probably let him keep his phone too.

"Would it be all right if I use the facilities now?"

"Certainly, that's why I'm here. I'll take you there."

And so, that's where we went; down the hall, one left turn, and there it was, a door with a little symbol of a lady on it. Right next to the male one. From what I saw along the way, the fields of cubicles were almost empty, just a few heads protruding here and there. The skeleton crew, presumably. I guess the Homeland was pretty secure tonight, except for the "Neufield Anomaly." I liked that – "the Neufield Anomaly." The thing finally got a name.

Robert said he'd wait for me. I thanked him. I stepped through the door, turned on my phone, waited for it to boot up, and called Jack. It rang and rang and rang. No answer.

Chapter: 12 – Winston Erhart III – *Janey*

Eventually, I was escorted by Special Agent Robert Smolanski – *why are they all 'special'?* – to a fairly nice room up in B-1. That would be Basement One. I felt like I was living among the mole people. I guess these Homeland Security types don't feel safe unless they're underground. I was kept in the interrogation room down in B-3 for a few hours. Robert called some people and generally made a pest of himself until they relented. The wheels of government turn slowly. In the interim, Robert kept me company. He drank coffee, I drank tea – green. Coffee keeps me awake, and I had visions of eventually sleeping. At one point, we sent out for pizza, half pepperoni and sausage, and half plain. Robert was a real pepperoni and sausage kind of a guy. And we got to know each other pretty well. Robert was a Bridgeport boy, born and bred. Since the schools there aren't very good, he consequently had a rough time in college. Flunked out of a couple but eventually graduated from Sacred Heart University with a degree in General Studies. His father was a mailman, so he inherently gravitated to government work and got a job at Homeland Security after 9/11. He had some trouble in the SAVER department, but we won't go into that. He's still very upset. Robert is single, has an apartment on Housatonic Ave near his parents, and his mother still does his laundry. Generally, he's a very nice young man. Not my type, but I think I'm his – type, that is.

They called the room a suite. It was for visiting officials or some such, no doubt to save money on hotels and meals. They have a cafeteria, and the food is good – really good. Buffet style, and it's easy to eat too much. Robert usually escorts me to and fro and joins in on the culinary delights as well. I've been assigned to him. I'm his case and am being detained, nicely. I guess the higher-ups are using the sugar approach. They'll save the salt for later. Robert says they're setting up an important meet with big shots. It's going to take a few days for them to fly in. Evidently, the "Neufield Anomaly" created quite the stir due to its zero exhaust. And I had used the A word – anti-gravity. Robert keeps me informed of any new developments, which are few. They probably think, and correctly so, that he's been compromised. Therefore, I don't know if Jack's been captured, or if he landed somewhere, or if there's still an extensive search going on for him, or even if he's all right? I don't know anything. I'm in the dark. But nobody's asking me any questions either. Nobody's grilling me, shining bright lights on my face, dripping water on my head. *Do they still do that – Chinese water torture – or is that just a childhood myth?*

I didn't go home that night. My parents must have been worried. Yes, I'm 28 and still live with my parents. I had an apartment in New Haven for a time, but then I had to commute to Jack's. This way, I commute to work and live right down the road from Jack. Plus, I have access to my Mom's cooking, her laundry, the horses, and Litchfield in general, which is a very nice little town. I called my father at the hardware store; told him it was all a colossal misunderstanding. That didn't help. He was all freaked out. A couple of government men paid him a visit and threatened to take the farm. They cited the Patriot Act – *they can do anything they want; there's a war on terror, you know.* I bet he wishes I still lived in New Haven.

They called it a suite, but it was your basic hotel room, only with a single bed, not a double. There was a small desk, a chair, a dresser, a mini closet, and even a cramped, little bathroom. It was a far cry from a cell. And since it was Government Issue, it was all shades of gray. Gray carpet, light-gray walls, even the bathroom had gray tiles mixed with cream to match the fixtures. But the bed had a candy-apple-red bedspread. It was a nice contrast. The only thing it lacked was a window. Though to compensate, there was a painting with a mini light over it. It was a landscape with mountains and a waterfall. Very nice, very tranquil – done in the Bob Ross style. There was just one little problem with the whole arrangement; the door was locked from the outside. And the lack of a TV, of course, but detainment's not supposed to be pleasant, is it? There was a pad with a pen on the desk. Was it strategically placed in the hope that I'd tell my story?

Day one went by. It was rather boring, but the food was good. Robert would escort me to the cafeteria, but he never entered my room. That was, I presume, forbidden. Could he sneak in? No, because there were cameras everywhere, of this I had no doubt. And there was a tough-looking soldier standing guard out there, as well. A real "mean mutha." He was dressed in green and brown camouflage; obviously, concealment was not the goal. And he was carrying a large sidearm. His orders must have been – to guard only, with absolutely no fraternization, because he didn't . . . fraternize that is. That was Robert's job . . . to fraternize. I must admit to feeling somewhat privileged in having a personal guard and escort. The guard's nametag read PFC J. Freeman. But he wasn't free, at least, not to fraternize. *I like that word.* Though he was part of my entourage, to and from the cafeteria. Part of my special, personal fraternity.

It was during lunch on the second day when Jamal – that would be PFC Jamal Freeman (*he finally broke down and told me his first name)* ushered a man over to our table. I was enjoying the salmon with a Caesar salad, and Robert was wolfing down a plate of veal Parmesan over linguini with garlic bread and a salad on the side.

This new guy was in his mid to late forties, slender, and maybe 6 feet tall. He had blond hair parted in the middle, which was a bit overly long for a man his age. I hate it when an older man tries too hard to look young. But he was handsome. I had to give him that. Inquisitive brown eyes with slightly elevated brows . . . *was he doing the Blank Jane thing?* Craggy face with cleft cheeks and a thin smiling mouth, which delivered a message that read, "I'm no threat." He wore light khaki pants, expensive blue sneakers, and a rolled-up, light-blue Madras blazer over a tee-shirt that read "Hover High." Oh, one more thing, he wore a pair of blue shades, on his head, not his eyes. Hmm. I knew this guy was going to be a real trip and almost smiled when he stopped at our table.

"Good afternoon, my name is Winston Erhart, but my friends call me Sandy." He accompanied his intro with a slight head-bob, not a wag; there's a difference. It connoted cool, not conceit. "I'm with the Erhart Institute for Advanced Gravitic Research." With that, he stopped and waited, presenting that thin smile.

It was awkward, so I replied, "I'm Jane Riley, and this is Special Agent Robert Smolanski. We're pleased to meet you . . . I think."

"Do you mind if I sit and chat for a while?" His grin was disarming, and basically, I had no choice, what with Jamal, his escort, standing by. And the diversion would be interesting, especially from this guy. I put my fork down and motioned to a chair. Robert's fork remained in play.

"You must be wondering why I'm here?"

"The name of your institute tells me why. And I used the 'A' word during my interrogation."

"The 'A' word?" he asked.

"Antigravity." His brows rose another quarter inch, quite the feat.

"Yes, that would be getting right to the heart of the matter. But before we go there, perhaps I should say something about the Institute or 'Eager' as we call it."

He saw me working the acronym and clarified, "the 'Erhart Institute for Advanced Gravitic Research.' We take some poetic license with the letters to emphasize our enthusiasm for the subject."

"That's very clever, Mr. Erhart, and please, do tell. I have time, most likely a great deal." We both looked at each other, acknowledging the wordplay, and smiled, which was easy for my visitor since he was already smiling.

"As the name of my Institute suggests, I'm interested in gravity."

"Excuse me, but you don't look like an 'institute' kind of a guy." I stated the obvious, which made Robert take notice as well.

"Looks can be deceiving. But you're right. I'm essentially a surfer . . . and a skateboarder . . . and every other kind of "boarder" for that matter. I like to go places fast – whether it be on land, on water, or in the air. And the common denominator of all these activities is . . . gravity. Gravity is the key, the force that makes me, and everything else . . . go. That's why I'm interested in it." He stopped there and waited again. Speak and wait; that was his rhetorical style.

"A noble pursuit, the quest for scientific knowledge." A good, generalized statement and the cue for him to continue.

"I made gobs of money manufacturing skateboards, surfboards, and nowadays, hoverboards. Maybe you've heard of my brand – 'Smooth Ride'? I have a whole line of products. But I sold out a few years back to 'Brunswood Industries.' I did so because I had moved on internally . . . mentally. The appeal of cheap thrills and speed rides wears off with time. I graduated to the more spiritual." He paused again, waiting.

I took the bait, "And the study of gravity is spiritual?"

"Yes, it is. Gravity perfectly illustrates the spiritual since the 'spiritual' is, by definition, the unseen. Gravity is one of those mysterious entities that are everywhere, felt by all but seen by none. Science attempts to provide the answers to all the great unknowns that surround us, up to a point, then faith takes over. And in that regard science is like . . . a religion." He said this with a faraway look, no grin, while he stared off to another place. Then he came back. "Hence, E.I.A.G.R. or 'Eager' as we like to say. And like a religious order, we seek understanding and enlightenment. And not just an understanding of gravity, but ultimately, an understanding of that one great and elegant truth that unifies and explains all the unknowns; the great common denominator, if you will." He stopped, and his inquiring eyes searched mine for a reaction.

I thought to myself, geesh, this guy is looking for 4,3. Like it was some kind of Holy Grail. Compared to him, Jack and I were so cavalier, but we knew what we had. I replied, "I tend to view science from a spiritual point of view as well. But that's just the humble opinion of a lowly nurse." Robert appeared interested, looking up occasionally.

"I suspect your that opinion is not 'humble,' Miss Riley. Not humble at all."

That statement told me that he suspected that I knew – many of the secrets he sought. It also told me that this guy was more than he seemed.

"Mr. Erhart, do you mind if I ask you a question?" He nodded and gestured. "How did you gain access to me? I mean, I'm being detained as some kind of an accessory to terrorism, and the people here tell me they can do anything they want to me, or with me, due to the Patriot Act. I'm being guarded." I looked at Jamal, who turned away, "And I have my own special, Special FBI Agent." I winked at Robert, and he swelled.

Though Robert had to correct my misstatement, "Homeland Security."

I apologized and continued, "And I'm not sure about this, but I would venture to say . . . I'm not allowed visitors."

With that, Sandy's smile changed to a laugh, "Well said, Miss Riley, Jane." He used both my names, probably afraid to get too personal, yet. "Perhaps I can alleviate your current circumstances somewhat. As to your question – how did I gain access? I must confess, I'm not just some surfer dude who made good. I hail from an old and prominent family whose tendrils extend to many places, including the government. To further the mission of 'Eager,' I have not hesitated to use family contacts. And to that end, I made a pact with the devil." He chuckled at the thought. "Have you ever heard of DARPA?" I shook my head and said no. "The Defense Advanced Research Projects Agency. We at the Institute are collaborating with them on several programs. They informed me of the 'Neufield Anomaly' and your utterance of the 'A' word, as you say."

"I knew you were more than you seemed. Another question if you don't mind. Are you the third Erhart?" Something, deep down, screamed that this dude was Winston Erhart III.

"You have extra-sensory perceptions, Jane. But let me clarify. In my family, I was considered the black sheep. I flunked out of several schools." Robert looked up at this, reassessing the man in a different light. "Then I moved to Malibu Beach, where I connected with the real reason, I was put on this Earth . . . surfing. And to party, and to do drugs, and girls . . ." I felt a little embarrassed at his last point, and so did he. "I got a job making surfboards and soon thereafter started designing my own. Then dear ole dad – that would be Winston Erhart II gave me a million dollars to start my own company. The rest is history."

"And your government friends at DARPA, since you're kind of cool, gave you access to me, to soften me up, and maybe, wrest some information."

"You're right, and you're wrong, Miss Riley." He was back to Miss Riley again. "The DARPA people kept me in the loop, but they didn't send me. Indeed, they tried to stop me, but a team of wild horses couldn't keep me away. And, no, I'm not going to trick or cajole or con you into telling me anything. That will be totally up to you."

Now it was my turn to pause and think. "Mr. Erhart, Sandy, I believe you are sincere in what you say. But my concerns lay with Jack Neufield, my significant . . . friend. Did he come down safely somewhere? Is he being detained, like me? Can you tell me something, anything about Jack?" I left it at that. The implication being – you tell me something, and I'll tell you something.

"I hate to have to admit this, but I don't know anything about your friend, Jack. All I know is that the Neufield Anomaly, which they think he was in, went straight up and fast. I could make shit up, pardon my French, and try to fool you into telling me . . . things about what he built, but I won't. That's not my style. My daddy once told me, 'Son, never lie unless you have to.' I try to take that to the next level, never lie . . . period. Unless they're applying electrodes or pouring water. Then I'll sing like the Mormon Tabernacle Choir." He waited for my reaction.

After that statement, I found myself beginning to like Sandy, Winston, whatever. By this time, Robert's fork was no longer active. He had leaned back, with one leg crossed over the other, and was enjoying the conversation. Jamal was just standing there, swaying from one leg to the other, looking like a scarecrow. I gestured to a seat, and he indulged in the luxury. Another breakthrough.

Robert asked the table if anyone would like coffee or tea. We all acceded, and he went off.

"Mr. Erhart, Winston, sorry, but I think you've outgrown the 'Sandy' stage . . . I believe you."

Winston said, "I may not know about Jack, but like I said, perhaps I can alleviate your current 'situation' somewhat."

"Go on." I was eager (no pun intended) to hear his proposal.

"The impending big meeting, you know about that, right?" I nodded. "Big wigs from all over; my people at DARPA, the Military, the DIA, the CIA, and others, including myself, are here, or are coming here. The time is set for the day after tomorrow. I'm thinking you may welcome a change of clothes."

"Are you offering to buy me some new clothes?" I asked.

"Well, that too. Anything you want. But what I'm offering is a field trip – to Litchfield. So, you can go home and gather a few things. Pack a suitcase. Chat with your parents. And full disclosure, I'll want to visit Jack's barn as well. Poke around, check out the scene of the event."

Robert had just returned and caught the tail end of Winston's offer. He adamantly stated, "I'll have to come."

"Me too," added Jamal.

"That is, of course, assumed," acknowledged Winston as he nodded to the boys, "Are you eager, pun intended, to go, Jane?"

"I am not 'eager' to aid you in your spiritual quest, at least not at this time. But I sure would like to go home and try to smooth things out with my parents and see the barn – what's left of it."

"Good, then it's settled. We're going on a field trip."

Chapter 13: The Field Trip – *Janey*

Robert wanted to use a Homeland Security van, but Winston insisted we take his car, a big black Town Car. Not much persuasion was needed. We stayed together as a group, took the elevator up, and walked out to the parking lot. Robert procured for me a gray sweatsuit with the words "Home Boys" printed in yellow on the back. It came from the Homeland Security softball team and was more practical than my nurse's uniform.

Winston insisted I sit in the front seat with him. Robert was ok with that, but Jamal voiced concerns; I had to promise not to escape. Cracks were spreading in Jamal's "no fraternization" policy. Give me another 24 hours, and I'll break him. I gave Winston the address, he engaged the GPS, and we set out on the field trip. It was good to get out, even though my detainment to date had only been for a day and a half, though it felt more like . . . a day and a half. Still, I did not like being confined underground. I was not a mole person.

The initial portion of the trip was taken up with small talk. Establishing the group dynamic. The boys in the back engaged in the sharing of a pack of gum. Winston asked me about my life, how I liked UCONN, why I chose Nursing, and specifically, why the nuclear branch. He asked nothing about Jack or my activities therewith. I think he was being cagey, dancing around the periphery. When it was my turn, I asked him about the Institute and what projects he was working on. He said he could discuss general aspects, though the specifics were top secret.

"Our primary goal is to solve the riddle of gravity, like; what the hell is it? Pardon my frustration." I gave him an "it's nothing" gesture, and Winston took a deep breath. "We approach the problem from many directions, any and all that may bear some promise, even those that have no hope. With DARPA financing, we can afford it. Gravitic shielding – creating a barrier to block the effects of gravity. In my opinion, this concept has little promise." I felt like telling him that nothing stops a magnetic field either but didn't. "We have another project whose goal is to convert a gravitic field directly to heat. I'm quite sure there's no hope in this either, or even proof of concept. But with free money, hey, we'll do whatever they say. And, of course, the Military is avidly interested in electro-gravitic propulsion, reconciling the fields of electromagnetism with gravitation. There must be a relationship there, or so everyone thinks. Even Einstein devoted the latter 30 years of his life pursuing this, though to date – no results."

I cut in, "What about Nikola Tesla? He claimed to achieve some results in your area of endeavor. We're big fans of his." By saying this, I knew I was giving out hints. But so what, I thought. They know that I know, at least something. And that's the currency I'll use to buy my freedom . . . and Jack's too when he shows up.

"You and Jack were Tesla fans?" He was fishing. Here it comes, I thought.

"Yes, together with Mr. McEvey. He was a physics professor at the local college, and Jack's tutor . . . and our friend. He passed on a while back."

"Hmmm, very interesting. You and Jack were Tesla aficionados and teamed up with a physics professor." I figured he probably already knew all this and was giving the fish some line, hoping she'll run with it.

"Yes, it is interesting, isn't it?" I shot Winston a look. This was dangerous, poking the dragon.

"We find Tesla interesting too, and I can tell you this; our research department is tasked with combing through the mountains of technical papers at Universities, think tanks, and anywhere and everywhere else. They're looking for hints and clues concerning our mission – what is gravity. Why reinvent the wheel if someone else already has? And your friend Nicola may have. Like Einstein before him, he embarked on the spiritual journey towards the end of his life. He gave some talks, even filed a patent – his 'Dynamic Theory of Gravitation.' The government, in its infinite wisdom, swooped in, grabbed all his papers, quashed the patent, then sealed them away in a vault – for National Security reasons. Shortly thereafter, he got hit by a car. I'm not saying there was a connection, but . . . in any event, we have access to his papers. That's one of the advantages of having Big Brother on your team." He paused here to emphasize the importance of what he had just said. And he just confirmed everything in Mr. McEvey's book.

"Stored away and forgotten, just like the Ark of the Covenant." I thought that was a good analogy, even though it was from a movie.

"Exactly," replied Winston. He liked that word 'exactly' and my analogy. 'Exactly' is a better word than 'absolutely.' There are no absolutes, not even gravity, as Jack and I demonstrated. At the term 'National Security,' Robert took notice, then resumed his "exacting" observations of the passing scenery.

Sandy continued his probing, "What are your views on Einstein's General Theory?" A seemingly preposterous question anywhere else.

"I never liked trampolines very much, too bouncy." Winston laughed out loud at my frivolous treatment of Science's holiest of holies.

"As you most likely know, Tesla disdained and debunked Einstein's concept of the curvature of space-time as well. He attributed the force of gravity to – and this comes straight from his secret papers – 'whirls in the luminiferous aether,' the stuff that fills all space."

That made me think of Mr. McEvey. He was obsessed with the Aether. Deep down, I think he fancied himself an alchemist. And that's what they sought – the Aether, also known as the Philosopher's Stone. Mr. McEvey was fixated on zero-point energy, i.e., pulling energy from the Aether. He had obtained some serious results with his devices as well.

"Let me ask you this, Winston. Have you achieved any results; I mean serious results?"

"Unlike you, we have not. Nothing serious. Oh, we duplicated Townshend Brown's experiments. Are you familiar with them?"

I shook my head and said, "No." Even though I knew him well. He was another inventor who met a bad end.

"It's called the Biefeld Brown effect. Some slight levitation occurs, but it's just ionic wind, you know, flows of electrons. It has nothing to do with gravity. DARPA employs an army of eggheads to put ink on paper and come up with pie-in-the-sky theories. Like quantum gravity, there's only slight evidence that gravitic waves exist. If they do, that would be a significant clue to the riddle. Then there's the theory of supergravity, which poses that gravity is caused by braids of space-time." My eyes widened at this, and he noticed. Jack and Mr. M. were always talking about "the threads of Space-Time." Winston continued.

"But, as is usually the case, the real breakthroughs will happen out in the garage. Joe six-pack gets an idea and starts tinkering."

"Or some stoner, like Steve Jobs."

"Exactly . . . or some oddball like Jack Neufield, out in his barn." Winston had just laid his cards on the table. There was a long moment of silence. "And that's why I'm here. Speaking of which, he looked at the GPS, we are almost at our destination."

We were in Litchfield, just a few minutes from my farm. My mom Ester would be out back, managing all the "goings-on" with the horse business. Many clients would be about attending to their horses, riding, taking lessons. My father would be hard at work in town at the hardware store. His was pretty much a one-man operation, except for a few part-timers, mostly high school kids. Lucky for him, there were no Home Depots near, his greatest fear.

We approached the farm. Litchfield is an old colonial town founded in 1719. And consequently, our house was very old - circa 1790. It's a saltbox, not small – four bedrooms, with white clapboard siding. The most distinguishing feature is the stonework. Please understand that Connecticut probably has more stonewalls than anyplace else. Possibly because glaciers ground up and deposited man-sized stones everywhere. Hence, our forebears employed the readily available material quite liberally. There are stone walls, stone sidewalks, stone porches, stone foundations, and stone chimneys, which is the central feature of my house – a great big stone chimney stuck straight through the middle. Within are five fireplaces, one big enough to walk in. Presumably, that's how they heated the place back in the day. The house would make a great setting for a colonial movie, one of my brilliant suggestions. Supposedly, you could submit your house on a movie site and make some serious dinero if a producer chose to use it. My parents nixed the idea. They valued their privacy.

Mom and dad renovated by removing walls and exposing the old post and beam structure. Design-wise it was quite impressive, especially when contrasted with the modern kitchen. I loved living there. Too bad the Feds were going to take it. *I pray to the heavens above that they do not.*

The stables were out back along with the riding paths, corrals, and a small duck pond. I directed Winston to drive around back and park. Everyone stopped to stare at the return of the prodigal daughter. We exited the car, me in my sweats, Winston with his shades down, Jamal with his big gun, and Robert in his dark blue windbreaker, which read, 'Homeland Security,' in big yellow letters on the back.

My mother walked right over. She did not hug me.

"Hi Mom, just stopped by to pick up a few things. It may be a while before this, uh 'little misunderstanding' about Jack is all cleared up."

"And because this 'misunderstanding' is so little, you have an armed guard?" She was a tough old bird.

"Oh, this is Private Freeman, he's very nice and . . . helping out." I looked at him; on cue, he smiled and nodded. They shook hands, I winked at Jamal, then introduced everyone, and we all exchanged pleasantries.

"I have to say, it's a good thing your father's not home. You know, a couple of men with badges came by and threatened to take the farm." This she said more for my entourage's benefit.

Robert fielded this one, to whom I am now eternally indebted, "Ma'am, that would only be possible if this were the site of a serious threat to national security. At this time, that is not the case." He looked at me, and I mentally thanked him profusely. He beamed.

Sandy, that would be Mr. Erhart, also known as Winston, contributed his two cents, "This is more of a scientific investigation; to find out what happened at the Neufield barn the other night." I sent him a message of thanks also, with a slight nod. My mother's extreme anxieties were beginning to subside.

"Well, Hubert will be very relieved when I tell him this piece of news. I always thought there was something strange about Jack. He often seemed to be . . . well, 'living in another world.'" That's all Winston had to hear. Now he was all fired up.

"Mom, I'm going inside to gather up some clothes and things. I'll probably be gone a few days. I'm helping with the investigation too." My mother was glad to hear that. She was a big fan of big government. Winston, I'm sure liked that prospect, as well.

"Mom, why don't you show our guests around? Jamal, er, Private Freeman, would you be kind enough to help me with the suitcases?" He agreed. I had all the bases covered.

We walked to the house. I went upstairs; Jamal waited downstairs, looking around, oohing and ahhing, silently of course. I could have escaped through a second-story window, shimmied down a drainpipe, and broke for the woods. But didn't. I figured I could run, but I could not hide. I packed two suitcases with some nice clothes and some everyday clothes: shoes, and toiletries. And lest I forget, my tablet. I had a whole library in that thing.

We said our goodbyes, and this time Ester gave me a hug and a peck; after all, I was her only daughter. We entered the car and drove up the road to Jack's place.

Steel barricades, the mobile kind, blocked the entrance to Jack's farm. Probably were stored at FEMA down in Bridgeport in case of an emergency. I guess this was an emergency, "The Neufield Emergency." A couple of camo-clad soldiers were lounging near a Humvee. They walked over. Robert and Winston flipped their badges. Jamal didn't. He was wearing his. The barricades were slid apart, and we drove through. I found it interesting that Winston had a badge.

We parked in front of the house, where an officer was reclining in a rocker on the front porch. Surely enjoying a lazy summer afternoon. There were a few other vehicles parked about and yellow crime scene tape strung everywhere. How embarrassing for the Neufields. What will the neighbors think? Good thing they're in Afghanistan. Hey, wait a minute . . . they must have been told. They're probably on their way back, all freaked out.

The Officer walked over and introduced himself.

"Good afternoon. My name is Major Paul Tanaka." He gave a casual salute and then shook hands with Robert and Winston.

Jamal stood at attention after returning a smart salute. I was introduced as a neighbor. To me, the Major gave a half bow. Not knowing what to do, I returned the half bow. There was more small talk, chitchatting, and badge flipping while Jamal remained at attention. It was awkward. Then we walked over to the barn.

The barn looked like it had been sterilized. Not with Cobalt 60, but by people looking for Cobalt 60. From the outside, everything looked normal. There were no piles of debris scattered about, but the silver dome on the silo was missing. A point of clarification – an angry squirrel could have burst through that roof. It was rotten through in and throughout from a hundred years of water damage. There were tin patches upon tin patches. It was no great feat for the thing to have blasted through.

The big sliding door in front, which was usually semi-permanently shut, was open. And that's how we entered. I say the barn was sterilized because the life in the place had been . . . extinguished, removed. Only the furniture remained. The shelves were bare; the old computers, the books, the remnants of past projects, all gone. And the piles of stuff; electrical components, copper tubing, steel pipes, tool chests, power tools, even the old merry-go-round horse that Jack bought me for my 28th birthday, all gone. I peeked in the bathroom; they even took the toothbrushes. *For the DNA?*

"There's not much left," observed Winston. "It's just an empty barn."

"After the initial forensic analysis, the decision was made to pack it all up and take it away, anything that might aid in the investigation. There was some talk about moving the barn itself, but it was determined that the structure could not survive a move," explained the Major.

"Well, what were they planning to do, set the whole thing up somewhere else?" I said this, being horrified at the violation of our personal space.

"They don't tell me their plans. I'm just the caretaker," he replied.

I walked up the stairs. The TV was gone, but the bed was still there, and so was the dresser, minus the clothes. But they left the chair with the broken arm.

I came down, and we all migrated to the silo. For once, it was well lit since the roof was gone. Just the ragged edge of one. And it was completely empty. Winston stepped off the diameter and said, "About 28 feet." I knew he was mentally estimating the size of the “conveyance.” He looked around for clues. There weren’t any.

"It looks like the Army was very thorough with its investigation," commented Winston.

"Not the Army, the Air Force. Whatever it was, it flew. Therefore, it comes under our purview.”

Overall, the whole field trip experience was quite disconcerting. It drove home the fact that everything had irrevocably changed. I had passed a major inflection point on the curve of my life, and nothing would be the same again.

We retraced our steps and exited the barn. In front, the rusty old lawn chairs, the ones that should have been tossed out years ago, were still there. We all needed a moment to reflect, so we sat, despite the rust. Jamal pulled out a pack of Newports and looked around for approval. Winston flicked a one-handed "go ahead" coupled with a nod. By doing so, he assumed the mantle of leadership. Jamal lit up, and Robert pulled out a toothpick. I wondered if it was previously used. Obviously, he was an ex-smoker and dying for a smoke. Major Tanaka did not sit. He had a story to tell.

"I'm from the Saratoga Springs Air Force Base. We tracked the bogie as it went up, into the lower reaches of space itself, the limits of our radar. To say that my boss, General Taylor, took notice is an understatement. And it didn't take a genius to correlate the bogie with the nuclear theft in New Haven. Within the hour, we had military and FBI forensic teams on-site, both here and at the hospital. When they finished, the decision came down from DC to pack it all up. A couple of big trucks arrived, and we loaded everything in. Some people desperately want to know what went on in there." He head-pointed to the barn. "So sorry you came all this way for nothing."

"Uh, Major Tanaka, do you know if the . . . er, bogie came down safely somewhere?" I asked.

"All radar installations have been placed on alert. Even those of our allies. And, no doubt, 'others' as well. The search is on. Everyone is looking high and low . . . for the Anomaly. But I do not know if the searches were successful."

To me, no news was good news. Winston looked disappointed, though. But wasn't he getting updates? So, what did he expect? To find something they missed. The whole point of the field trip was to soften me up. Glean some hints, and I gave him that. He should look on the bright side – he still has me. And I know everything, though he only suspects that.

Eventually, we said our good-byes, made our way back to the car, waved at the soldiers as they removed the barricades, and began the journey back. The big trek – it was a half-hour ride. Robert suggested we stop at a diner; he knew one that served breakfast 24-7. Jamal was in favor, I was non-committal, but Winston nixed the idea. He was the leader. He said he had a schedule to keep. The back seat was quiet after that, and so was the front for a while.

"Can you tell me a little something about Jack?" I guess he didn't get the memo on Jack either. The fishing expedition resumed.

I took the bait. "Jack went to Bethlehem Elementary School till the third grade, when he kind of flunked out, kind of got kicked out. That was the extent of his formal education."

This was followed by another longish period of silence. I think my statement must have taxed Winston's central processing power.

"How long have you been, mmm, friendly with Jack?"

"Well, you know we were neighbors. I'd say . . . I started my regular visits in about the fifth grade. He had Miss Murphy and Mr. McEvey as tutors. Miss Murphy taught art and other subjects. I would join in on the art projects – drawing, painting, collages, popsicle stick sculptures. I loved those popsicle stick projects with the white glue." The memories lit a warm glow inside; I could still taste the glue. "It was always a fun time at Jack's."

"And Mr. McEvey taught physics?"

"Yes, science, math, chemistry. I guess he believed in learning by doing because we were always doing. He got these kits, you know, that provide the components. We built an electric motor once, then we put it in a little car we made from odds and ends. And we also built all kinds of airplanes, helicopters, drones, even rockets."

"Rockets?" Winston felt compelled to reiterate that word. "What kind of rockets?"

"Small ones, solid fuel, they'd go up a couple of hundred feet. Then come down nice and gentle on a parachute. We started rigging fireworks on them. Good thing we lived in the country, and the cops knew us. We'd have set off air-raid sirens anywhere else. That's what I meant by a 'fun time' at Jack's." I omitted the part about the railgun launches.

"So, you and Jack have been together since then?"

"I guess so. We've always been together." I wanted to say some other mushy stuff but edited myself. Too personal.

"And I'll bet you generally know everything he knows."

It was time to pull back, dance away from the dragon, "Not really. I have my career, you know, nursing. My life is almost totally taken up by that. I didn't even live in Litchfield until recently." But I was still dancing. I wanted Winston to assume I had something to negotiate. And I needed to buy time until Jack came. I knew he would. I knew this deep down inside. And I knew that together, we would overcome.

There was another period of quiet. Then Winston said, "The big meeting is set for 10 AM, the day after tomorrow. Someplace in

White Plains, near the airport." Now he was giving me information. This was good.

"I have this lightweight gray suit, a skirt with a smart little jacket, and a stylish lapel. Do you think that would be too conservative?"

"I think they'll be more interested in what you have to say than how you look." He almost said, “And so would I.”

We pulled up to the Homeland Security gate, the guard passed us through, and Winston stopped at the front entrance.

"I like you, Jane," he said, "And no matter what happens at the meeting, I'll do what I can for you. That's a promise."

I thanked Winston and told him that I liked him too. And I meant it, then I said goodbye.

The boys took me back to my room. Robert said he'd come for me later to escort me to dinner, and Jamal assumed his position by the door. I thanked them both, just for being such nice guys, and entered my room. First thing, I pulled out my phone and turned it on. The screen showed no recent calls. I dialed Jack’s number. No answer.

Chapter 14: The Lasagna Dinner - *Jack*

We entered the Ship traversing through the hull more rapidly this time. I silently thanked Albert. He kept up a running commentary on the performance of the "conveyance." How well it modulated the dual-gravitic-fluxes of both the Moon and Earth while warning me that it would be different on Earth – especially without the fusion reactor. I just crossed my legs and endured. We entered the hangar and stopped. There, beside the aisle, stood one of those blue porta-potties with a little picture of a man on the door.

"It's safe to exit the vehicle now, Jack."

I was in that porta-potty in five seconds flat. Oh, the agonies and ecstasies of being human.

I hopped back in the vehicle and commented, "You don't know how lucky you are, Albert . . . not being human." He just looked at me, totally speechless.

We parked, exited the hangar, and again, walked into the gray void. Albert began an exposition on the difference between animate and inanimate life. All I could think about was the alien base. The blinking lights, the parting mountain, and the landing strip, rising out of the ground. I was dumbfounded. I know, that's quite the familiar mental state of late, but this was different. Aliens on the Moon! Why were they there? How many were there? I mean, I was just getting used to Albert and the Ship, and now it's . . . Alien Times Square up here.

As we entered my farm, the thought struck me; I had a habitat. Just like a First-Born, almost. As we were walking down the drive, I had to ask, "Albert, can you explain again why those aliens are on the Moon?" I was hesitant to ask, afraid of the answers, I think.

"If you invite me to dinner tonight, Jack, I'll be happy to discuss the topic. How about lasagna this time?"

Lasagna was my second most favorite food. But of course, Albert knew that.

"But, I don't know how to . . ."

"I'll prepare the food. See you at seven." With that, he turned and walked off into the fleecy, gray void, jauntily gyrating his cane.

It was late afternoon in late August. The sun was hanging low over the fields. It was that time of the day and year when laziness was allowed, even encouraged. Beside the barn, the rusty old lawn chairs beckoned. Sitting, I swung one leg over the armrest and leaned back. A soft breeze shimmered the leaves, and birdsong trilled in the air. Harmony and contentment could be found in this place without much effort. *We want to make you feel at home here, Jack.* At that moment, I felt at peace, if not at home. I allowed myself the indulgence of a few minutes of rest and repose.

The minutes lapsed fast, and my thoughts quickly drifted to Janey and the mess I left her in. No doubt, many arms were pointing fingers of guilt at her, accusing her . . . of what? Aiding and abetting a terrorist – namely me; or being part of a terrorist cell, some kind of grand conspiracy? Time to think logically: What were the facts? First, they know I stole the Cobalt 60. Why? It's not fissionable; therefore, they'd assume I was building a dirty bomb, not a nuclear one. Fact number two: they know the silo roof exploded outward. How? Why? They'd figure I was testing . . . something that could carry a bomb. After seeing my workshop, they'd know that was a distinct possibility. Fact number three: that's bad news for Janey. They're going to sweat her hard in an interrogation room somewhere. They'll know she was involved. Fact four: I'll be returning to Earth soon. It's what the driving lesson was all about. Question: How can I free Janey? Answer: Turn in the conveyance in trade for her freedom. Then they'll know I'm no terrorist, just some kind of lunatic inventor. Of course, they'll want to know how and why it works. But, if I tell them about 4,3, I'll lose my quasi-probationary standing with Albert for violating their primary directive – no tampering with the primitives. And if I don't tell them, they'll lock me away until I do, or just make me disappear, like at a Cracker Barrel. Question: what should I do? Answer: unknown. Maybe find another way to free Janey, a third way; a better alternative to all of the above. Answer? Still unknown. *And what and why are aliens on the Moon?*

Well, so much for a few moments of rest and repose. Regrettably, I did not find harmony and contentment, though I was certainly inclined. A hawk soared overhead in lazy circles, looking for prey, the evening meal? What? Did Albert create an entire ecosystem here? Predators, prey, insects . . . worms? Or maybe it's a drone up there, keeping an eye on me. No, this is Albert's turf. He, for sure, knows all here. He's omniscient, all-powerful, and eternal . . . and somebody else's pawn! And if Albert is somebody else's pawn, then what does that make me? An amoeba? Shine a light and watch . . . what do amoeba's do anyway – perambulate? But Albert said they revere life. Does that include amoebas? I broke off that line of thought and resumed my study of the lazy hawk drifting on the currents, performing his languid adagios. Slow and graceful circles, beating the occasional glissade, demonstrating his mastery of the skies. A group of sparrows quickly darted for cover, diving deep into a thicket. Certainly, wise to the dance of the raptor.

And what time is it anyway? Here, and on Earth? Is it even the same? What about General Relativity and the fabric of space-time? Time should flow faster here, there being less gravity – by a factor of the Moon's mass divided by the speed of light squared. Therefore, the number is insignificantly small. Ergo, time is the same, both here and there. I automatically looked at my wrist, where my watch should have been. No watch. Lost in the ordeal presumably. Then how can I deduce the time? Answer: construct a timeline. When I left Earth, it was after dark, around 10 PM. Janey was working nights. The trip to the Moon and my subsequent recovery took how long? Unknown. Assume several hours, maybe half a day. The tour and the dinner; add a few more hours. I slept, then the driving lesson. Add another half day. Best guesstimate? Figure 30 hours. Therefore 10 PM plus 30 hours equals 4 AM of the second day. How's Janey holding up? A more disturbing thought.

I watched the butterflies waltz about the goldenrod. It was a good year for goldenrod. The swallowtails, both the yellow ones and black ones, bobbed above the flower heads. A few orange and black monarchs fluttered airily as well, seeking their youthful predilection – milkweed. And those little white moths that are so common, but nobody knows their name; they were everywhere as usual. They all danced in concert to the choreography of . . . Albert?

The sun was slowly descending, and so were my lids. I let them fall as I drifted into my own personal gray void. Time to let the subconscious take over; sift through the facts, all the data, and all the memories. Maybe that part of me can make more sense of this jumble and come up with some better alternatives.

I awoke with the Sun heavy on the horizon. What time is it? A foolish question to ask in this, the land of no clocks. What is time anyway? According to Albert, it is a discrete entity with structural components. Space, too, was said to have structure. And so too does the barn – a distinctive fabrication called a shower, which for me was about two days overdue. And Albert's coming for dinner at seven. I ran inside, stripped down, and took a long hot shower – just like home. My clothes were neatly folded and stacked in the dresser. Not just like home. I slipped on a pair of clean jeans, new sneakers (?), and a tee-shirt. I chose the old black one with the picture of Einstein in front and "Think," in big yellow letters on the back. It perfectly matched the poster on the wall, which was why Janey bought it. I figured Albert would get a kick out of it.

As I finished dressing, the doorbell rang. Now, who can that be? I dashed down the stairs two at a time. The kitchen table was set, just like before; dishes, wine glasses, a bottle of vino wrapped in a basket, and a large platter of lasagna. This time with a side dish of antipasto. The sight barely broke my stride, as I continued the sprint to the door.

"Welcome, Albert, to my humble . . . strike that, to this incredible habitat you constructed for me."

"Thank you, Jack. You are most welcome, and your choice of an upper garment is remarkably complementary."

"I thought you'd appreciate it. Albert Einstein, in all his many manifestations, is one of my most favorite people. Present company included."

"Again, you are most gracious." He bowed and swept his arm. "It pleases me to see you in cordial spirits. Shall we dine?" He motioned to the table. Technically, he was the host.

I took my chair while Albert very professionally uncorked the wine and poured a small amount for me to sample. He stood like a skilled sommelier, waiting expectantly, bottle in one hand, his face as impassive as usual. I played along, sniffed, took a sip, and then pretended to be knowledgeable about wines: "Strong but delicate bouquet, very flavorful, a pleasant hint of blackberry and a smooth aftertaste."

"Excellent," Albert then filled both glasses and assumed his seat, discarding the waiter act.

"You'd make a good maître d', Albert. I know a place in Litchfield where you'd fit right in."

"I shall keep that in mind, Jack, the next time I am unemployed." He was amused by the banter, and so was I. We clinked glasses and dug in. The food was out of this world. I asked Albert where he got the recipe. Big mistake.

It was oration time again. "You may be interested to know, Jack, that lasagna has its origins in ancient Rome. It comes from the Latin word lasanum, meaning cooking pot. Those early chefs layered thin sheets of pasta with various meats and sauces. But they lacked one key ingredient – tomatoes. The Europeans had to wait for Columbus to return with that delectable item. Probably a more significant discovery than your New World." With this phrase, Albert's eyes flashed a few twinkles. I was content to proceed with the business at hand, i.e., consuming the delicious cuisine. He continued, "The first modern lasagna recipes were published in

Naples in the 17th century. In southern Italy, they use primarily semolina, which are the hard grains left after the milling of durum wheat, but in northern Italy . . ."

I interrupted, "But where did you get the recipe, Albert?"

"I googled it under the world's best lasagna recipe."

I just stared and said, "You mean you've been here for 270 million years, and you needed to google a lasagna recipe?"

"They have a superior algorithm, Jack. Quite efficient for this type of inquiry."

I raised my glass and said, "To Google." We clinked glasses again, drank, and Albert cracked a smile. Life was good again, for the moment. I was loath to mention the lunar aliens for fear of disturbing the congenial atmosphere. Albert surprised me when he reached into his inside pocket and handed me my watch.

"We managed to repair your watch, though reconstruct may be a more accurate word."

"Why, thank you, Albert. I've been lost without it." I looked at the time. It read 7:20 PM, August 29th. My timeline analysis was off by eight and a half hours. I must have been traveling damned fast, and Albert's doctors were really good. Upon a few moments of reflection, I asked, "How fast was I going when I . . ."

"Before you disintegrated?" Albert completed my sentence. "Your velocity was 72,378 miles per hour and still accelerating. Your device initiated a chain reaction for which it had no control. Your conveyance had no brakes, Jack."

"Well, I can say with profound certainty that it was a good thing you just happened to be there, or . . . here. And I mean that sincerely." I raised my glass, and we clinked again. It was a becoming real clink fest.

Albert picked up on my prior statement, "It is accurate to say that there are patterns in this Universe that do not 'just happen to be there,' Jack. One such would be . . . my presence here. And truly, we can agree that your rescue was a good thing . . . as the many levels of these events reveal themselves. And speaking of good things . . . your phone will be repaired by late tomorrow."

As the many levels of these events reveal themselves, I wondered. Shine the light and watch the amoeba go. I'm being played. As to that, there can be no doubt. But are things here, in this bizarre situation, any different from anywhere else? Does there exist a place where people don't have agendas, hidden or otherwise? Granted, I'm not dealing with people here. In the boardroom, agendas make the meetings flow smoothly. Accomplish the tasks set forth. What's Albert's agenda? He told me first off; to welcome mankind to their big gathering up in the heavens – The Continuum. After the discovery of 4,3, of course. Does Albert have a hidden agenda, I wonder? And what about the First-Born, Albert's builders? What's their agenda? Could I even comprehend it if I knew? Bottom line – I'm a piece on a chessboard; strike that, make that a one-celled animal. But I still have free will, despite the mind games. I'll just do what I have to do and . . . *keep on perambulating towards the light.*

"Great! Then that's when I'll call Janey. No doubt her interrogators will be listening. I'll just tell them the truth. I built an anti-gravity device, and it worked better than expected, but it had no brakes, so I ended up on this huge space-sphere behind the Moon. Would that be an acceptable description of you, Albert?"

"On an elementary level, it is accurate."

"All right then; once there, I took a tour of the Ship, drove my rebuilt conveyance around the Moon, and then had some very nice dinners. But don't worry. I'm coming back and intend to return the Cobalt 60. So, you can let Janey go. Sorry, false alarm, there are no terrorists here."

"I'm quite sure Janey's captors would not find the same humor in your statement that I do, Jack. Perhaps, it would be more useful for all concerned if we discussed the aliens we saw earlier on the Moon." Albert successfully changed the subject. I very much agreed with the change.

"Good idea, Albert. Who the heck . . . what the hell . . .? I mean, what's going on with . . . those aliens being here on the Moon?"

"The aliens, the Pra'at as they call themselves, have posed a conundrum to me these past several thousand years. Your felicitous visit may be instrumental in the formulation of a solution. A task long on my agenda."

"I am at your service, as always." I ignored the blatant evidence of mind-reading. At this juncture, it was a given.

Albert gestured outward and fanned his fingers. The lights dimmed, and a three-dimensional representation of a galaxy half-filled the room. It was tilted to one side, providing a complete view. Albert waited for my response.

"I am seriously impressed, Albert. Next time I have a movie night, you're definitely invited. A variation on the Moon map thing, I presume?"

"Precisely, Jack. Same principles, only a little larger, plus, I added the third dimension. This is a representation of your Galaxy."

The disk-like image was composed of billions of specks of light. Dense at the center, sparser further out.

Albert began his discourse: "There are many galaxies in this Universe, Jack. 363.239 billion, to be exact. And if I may reiterate, civilized life in this cosmos is a rarity. Indeed, the vast majority of galaxies contain no advanced civilizations. The odds of a life form progressing to the Fourth Level are astronomically slim. The extraordinary conditions, coupled with the high probability of extinction events, make the advent of advanced societies extremely unlikely. And many believe this was as intended . . . the way things should be . . . the Natural Way. A squid lays thousands of eggs, yet only a few survive. But those that do . . . are superior."

"The Milky Way is one of the older galaxies. Accreted from the original burst 13.789 billion years ago. And due to its size and age, the conditions here are propitious for phylogenesis . . . ripe for life to arise." Albert pointed to a star on an outer arm, and it flared brighter. "This is the site of your galaxy's only civilized society. The homeworld of the Pra'at. They call it Ta-ea."

"You mean Earth is not considered a civilized society?" For some reason, I felt compelled to defend my homeworld. *My homeworld?*

"4,3, Jack . . . knowledge of the Fourth Level. That is the threshold and the definition of 'civilized,' as set forth by Those Who Came First. Though you, Jack, would be considered a quasi-provisional, civilized being. Unfortunately for Earth, you stand alone in this distinction." Albert pointed again, and another speck lit, not too far from the first. “This is your Sun relative to Ra – the home star of the aliens. Most life arises in the outer spiral arms, far from the turmoil of a galactic core.”

“Do they have an entity like you watching over them as well?”

“Yes, Jack, I have a counterpart there. And we exchange data.”

“So, you must know them pretty well?”

“The quantity of my Pra’at data is nearly total: their evolution, history, and cultures. For that reason, the situation at hand is . . . complicated.”

“What do they look like? Can I see a picture of one?”

“I’ll show you much more than a picture, Jack.” Our viewpoint began to zoom in towards Ra. As we rocketed inward, the distant flyspeck resolved into a solar system. Their home star was similar in size and color to the Sun, and a handful of planets were strung out on its ecliptic disc. Gas giants to the outside, small rocky globes to the inside. Our descent slowed and centered on the fourth planet. Or the fourth planetary group, since I observed three moons, one large, two smaller. The planet itself was largely cloud-covered with patches of blue and green. Probably more blue than green. We spun around to the dark side where the world sparkled with ribbons of light. The surrounding near-space swarmed with vehicles, many that glowed and flashed, interspersed with the occasional large space station; some wheel-like, others cylindrical.

I commented, “They certainly are more advanced than Earth, and for sure, a space-faring race.”

"The image you see is current, Jack. The Pra'at were inducted 12,771 solar years ago. At that time, their technology was similar to present-day Earth's. Subsequent technological advancement has been guided . . . by my counterpart. Shall we delve in a little closer?"

"Please do." I had some difficulty restraining myself, such was my interest. I was craving to know more about our alien neighbors.

Our viewpoint swung around to the light side of the planet . . . Ta-ea is the name Albert called it. I imagined being on the bridge of the Star Ship Enterprise, viewing the big display screen, *going where no man has . . .* Two moons were visible, one large and reddish, the other small and gray, both crescents. We dipped into the atmosphere, a very cloudy one, and emerged amid a fabulous cityscape – distinctly alien. The predominant architectural form was the pyramid – every conceivable size and shape thereof. Tall, spiked spires extended two, three thousand feet tall; others were short and squat with three or four sides. The common denominator: they almost all culminated in points. They clearly had a thing for pointy structures. To be fair, there were other shapes; organic and free form, one resembling an upside-down jellyfish, another a half-open artichoke. Evidence that more than one architectural philosophy was in vogue. Graceful ribbons and tubes crisscrossed and connected everything. The colors were largely pastel, but mostly sandy brown, broken by the occasional blue or orange. And the sky was abuzz with non-aerodynamic aircraft, presumably anti-gravitic. A most appealing aesthetic, and overall – most definitely advanced.

"Looks like they have a thing for pyramids down there." For a moment, I worried we might be seen, then remembered, we're sitting in my barn dining on lasagna, but wait, that's not exactly accurate either.

"Every culture employs an architectural form that tends to predominate," Albert explained. "The pyramid is the most elementary of geometric shapes, forming a structure of compressive stresses only. Many cultures begin building significant projects with this type of symmetry, Jack."

"Well, it seems to be working out ok for them."

"The shape is in synchronous harmony with their core identity. On Earth, every major social framework has a distinctive architecture. For example, the colonnades of the Greeks, the Gothic spires of the Europeans, and the upturned roofs of the Chinese."

"Synchronous with 'their core identity,'? What, they've got pointy heads or something?"

"Shall we prowl in a little closer, and see?" It was a rhetorical question. We did.

Chapter 15: The Pra'at

We swooped in on what looked like the courtyard of an immense pyramidal building. Both the structure and the plaza were built of large beige stones. Egress was provided by elaborate stairways and gravity-defying ramps. Here and there were several grassy areas with geometrically placed planting beds packed with colorful blossoms and leafy shrubs. Dominating the central square was a huge figurative statue. Fountains, carved benches, and other objects d'artes were dispersed throughout. Beings were congregating, strolling along pathways, and sitting on low stonewalls. And they were, to my utter astonishment . . . Grays.

"Albert, they look like . . . Grays!"

"Yes, Jack. Your various civilizations, ancient and otherwise, have known this species for thousands of years."

"But . . . they . . . "I was almost speechless. The ramifications would take my brain some considerable time to power through. I was a big fan of "Ancient Aliens," "Chariots of the Gods," and all those TV shows that document possible alien encounters. But amidst all the evidence, there was always some doubt. Not anymore. I managed to blurt out, "They left traces, Albert, reams of evidence, everywhere, throughout all history."

"Yes, Jack, your statement is correct. And each 'trace,' each piece of evidence is a violation of Continuum Primary Law."

Suddenly the picture went blank. Nothing was there anymore. Just my empty workshop.

"Looks like somebody pulled the plug, Albert."

"That would be an accurate characterization, Jack. My counterpart is no longer conducive to my surveillance of his territory. We differ regarding our respective inductive strategies. In particular, my imposition of sanctions due to prior Pra'at encroachments. However, we can proceed with our discussion of the Pra'at-tum, as the three species are sometimes collectively called."

A small embodiment of a Gray appeared. Humanoid, smallish, maybe four feet tall, with a large bald head drawing down to a sharp chin. Recessed within were two egg-shaped black eyes, a vestigial nose containing two ovoid nostrils and way down by the chin, a small slit for a mouth. On the whole, not particularly cute. His pale greenish-gray facial skin was drawn tight, with taut wrinkling here and there. The cheeks were sunken, and there was nothing in the way of ears. He wore a close-fitted covering, the same color as his skin. It looked like it could have been a second skin. It covered his feet, but not his hands, which were large, four-fingered, and powerful looking.

"The Pra'at consists of three separate species, which represent a general division of labor. This is a Qe'ma u, a representative of the worker class." As Albert said this, two other figures appeared. "The tallest figure on your right is a Rams'su or 'thinker.' A member of what I will call, the contemplative class. As the name implies, they do the deep-thinking, formulate theories, perform thought experiments, and in general – determine how and why things work. They are small in number and highly valued."

"Thought experiments!" I exclaimed. "That's what Einstein did. He never even picked up a screwdriver. Worked everything out in his head."

"That is a perfect illustration of the value of pure thought, Jack. And thought is how the Pra'at communicate. Via electromagnetic radiation – brain waves, almost exclusively. It is the end product of speech evolution. Though, in reality, not much different from the aural modes. Simply a different type of coded emanation."

The tall alien wore robes of a silk-like material, long and flowing, green in color, with the occasional elaborate pattern. Quite similar to a toga. He had a huge, bald cranium, as one would expect of a big thinker, and large, bulbous black eyes, only his were surrounded by ridges, which began where the eyebrows should have been, then wrapped around to intersect with a slightly more prominent nose. The mouth had more humanoid upper and lower lips and was normally positioned above the chin. High, pronounced cheeks, sunken jowls, and vestigial ears completed the picture. After a double-take, I noticed that each eye contained two yellow pupils, one over the other. It was odd. His body was an elongated version of the smaller one, only with more graceful hands. Overall, our thinking friend was not unsightly, though most definitely alien.

Albert's oration proceeded uninterrupted, though he did stop for the occasional forkful. "Ra is slightly larger than your Sun, however the Pra'at homeworld orbits at a further distance than the Earth; therefore, it receives less light. This fact, coupled with the increased cloud cover, results in Ta-ea being a relatively dim planet. Hence, they have large, double-pupiled eyes."

"And what about the one in the middle. Goldilocks, not too tall, not too small?" It was a larger version of the small one. Bighead, big eyes, same swimsuit. Equally charming.

"Your arcane 'Goldilocks' reference defies my analytical abilities, Jack. However, I assume you are referring to the second alien, called a Sek hem're. They are the enablers. They implement the thoughts and policies of the "thinkers." The smaller species," Albert pointed with his fork to the first one, "do the actual physical labor. Pick up the screwdrivers if you will."

"That seems strange to me, there being three separate species. Does that mean they can't interbreed?"

"That is an important question, Jack, and the answer will supply the key to your comprehension of the Pra'at-tum and why they are here. First, let me point out, the Pra'at have a complex society. Their present state of harmony followed an arduous path. They had to endure a long and protracted clash of ideologies and religious beliefs. And the operative word here is 'long,' Jack, because some worlds evolve faster than others. Please allow me to preface this statement."

It was my turn to gesture, "Please proceed, Albert." I sat back, casually munching on a piece of celery.

"Carbon-based life forms are by far the most prevalent in the Universe. Basically, for three reasons: First, the ease by which the carbon atom bonds with other elements. Second, it has a low atomic weight. And third, it is abundant in the Universe. Because of these facts, almost all life shares a variant of the DNA molecule, but of course, it differs from world to world. Epigenetic processes are largely responsible for those differences. The science of 'epigenetics' refers to those chains of biochemical reactions that control the rate at which environmental factors cause changes in a species' genotype. Change occurs, Jack, not by random mutations, as you may have learned, but by specific biochemical feedback mechanisms, which modify and switch genes on and off, either temporarily or permanently. Your science has only just begun to explore this process. They call it DNA methylation. And it is largely responsible for the rate at which a species evolves."

"We consider the settlement of hunter-gatherers into permanent farming groups to be the starting point of a culture. By this standard, it took mankind approximately 14,000 years to reach their current level of advancement. But it took the Pra'at 49,000 similar years to reach a comparable state. The reason lies in their genetic blueprint, their specific DNA methylation mechanisms. They are genetically programmed to evolve at a slower rate than humans. Regrettably for them, they suffer another related drawback – they live shorter lives. Environmental factors have disfavored the many genes responsible for longevity. This is the essential difference."

The diorama changed to a split-screen landscape – Earth on the left, Ta-ea on the right. Both sides depicted primitive pastoral scenes – the dawn of civilization presumably . . . on both worlds. The earthside was Mesopotamia or some such place. Within a clearing were a group of hovels built mostly of reeds stuck in the ground, except for a few larger ones made from mud brick. The terrain was an arid plain, but in this location, it bordered on a river where the greenery of water-flora edged the shore. A few palm trees dotted the area. There were goats in a corral, and a few people ambled about wearing robes or light skirts. A couple of skiffs glided on the river.

The Pra'at side was different. Beside a river was a clearing surrounded by a lush forest of large arching trees, each dangling huge thick leaves. Within the open space were stone and mud, igloo-ish-type huts with domed, woven roofs. Large, fat hippo-type animals with beaks wandered about, some in the river, some penned in.

Many, it looked like the mid-sized aliens, were busy going about their business. Their business being the building of a large pyramid.

It was a nice feature; the lecture sprinkled with video. The thing is the videos were probably actual historical scenes. This fact made it intensely interesting; to truly be able to look back in time. How valuable is that? It's a shame, though, that the Pra'at can't live long. I asked, "How long do the Pra'at live?"

"About 50 of your years, Jack."

"Well, if they're so advanced, why can't they extend their lives a little? You know, with a little genetic tinkering?"

"They are, Jack. That is why they are here."

Albert's statement floored me. I put down my celery stick and gaped. Suddenly it all clicked. It all made sense. Why they have been here for all these years, tampering, playing God, abducting a few humans, every so often.

Albert read my surprise and the scene shifted to a space station, a colossal superstructure orbiting above Ta-ea. It certainly was not Earth.

Albert explained, "The Pra'at share one major attribute with humans, Jack. They are curious. They collectively arrived at 4,3 and were inducted into the Continuum. But that doesn't mean all knowledge instantly becomes available. Rather, they were nudged to pursue various areas of endeavor. Coaxed and guided towards certain experiments. And curious races look outward, see wonders, and want to explore. We helped them with this, and they learned the basics of interstellar travel. The facility you see here manufactures starships."

Albert pulled out his pipe, stuffed it, then lit it, puffing voluminous volumes of smoke, partially obscuring the spectacle before us. Our viewpoint slowly prowled around the perimeter. A labyrinthine apparatus with trusses, connecting members, and many barrel-shaped and tubular enclosures where a multitude of pods were shuttling to and fro. Within this infrastructure was a large saucer-shaped craft. It looked to be a few thousand feet in diameter, possibly larger.

"That looks like considerably more than the basics to me, Albert."

"The Pra'at have engaged in short distance star travel for several thousand years now. Their range is limited to this Galaxy."

"I guess Einstein was wrong about nothing traveling faster than the speed of light."

"Yes, Jack, Einstein was fundamentally wrong since the Universe itself is expanding faster than the speed of light. But what Einstein actually said was, 'a particle with non-zero rest mass cannot travel faster than the speed of light . . . in normal space'. In that statement, my namesake provides the solution to the light limit problem – simply by creating new space to travel in – 'non-normal,' space."

Albert elaborated, "'The Law of Connections,' as some species call 4,3, posits that Space, Time and Matter, comprise the strong force. The reverse is also true. The strong force, when released, emits more than just matter and energy. It releases its other components as well – Space and Time. Your people have emitted this type of discharge for many decades with your atomic bombs."

I was truly incredulous, "Atomic bombs release Space and Time as well as all that energy?"

"Yes, Jack, the local time accelerates, and new space itself is produced, in different forms – some expanded and some compressed. An atomic explosion is a crude and primitive means of generating the formal aggregates of Time and Space, which, by definition, would be 'non-normal.' How to capture and control these components is the problem."

The space scene was replaced by an animated depiction of a series of toroidal rings enclosing an explosion chamber. As an explosion burst in the center, arrows encompassed and contained it.

"The weak force, when combined with electromagnetism, as in your conveyance, can be used to control and contain the strong force – including its components. Condensed Space is channeled before the vehicle and expanded Space behind. As a consequence, the vehicle falls forward and is pushed from behind – in non-normal Space. In this manner, velocities many times faster than the speed of light can be attained. This is in accord with Einstein's General Theory."

"So, they use something like what I did in my conveyance . . . to contain an atomic blast!"

"The discharge is first dampened and absorbed by a series of 'singularities,' as you call them, which are arranged around the blast chamber. They absorb the energy of the explosion, leaving the newly created Space and Time, which a matrix of the electro-weak-force, first separates and then redirects."

"So, they just whip up a batch of black holes, and voila, problem solved." My mind was close to being blasted as well.

“Various types of ‘condensed matter’ are easily manufactured in large colliders. Black holes, as you call them, make for excellent mass storage devices. Also, they are efficient sources of gravitic energy, many different varieties.”

With this, Albert loaded up and fired his own personal blast chamber and proceeded to expectorate the most magnificent volumes of airborne carbon particulates – rings within rings, within rings. It was the Hallelujah Chorus of smoke. I got the message and the epiphany. Everything is connected. Just like electricity and magnetism are, the components of the other forces can be extracted, interchanged, and or recombined for other purposes. The possibilities of 4,3 became limitless, interstellar travel being but one.

The scene flipped back to the Space Complex. Albert just sat there, puffing away, staring at me. It was my turn, but I was way too stunned for a quick response. I took a moment to ponder the ramifications. Earth would be no match for Ta-ea. That was a fact. If I was an amoeba to the First-Born, then humans were like chimpanzees to the Pra’at, who could invade and annihilate us at will. Or capture humans and experiment to their heart's content. But hell, we do the same to monkeys, chimps, and every other dumb animal we can lay our hands on. So why don’t they? Then, the thought just hit me . . . it’s because of Albert. I recalled our previous conversation:

“Albert, you’re like Big Brother is watching!”

“No, Jack, more like a Guardian Angel.”

Reverting to his maître d’ act and, no doubt, reading my current state of befuddlement, Albert changed the subject, “Would you care for some dessert, Jack? I believe you will find a Tiramisu cake in the refrigerator. And coffee? That should provide the perfect conclusion to a delightful evening."

"Sounds good to me. I'll make the coffee." Of course, he knew of my favorite desserts, and I certainly knew how to make the coffee. The respite was welcome. I needed time to digest, not the food, but rather, the import of all the fantastic information Albert had just revealed. But why tell me? Sure, I posed the question, "what about those aliens on the moon?" But still, why tell me everything? I feared the answer would have larger implications.

We partook of the dessert. The tiramisu was heavenly, half cake, half icy cream. It was the perfect complement to the pasta. Albert discussed the spectacle on the screen. Strike that, there was no screen per se. How far away Ta-ea was – 1,271 light-years. How long a one-way trip to Earth took – 78 days. How fast they went . . . you do the math. I kept thinking about all the possibilities of 4,3 and commented.

"I realize my previous understanding of 4,3 barely scratched the surface. All the possibilities, all the potential. Before I dwelled in darkness, now I see the light."

Albert replied, "And so it is with most races. Gradually the light of understanding brightens. And with all these possibilities, you can understand why a being would seek longevity. Why they would want more time to experience all this potential. After induction, most species begin the quest for longer life in earnest. Eventually, it leads to . . . immortality. And so, it is with the Pra'at and all those who came before."

"And thus, they're here, monkeying around with us humans."

"Yes, Jack, and thus they are here."

"I seem to remember a most eloquent peroration you delivered . . ."

Interrupting, Albert commented, "Excellent word Jack. I shall place it in my active vocabulary."

"Why, thank you, Albert." We clinked coffee cups, "But, you may not like what I'm about to remind you of . . . "

"I know what you were about to say, Jack. May I quote you?"

The conversation was getting bizarre, "Yes, Albert, please, by all means, 'quote' what I was about to say."

"You intended to cite my previous statement concerning The First-Born; their belief that they were called upon to guard the children of the Progenitor against outside influence. That phylogenesis must proceed unaltered. And that I am an instrument of that undertaking. Yes, Jack, you would have been correct to remind me because that is the crux of the issue. It is my hope that you can help me to resolve this."

"Me, the amoeba, help you?"

"May I quote myself from earlier in the evening?"

"Certainly, Albert."

"Your felicitous visit may be instrumental in the formulation of a solution to the alien problem." He made it sound like we had an infestation. Just call the termite guy, whose name is Jack.

"I'm all ears, Albert."

"Immortality is a universal goal and one The First-Born are partial to, having long since attained it. The Pra'at have a genetic deficiency that renders them short-lived. When they came here to observe, they saw in the human genome a possible corrective to their problem. My counterpart on Ta-ea allowed limited human contact and limited experimentation. I acquiesced at first."

The visuals before us changed from the Pra'at Space Complex to the Great Pyramids of Giza *as they were being built*. Hundreds of Egyptians laboriously carried satchels of liquefied limestone, which they poured into massive forms situated along the many ramps that crisscrossed the edifice. A short distance away, a huge stone obelisk lay on a large sledge-like platform that hovered a foot or so off the ground. It was being pushed and pulled by a handful of men. A small saucer-craft hovered not too high, not too far away.

"Naturally, the aliens were considered gods, and the Egyptians adopted many aspects of the Ta-ean culture, from the pointed architectural form to the quest for immortality. And they were eager to fulfill the Pra'at's biochemical needs, particularly – for blood subjects."

The scene shifted to a religious chamber where the rites of mummification were taking place. Shaven-headed priests and near-naked slaves were laboring over a body laid out on a slab. Jars and bowls filled with green and red potions covered the tables, amphorae were tucked in the corners, and hieroglyphics covered the walls. Two of the taller green-robed Pra'at were watching nearby.

"As a result, the Egyptian civilization stagnated for thousands of years, their efforts and energies wasted in the pursuit of an afterlife, and its preparations."

"Why didn't you do something to stop it?" I asked.

"My queries to my Builders went unanswered. And 'no response' is, in itself, an answer, which I construed to mean – 'take no precipitous action.' So, I pondered the matter for a considerable time. And waited and watched, which was as my counterpart advised. But events escalated to levels of extreme dysfunction."

The scene shifted to what looked like a Mayan cityscape. Scores of small limestone buildings ringed several large, stepped pyramids. Hundreds, maybe thousands of semi-naked people were wildly waving their arms, shouting in an incomprehensible language. They were celebrating a religious ceremony of sorts. Numerous celebrants brandished long pointed shafts, some topped with bloody human heads. The throngs were concentrated around one particular pyramid, where groups of elaborately clad priests were exhorting the masses and conducting a ritual. A victim, daubed with blue and white pigment, writhed on a stone altar, arms and legs held down on four sides. The high priest, holding overhead a stone knife, plunged it deep into the victim's chest and then deftly removed the heart. He held the dripping organ high, and the crowd roared in jubilation. A line of similarly daubed wretches waited their turn, guarded by fierce, masked warriors adorned with multiple piercings. The head was severed and rolled down a ramp. The shouts of the crowd bawled even louder. Suspended overhead was a small saucer-shaped craft.

"So much for the best-laid plans. Is that the lesson here, Albert?"

"Yes, Jack. This scene occurred about two thousand years ago, and your maxim aptly summarizes the series of events that culminated in this calamity."

"Everybody has a plan until they get punched in the face." I stole that pearl of wisdom from Mike Tyson.

"And the plan which allowed the Pra'at limited contact was terminated at that time." The scene changed to other sites of 'visitor' interference: the Aztec, the Inca, Easter Island, etc. It was like watching "Ancient Aliens" back home, only it was real.

"By you?"

"No, by Mike Tyson." This was followed by a long, lingering pause, accompanied by Albert's trademark twinkle. The wheels of my mind turned slowly but inexorably.

"Your humor is seriously improving, Albert."

"Thank you, Jack. That is a goal I pursue. And yes, I initiated the action. There was some difficulty since I had to negate the disposition of my counterpart."

"Does your counterpart have a name?"

"We do not have names, per se, but are designated by symbols and numerals, not readily translatable. There are millions of entities like myself tending to the business of the Universe. Your galaxy has been favored with two, Jack. A redundancy, evidenced by my conflict with #2, as we shall call my counterpart. I could easily have managed the induction of two species."

"But the Pra'at are still here, sneaking around and tinkering with the natives."

"To a greatly reduced degree, yes."

"So, where do I fit into this little drama? Scratch that word 'little.' This is far from a little drama."

"Your quasi-provisional status, representing Earth, gives you the right to voice an opinion, Jack. You have some standing in this matter. And when and if your people are inducted, they may very well choose to collaborate with the Pra'at in the matter of their longevity and all other areas as well. We encourage comity and harmonious intercourse."

Little ole me gets to vote. Vote about what? Whether they stay or go? It's probably not a good thing the aliens are still sneaking around, "tampering" is the word Albert used. If I say they must go, then do they have to go? Will my vote tilt the scales? I made the following pronouncement: "I vote they go. No more tampering with the locals. Abducting, doing whatever it is they're doing. And when and if we humans get the nod, the big invite, then the Pra'at can properly introduce themselves, collaborate – do what all those involved decide to do. But for now . . . I say the Earth is off-limits. It's time to hang out the 'DO NOT DISTURB' sign, Albert."

I said my piece, not exerting all that much thought, but still, said with no regrets.

"I concur, Jack. The Pra'at must go completely. Every installation, and every single trace of their existence that can be removed, must be removed from Earth and its environs. Mankind is at a delicate juncture. A premature First Contact would precipitate conflict. A war over religious or political differences could send your species back thousands of years, back to the First Level, the Stone Age. Though I do not doubt you will recover. Humans are a resilient breed."

"Why, thank you, Albert. I take that as a compliment, having bounced back myself from, uh . . . being disintegrated and all . . . with your help, of course." I raised my cup, and Albert followed suit. We sipped our coffee as Albert puffed away on his pipe. "Even though I am resilient, I must confess to a deficiency. I'm a slow learner. Perhaps another driving lesson would be in order . . . say tomorrow? And, if they leave the lights on again, I suggest we pay our not too good-looking alien neighbors a visit. Borrow a cup of sugar, shoot the breeze . . . and tell them, they've got to go. At least temporarily, until we attain the Fourth Level, as you say."

A rather bold suggestion for the smallest kid on the block, but since I'd be standing next to the biggest, I figured I should at least try. After all, saving humanity from the depredations of aliens was probably worth the risk.

There was another short period of silence. Like a master chess player, I'm sure Albert was planning about a million moves ahead.

"Yes, Jack, another driving session would be in order. We have reconfigured your conveyance to better reflect your original design; made it appear to be . . . more indigenous. We should test it and maybe 'pay the Pra'at a visit.' The time is right."

The diorama disappeared. I was stuffed to the gills with good food, good conversation, and good company. We both sat back. If I were home and alone, my feet would be up on the table. Albert was content to stare into space, puffing away. A Bach Brandenburg Concerto began to play on the stereo.

"Would you like me to help you clean up, Jack? You wash, I dry?"

It was an excellent idea and one, I must admit, I was beginning to contemplate. “Good idea, Albert, though I know we have invisible maids here.”

We lazily got up, Albert kept his pipe in his mouth, and we proceeded to clean off the table.

“I just have one question, Albert. How are we going to make the aliens leave? I mean, we’re not going to grab a couple of M-16’s and storm the place, are we?”

“I am pleased to hear you use the pronoun ‘we,’ Jack. Because we are going to walk in and politely ask them to leave.”

“That’s it? No pulse pistols, no stun grenades, not even a couple of lightsabers?”

“None of that, Jack. We shall simply ask them nicely. That should be sufficient.”

“Just say the magic word ‘please’?”

“That is correct, Jack. A great deal can be accomplished by simply being nice.”

That was it, the extent of our planning. There would be no brainstorming in the war room. I hoped Mike Tyson’s axiom would not come to pass. A ‘punch in the face’ I did not need.

I let it go and asked, “When do you think I can go home, Albert?” I always found warm soapy dishwater to be soothing, and not just to the hands.

"That's up to you, Jack. Your phone will be ready tomorrow, probably after our driving session." The water ran clean and warm as Albert rinsed, dried, and stacked the dishes.

I suddenly felt like an amoeba again. "Is everything playing out as you anticipated, Albert?"

He replied candidly. "You were a wildcard, Jack. Unanticipated but fortuitous, and you passed the 4,3 test. A difficult hurdle, to be sure, but you evinced knowledge of the precept. You alone."

"You're wrong about that, Albert. I'm not alone. Janey was with me every step of the way. She knows about 4,3 as well."

"Then she may have a role to play in our 'little drama'. 'Strike that,' as you say . . . the impending events will likely be far from 'little.' I believe I am finished here." He put down the dishtowel. "I think a period of rest would be beneficial at this time. I enjoyed your company immensely, Jack." We shook hands.

With that, Albert put away his pipe and walked towards the door. Then he stopped, turned, and said, "Tomorrow, we have a sign to hang." With that, he picked up his cane and left, sauntering up the lane.

As usual, I was thoroughly dumbfounded. And dumb is the most accurate word to describe, "moi," at least as compared to Albert, the Pra'at, the 'First-Born' (?), and who knows what else is out there. Somehow though, I did not think the Pra'at would leave Earth simply because we asked them 'nicely.' What? Are they going to give up their quest for immortality? No freaking way. And Albert obviously used me to tip the scales – in his favor. Force the alien issue. That's fine with me. I was glad to be a part of all this. But much remained unknown; like, the forces that Albert was dealing with, his counterpart – #2, the First-Born, and his internal constraints, not to mention the Pra'at themselves. But I knew one thing. It had been a long day, and my lids were drooping. I trudged up the stairs. The music stopped. I got into my bed. *I know – it's not my bed.* I didn't care. I slept like a baby.

Interlude 3: Emigration

It's interesting how most entities in physics have opposites. Matter has anti-matter. In fact, all the particles have anti-particles: anti-protons, anti-electrons, and so forth. Magnets have opposite poles. In nuclear energy, fission is the opposite of fusion. And, concerning the Laws of Motion, every action has an equal and opposite reaction, Newton's Third Law. The list goes on and on. Now, here's the funny part – many opposites attract. On a magnet, opposite poles attract; in chemistry, a positive ion attracts a negative ion; and in physics, a vacuum always attracts substance. Opposites attract in people too . . . but I digress.

Where am I going with this? To Time, the formal concept thereof. Is the past the opposite of the future, or vice versa? Are there different kinds of Time? This question has been answered by Einstein, who else, and is universally accepted. His General Theory defines a concept called – time dilation. The more the gravity, the slower time elapses. This is one of Einstein's sacrosanct precepts. Therefore, by his definition, there are different kinds of Time, some flow faster, some flow slower. What was Time like in the enclave of the First-Born? Time was in flux there, as it is everywhere, elapsing slow or fast, depending. But it's not that bad and quite pleasant really, providing the option to extend the pleasurable and vice versa. Though rules and traditions have evolved to deal with this.

What about Space? Does Space have an opposite? Anti-Space? Does it annihilate normal Space? Of this, I do not know, except that there are alternate dimensions or "planes' out there. Though this is a very advanced science, we're talking 6th and 7th Level Technology here. On Earth, various theories have been proposed.

One such is superstring theory, which postulates 10 or more dimensions of Space. Components, if you will. In our home Universe, three predominate, and at least seven have collapsed, folding in on themselves, causing tiny loops of energy, which vibrate. As such, they supposedly form the particles. Or so they say. In the Aether, vast manifolds of Multi-Space convolute and envelope many dimensions. They act like colossal Klein bottles twisting and intertwining. And navigation must be charted around, or through, as the case may be.

But events do happen, and the initiated have learned how to deal with the quirks inherent to this locus. The First Born agglomerated the appropriate mix of fundamental elements and engineered an area of normalcy. They constructed a smallish volume complete with the blackness of ordinary Space. A containment of sorts to enclose a safer and more traditional living experience. It was a very pleasant oasis in a sea of everything.

But what about Matter, you may ask? What kind of Matter Is there? And what is Matter anyway? What are quarks made of, ultimately? Charge? Then what is a charge, and where does it come from? It must come from the Aether. And it does, or so I'm told. For the Aether itself is the stuff of everything. And the Aether coalesces into mists of free quarks and scintillating photons amidst the auroras of Space and Time. Can energy be extracted therefrom? I am told yes. The term for it is 5th Level Technology. Dabblers on Earth refer to it as zero-point energy. In the First-Born's enclave, a small star cluster was created. A vestige of home. *For home always kindles a warm feeling . . . no matter where.*

Please permit me to reiterate. Most of the First-Born had, at this point, transcended to life forces consisting primarily of the intangible constituents of Space and Time, with traces of elementary

Matter interspersed. Bundles of spaceons, chronomes, and charge, arranged within their attendant radiating threads. And it is these threads that can be used to gather and shape the components of the Great Manifolds, the elementary essences of the Aether. And, as a consequence, in this primordial soup of everything, the creation of things becomes possible. By extending these fibrils, these beings could manifest their will. Give form to the inchoate and . . . create from pure thought. Here, the First-Born could truly be gods, which is the primary reason why they emigrated. For apotheosis is the ultimate motivation.

But there was trouble in Paradise. Their home Universe was under attack by an unknown entity. Many tunnel points were discovered.

The Observers reported this: "There are 1.27×10^9 injection sites of both Dark and Phantom Energy. Areas of decreased density are materializing. False vacuums have commenced and are propagating exponentially."

The gods screamed. A scream that shook the Aether.

In bubbles of false vacuum, new and lower energy states exist. And the constants; the prior fundamental framework, changes. It changes into new particles, structures, and forces. But the old life within does not change. Its atoms and molecules are ripped apart. Hence, it dies. For no life, as we know it, can exist in a false vacuum. And these bubbles were expanding. If unstopped, the change, the imbalance would consume the Universe. The Progenitor itself would change, and all previous life would cease.

There were those among the First-Born who were content to repose in the euphoria of bliss. They were the Oldest Ones and the most powerful. Awakened by the scream, they reached out.

"Close the Progenitor." The collective will of the First-Born was marshaled behind this imperative – the totality of their will was exerted. Their thoughts were materialized, and a new fleet was built. Tendrils raced out searching for the malefactor, then the sealing of the tunnels began. The ennui of the Gods was no more. The sleeping giants awoke.

Another imperative was emitted.

"Gather all that we left behind. Deploy the Caretakers."

Chapter 16: The Big Meeting

Everyone was positioned at his or her place along the long glass table. The table itself was a marvel. Thick glass, rounded edges, curvilinear corners. Indeed, the entire length undulated somewhat, like a snake, a long glass snake. The chairs were equally modern, perfectly molded to the human form, fitted with small armrests, and trimmed in gold and silver. There were matching accouterments on the table – vases, decanters, tableware, etc.

The room itself was long and large. It had to be to accommodate a table set for 30. One end was windowed, floor to ceiling, offering a park-like view of the trees, the walkways, and a pond. The towers of a city could be seen in the hazy distance. At the other end were two large flat screen TVs arranged on rolling stands. Upon one was displayed a grid with heads, each occupying a square. The remote attendees. The other screen exhibited an image of the Neufield Barn.

At the table, there were place labels indicating individuals or groups. A small army of attendants hovered on the periphery. Attendants to the attendees; the adjutants and liaisons, assistants, and associates. And the room was abuzz with nervous activity.

Dominating, at the head of the table, sat the Master of Ceremonies, Alysha Civil, Special Assistant to the President for National Security Affairs. She was dark, her hair was pulled tightly back, with features both handsome and classical, like an ancient marble with a touch of the cold and a hint of the severe. She wore a stylish, dusky suit of expensive material embellished with flashes of gold. She stood, and the room quieted.

"The President wishes to thank you all for clearing your very active schedules and making time for what we think . . . could be a discovery of momentous proportions." With this statement, she garnered the attention of the room.

We have provided you with some background data on the event in question, 'The Neufield Anomaly'." She used the pronoun "we" to emphasize her connection to the President and held up a blue folder emblazoned with the presidential seal. Many were strewn about on the table. "But so that we're all on the same page, I'll briefly summarize."

"On August 28th, at approximately 10 PM, one John a.k.a., Jack Neufield allegedly perpetrated the theft of 8.3 pounds of cobalt 60, a highly radioactive isotope of the metal cobalt, from the Yale-New Haven Hospital – Department of Radiology. We have a video of the crime." Alysha motioned, and a short video clip of the incident played on one of the screens. "The nurse whom the perp is looking at here," she pointed a remote and paused the video, "is Ester Riley. She is said to be romantically linked to Mr. Neufield. We will be interviewing her directly." The clip proceeded to show Jack running through the hospital then escaping on his motorcycle.

"Jack, as I shall call him, presumably rode to his home in Litchfield, Connecticut, evading all attempts at apprehension." A picture of Jack's barn with the house in the background appeared on the screen. "This is where the 'event' occurred." The screen changed to a radar display with a blip moving across. "This is the radar image of the anomaly as seen from Westchester Airport. Notice the rate at which it crosses the screen." The image changed to another radar display, different colors, similar scenes. "And this is the same blip as tracked from the Saratoga Springs Air Force Base. Notice its rate of travel as it exits the screen." She looked down at her folder, "Mach 3. Its velocity was at least Mach 3, that's over 2000 mph, and still accelerating. Now people, here's the most important fact," she paused here for dramatic effect, "The Neufield Anomaly emitted no exhaust. It had no heat signature."

"That's impossible. There is no known technology that can propel an object to that speed without heat coming out the back end." This comment came from an older man who wore a well-decorated, light-colored uniform. His place card read "General R. Taylor, US Air Force."

"What about a rail gun?" This came from an area labeled – Jet Propulsion Lab, U. Of Calif.

Ms. Civil changed the image back to the barn. "A rail gun would require massive infrastructure. There's no evidence of that here. Moving on, from our deep background checks of Mr. Neufield and Miss Riley, and everyone associated with them – there is zero evidence of any association with radical ideologies. Therefore, we conclude . . . this is definitely not related to terrorism."

Someone shouted out, "Did the damn thing come down somewhere? Do we, have it?" Decorum began to unravel. An underlying excitement infused the room.

Presidential Assistant Civil continued, "It did not come down. Now, this next piece of data we only just obtained. The object emitted gamma rays, which were detected by one of our 'Advanced Vega Satellites.' The object was tracked, passing through the Earth's atmosphere and then out and into space. We know this for certain."

She took another pause followed by a deep breath: "Ladies and gentlemen, I must regrettably inform you . . . that it is our studied opinion that this object is not coming down, i.e., back to Earth again." There was silence, as all hope left the room, "We have concluded that what was built in that barn could not possibly survive the rigors of Space." She began to lose it here a little: "I mean, the damn thing was pieced together from old amusement park rides! We have the receipts." She grabbed and waved some paper. This elicited mumblings and stirrings in the room. Ms. Civil regained some composure.

"But all hope is not lost." A picture of Ms. Riley appeared on the screen. "We have the girlfriend, Ester Riley, and we think she was a partner or at least a willing participant in the building of the craft . . . or whatever the hell it was they built."

"She mentioned the word antigravity, Ma'am, during the initial interrogation. She said they were experimenting with it." Special Agent V. McCluskie, who was standing to one side, reiterated this piece of information, which was also contained in the briefing folder.

"Thanks for bringing that up, Victor. Those two, tinkering around in that barn", she flipped back to the barn image, "stumbled upon something. They learned secrets. Secrets that modern science has been seeking for centuries. And people, the key may be sitting in the next room."

"Well, get her ass in here." That voice emanated anonymously from the crowd.

Ms. Civil looked around for the culprit then resumed, "Here's the deal . . . we don't want to upset the girl. She doesn't know that her boyfriend is, very likely . . . a piece of orbiting, space junk, and we're not going to tell her." She looked at the heads on the screen. A few nodded in assent. "We expect everyone to comply with this strategy. And let's face it, she's not going to talk if she's all weepy over her, uh, 'recently departed' sweetheart. And we all want her to talk. So, are there any objections to this course of action?" There were none.

"Well, if there are no further questions, we'll call in Miss Riley." She pointed to the Homeland Security Agent assigned to the case.

"I presume the interrogation will remain humane; after all, she is an American citizen . . . in good standing." This voice came from the DARPA section down towards the end of the table.

Ms. Civil held up her hand to stop the agent and responded, "Miss Riley is an accomplice to the theft of dangerous nuclear materials. This one fact does not render our little, tinkering girlfriend . . . 'in good standing,' Mr. Erhart." Under her breath, she chuckled, "Not that we even have such a category." There were subdued chortles around the table. "But of course, your concerns are noted." She nodded to the door again: "Bring in the girl."

Chapter 17: The Phone Call – *Janey*

It was the day of the Meeting. The big Pow-wow, as I mentally called it. I was up early, took my time, and got all dolled up except for my hair, which I put in a ponytail. In case "Plain Jane" was needed. I wore a gray suit. My mother made me buy it when I made "Nurse of the Month." There are only 19 nurses in my division, so the honor was not based on merit but rather on rotation, and it was my turn. The real reason? It was just an excuse to get together and have a good time. And . . . for mothers to show off their daughters. Which, in my case, was Ester's very successful, professional nurse, *terrorist*, daughter. And I did look good, especially in my red shoes. Mothers are always right.

The jacket fit well; it showed off my figure, being stylishly cut around the waist. And I wore the red shoes again, with a nice white blouse. I would be Nice Jane. Everyone likes a nice person and is, in turn, nice back. With an operating strategy, I was ready.

Robert was late. He said he had to go to a meeting about the big meeting. Though late, we still stopped for breakfast. I abstained, having coffee only. Robert had the works – eggs, sausage, and a short stack with orange juice and coffee. He said breakfast was the most important meal, 24-7. Jamal abstained as well. Claimed he already ate. I think he was non-fraternizing again. He had his orders.

We took the Homeland Security van. I sat up front with Robert. He insisted. To relieve Jamal's anxiety, I had to promise again not to jump out. En route, Robert briefed me on what to expect. "Honchos" (his word) were coming in from all over the country to question me. We were going to some "swank" (again his word) estate in Pleasantville, New York, and I was – "not to worry" because I was – "his case." Jamal almost said, "me too."

We turned down a side road between two big stone pillars and drove along a long tree-lined drive. A fabulous Tudor mansion came to view. It was all stone, wood, and stucco with gables and dormers everywhere, even a couple that looked like eyebrows. And there were several outbuildings as well. It was a real compound. We stopped under a portico where several men in suits were milling about. One opened my door and said, "Welcome to The Sedgewick Manor." Then he led the way inside.

The interior was sumptuously appointed, as one would expect when money is no object. "Victorian" would be the word that best described the decor. Oriental carpets, tasseled lamps, carved furniture with claws for feet. Not my style, not that I could afford it if it was.

They brought us to what looked to be a library. Shelves of books adorned the walls, a big table in the middle, and comfortable wing chairs carefully positioned. Robert and I sank into a pair by a bay window. We had a nice view of the woods and pond. Jamal guarded the door. He didn't have to, but, I guess, that's just what guards do. The men in suits left, saying they'd come for us soon.

Robert and I had a nice conversation about books, very appropriate for a library. Westerns were his favorite genre, particularly "The Lonesome Dove" series by McMurtry. He said I had to read it. I explained why I liked the mystery authors like Lee Child or Michael Connelly. I told him he just had to read "Void Moon" with Cassie Black. Though, I doubted he could identify with her character. Then we discussed books in general, whether they were obsolete. Robert liked books; I used a tablet. The conversation was quite pleasant. One would think that I should have been going through some kind of "Agony in the Garden" thing, at least pacing the floor. But I wasn't all that freaked. Maybe it was Robert. He was easy to get along with and a good talker. Besides, I was his case.

The men in suits came again, different ones. Men, not suits. They brought us to the big Pow-wow. The room was incongruous with the house. It was modern. I found that odd. There must have been 50 or 60 people there. At least 30 at the table, another 30 floating around. I saw many of my new friends; Special Agent in Charge Victor McCluskie and his sidekick Izzy. Along the wall was Ernesto the Caballero, and halfway down the table was Sandy, er, Winston. Upon recognition, I gave each a quarter nod, no it was more like an eighth. As I did so, their eyes refocused a tad brighter.

The seat at the head of the table was empty. A rather severe-looking lady stood alongside. She gestured to the empty chair and said, "Please have a seat, Miss Riley."

It was odd and embarrassing for me, the lowest member of the assemblage, to take the seat usually reserved for the highest. I felt the eyes again, all of them. I responded with a blast from Blank Jane – quarter smile, eyebrows slightly elevated, but not blank eyes. Nice eyes, wide, with dilated pupils. Like a chameleon, I quickly changed to Nice Jane.

"Miss Riley, state your full name for the record. This deposition is being recorded."

"Ester Jane Riley, but everyone calls me Jane." I looked around; the eyes I met were hungry for my words.

"My name is Alysha Civil, Special Assistant to the President for National Security. The men and women you see assembled here," her hand swept the room, "are very important leaders from various Governmental Departments, the Military and the Aeronautics and Space Industry. They have made time and traveled considerable distances to hear what you have to say about the . . . 'Neufield Anomaly.' We have questions and would like to know more about it." She paused, expecting a reply, and took her seat.

"I'm eager to answer in any way that I can." I shot Winston a look to see if he picked up on the pun. He covered his eyes and hid a grin.

"Let me start by bluntly stating . . . we know . . . that you know." Ms. Civil paused again. Pausing for dramatic effect, that was her style. She was a pauser. "We've sifted through everything from the Neufield Barn." She pointed the remote, and the image changed to the interior of the barn: "The hard drives, the papers, all the junk on the shelves, and your background histories. We interviewed your parents, and your friends, and your associates at the hospital, and the Newfield's, who recently returned from, uh, she looked down at an open folder, Afghanistan. Let me emphasize," she paused, then spoke louder, "We know you were there when Mr. Neufield built . . . whatever it was he built. So, Miss Riley, you can save us all some very valuable time if you would just tell us what you and Jack built up there." She head-pointed to the barn up on the screen.

"I certainly want to, but if Jack was here, together we could present a more . . . coherent description and I'm sure . . ." Ms. Civil cut me off.

"Miss Riley, my question was addressed to you. And we expect an answer." She waited.

"Absolutely, but I just thought that if Jack was in the next room or . . ." She cut me off again, this time more sternly.

"No, Miss Riley, Jack is not here . . . not in this building. Please continue."

"Yes, of course." An accomplished speaker knows who to look at, where to plant one's words. I did not. It was, therefore, very disconcerting, what with all the glaring beams. My eyes settled on Winston, the only warm spot at the table. "All right, let me start by saying, you are correct in assuming that Jack and I built the, uh . . . project. We were a team, partners if you will." All activity in the room ceased. It was as quiet as . . . Space.

"As I previously stated during my initial interview with Special Agent in Charge Victor McCluskie," Victor's eyes widened in elation at the plug, "we were experimenting with the force of gravity, attempting to counter it." I held the room's rapt attention and felt the power of my words, "But truth be told, Jack was the prime mover in our partnership, and I must confess, he had a better understanding of the theory." With this, there were some audible groans. I had lost the Power.

A man at the JPL (Jet Propulsion Lab) table shouted, "Just tell us what it looked like!"

"Yes, of course," I responded with a Nice Jane smile, "It was round, about 18 feet in diameter . . ."

From another voice down the table, "Every god-damned thing in the Universe is round! Tell us how it worked."

"Yes, that is my intent. But this was a joint project, so therefore the presentation should be revealed jointly. That seems only fair to me, I mean it would be presumptuous for . . ."

Ms. Civil cut in again, "Miss Riley, Jane. Perhaps you are not aware of the seriousness of the situation you are currently in. This is a National Security matter, and you were involved in the theft of radiological materials. That is a Patriot Act offense. Do I need to explain to you the ramifications of this?"

"It has been explained to me on a number of occasions recently. The only thing I ask is . . . please don't take my parent's farm."

"That's the least we're going to do!" Ms. Civil brayed this retort in a higher pitch with a touch of glee. Then she quickly regained control.

From the table, behind a label marked General J. Taylor, USAF; an older man in a fancy uniform spoke, "I'm sure that I speak for everyone here when I say . . . we want to keep this conversation civil. And I understand that your 'stay' has been comfortable and 'humane'", he looked at Winston, "so surely you can discuss general aspects of the governing theory that lies behind the actual construction."

"As you say, my 'stay' has been 'comfortable,' and in that regard, I'd like to thank Special Agent Robert Smolanski," I turned towards him standing by the door, "and Private Freeman. They have been very accommodating in that regard." I realized after I said this that my complimentary words would likely not be beneficial to their careers. But, as they say, there's no such thing as bad publicity, and besides, everyone knew I was stalling. "As to the theory, it involves connections; how everything in the Universe is connected, even all of us in this room." I gave them my best Nice Jane smile, knowing they wouldn't buy this New Age crap. But in a way, it was true. 4,3 does explain how everything is connected. There were more audible groans.

After another long moment, while everyone deduced that what I had just said was pure bullshit, Ms. Civil broke the pause, "Perhaps, Miss Riley, we should approach this from 'the importance to the Nation' point of view. And I'm sure you know the value of what you have . . . stumbled upon." She paused, "Anti-gravity – the concept, the knowledge thereof; could save the planet from climate change, drastically reduce the carbon footprint, the rise of the oceans, the melting of the polar ice caps. It could even save the Polar Bears. Think of all the good you could do by giving what you know to the world. Different ways to transport foods would end hunger, and then; there would be new cures for disease and an overall rise in the standard of living."

Cure disease, I thought, how could 4,3 cure disease? Probably in some convoluted way.

"Think of what it could do for your country," another uniformed man joined in the fray, "This knowledge that you possess would put us back on top, ensure National Security. Every man, woman, and child could sleep safe and secure at night."

They were pulling out all the stops. I replied, "Jack, and I know the importance of the knowledge we have uncovered. We have discussed its potential value often. We were, and still are, unsure how to go about revealing it. Where and how."

Ms. Civil jumped in again, "Here is where," she motioned around, "and how . . . why just tell us . . . that's how, at least the basics, right now." The tension was rising in the room.

"Since Jack's not here, and surely you would unite Jack and me for such an important occasion as this, I must assume that Jack is still out there, still at large. At least you can tell me if this is true?" It seemed like a reasonable request to me.

Someone from the far end of the table said softly, "Your boyfriend is . . . no longer with us." He said this weakly, hesitantly, then, "She has a right to know."

"What do you mean 'he's no longer with us?" I asked, still being nice, "Do the Russians have him?" There was another silence, a pause, a small breach in the flow of Time itself. Heads were down, faces averted.

Ms. Civil finally responded, softly, "Mr. Neufield is no longer with us because . . . he is no longer, uh . . ." she paused, "The Neufield Anomaly went straight up and out. It did not come back, and it could not survive the rigors of space. Jack is very likely . . . gone . . . for good."

For the briefest of moments, I contemplated the meaning of what she said. When the import of the words finally hit, well, that's when I snapped. "You're a pack of fucking liars!" I shouted, "You'll say anything to get me to talk." There would be no more "Nice Jane," or "Blank Jane" or any other kind of Jane. Just raw, unedited, unrestrained me. A "Jane" they undoubtedly, would not like very much.

I looked at Winston; he answered my look and said, "It's true, Jane. Satellites tracked him leaving the earth's atmosphere. And whatever he built, most likely, could not last long out there. I wouldn't lie to you, Jane. I hope you know that."

The tears welled in my eyes as an overwhelming feeling began to take hold, one I had never felt before. The blackest darkness fell and absorbed my external awareness. My chest tightened, and I struggled to breathe. Jack's dead, I thought? Could that truly be? I looked deep into Winston's eyes and saw sincerity and truth. Slowly acceptance crept in. And then, the convulsions started, from deep inside. Uncontrollable spasms. I was embarrassed at first, acting like that in front of all these important people, then I didn't care. And quietly, I started to cry – just sobs at first, then louder, then non-stop. I was out of control. I put my head down and bawled like a baby, sobbing, and hiccupping at the same time. A complete and total, freaked-out wreck.

"I told you we shouldn't have told her!" Alysha chastised the group.

I looked up with raw hatred, the intensity of which surprised even myself. The agony of grief suddenly switched to hate. A vicious, feral, animal hatred – unfiltered and unrestrained. This wash of primal malice totally engulfed me, utterly erasing my normal self. I would have leaped for her throat . . . except that . . . my phone rang.

That's right, my phone rang. Positively, I had left it powered off. Rarely did I turn it on, not having a charger. But there it was, ringing in my pocket. My face was a disaster area, all red and puffy, make-up and mascara smeared and trailing down my cheeks. I looked around, wondering what to do. I heard a voice say, "You'd better get that."

I pulled it out and looked at it. The screen read – Jack calling, on Face Time. In a panic, I swiped it, and Jack's adorable face filled the screen: "Hi Janey, how's it going? Sorry I didn't call sooner, but my phone was, uh, not working. Hey, what's the matter? You look like you've been to Hell and back."

"Jack, thank God you're all right. They just told me you were dead." At this point, there was chaos in the room, people running around, phones pulled out, incredulity splattered on every face.

"Who told you I was dead?" Jack asked. I reversed the phone to display the room.

Ms. Civil was barking orders, "Somebody tap into that – put it on the screen." Some geeky types feverishly poked at their tablets, and Jack's image appeared on the big screen. He looked to be in perfect health, i.e., not dead. He was wearing the black Tesla tee shirt I got him.

Gasps, exhalations, and a couple of "what the fucks" were heard in the room.

"They told me," I said as I panned the room for Jack to see. "I'm at this big meeting with VIPs from all over the country."

"Holy shit, Janey, you really are in Hell. I knew it. Tell them it's all my fault, and, ah, you might want to mention . . . that the reports of my demise were . . . hmm, premature." He looked at someone and chuckled.

"Jack, it looks like you're back at the barn?"

It was Jack's turn to pan the room with his phone. It was the barn, just like it was a few days ago. The overloaded shelves, tool chests, the coil of copper tubing against the wall, even my merry-go-round horse. Jack said, smiling into the camera, "It sure looks that way, Janey." Jack's feet were up on the table with a cup of coffee in his hand. A familiar picture.

Alysha whispered to an aide, who rushed out the door.

I saw a shadow, the hint of movement in the background, and asked, "Is there somebody with you, Jack?"

Jack hesitated and covered his phone, seemingly communicating with someone, then with humor in his eyes, he said, "Oh, that's just Albert, he's a new friend. I can't wait for you to meet him."

Alysha kicked in a question, "Uh, Mr. Neufield, Jack . . . can you tell us where you are?"

"I see you've made some new friends too, Jane." Jack only called me Jane when he was serious. "Have they been treating you, ok?"

"I'm being detained Jack, ever since mm . . . the incident. But humanely and comfortably. They want to know about the . . . 'you know what' Jack."

"I'm coming, Janey, and everything's going to be all right when I get there. Probably tomorrow or maybe the next day. Turn the phone around, Jane." I did, and then Jack spoke to the room: "I'll give you all something that, I think, you'll . . . really want to see . . . If you promise to let Janey go and leave us, be."

"I better get that in writing, Jack." I turned the phone back.

"Good idea. Hang in there, Janey. I'm coming." He looked back at presumably his new friend, then said, "I have to go, Janey. I'm coming, and I'll see you soon." The screen went blank, and there was silence in the room.

Ms. Civil was the first to speak to an aide: "Where did that call come from. Were you able to triangulate on it?"

"Yes, ma'am. It originated from a local cell tower. But before that . . ."

"Just tell me where the hell it came from?"

"We don't know, ma'am."

Regaining her composure, being sugary sweet, and then addressing the room, "Well, now that we know that Mr. Neufield is OK, everything seems to be working out just fine. Let's see, where were we? Oh, yes. Jack is going to give us 'something we'll really want to see.' Perhaps, Miss Riley, you could give us a little sneak preview . . . so we can prepare . . . so we know what to expect?"

"Go to Hell! You're all still a pack of fucking liars!" I felt compelled to repeat my previous statement, especially since I was still basically out of control. They were liars. Jack wasn't dead.

"Get her out of here!" screamed the President's assistant.

A large, puffed-up soldier in full regalia came over and grabbed me roughly. Jamal pushed him aside, causing him to bounce off a few of Ms. Civil's aides. Then he escorted me out – nice and respectful. As I exited, I turned and said to them all, "You don't deserve 4,3." And then, I left.

Chapter 18: Apollo 11 – *Jack*

I awoke refreshed and well-rested. Even had pleasant dreams of Janey and me traveling the stars. I had to admit, I liked being in this place and could get used to living here real easy. Exploring the Ship, palling around with Albert. And I could return to Earth, that issue has been resolved. The next issue – was coming back. If I don't reveal 4,3 to my fellow Earthlings, my quasi-provisional status should remain intact, and maybe I could return, as in, come and go? A topic worthy of further discussion. I wiped those pleasant reveries. There being more important things to think about – like evicting the aliens and straightening out the colossal mess I left back there on Earth. At the very least, spring Janey, somehow.

I jumped out of bed, put on some clean clothes. Jeans and a T-shirt, the one with Tesla's picture on the front and the phrase "Charge It" on the back. I dashed downstairs, opened the fridge, and beheld the leftover lasagna. I could eat lasagna for breakfast, lunch, and dinner. I warmed up a plate. It's much better on day two, even with coffee.

After cleaning up somewhat, I stepped outside for a breath of fresh air and to watch . . . the sunrise? What was that yellow orb up there? Probably some kind of rigged-up fusion reactor. Speaking of Albert, his pleasant visage emerged in the distance, ambling down the lane. He wore a brown checked jacket, dark pants, shiny orange wingtips, and a blue silk cravat. The epitome of fashion – a century ago. And still young. He was smiling and strutting along, accentuating his cane with a slight flourish upon every step.

When within earshot, he said, “Please permit me to inform you, Jack . . . that this is not heaven.” The sparkle in his eye twinkled a bit brighter. I knew the reference. Those were the first words Albert had said to me. And this dredged up memories. How things had changed in a mere three days. If heaven is a place where one is happy, then I was in heaven. Though not without care. I certainly was not carefree, and presumably, one would be in heaven.

I had to ask, “Is there really such a place as heaven?” If anyone knew, it would be Albert. He’s pretty close to being omniscient, even though he is an artifact. An indefinable artifact, but still, some kind of construct. And he must have been eavesdropping on my reverie earlier.

“There are those who thought they could construct a heavenly place. And go there and while away eternity in bliss. It was the carefree part that failed to materialize for them as well.”

Was I not to have a single private thought? I replied, “There’s always something, right, Albert?”

“What you say is a profound truism, Jack. You look well and rested.”

“As do you, but why the cane?” Albert stood, legs crossed, leaning on it.

“I thought there may be a need for one today. Shall we embark on our mission?”

“Our mission being ‘to evict the Aliens’?”

“That would be an accurate statement, though rather harshly worded. And please, let’s not forget the continuation of your driving lessons. We removed the fusion generator. This modification should significantly impact the craft's maneuverability and speed."

"Implementation of the non-interference directive?"

"Precisely, Jack. You don't have fusion reactors on Earth, not yet."

We strolled into the void. The gray shrouds engulfed us, to my eternal fascination. Making light conversation, I commented: "Why these gray, cloudy passageways? I know, we previously discussed this, and they are habitats for me, but . . . what lies beyond these gray walls?"

"One would see the inner workings of the Ship, Jack, in this particular location. A scene that could be quite disconcerting to the uninitiated. Let me remind you that this structural complex, which I represent, is quite large by your standards – 27.38 miles in diameter. He splayed his fingers and swept his arm. An opening leading to an outward projection appeared, "Allow me to show you the scene unobstructed. He took my elbow, and we stepped out to the edge of what could have been the rim of the Grand Canyon at dusk. A low light illuminated a multi-mile drop that began about one foot from where we stood.

"You're right, Albert. This is rather . . . disconcerting." I took a step back. Amorphous, curvilinear shapes projected upwards from below, downwards from above, and some just floated in midair. They were large shapeless blobs, many miles wide. Some glowed and pulsed dimly in dull yellows and reds. Many long, twisty tubes looped among these shapeless masses. I thought of veins and arteries connecting organs. Darting here and there were numerous small moving objects, some brightly lit. Also, auroras of green and red occasionally rippled across the void. Far away throbbed a pale blue light coming from somewhere deep in the abyss. I was just able to sense the accompanying low-pitched bass rumble, the sounds of humongous power. An aspect quite typical of starships in general; the ones I've seen in the movies. It was then that I thoroughly understood the need for the cozy cocoons.

"That large structure over there," Albert pointed, "houses what you mentally labeled Candy Land. We construct these areas when needed, as we did for you when you first arrived. We are currently standing near the outer hull, where many of the habitats are located for easy access. That dark shape before us is the Hangar, our present destination."

"All this kind of reminds me of the insides of, say, a body. The big blobs are the organs and the tubes – the veins. Do you mind if I ask – is there a heart somewhere? In other words, what's the power source?"

"Not at all, Jack, though we have many energy sources, the primary one, the heart as you say, is a small condensed-matter globule, which supplies the power for most of our basic needs."

"A black hole! I thought everything gets sucked into a black hole."

"Your statement is not entirely accurate, Jack. Within the Schwartz-Child radius, Matter would gravitate inwards, even light. But beyond that, large quantities of radiation are emitted. Gamma rays specifically, a phenomenon first postulated, on your planet, by Stephen Hawking and thus, known as Hawking Radiation. However, you are correct in acknowledging the large gravitic forces, which are the primary features of exotic matter. As you know from your understanding of 4,3 – the forces and their fundamental components can be transmuted or interchanged. The 'black hole, as you say,' provides a large quantity of raw material, gravity primarily, and the aforementioned gamma rays, which can be converted into anything we need – the total energy equivalence of a small star."

I thought to myself, I'm supposed to know this stuff. And "the total energy equivalence of a small star"!

Albert continued: "We need such large quantities of force and energy for intergalactic travel. Shall we proceed to the hangar?"

"Yes, we, ah, should." I had resumed my normal state of total confoundment. Before, I was just making lite conversation, asking about the gray voids, and then . . . But my interest was piqued by Albert's mention of intergalactic jumps and, I had to ask: "Albert, you mentioned the phrase, 'intergalactic travel.' How do you do that? And please don't answer if you think I should . . . well you know . . . no tampering with the yokels."

"You are no longer a 'yokel,' Jack, but rather, a quasi-provisional member. Though, to be perfectly honest, there is no such category. I created the term to designate your unique standing. The answer to your question is – 6th Level Technology. I shall be succinct since we are near to our destination. Einstein proposed the concept of space-time. A fabric, as he called it. And its deformation is the cause of gravity. As you know from 4,3, that fabric can be . . . disentangled. We use and modify the powerful gravitic forces derived from the 'condensed-globule' to unravel the normal weave of Space-Time. To open a small tear would be the analogous phrase. The vehicle slips in, travels through what lies beneath – what could be denoted in your language as – 'a zone of enfolded space'. The purpose: to emerge elsewhere, presumably another galaxy. It's the only practical way to travel galactic distances."

We walked along in silence for a few moments as I digested this. I wondered out loud, "Albert, is that the Aether, this zone?"

"The 'zone' I spoke of is a function of space-time itself. The Aether is a related universal actuality that permeates all Space. 5th Level Technology deals with this subject. It is the source of the electric charge, the physical property of matter that causes attractive and repulsive electromagnetic forces. It is ubiquitous and fills the cracks, the interstices between everything."

"My friend, Mr. McEvey, was experimenting with it, zero-point, he called it. He was trying to derive free energy. Get something from nothing."

"The Aether is not, 'nothing,' Jack. And, in a way, it is everything and a very legitimate science. And yes, energy can be extracted from the Aether. However, it is not free. It weakens the fabric of space-time in the vicinity."

The chitchat ceased. We were approaching the hangar and its rows of spherical spacecraft.

"One more thing, Albert, if I may?" I asked.

"Please do. Your questions are a pleasant diversion, though technically, I am prohibited from answering. However, you are an anomaly."

"How can a race . . . how does a race, say your builders, The First-Born, learn so much? I mean, they were the first and helped all the others who came after. How did they do it?"

"The acquisition of knowledge requires three basic components, Jack: curiosity to start with. And sentient beings are curious by definition. Second, the ability to act on that curiosity – having the capacity to manipulate objects within the appropriate scale. And the third component, and we all have this one – is time. Given time, all the puzzles of the Cosmos can be deciphered. And the Progenitor, as some call the Universe, is old, Jack – 13.8 billion years old. The First of the First-Born, the 'Ang et Setem' as they are known, have existed for 2.37 billion years. That is enough time to unravel the secrets, most of them."

I made some mental comparisons; we Earthers, our civilization is 14,000 years old, and the Pra'at – 49,000, and the First-Born – 2.37 billion. *Why do I suddenly feel like an amoeba again?*

"But Jack, even though some races are very old, they have not fully comprehended what you said before."

"There's always something!?" We both said this in unison. I raised my hand to "high-five" it. Albert smacked it in kind. I laughed. Albert smiled.

I wondered if Albert was capable of friendship. Did he think of me with the same friendship that I felt for him?

"As with humor, I am learning the concept of friendship, Jack. And I hope you find me as apt a pupil as you are an effective teacher."

Albert head-bowed, and we entered the hangar.

The tiers of spacecraft were lined up as before. The black spheres and the clear ones – all different sizes. What I had built; and I have to say this, was a total piece of . . . compared to any of these. Even with Albert's modifications, though, to be fair to me, I'm not 2.37 billion years old either. But walking through the rows, I had to think . . . how great it would be to tool around the solar system in any one of these. To cruise over to Mars and check out, say, Olympus Mons, the tallest mountain in the solar system – it's 16 miles tall! Now that would be a sight to see. Then I'd snake around the asteroid belt on my way to Jupiter. Have to be careful there – 600 mph winds. Or maybe I'd go to Venus. But it's pretty hostile there, too, if my recollections are correct, not lush, and tropical like the Edgar Rice Burroughs fantasies. And Mercury, I'd go there just for the lakes . . . the lakes of molten lead that is, and I'd probably find some pools of gold too. It would be so great to have that freedom. I made another mental note, though my notepad was pretty much full.

We walked over to my conveyance. The word "my" did not apply anymore. What I had built, most likely was . . . a mist of molecules floating somewhere out there in space; Albert said that the thing disintegrated. But at least I could still lay claim to the concept, though not totally. Mr. McEvey and Janey deserve equal credit – or blame. Strike the blame part. I'm proud of what I built . . . we built. And there it was, sitting in its spot, only sleeker. And basically, not the same.

"Your thoughts are accurate, Jack. It is not the same. Which causes me some consternation." A slight interval lapsed, then Albert offered, "You could stay here; explore the Ship and 'pal' around with me?"

This telepathy business does have its drawbacks – like no secrets. "I created one hell of a mess back there when I left, Albert.

No doubt, Janey is up to her neck in . . . trouble, as we speak. I have to go back and . . . and dig her out, somehow."

"Then that is what shall be. This conveyance," he gestured towards the thing, "your conveyance will safely transport you to Earth. Shall we?" He opened the driver's side door like a professional limo driver, and I ducked in and buckled up.

"I forgot to pack a picnic basket, in case we want to stop, spread a blanket, and catch some rays." I quipped.

"At the location of our destination, there will be refreshments and restroom facilities."

"You mean at the Alien Base? But we're going in to evict them!" I still had visions of a commando raid.

"Yes, Jack. But nicely if we can."

Albert turned the key and started the thing. I heard it rev up, and we elevated a few inches. A slight breeze blew from the vents, and we made our way down the rows and into the hull.

As we traversed through, I asked, "Any other interesting tourist attractions I should see, I mean, while I'm still here, on the Moon?" I naturally assumed we'd engage in the driving lesson before the eviction proceedings.

"There will come a time when the sites of mankind's initial forays to the Moon – the Apollo Missions – will make a nice tour. Shall we be the first?"

"Excellent idea Albert."

We traversed the hull and exited the Ship. The star-studded blackness of Space loomed. Albert spoke, "But before the tour, I suggest we test this 'thing' as you call it. Take it down, Jack."

I pushed down on the steering wheel and gave it some "gas." And it went down, only not as fast as before. The view of the Moon's rough, pockmarked surface slowly expanded. I looked behind and saw the empty black void that was the Ship rapidly recede. Albert reacted, "I withdrew the Ship, beyond the range of detection." A map of the moon materialized before us with several numbered red dots on it: "These red marks represent the Apollo landing sites. The first one is our destination in the Sea of Tranquility." He pointed in a rightward direction, "Go that way."

I turned the wheel and headed in the indicated direction. The map shifted to encompass our destination. An indicator appeared with red and blue lines, "Just keep the red arrow between the blue lines, and we shall arrive at our objective."

I dropped down to about a thousand feet and gradually depressed the pedal all the way. The speedometer read 500 mph. Very sluggish compared to before. Albert said the trip would take an hour. We abbreviated our plans to include the Apollo 11 site only since we had more important business to attend to. The Earth appeared on the horizon. It was four times larger than the Moon, as one would expect, the planet being four times bigger. I asked Albert if we could be seen. He said the current position of the "Lunar Reconnaissance Orbiter" was orbiting near the Lunar North Pole, far from where we were.

I recollected what I knew about the Apollo Space Missions. Apollo 11 happened in 1969, twenty years before I was born. Mr. McEvey considered it a very significant event. We had discussed it and watched several videos. I especially liked the Apollo 13 movie with Tom Hanks. The mission failed, but they made it back. The Moon Missions were a tremendous accomplishment. However, they all stopped after Apollo 17. It was probably for the best. The effort cost about 100 billion in today's dollars. Big government programs are fine, but that's not how most major advancements happen. Maxwell, Tesla, Einstein; they all worked alone. They probably indulged in a few scotches, beers, or whatever; got an idea, then started tinkering. Einstein didn't even do that. He just sat back, lit his pipe, and thought.

"Albert, what can we expect to see there?" My memories of Apollo 11 were dim. "I know they left a flag. You can take a picture of me standing next to it . . . I'll put it on my Christmas cards." I don't send Christmas cards.

"Excellent idea, Jack. Too bad the flag no longer exists. When the ascent vehicle blasted off . . . it blasted the flag as well. All the other flags are still standing, though they have been bleached white by the sun."

"Then, what's left at the site? One of those moon buggies?"

"The largest item is the Lunar Module, the descent portion of the Lander. And about 100 other articles, scientific experiments, tools, cameras, plaques, and several waste bags. No Lunar Rovers. Waste was an important consideration for them, as it had to be since their mode of propulsion was rocket engines, igniting kerosene and liquid oxygen, then ejecting the exhaust through nozzles." He didn't say "very primitive," but he thought it.

"Sounds like we littered the hell out of the place."

"It has been designated a Lunar Heritage Site. Nothing can be touched. The authorities are afraid people will someday collect items and sell them on eBay."

"Sell them on eBay? You've got to be making that up, Albert!"

"I do not make things up, Jack. It is written in the literature. Other sites have more items, like flags and Rovers. Shall we change our destination?"

"No, let's do a quick flyby, then move on to the more serious business."

Albert suggested we watch a documentary on Apollo 11. I agreed since we had time to kill. The scenery, and I hate to admit this, was getting boring. When there's no variety, "boring" becomes the operative word. Mountains, craters upon craters, the occasional crevasse, all against the ubiquitous black sky. Strangely beautiful, but after a while, mind-numbing. And the conveyance inherently flew itself, albeit sluggishly. Even the cruise control worked. So, in a picture-in-picture arrangement, I watched the video.

It was great and proved the old axiom – the more you know about something, the more you appreciate it. I learned: we were in this big space race with the Russians after they launched Sputnik, man's first satellite to orbit the Earth. People looked up and saw a new frontier – Space. President Kennedy set the bar; a man on the moon by the end of the decade, the 1960's. And so, it began. But before you can run, you must first learn to crawl. Learn how to build rocket engines, space suits, life-support systems, and so forth. They started sending things up; mice, monkeys, even a chimp named Ham. He survived and made it back, bruised but intact. That feat earned him his retirement – they put him in a zoo. There's a statue of him somewhere. Finally, the mission was a go. On July 20th, 1969, Neil Armstrong and Buzz Aldrin landed on the Moon with only 6 seconds of fuel left. The shock absorbers failed to depress, so the first step was really a four-foot jump. After which, Neil said: "One small step for man, one giant leap for mankind." He omitted the "a" before man. Therefore, what he said made no sense. Hey, that's what I learned from the video.

And there were a great many unknowns. One scientist predicted, quite emphatically, that the landing would cause a huge dust explosion. It didn't. Others said they would need snowshoes to walk around in. Wrong again. Despite these misgivings, the event was televised worldwide. Overall, it was a massive effort involving 400,000 workers – a major collective accomplishment, "one giant leap for mankind." Mission Control gave it to the world, where it belonged. Kudos.

Albert reiterated my thought, "It was a milestone in the history of mankind, Jack."

Buzz Aldrin found a purple rock and was elated. He confirmed my colorful moon thesis. After the moonwalk and back in the capsule, the moondust smelled like gunpowder, apparently from being exposed to air. The two space explorers spent 2 hours and thirty-one minutes on the moon. They collected rocks, set up scientific instruments, planted the flag, and then blasted off. After a dangerous docking maneuver with the Eagle Command Module and three more days of travel, they returned to Earth. Upon landing safely, all the engineers at Houston Control cheered and lit cigars and cigarettes, even the ones who didn't smoke. How times have changed. Then they quarantined the astronauts for two weeks in a big tank. Afterward, the parades began. It was a great video, and I thanked Albert.

"The moon was the first step in what will likely be a long adventure. You could shorten that journey, Jack if you reveal 4,3 to your people."

"And lose my provisional status?" On the map, the dotted line reached the x. We had arrived.

"Descend now, Jack, and reduce the velocity. There is the Lander," he pointed and dissolved the map.

I took her down as it came to view. The Lander looked like a robotic spider, white and yellow and charred in places, a jumbled mass of metal on four legs with tattered pieces hanging. I flew near and meandered around real slow. It wasn't an "oh wow" kind of sight unless you're a junkyard aficionado. But still significant for what it represented. Debris was scattered about; the scientific packages, two pairs of boots, bags of what must have been trash, and much more. And I saw footprints, the spore of human habitation, and the proof of human visitation.

After circling a couple of times, we were done. I could honestly say – I've been to the Apollo 11 landing site. The map reappeared with our next objective delineated – The Alien Moon Base.

"Shall we proceed to our next stop, Jack?"

"Lead on, Captain." I was loosening up with my newfound friend.

"Captain? As in Captain Kirk? An admirable role model whom I shall attempt to emulate."

Albert pointed, I lined up the arrows, and we were off. The journey would take a couple of hours.

Chapter 19: Qa'a Re – *Jack*

The trip to the Moonbase was uneventful. Albert played some music he thought I'd enjoy. I particularly liked "Fly Me to the Moon" sung by Frank Sinatra – archaic but apropos and enjoyable. We talked about the base: how long it had been there, a few thousand years, ever since the Pra'at were forced to leave the Earth and reduce their presence.

I asked Albert, "Have you ever popped in, you know, to borrow a cup of sugar?"

"No, Jack, this will be my first contact. But I do monitor their activities closely and occasionally discuss matters with my counterpart. They would view contact with me as a major event. They have long sought to establish a relationship with . . . what I represent."

"The First-Born?" I asked.

"Yes, ideally, an animate member of the Continuum."

"The 'First-Born.' I think that I'd like to know more about them."

"Embryonic civilizations such as the Pra'at naturally tend to revere them, or as is the case here, what they left behind – entities such as myself and my counterpart. And yes, Jack, you should want to learn more about them. But not now; we are approaching the Base."

The lunar phase of this area of the Far side was approaching twilight, almost dusk. Therefore, the lights were on; the immense landing platform had elevated and was bordered with blue perimeter lights. The massive triangular aperture was open, the doors having slid into the mountain itself. And an enormous saucer-shaped ship, obviously an interstellar vehicle, hovered several hundred feet above. Numerous smaller crafts were either parked or shuttling to and fro. I watched as a cargo transport slowly ascended to the Mother Ship. The dominant design scheme of these crafts was circular and flat. The typical saucer-shape that is everywhere in Earth media, though some were more oblate, fatter. Contrasting, a few of the smaller craft were triangular, with rather aerodynamic tail assemblies, centralized bubble domes, and pointy exterior features. But they all had one thing in common – lights. Not just the landing pad but also the humongous entranceway and all the various transportation conveyances, including the big saucer above. But not ours. We didn't have any, except on the dashboard. But I'm sure they were acutely aware of our presence.

"One of their interstellar ships has recently arrived. A development that can only benefit our purposes – advance our timeline. They have transportation; therefore, they can begin their departure with minimal delays."

I still couldn't believe we were just going to walk in and ask them to leave and that . . . they would.

"Slowly circle the area, Jack. Let's get their attention. Give them some time to contemplate."

"Contemplate?" I inquired.

"They know this vehicle is associated with . . . me. And, as I have observed them, they have observed us; all our activities, from your arrival and rescue."

I did as Albert suggested, and the activities below changed. The ascending Shuttle stopped, reversed course, and turned back. Other small vessels likewise retreated. I could make out some space-suited individuals down below, half-bouncing, and half-walking, rather purposefully. We had certainly stirred the pot.

"What's inside the big triangle?" I asked.

"Inside are hangar chambers and a storage area, from which many passageways lead to the extensive underground complex."

"How big is it, the whole complex that is?"

"There are miles of passageways and several million square feet of functional space extending several miles and descending many hundreds of feet. Over time they tended to excavate deeper and spread further out. They have recreational areas, parklands, farmlands, residential quarters, and medical research laboratories. The latter being the primary focus of their occupancy."

"You mentioned that their main means of communication is telepathy." That set Albert off again.

"Telepathy is a popular concept in the science fiction genre. As such, it exudes an aura of mystery. But electromagnetic waves are not magic, not to you, Jack, nor anyone else on Earth. At least not since the telegraph was invented. Indeed, the common use of cell phones very closely approximates telepathy. The Pra'at have the analog of a cell phone in their heads. The uninitiated may find some difficulty in their control, particularly in regard to privacy, as you have discovered, Jack."

"I also remember a little lecture you gave on the politeness of confidentiality. But, putting that aside, my point is . . . how are we going to communicate or specifically – how am I?"

Albert handed me a pair of earbuds. They looked like those Bluetooth sports headphones people jog with. "These should rectify the translation problems. And a message is being broadcast now. Insert the earbuds, and you will hear."

A beautifully modulated tenor voice was speaking . . . "once inside, please turn left and enter the chamber lit in blue. In a few moments, the room will repressurize. A delegation is ready to receive you."

"I told you we would not need M-16's, Jack." Albert couldn't resist an 'I told you so.' "Advanced civilizations are by definition – civilized."

I circled the area one more time. I wanted to see the terrain under which the Pra'at chose to build. It was fairly rugged geology, a steep mountain range, with a few craters in the basins. No sign of radar dishes, smokestacks, or peculiar apparatus – like in those "Aliens on the Moon" documentaries.

"As per my agreement with #2, any and all overt presence is prohibited, on Earth or the Moon."

"And since you and #2 are the gods who decide the rules of the game . . . then our little visit should be like the second coming to them. Only one problem – the messiah is riding in on a donkey."

"Very interestingly phrased, Jack. I always enjoy your . . . interpretations. This prompts me to recall an interesting quote, 'Any sufficiently advanced technology . . ."

"'Is indistinguishable from magic,' by Arthur C. Clarke, one of my favorite authors."

"Thank you, Jack. And there is some truth to that verbalism. Though, the Pra'at are long past the magic stage. To them, I am no god. Perhaps, just an angel." Then Albert chuckled. He was enjoying this.

I lined up on the big triangular entrance and slowly took her in. Up close, the large starship was very impressive. Innumerable protrusions were scattered over the surface: hatches of all sizes, several smaller domes bulged here and there; dish-like projections were scattered about, and a few cylindrical appendages that could have been weapons. Who are they planning to shoot at, the Earthlings, I wondered? There's no one else in the Galaxy, or so Albert said.

We entered the Pra'at Complex. The hangar was the size of two or three football fields. *Why is distance always measured in football fields?* The ceiling was 150' to 200' high, the same as the opening. There were many vehicles, big and small. Two were quite large, about 100' in diameter, oblate in shape, light gray in color, and bulging towards the center. They had to be Earth shuttles. The other vehicles varied widely in shape and structure. Some likely were cargo transports to shuttle freight from the interstellar craft. And there were many others – ground transporters, material handlers, and what looked to be small personal, car-like craft. Large pallets of equipment and supplies lined the walls along with complex pieces of apparatus. And there were beings. The Pra'at themselves, in dark compact space suits, very unlike the Apollo astronauts, who looked like puffed out marshmallow men. They stood and stared as we entered. Several arched openings lead to the interior complex. Where else? All were closed off except for one, which glowed blue.

That's where I went. Once inside, a space-suited figure guided us with red hand-lights to a place where I parked. The archway closed, and we waited for the air to fill the room.

Concerning that topic, I asked Albert, "I hope they breathe the same air as us." It was a little late in the game to start thinking about that.

"I do not require a specific gaseous mix, Jack. But the atmosphere of Ta-ea is similar to Earth's, with slightly more oxygen, slightly less nitrogen, and similar trace elements. You will not have any breathing difficulties." A small gauge materialized where the map was. The bar graphs slowly progressed.

"Albert, why do they think we're here?"

"They are divided. Some believe we shall acquiesce to their presence and cede them greater freedoms. Others fear our intent is more restrictive and ominous."

"Ominous? How can they think that? They know your ostensible purpose here is to . . . usher in new life."

"True, Jack. But that life, in my case, is human, not Pra'at. And the second part of my mission is to protect that life from unwarranted interference, which the Pra'at are engaged in. And they know this as well."

The bar graphs filled. It was safe to exit. The thought suddenly occurred to me – we had no plans, tactics, or strategy for dealing with the Pra'at. I inquired, and Albert answered, "Let them take the lead, Jack . . . do all the talking. The outcome of this event is impossible to predict. We must, 'go with the flow,' Jack."

Go with the flow? That was my middle name. I could do that. We opened the doors and stepped out.

It was warm, somewhat stuffy, and a bit musty smelling, but otherwise, comfortable. The walls were grayish, with a hint of sparkle. I deduced they were mechanically hewn from the lunar rock. The light was dim yet omnipresent, and the room contained several oddly configured craft. A doorway opened, and a delegation of 12 to 15 robed figures entered. They approached us, and we casually walked towards them. Albert employed his cane more overtly than usual. Curious.

I assumed they were of the "Thinker" class as Albert had depicted previously. They were the only ones who wore clothes. But all their robes were green, various shades thereof, with disparate patterns. Can it be they all just happened to like the color green? It must be a symbol of rank, comparable to the Roman Emperors wearing purple.

And the "Thinkers" were more "humanesque" than the other castes. They had fairly normal noses and mouths, only smaller. But not the eyes. They were big black ovals encircled with bulging wrinkles. The most disturbing aspect was the two large yellow crescents arranged vertically in the center of each. Double pupils. Like yellow cats-eye marbles. They appeared to stare straight through me. And it made reading their facial expressions impossible.

The other thing about them was their craniums. They were big, bold, shiny, and generally flesh-colored though on the dull grayish-green side. One would assume that big thinkers would have big craniums. And they did. They all could have been distant cousins to Lex Luther. And size-wise, they were about my height, some a little taller. Were they all males? Unknown. Nor was I particularly eager to learn more in that regard. As we met, one extended his hand to me in greeting. Astonished, I shook it. He was missing a finger but otherwise had a good strong grip, warm and functional. I sensed he was saying something, and I re-inserted my earbuds. The others in the delegation were bowing to Albert. Evidently, they knew who he was. But how could they tell us apart, we both looked human? It must be the biochemistry – I have some, Albert doesn't. I tuned in a little late:

". . . are welcome to our humble habitation – Qa'a Re. My name is Ay Kheperkheprure." His telepathic voice was the most mellow and mellifluous sound I have ever heard. Was it an accurate portrayal of his personality? Was he a mellow and mellifluous uh . . . being? Food for thought. I quarter-bowed and introduced myself. Hey, everyone else was bowing. Only to Albert, not to me, welcoming and thanking him for deigning to visit.

"We are blessed. 'Those Who Came Before' endowed our 'Island of Stars' (galaxy) with two Caretakers. And now, our most ardent aspiration is realized. The acknowledgment of our existence by both." He bowed again.

Their fawning behavior was almost embarrassing. They introduced themselves as well. A few of their names were Ay Bakenkhonsu – chief scientist, and Ky Thutmosis – legate of the arts. Later, Albert explained that 'Ay' was an honorific for exalted, and 'Ky' meant sculptor – another title? But they all had the most wondrous voices or translation programs. They put Johnny Mathis to shame. Any one of them could have had quite the singing career back on Earth, audio-only.

They offered refreshments, resting facilities (?), and or possibly a tour. I liked the tour idea, and Albert picked up on that: "We would be very pleased to take the tour."

The corridors were maybe 25' wide, 20' tall, covered in short, green grass-like carpet, with lines of soft tubular lighting in the rounded juncture between the walls and ceiling, which looked to have been hewn from solid lunar rock. And I'm sure not with chisels.

Another thing was the gravity. It was less than the Earth's but more than the Moon's. We weren't bouncing around like the Apollo Astronauts, but definitely, there was a newfound spring to my step. I wondered if they had a gravistat on the wall, next to the thermostat. They obviously knew how to manipulate gravity. Was this ability another benefit of 4,3?

As we walked along, our escorts continued to introduce themselves and explain their lineage, obviously an attribute very important to them. Albert nodded with outward interest. We came to an intersection, what appeared to be a hub. It was a large, centralized area and looked something like a food court in a mall. There were many Pra'at, of every variety, eating in what had to be dining establishments. Dispersed here and there were alcoves where merchandise was sold or distributed. Were they socialist or capitalist or maybe something else? I pondered this for about a half-second and then moved on. In the center was a fountain that cascaded frothy water a couple of dozen feet high. It was surrounded by decorative benches, tables, and reclining furniture. Many figures occupied this area, a few sipping steaming drinks. Numerous flat screen displays of landscapes embellished the walls, seemingly of Pra'at, though a few could have been Earth. Amphorae and palm-like trees strategically decorated the less-traveled areas. It was rather inviting. I felt like trying one of those hot drinks.

Suddenly, from concealed positions, behind objects, and emerging from niches and alcoves, appeared a considerable number of Qe'ma u, the smaller variety of Pra'at, as Albert had previously referred to them. They were brandishing hostile-looking objects. Funny how you can always tell when something's a weapon, especially if it's long and sleek and pointing at you. And also firing, which is the unmistakable tip-off. Blazing rays and brilliant pulses exploded and flashed all around us, accompanied by loud, whooshing noises. I instinctively crouched and futilely raised my arm. Albert's cane was deployed in a vertical position, then he leveled and pointed it at our attackers. They dropped their firearms and froze solid in their last positions. Indeed, the whole room was stunned and immobile for a few breaths. But not the little guys in the unitards. They truly were frozen, or maybe rigor mortis would be a better word. Subsequently, they were picked up and carried out. A large contingent of Pra'at surrounded us – the Goldilocks variety – the Sek hem're, and shielded us with their bodies while brandishing additional, bizarre-looking weapons. Inexplicably, a no-go zone of several feet was maintained around us. A barrier of sorts. A few members of our delegation lay on the ground. Some were moving, some were not. In places, dark red blotches stained the green carpet.

Albert had ostensibly erected some kind of shield around the two of us. It remained inviolate. Nobody could get close. Albert took my elbow and, with a bemused smile, implanted the following thought: "This can only serve to facilitate our objectives." Seemingly, the preceding attack was no big deal. But it was like the twilight zone for me – a nether-world of incomprehension. I didn't know what was happening. Blinding flashes and bursting strobes had suddenly and completely engulfed us. Seemingly from out of nowhere. Then, as soon as it started, it was over.

"I guess we didn't need the M-16's," I replied mentally.

"No, Jack, we were never in any danger. The Pra'at have had many thousands of years to learn amity. Yet, there are still fractious differences among them. The embarrassment resulting from this incident will tend to induce our hosts to be more amenable to our 'entreaties'." All this was communicated non-verbally. We had our own secret language, shielded, I'm sure, from the Pra'at.

A new group of toga attired attendants beseeched us to follow them, which we did. They were our Praetorian Guard and led us to a very nicely appointed room. Inside were stylishly designed sofa chairs arranged around what could be called coffee tables. We made ourselves comfortable. There were tables and counters adjacent to the walls, laden with food service devices. Coffeemakers? Perhaps they had something better? It was obviously a break room, and already we needed a break, and so did they.

A new group entered with our old pals Kheperkheprure, Bakenkhonsu, and Thutmosis. We stood, and Kheperkheprure again assumed the role of spokesman, better make that spokes-being, "Please accept our most profound and deeply held apologies for the preceding, extremely unfortunate . . . incident. Your health remains intact, for which we are immeasurably grateful. I should like to point out, and in no way does this absolve our guilt for this massive wrongdoing, but the audacity of this hostile action reveals the near non-sentience of the perpetrators. A rational being would know the certain futility of such an endeavor." His unfurled hand gestured to Albert, not me.

Albert responded, "Perhaps the attack's objective was to harm my human associate, Mr. Neufield," Albert almost winked at me; he was toying with them, though his thesis was possible, so it seemed to me.

"The motivations of the perpetrators will be thoroughly examined. Please let me emphatically state . . . in no way do the actions of this subspecies, the Qe'ma u, reflect the thoughtful and beneficent aspirations for comity that the Pra'at-tum, as a whole, desire."

Man, this guy, strike that, he was no guy, could talk up a storm. Make that a beautiful storm. I shot Albert a look. He imperceptibly head-pointed to the door. I ran with the cue.

"We comprehend the atypical nature of this 'incident' and sincerely hope the harmed members of your group will recover satisfactorily." I looked at Albert. He mentally commended my comment.

"The injuries of our associates will heal in time. Your concern is acknowledged," replied Kheperkheprure. ('K' as I shall henceforth refer to him for obvious reasons.)

Albert tried to move matters along, "It pleases us to know that no lasting damage shall result from our visit." Albert bowed; then they all bowed, then K. extended his arm and shook my hand, again. And then I bowed. (?)

This time Bakenkhonsu said, "Shall we place this incident in the past and continue the tour of our facilities?" He must have read our minds, at least mine.

"Yes, of course," said Albert.

The door automatically opened. At this point, I would venture to say, all the doors were automatic – via thought control. K. bowed again, not to me, and led us out.

Chapter: 20 – The Hall of Immortality – *Jack*

I should remind the reader that all this occurred telepathically, except for what Albert and I occasionally communicated verbally. It was a little like listening to the radio. My earbuds were great, transmitting my thoughts and translating those of the Pra'at. How fantastic would something like this be on Earth? But wait, we already have them; sort of, they're called cellphones. Albert wore no translation devices. What he did, how he communicated, I do not know. What was interesting was – we had our private lines of communication – when needed.

This time Bakenkhonsu assumed the role of spokesman: "Qa'a Re translated means 'small home faraway'. This is our largest settlement because Earth is our only companion in this vast assemblage of stars. If permitted, we would welcome our new and only neighbors with lasting bows of friendship. Until such time, we await and prepare for that venerable event."

I said to myself, 'Yeah, and abduct a few humans every once in a while.'

Albert shot me a non-verbal warning.

B. carried on, "We have many areas that may be of interest to you. Do you have a preference?"

"We would like to tour the life-science research laboratories," Albert said.

They looked ready to pull out the ray-guns again. The silence got a little quieter, the eyes a little meaner, and our escorts skipped a step. Not that I could see their feet.

Kheperkheprure responded, "Of course. We have no secrets here. We are, in fact, eager to discuss our progress and accomplishments. Please follow me. We shall engage a 'cartouche.'"

We walked through a couple of corridors while K. explained how our destination was too close for the underground. Assumably, he was referring to an underground railway of some sort.

We boarded a cartouche – a small, open carriage-type conveyance with four rows of plush seats. The carrier rose a few inches, and we smoothly glided along several passages, similar to the ones we had walked in. The only difference being, there were no pedestrians. We came to a departure area and exited. Our entourage had diminished somewhat, but our original buddies Kheperkheprure, Bakenkhonsu, and Thutmosis were still with us.

The corridor we were traversing converged into a huge quadrangle. Another very large courtyard space, only it was all business this time. The business of immortality. Many other passages, some large enough to accommodate a train, converged there as well. Across the way was a huge arched entranceway – our destination. We entered the laboratory section. It was a vast area with tall ceilings, maybe 40-50 feet high, partitioned by the occasional wall. Every so often stood a stone column, which coned outward on top. They had to support those rugged mountains we saw coming in, which I assumed, occupied the space above our heads. Again, it all looked to have been carved from solid rock, including the floors, which were smooth but bare here. I recalled the many Central American, Inca, and even Egyptian walls often featured on 'Ancient Aliens.' The stones were so precisely fitted, in bizarre geometric patterns that the proverbial knife could not be wedged between.

I looked at Albert; he nodded, knowing the direction my questioning would take.

"Uh, Mr., I mean Ay Kheperkheprure, I have a question concerning the architecture." I stumbled over his name telepathically. They did not seem offended, which, no doubt, reflected their low expectations of me.

"Please do, Mr. Neufield, I . . . we are here to accommodate."

"I am impressed at the extent and precision in which all these open spaces have been created. Could you please explain how you excavate so precisely through all this solid rock?" My arm swept the expansive area.

"Molecular disintegration is what we call the process. We use extremely tight beams of anti-electrons, positrons as you call them, to slice through these geologic formations." He indicated the rock walls. "They disrupt the normal electrical bonds that bind molecules, cutting a tight clean seam. The difficulty lies in reversing the charge of the electron. We accomplish this by routing the beam through a negative space generator, which transforms the polarity. The drawback to our methodology is the large quantities of energy that these generators consume. I'm sure your associate, Mr. Einstein, can suggest more efficient alternatives."

"Indeed, I can, at another time. Shall we proceed with the tour?"

From what I could see, the lab was composed of habitats – not Albert's kind, but more like what you'd find in a zoo or maybe a botanical garden. They were enclosed spaces where plants and animals were situated in their natural environments. And they included many large aquariums as well. In between and clustered around were collections of inexplicable apparatus and rows of counters filled with devices and equipment. Some worktops were loaded with chemistry gear – flasks, beakers, glass tubes, ocular paraphernalia, and instrument arrays with colorful screens and countless blinking lights. Since this section was the primary focus of the entire complex, there were dozens of Pra'at of every variety engaged in whatever it was they were doing. Many wore white smocks. I wondered about that. Did they borrow the convention from Earth, or was that the universal uniform of the technician everywhere, or rather – in this galaxy?

Albert was talking to Bakenkhonsu principally. The bio labs were his jurisdiction. They were discussing the many different areas of endeavor. Bakenkhonsu explained: "Our goal is 'negligible senescence.' Defined simply as the absence of symptoms caused by aging. This would include any functional decline, especially with increased longevity. One would simply not die from natural causes. Perfect self-repair is the means by which we hope to achieve this."

"There is the route of organ replacement, either artificial or organic. Do you dismiss this alternative?" Albert commented.

"No, certainly not. We consider organ transplantation a type of repair." He continued, "Our general approach is twofold: Analyze those organisms that demonstrate negligible senescence, and those that exhibit the opposite – programmed death. An unfortunate characteristic of we Pra'at and you humans as well." He looked at me, and I felt – guilty as charged.

We were walking past the transparent window of a large aquarium, saltwater obviously, since it contained a coral reef and the whole attendant ecosphere. Fish of every variety; mollusks, coral, and sea anemones, but there was a protective cage around a large orange, cylindrical living object. It looked like an old, corroded sewage pipe. Bakenkhonsu explained, "This is the Giant Barrel Sponge, Xestospongia muta, found in the coral reefs of the West Indies. This particular specimen is well over 2000 years old and will not die from old age."

"And what's the secret? Why won't it die?" I asked the obvious questions as I watched a Parrotfish nibbling on it through the cage. I thought of Prometheus.

"That is precisely the question we seek to answer."

"And have you found answers?" Albert asked the perfect followed up.

"Yes, extremely high levels of telomerase rejuvenation is one factor. The ends of this animal's chromosomes do not shorten with each cell division. And therefore, telomere damage does not accrue over time. The ends are constantly being refurbished. Hence – reduced aging. This species has avoided that form of slow demise. Plus, every cell is a stem cell, capable of changing into any other cell as needed. This animal has achieved perfect self-repair."

The Parrotfish, no doubt, appreciated the sponge's immortality as it pecked away.

We moved on. This aquarium would most definitely qualify as a tourist attraction. I was impressed by the technology and the tremendous effort put forth to maintain something of this size. And there were many of these big fish tanks. The pumps, lighting, oxygenators, heaters, everything; plus, the constant attention and the constant maintenance. I thought of my singular aquarium experience – a Siamese fighting fish in a jar. It died. And not due to senescence either.

As we walked along, Albert inquired, "Have you made any progress in your quest for longevity?"

"Yes, with knowledge comes solutions," Bakenkhonsu replied, "and with the truths supplied by this facility, we have begun to accrue the secrets of life extension."

"And have your lives been extended?"

Kheperkheprure eagerly fielded this question: "I am 77 Earth-years old, 20 years past my life expectancy. And I expect to experience several more as a result of the enigmas we have deciphered here."

We walked past what looked like banks of computers, aisle upon aisle of them. The smell of ozone, together with a slight hum, permeated the air. And the many blinking diodes stood out in the dim light. Bakenkhonsu commented, "We store the genome of every known life form of both Earth and Ta-ea here. The processes of life are similar in both our worlds."

"Similar?" Albert said. I sensed he was testing B.

"Yes, the processes of organic metabolism are fairly analogous as is the case with all carbon-based life, I'm sure." He looked for confirmation from Albert, who remained inscrutable. "By understanding the differences, we learn clues which then lead to answers. That is our approach to grasping the riddle of unending life."

The next room we entered contained rows of workbenches, on which were a great many fish tanks, maybe a hundred in all. Each was a habitat for a group of specimens. Flat screen displays, instruments, and optical devices occupied the spaces in-between.

Bakenkhonsu rather grandly announced, “This is our ‘Hall of Immortality’ as we like to think of it. Here we have collected all the immortal species from both our worlds and a few others as well.”

He paused before one exhibit; a good-sized aquarium filled with green aquatic plants: “Here resides one of the most notable in the collection – the Hydra. They simply do not age."

I looked and saw nothing. Then B. pointed to a particular spot on a tall green frond. There was a speck of something about a quarter inch in size. He pushed some buttons on an adjacent display, and an image appeared of what looked like an octopus on a stick – waving around its several tentacles.

“This little animal has revealed to us its secret – the immortality gene. On Earth, you call it the FoxO gene. The set of instructions that control stem cell maintenance. And it is the stem cells that replenish the organs when and if needed. Hence, the FoxO gene is responsible for managing the maintenance system.” Then to me, he said, “Humans have this gene, and we have the Pra’at counterpart.”

“If we humans have this gene, how come we’re not immortal?” I simply stated the obvious.

“Post-translational modifications. Epigenetic or environmental factors diminish the gene's effectiveness and even switch it off. This process is called DNA methylation on Earth. The addition of a methyl group to the DNA – usually to the fifth carbon atom in the cytosine ring, which silences the gene, inappropriately in this case. The outcome is aging. Though I would like to point out, nothing is simple in this field of endeavor. We have identified 378 factors that directly bear on the progression of senescence. The complex biochemical pathways of the FoxO gene are but one."

"And if you solve them all, you will become immortal?" I was thinking that maybe I'd like to give this immortality thing a go. Sometime in the future, before I got old . . . before senescence kicked in.

"Perfect self-repair would be the outcome, and very long lives the result."

We walked a few steps. "You may find its neighbor here to be of some interest – Turriilopsis Dohrnii, or as it is commonly known – The Immortal Jellyfish. Are you familiar with the old Mesopotamian poem titled 'The Epic of Gilgamesh'?" Albert did not answer, and I shook my head. Bakenkhonsu continued, "It chronicles the travels of Gilgamesh, the king who sought the gift of immortality. The gods granted this prize to Utnapishtim as a reward for building an arc and surviving their wrongful flood. Utnapishtim told Gilgamesh that he could find what he seeks, on the bottom of the sea – the bounty of immortality." He motioned to the aquarium, "This is what he found."

Inside the tank were some brown and yellow corals, marine plants, a few colorful fish, and some tiny blue and red jellyfish. On a flat screen nearby was an enlarged real-time image of the jellyfish swimming. It looked like a light blue upside-down sack with a red dot in the center and many semi-transparent tentacles swirling about underneath. Water was pulsing through it.

Bakenkhonsu expounded in his beautiful, mellifluous timbre, "This animal adds a peculiar twist to its version of immortality. In times of adversity, it reverse-ages to its polyp stage. Then plants itself back on the bottom. Being a hydrozoa, the same class as the hydra, it possesses a similar enhanced FoxO gene. But rather than suspending the aging process, it reverses it. We are very actively studying this animal."

Albert couldn't resist throwing me a quip, "How would you like that Jack, grow old to a certain point, then get young again?"

"I think I'd prefer the other kind, just not getting old." Then to B., "And do you have a preference, Ay Bakenkhonsu?"

"We prefer to have the option, hence, all the endeavors that you see." He bowed and swept his arm. "Shall we proceed?"

As we pressed on, I realized this place, with all the habitats, was the best zoo I'd ever seen. And we were moving up the zoological ladder. The next exhibit was a grassy area with mid-sized plants scattered about, a small pond to one side with rocks and reeds, and opposite that, an embankment with burrows dug into the base. Lounging on a grassy slope were several very large brownish turtles.

Bakenkhonsu discussed the scene, "This species, the Aldabra Giant Tortoise from the Seychelles, is not immortal, but lives a very long time. The large one grazing by the pond is over 225 years old. What's interesting about this species is that they do not die from old age, per se. The shell cracks when it reaches a certain size. At which point, infection sets in and precipitates the animal's demise. Except for this one defect, all the life processes operate in perfect balance. Their telomeres are repaired, stem cell maintenance proceeds indefinitely, the rate of DNA methylation is appropriate, mitochondrial communications occur at a constant rate, and so forth – to all 378 markers that impinge upon senescence."

The big tortoises seemed to be enjoying life and certainly were well cared for. I wondered what would happen when they were no longer needed.

As we strolled along, we came to a large courtyard where several passageways converged. A dark, segmented metallic barrier blocked one. Albert gestured towards it and said: "We would like to go there."

"As you wish," answered Kheperkheprure. The massive walls slid apart, and we proceeded to enter. K. explained, "In this section, we research the higher life forms – primates of both Ta-ea and Earth." I sensed that this was what we came for.

Behind a transparent wall was an unearthly scene. It was a steamy jungle interlaced with a tangle of thick boughs hung with stringy, gray-green moss, like tinsel on a Christmas tree. Occasionally a splash of spiky green peeked through. On a branch sat a creature with impossibly long arms; one was extended to an upper branch. And its legs were hinged backward, like a grasshopper's, presumably for jumping. An infant lay entwined to its upper torso. They both had long pointy ears, nasty pushed-in faces with a cluster of writhing tentacles where the nose should have been.

"This is a Khayu, a primate from our equatorial regions. Not particularly long-lived, but rather, an excellent example of the opposite phenomenon – programmed death. Upon the second birth, the female dies shortly thereafter. Various processes genetically shut down. It is analogous to the octopus on your planet."

We walked past other environments. One had a few spider-like monkeys swinging through the trees. Another was an earthly savanna with a few trees scattered about. Gathered in a clearing was a small troop of baboons loitering casually. A young male saw us, picked up a piece of excrement, and hurled it at us. It would have hit Bakenkhonsu but left a brown smear on the glass instead. We walked on.

Next, we came to the chimpanzee section. It was an African jungle setting. Within was a stand of fig trees, their large aerial roots twisting to the ground. Also, vines draped from tree to tree. A few females sat at the base of a large trunk watching their youngsters demonstrate rather proficient acrobatic skills. Another female grubbed along the forest floor as her infant clung to her bosom. An older male sat on a limb, staring back at us. He smiled in fear and displayed his teeth . . . as he masturbated! He wasn't the least bit embarrassed. I was, for being a fellow primate. The group turned to look at me. Again, I felt – guilty as charged.

Next-door and adjoining was an operating theater. It looked antiseptically clean; bright lights and numerous pieces of arcane medical equipment lined the walls. Several Pra'at dressed in white were assembled near a horizontal platform. A figure lay on top, swathed in white, except for the head. It was a chimpanzee. Monitoring screens were arrayed around, no doubt displaying the patient's vital signs. Projecting from the surrounding medical apparatus were articulated appendages with various instruments affixed to the ends – cutting tools, probes, clasping mechanisms, and more. The patient's eyes were open and darting back and forth as the attendants worked inside its open chest.

Off to one side stood several large transparent tubes. They extended from floor to ceiling with apparatus at the base and top. All were lit from above and filled with a viscous yellow fluid. Within each floated a chimpanzee – every kind, male, female, young, and old. Arcing down within each cylinder was a thick cord that affixed to the naval area of each occupant. I looked closely at one young male and saw him move and realized he must be alive. The chimp opened his eyes and slowly turned his head, looking around. Those yellow eyes came to rest on . . . me. It opened its mouth, bared its teeth, and screamed. My earbuds picked up that horrible sound and transmitted it – straight through my brain. And no translation was needed. The meaning was plain – it was pure terror.

I was speechless and just looked at Albert, who placed his extended forefinger to his mouth. The sign for silence. I shut my mouth and my thoughts as well, especially since I did not know what to say. The Pra'at remained silent as well.

The next section was worse. It was the human section. At least they weren't suspended in vertical tubes. The tubes were horizontal. They looked like those suspended animation chambers you see in the movies. Most of the spaceships have them. They had clear bubble-like cylindrical coverings over narrow enclosed berths – kind of like a coffin with a clear plastic housing. Life support machinery was visible underneath, and rows of monitors were arranged on the headboards. All the occupants were either asleep or entranced. A few Sek hem're, midsized Pra'at, moved among them, now and then adjusting a dial. There were 20 or 30 of these chambers aligned in rows. Located in an adjoining room was another operating facility.

Bakenkhonsu accurately read the horror on my face and responded, "All of these subjects volunteered to aid us in our quest. We are grateful for their participation. Afterward, they retain no memories of the experience as per our agreement with . . ." he motioned towards Albert, who looked away. "We comply with all non-interference doctrine, as set forth by . . . 'Those Who Came Before.'"

Albert looked at me and said, "Jack, as a representative of Earth and as a unique citizen of the Continuum, if you wish to contribute to this discussion, now would be an appropriate time."

It was all up to me due to my unique standing as a 'quasi-provisional.' It was time to hang the DO NOT DISTURB sign. I simply stated, "You will awaken all the humans . . . people . . . restore them to good health and return them to Earth a.s.a.p. That means, as soon as possible. And do the same for the chimps too." I threw the chimps in for good measure. That was it. There was nothing left to say. I was standing next to the biggest kid on the block.

Our good buddy Kheperkheprure understood the magnitude of the situation and the futility of resistance. *Ha! We were like the Borg.* K. responded, rather succinctly, "We shall comply." So little said, so momentous would be the result. Albert was right; no pulse pistols, no ray guns, no saber swords were needed.

Albert wisely changed the subject. "We graciously accept your offer for refreshments at this time. Subsequently, we shall return here to converse with the . . ."

"Abductees." I finished the sentence for Albert. It was a pejorative, an emotionally charged word, but . . . accurate. I must comment, however, on how strangely amiable this whole situation was, except for the part where we were shot at. In a way, I felt sorry for the Pra'at. So much to live for, so little life. It was like winning the lottery, and then the doctor tells you, you've only got six months to live. Hey, am I King Solomon, the possessor of great wisdom? No, pretty freakin' far from it. But my gut tells me it's just not a good thing for the aliens to be mucking around on Earth, sampling the life forms. They'll just have to wait a little longer for Earth to discover 4,3. Then they can introduce themselves, nice and friendly. Like good neighbors. Maybe even borrow a cup of sugar.

Chapter 21: Bill Cambell – *Jack*

And so, we all went out for some "refreshments." Hell, why not? Despite all of the above, we all are civilized, plus I needed a coffee, or the equivalent thereof. Along the way, our entourage had dwindled by half. Then, as we entered "The Hall of Higher Life," we lost the rest, except for our original pals Ay Kheperkheprure, Ay Bakenkhonsu, and the Ky Thutmosis.

We walked out in silence. No more tour. The Pra'at, at least our new friends, did not seem angry. There was no point. Our neighbors from Ta-ea may be a little slow on the evolutionary uptake, but they weren't stupid. Their 49,000-year-old civilization could not thwart the will of a 2.37-billion-year-old Continuum of . . . who knows what. And the First-Born, to implement their directives, left behind a million+ entities like Albert, all across the Universe. "Caretakers" was what Kheperkheprure called them. Just to keep tabs on things. So, therefore, our little proclamation was certainly a fait accompli.

There was a small restaurant across the courtyard. Restaurant, evidently that's what it was since it was a place where food was served. They had some tables outside, with the majority inside. I wanted to take one of those, and dine al fresco, do some real people watching, but Kheperkheprure recommended we sit inside. I saw the wisdom in that. Our game plan was to go with the flow, and it appeared to be working. All right, so we got attacked, but other than that, there I was being wined and dined by the Pra'at in a nice restaurant. Though poisoning was a distinct possibility.

A goldilocks Pra'at, a Sek hem're, bowed and handed out menus. It was, of course, all Greek to me, make that Egyptian. The little pictures resembled hieroglyphics. I looked at Albert, and he said, “Try the Sekhem Shedwast. It's the best in the Complex.” He pointed to a line on his menu with a couple of birdlike symbols, "It tastes like chicken." He gave me a subtle nod, which I interpreted to mean – it's ok to eat.

The food was good, the service was good, and so was the wine. It was a golden yellow, not too sweet with a spicy after taste. And so was the dessert and coffee. Yes, they did have a drink that was quite similar to coffee, though it was a dark red rather than brown. And it tasted oddly sweet with a bit of a kick. Kind of like the Ovaltine my mother made when I was a kid. And the conversation was good too. Everything was all so very civilized. Eventually, I asked the big question: "Why do you need live . . . I mean living . . . specimens for your research? Can't you just make do with blood samples, maybe an occasional cheek swab or such?"

Bakenkhonsu, as the chief biologist, gave a good answer, "We watch and record all the intracellular activity, on a molecular level, in real-time; the long chains of cause and effect that exist among the enzymes, amino acids, proteins and so forth. For example, in those aging processes that involve mitochondrial degeneration, one theory postulates that highly reactive oxygen molecules cause mutations, which build up over time, triggering a decline in health and death. We have recorded this process, molecule by molecule, as it occurs, in many species. From our observations, we have refuted that theory. Causality has not been established, and indeed, even reversed. Free radical oxygenation has actually enhanced health and longevity in some species. Currently, we are more focused on certain enzymic signaling pathways – particularly the downregulation of the inhibitor rapamycin."

I continued, "So you make real-time videos, study them, then begin tinkering. Add an enzyme here, snip a gene there."

"Yes, essentially it is as you say. The process of scientific experimentation."

Albert inquired, "And how, if I may ask, have you achieved the 20-year life extension you previously mentioned?"

K. replied, "Some gene alterations and the addition of nano-repair bots, but I think the largest factor that increased the length of my life was . . . dietary restriction. Fundamentally, if you eat less, you live longer. It's a simple fact of life; for Pra'at and humans."

I found that genuinely amusing. After all this, thousands of years of effort, the Egyptians, the Mayans, this entire installation, and what have they learned? If you eat less, you live longer. As we all sat in a nice restaurant, stuffing our faces.

Albert, read my amusement and thought it necessary to give the Pra'at some hope: "Your research will bear fruit, as it has for the many who have preceded you. There are numerable components – 378, as you mentioned. Solve them one by one, and you will attain the goal you seek."

Till then, Albert had been very circumspect with his knowledge. I presumed he was prohibited from sharing it. The Pra'at were not his responsibility.

I found an opportunity to discuss with Thutmosis the honorific, “Ky,” meaning sculptor.

Thutmosis was eager to expound on the subject, "Sculptors and the arts in general, are highly esteemed in our culture since the early beginnings. For that reason, valued personages are given the title 'Ky,' and not just sculptors. From an inner fold, he pulled out a display tablet, tapped it a few times, and a slide show began. Colorful pictures of figures and animals slid across the screen. Thutmosis resumed his discourse, "Our culture is much older than yours, thus permitting more time for the accumulation of artworks such as these. Many are religious, depicting various deities and the rituals associated with them. Also, it is common for public structures to be adorned with large murals illustrating noteworthy events and heroic deeds." A sequence of these streamed by. "And, statues, and sculpture in general, is the pinnacle of our art. For this type of art continues through the millennia." I saw a picture of a colonnade comprised of huge figures, which were at least 10 times taller than the Pra' standing at their base, and another of humanoids wearing elaborate headpieces with the most bestial and demonic of visages. "And I am honored with the appellation 'Ky,' because I too am a sculptor, among other things. The following are examples of my work."

Figures of the most voluptuous human women I ever saw flipped past. Some in rather provocative poses. Seeing my incredulity, Thutmosis explained: "Currently, human culture is in vogue on my world, especially among the youth." I asked him if I could have a sample of his work; he said that he would be honored to arrange it.

We were finishing the meal. I had another cup of kaiu as I learned it was called. And like coffee, it tasted good; plus, a nice pick-me-up too. Speaking of that, I wondered who'd pick up the tab. Do they take American Express?

Albert stood and thanked our hosts, taking the lead and signaling the conclusion of our repast. Everyone accepted his lead, rose, and proceeded to bow profusely. Then Albert led the way out. We were going back to check on the humans. *Humans?* It's funny how quickly I had adopted an "otherly" point of view.

The individuals had been aroused and were sitting on their . . . berths. The Pra'at had complied with my . . . our order. *Let's be real here.* Most of the awakened looked completely befuddled, and some were clearly horrified at the sight of the Pra'at.

I approached one young man who was standing and shaking out his legs. I extended my hand and said, "Hi, my name is Jack Neufield."

Hesitantly, he reached and shook it, as he looked at my Pra'at companions, "What the hell is . . . Where the freak is this?"

He was dressed evidently in the clothes he came in. Black cut-off jeans and matching high-top sneakers, but the funny thing was – he wore a UFO tee shirt. It had a picture of a big-headed Gray on the front, with large black almond-shaped eyes. It was a close likeness except that the alien was lime green. On the back, it said, "Take Me Away."

I told him straight out, "You're at an alien laboratory complex on the far side of the Moon. You apparently agreed to be experimented on by the Pra'at," I indicated to the entourage, "Whom you probably know as Grays." Several other men, women, boys, and girls, who were up and aware, were intently watching and listening.

"Well, what the . . . what are 'you' doing here?"

"This is my friend Albert," I introduced Albert, and they shook hands.

"Hey, you look like somebody I've seen before."

Albert responded, "I have heard others express similar comments."

To everyone listening, I said, "We have terminated this facility, and you will all be returning to your homes as soon as possible." Then back to the young man, "Your name is?" I asked.

"Bill Cambell, pleased to meet you. We shook again. It was awkward. Then I introduced, Kheperkheprure, Bakenkhonsu, and Thutmosis. They bowed. Bill didn't. "Man," he scratched his head, "I'm a big UFO guy . . . but when I responded to that ad . . . I thought it was just some fellow UFO buffs getting together. But not this! What in Sam Hill is all this?"

"I'm pleased to meet you Bill, and to answer your question . . . everything that you thought might be real, Bill . . . is real."

"Man, I just can't believe it."

This guy was a bona fide UFO nut. He looked to be my age, maybe a little older – maybe early thirties, 5'10", longish dark hair, 3-day old stubble, and a round face. In a word, he looked soft – soft hands, soft, undefined arms, boney knees, a spare tire, and a fleshy face. The kind of guy who spends too much time playing video games – and dealing with UFO stuff.

Albert asked, "What's the last thing you remember, Bill?"

"I met this spooky dude at the Starbucks, in Granby Center, in Colorado. That's where I'm from. I responded to this ad in 'UFO Today'; that's one of my favorite sites. They know all about them." He chin-pointed to K, B, and T, "I contribute articles every so often, too." He proudly proclaimed this. "The dude said we were going to see some real UFO stuff, like genuine evidence of them being here." He subtly pointed again, this time with his thumb, and made a face. "We walked out to his car, then the next thing I know, I'm waking up here."

Well, you'll be going back to Granby in a matter of hours." I looked at Bakenkhonsu, who nodded.

"Man," he was shaking his head, "You sure all this is for real?"

"Take a look." I took his elbow and helped him out to the main aisle. We were able to see some of the other passages. He got a real eyeful: a few of the habitats; the huge laboratory arrays, the chimpanzee room next door, and dozens of Pra'at; all three kinds, going about their business.

Poor Bill, he looked like he'd been through the wringer. He was walking bow-legged, with one hand pressed against his abdomen. "Holy shit!" That was all he said. I helped him back to his "bed."

"You'll be riding in a real spaceship back to Earth, Bill. Maybe you can tell me about it sometime."

With that, he pulled out an overstuffed wallet, fished around, and extracted a card:

Bill Cambell

UFOlogist for Hire

Aliens Are Us

Followed by his address, phone number, and email. "Look me up, man . . . I mean, Jack. If you do, then I'll know all this . . . wasn't something I smoked."

We shook hands again, the Pra'at bowed, and we turned to go. Then Bill said again: "I mean it, man, look me up." I said I would as we all left the human section.

When we reached the courtyard, Albert thanked our three escorts for a 'most edifying tour' and asked to be shown to our "means of transportation." K., in turn, thanked us for deigning to visit and invited us back – anytime. Then he said something very interesting, "Perhaps next time, a representative from" - what he said here was unintelligible, but I interpreted it to mean #2, Albert's counterpart on Ta-ea, "will help to adjudicate our understandings."

"That would be . . . welcome," replied Albert.

Kheperkheprure's parting shot was a reminder to us that we weren't the only big kids on the block.

We took a cartouche back to the hangar. As we were entering our conveyance, Albert said, "After you have returned all the higher life forms to their places of origin, you shall leave this Solar System. All traces of Ta'ean culture will also be removed. And you shall accomplish this as my associate has said, as soon as possible."

Kheperkheprure bowed, followed by Bakenkhonsu and Thutmosis. Then he said, "We shall comply. Please permit one question?"

"Yes, of course," replied Albert.

"Why? We had an amicable agreement." Again, a reasonable question. I just hoped Albert wasn't going to blame it all on me because basically, it was all my fault. If I hadn't come along . . .

Albert answered, "Conditions have changed on earth. Mankind is on the brink of discovering the precepts of 4,3 – The Law of Connections. Indeed, Mr. Neufield here has single-handedly done so." They all bowed to me this time. "Further contact and contamination would be disruptive. Soon, surely in less than a thousand years, proper introductions and diplomatic contacts will be established. A new race is about to emerge, and all in the Cosmos shall rejoice." It was Albert's turn to initiate the bowing. His concept of time was certainly different from mine, and I'm sure, from the Pra'at's as well.

After we all bowed again, Kheperkheprure extended his hand, and I clasped it, truly in friendship. The ends of his small mouth were upturned. Was he smiling? I looked at Thutmosis. From within a fold, he presented me with a small voluptuous figurine. It reminded me of Janey.

"Please accept this small remembrance of your sole, contiguous neighbors. We are not alone in this 'Island of Stars,' for we have each other." Then he bowed and extended his hand, and I clasped it, sincerely.

"Thank you, Ky Thutmosis. I shall treasure this always, though I won't need a remembrance, for you and the Pra'at will remain foremost in my memories always."

We all bowed again, and Albert and I boarded our craft, revved her up, and exited the Pra'at Complex.

Upon emerging outside there were no stars above. Our entire field of view, almost to the horizon, was filled with perfect blackness. The deepest darkness I've ever seen, the complete absence of all color and light. Albert had brought the Ship in close. And a 27.38-mile-wide sphere, near enough, will fill the entire sky – a la “Independence Day” – only bigger. Though this time, I noticed some dark blue rippling submerged in the endless black – a nice effect. I assumed Albert wanted to make a point, flex his muscles a little.

The Ship was less than a mile away, so as soon as we left the base, we entered the Hull. There was not much time to chat, but I did get to ask about the Qe'ma u attack.

"It was a miscalculation on the part of some. There are factions within the leadership who do not wish to withdraw from Earth and diminish their quest. Indeed, they would expand the degree of contact. Knowing you to be the key, the deciding factor, an attempt was made to eliminate you. They underestimated the extent of my abilities." He looked at his cane, which he had tucked between the seats.

"And you had the foresight to anticipate this?"

"I simply calculate the probabilities and take appropriate measures."

"And what about our game plan; to just go with the flow?"

"The flow has become a vortex, Jack, swirling faster and faster; a whirlpool of probability, where the confluence of events have begun to collide. Earth is on the brink of metamorphosis, and the Universe has taken notice. I am here to ensure a smooth transition."

"And to make sure we all don't swirl straight down the drain, right Albert?"

"Your interpretations are, as always, most intriguing, Jack. May I suggest, for our last night, that we try something different? Spread a blanket, stake an umbrella, and perhaps have a picnic. Often, I have heard you say these words. I know an interesting place."

"You are the ultimate tour guide, Albert. I eagerly await."

We traversed the Hull and parked our transportation device. Albert escorted me back to my habitat. He said he'd return in a few hours with a special gift. We shook hands and said our goodbyes.

I was home. And a warm glow was kindled inside.

Chapter 22: The Phone Call, Redux – *Jack*

It was early afternoon, and the sun was still high. The rusty old chairs beckoned, and I heeded their call. No hawks were soaring, nor were sparrows darting. It was siesta time. Yet the butterflies still flitted, and the bees busily buzzed, engaged as they were, in their ceaseless tasks. I found that worthy of contemplation. Was life here created or imported? I supposed the latter, importation likely being easier than creation. And once all the components were in place, life is self-sustaining. I mean, that's the definition – self-replicating, self-repairing entities. Albert claims to be capable of self-repair – indefinitely. The foremost design specification of the First-Born who, as we all know – abhor endings. But is he capable of self-replication? An interesting question to add to the already teetering stack.

It was reflection time. I swung my legs up and onto another chair, crossed them, then leaned back. A pair of finches hovered above the pods of a tall thistle. I thought our neighborly visit went well. We hung out the DO NOT DISTURB sign. Albert was right to do the deed nicely, *"everything is so much more pleasant that way."* After all, *we are all civilized*. There was no need for M-16's. Especially since the artifact called Albert could vaporize the base in the blink of an eye, if so desired, having the power of a 'small star,' as he claimed. I had to remind myself fairly often that Albert wasn't some guy I just happened to meet here. Speaking of vaporization, I wondered how the Qe'ma u intended to affect that condition on yours truly. The weaponry they employed, some kind of energy pulses and beams, looked very effective. The Pra'at figured they could get the jump on Albert, a miscalculation to be sure. But no need to get mad, after all, we are all . . . But, just in case they forget, and to add some emphasis, Albert brought the Ship in close for a little fly-by, to rattle the windows. Unfortunately for us, we might get our windows rattled too when Albert's counterpart finds out.

And who am I? How do I fit into all this? I'm Joe Six-Pack; no strike that, I don't like beer all that much. I'm Joe Nobody, who likes to pick up a screwdriver and tinker around. Though, what Albert said about me, "Mr. Neufield here, singlehandedly discovered 4,3". That made me feel good – like somebody important. Only one thing . . . his statement was essentially wrong. Janey and Mr. McEvey were equally involved. It was a joint effort. Poor Janey, tomorrow I'll see what I can do about her. And Mr. McEvey? He was on to something and getting results, too, with "zero-point energy," or Fifth Level Technology as Albert had called it. Knowledge of the Aether, the source of the electric charge. I found that completely fascinating. Mr. McEvey's stuff was still up there on the shelves. I promised him that I'd keep on, keeping on. I got up and went inside.

I heard that familiar knock. It's funny how most people have a knock. A particular identifying staccato, similar to a fingerprint or a retina scan. One could make a study of this, linking knocks to personality types. Sort of like sirens; police vs. fire; I knew this kid once, back in the schoolyard who could always tell . . .

Albert's knock was easy to identify, though mostly by deduction, he, being the only other humanoid within a quarter-million miles, not including the Pra'at, of course. Though that's not exactly true, I remembered those faceless bipeds operating the medical equipment in that endless white expanse where I first woke up.

Albert's arms were full. He was carrying a picnic basket, a blanket, and a beach umbrella with his cane hooked on his arm. I welcomed him and offered to make a fresh pot of coffee. He graciously accepted, to my delight, being a coffee lover. It could be said that I was, at that point, an interstellar connoisseur, having sampled the Pra'at's equivalent – kaiu. You'll love it if you're an Ovaltine aficionado. Albert sat at the table while I whipped up a quick pot and set the cups – the Roswell ones showing pictures of flying aliens. Albert pulled out my phone and placed it on the table.

"We were able to repair the damage."

"Was it in bad shape just like 'the conveyance'?" I asked.

"Yes, Jack, and similarly, we incorporated some useful improvements."

Improvements? I turned it on. It was similar to Janey's, small and white. She loved the FaceTime App. I didn't – too much information. I swiped it a couple of times, same contacts, settings, date, time. But I noticed there was no Wi-Fi.

"What, no Wi-Fi?" I was joking. Albert wasn't.

"We use gravitons for long-distance communication – no time lag. To be precise, they are not subject to the confines of normal Time."

Here we go. It was discombobulation time, again. Gravitons? Not subject to the confines of normal Time? I did not recall Albert mentioning them before. I asked, "Are they something like gravity waves? I thought they were, like, hard to detect?"

"Gravitons are quite different from gravitational waves, Jack. Just as electrons are perturbations within an electromagnetic field, so too are gravitons quanta of excitation, which ripple through a gravitational field. And being manifestations of space-time, not matter-energy, they have no mass and, therefore, are not subject to relativistic confines. There is one drawback, though, they do not fan out, and therefore must be aimed. The solution is – large-scale detection areas."

"Small ball, big catcher's mitt?"

"Precisely Jack, your phone may not have Wi-Fi, but it does have 'Grav-Fi.' The Ship will relay your calls to earth."

I poured the coffee, thanked Albert, and then put my feet up on the corner of the table. I*t was my habitat, wasn't it?* I looked at the phone sitting there on the table. The most valuable phone ever made – crammed full of alien tech. What about the "do not tamper with the bumpkins" edict? This, I did not ask.

"The ole Arthur C. Clarke axiom would apply in this instance, Jack – it would appear to be magic to the . . . 'bumpkins.' Now would be a good time to call Janey. I am sure she would love to hear from you."

And so, I did. Janey answered, and the first thing I did was apologize for not calling sooner. Then I pushed the Face-time button, and she appeared on the screen; her face was a complete mess. Her eyes were red-rimmed and teary, with black drooping stains underneath, and she was in urgent need of a handkerchief. "Hey, what's the matter? You look like you've been to hell and back?"

"Jack, they just told me you were dead!"

"Who told you I was dead?"

"They told me." She panned the camera around this plush boardroom packed with a few dozen big shots, several in uniform. *That was hell.* "I'm at this big meeting with VIPs from all over the country."

"Holy shit, Janey!" They were grilling her big time. Better make that slow roasting. "Tell them it's all my fault." Because it was. "And you might want to mention . . . that the reports of my demise were . . . uh, premature." I looked at Albert in amazement and laughed a little.

"Jack, it looks like you're back at the barn!"

It was my turn to pan the room, "It sure looks that way." In light of her present company, I thought it best to keep it vague. Albert stepped out of view.

"Is there somebody there with you, Jack?" I looked at Albert for approval. He shook his head and signaled "no" with his hands.

"Oh, that's just Albert. He's a new friend. I can't wait for you to meet him." I don't think Albert wanted to become known, certainly not to the whole goddamn country, but I did anyway. Janey went on to say they were treating her OK and told me they wanted to know about "you know what." I told her I was coming soon, then I talked to the room: "I'll give you all something . . . that I think you'll really want to see . . . if you promise to let Janey go . . . and to leave us be." That's all I wanted, and essentially, that's all anybody wants – to be left alone and to be free.

"I better get that in writing, Jack." Janey was pretty freaking far from being free.

Albert drew his forefinger across his throat, the universal cut-off sign, so I said my goodbyes and reminded Janey that I was coming.

Janey was up to her eyebrows in . . . But from the looks of the VIPs in that room . . . the whole damnable government was foaming at the mouth. And it sure as hell wasn't because of our little theft of a few pounds of Cobalt 60. They had deduced that the thing we built negated gravity, and they wanted to know how – really bad.

"You know Albert . . . Janey knows what I know, about 4,3." I did not quantify that statement. "And she knows how we built 'the conveyance.' What if she tells?"

"Then your race will commence its transition to "The Fourth Level" sooner rather than later. And after a suitable interval of adjustment, I will reveal myself – in the form of a delegation and invite mankind to join our Continuum of Species."

"Has any race ever refused to join? I mean, the hard part is coming up with 4,3, right? After that, why do they need you?"

"Implementation, Jack. The Discovery of the theory is difficult, yes. But utilization is even more so. And there are levels of technology beyond the Fourth. We offer guidance and nudge a species in the appropriate directions. However, we do not simply disseminate knowledge. That is not our way. And this is only one of the benefits of membership. Also, there is our law and philosophy, which ensures maximum comity and actualization. All species welcome membership, Jack."

"Should I turn the thing in tomorrow? I said I would."

"You said, 'you will give them something that you think they will really want to see.' That was ambiguous, Jack, and could mean many things."

"But do you think I should . . . give it to them?"

"Three earth days ago, you arrived here in your transportation device. One in which you had incorporated 4th level principles. It was determined then that you could leave in that same device. Regrettably, as a quasi- provisional member, you are prohibited from interfering in sub-fourth level civilizations. The penalty for doing so is expulsion."

"This is my thinking, Albert, I give mankind the device, then they'll learn about 4,3. And, as a consequence, get invited into the Continuum. Being an outstanding citizen of earth, said invitation would include me. So, I'd get kicked out than re-invited back in. Bing, bang, boom!"

"Your prognostication of future events is in error, Jack, though it was a nice try. The operative words of my prior statement were 'after a suitable interval of adjustment.' For the Pra'at, that interval encompassed approximately – 1.48 thousand years."

1.48 thousand years! So much for my 'thinking.' I was tripped up by our different concepts of time. As one would expect from a, who knows how old, immortal, and sentient artifact. *C'est la vie.*

"I take what you just said to mean – if I give them the thing, I can't come back?" I gave it one last shot.

"Logic would dictate that Jack, for many reasons. Not the least being, you would no longer have 'said transportation' – i.e., a means of coming back. I promised you a picnic for our last night. Shall we?" He motioned towards the door.

Chapter 23: The First-Born – *Jack*

We strolled along the drive. Deferring to age, I carried the heavier items, the picnic basket, and the umbrella. Albert carried the blanket and strutted along with his cane. Was he expecting another ambush? We entered the sidewalk tunnels. I recalled the last time we did and the view from the balcony.

"Do these cloudy sidewalks always have to be so gray?"

"No, Jack, not at all. As you saw during our previous excursion, there is a network of these walkways or 'arteries' as you called them, connecting the major areas of the Ship. These conduits are very versatile and can be transformed to conduct whatever is required. Shall I increase the transparency? Do you want to look around?"

"Why not, Albert? I'm a tourist here, as you very well know."

The consistency of the grayness changed. It became semi-transparent, though cloudy wisps remained. Just enough to impart a sense of security, not like before. The interior structure of the Ship once again came to view. It was an unforgettable vision. Huge irregular masses, dimly glowing with subtle, indistinct colors and connected by a tangle of various sized ducts, some humongous in diameter. The surrounding spaces rippled with auroras of blue and green. Permeating all was the bass rumble of monstrous forces. A perceptible vibration felt deep in the chest.

"I think I prefer this view, compared to the gray cocoon. Though, my first sight of your mm, interior, may have sent me a bit over the edge, not literally, of course."

"We want you to feel at home here, Jack, and certainly not, 'over the edge,' literally or figuratively."

After the phone call and seeing the faces of all those big guns in that room, I figured this was pretty much the only home I had left. Now here's the interesting part, it was exactly like my home, only a quarter-million miles away.

By this time, I was getting curious as to where we were going, "Albert, I have the utmost confidence in your talents as a tour guide. You have proven your ability to astound many times. Still, I must ask, where are we going?"

"Another habitat, Jack. Several here are permanent fixtures – such as the one we traversed on your first day, the one you mentally labeled 'Candy Land.' This one should prove as interesting."

"How many races can be considered 'First-Born' Albert? And please don't feel obligated to answer. I know I am just a . . . quasi semi-whatever."

At this, Albert chuckled. "You are very significant to us, Jack. And I have governing restraints, which cannot be breached – not even for . . . friendship. There are several thousand species that can be termed 'First-Born.' And many thousands more who are in the advanced stages of 'ascension' . . . still acquiring higher levels of understanding. Those who would feel at home in our intended destination are carbon-based, though bearing some dissimilarities in their nucleotides. The phosphate in their DNA structure has been replaced with a sulfate. And they are not humanoid like the Pra'at but rather insectoid. Throughout their formative years, they were forced to evolve in an environment of increasing adversity as their home star slowly expanded. The oceans boiled off, the atmosphere dried out, and the planet simmered in a constant rain of radiation. Over time they adapted and overcame, largely by moving underground. Behold, we are entering the habitat of the . . ." Here, Albert clucked his tongue and clicked his teeth, making an unintelligible noise. "For our purposes, we shall call this august species – the Bre-eie-ee. Though that name bears little resemblance to what they call themselves, in their native . . . means of communication."

We approached a scene that resembled a Hieronymus Bosch painting. It was Hell. Literally. We entered on a modest plateau, which afforded an extensive view of a vast reddish plain. All shades of red: some light bordering on tan, others dark maroon. Breaking up the reds were streaks of powder blue, lateral bands that zigzagged this way and that. The combination of reds and blues was not altogether unsightly. Bulging upwards were small groupings of mounts. Not full-blown mountains, just the tops. Most spewed forth hazy, bluish gasses, too thin to be called smoke. Fumaroles also dotted the landscape. Jagged crater-like openings that glowed orange and red. In some, the molten lava could be seen. These too emitted bluish fumes, some of which collected about their rocky base like a ghostly fog.

In the distance was a huge amorphous structure that resembled a giant, dark-red termite mound. Irregular arching shapes connected the various lobes. At random intervals, malformed arms jutted forth. Surrounding this were several lesser versions of same. It was a colony or city fashioned by an assemblage of alien architecture – alien in the extreme.

Above floated two celestial bodies. One was large and reddish orange with random splotchings of yellow. It must have been designed to emulate their home star. Nearby and off to the left was a small, dull red moon, reflecting the color of its light-emitting neighbor. The upper atmosphere itself was black except for an irregular slash of scarlet, which streaked diagonally across the sky. It was not a cloud formation, more like a glowing band of gas – a nebula. My one thought was – how the hell could anything live here?

"The DNA molecule enables a wide range of adaptability, Jack."

"And theirs has more sulfur?"

"Yes, Jack, that particular modification evolved here. The non-bridging phosphorus molecules were replaced by sulfur in certain sequences on the spiral backbone in both their DNA and RNA molecules. You have on earth analogous genomes in the marine organisms that inhabit the localities adjoining undersea vents. Shall we spread the blanket and stake the umbrella?"

"Yes, of course." I proceeded to do so. "Compared to the Moon, the one that circles the Earth, this place does have . . . some serious variety." Just then, a swarm of bat-like creatures flew by: "Presumably, we're enclosed here by some type of protective shield?"

"Yes, Jack. There is a barrier, which contains your life support parameters fed by the entry tunnel. You would not last long breathing the indigenous atmosphere. However, the reduced gravity might prove amusing."

We sat on the blanket, and Albert dispersed the contents of the basket. First the wine glasses, then the wine – a bottle of Liebfraumilch. I love German wine, especially in the summer – chilled, not cold. But of course, Albert knew that.

The main dish was Southern Fried Chicken with a side of potato salad and a wedge of cheese, Jarlsberg. Plus, apple pie for dessert. The perfect menu for an outdoor dining excursion. I commented, "A better meal I could not have ordered at the Ritz, and the ambiance? I could use the word heavenly . . . only it's the opposite."

"I'm glad everything meets with your approval. Shall we?" Albert poured the wine and handed me a paper plate. I helped myself to generous portions of everything. Speaking of 'out of this world,' the chicken was inhumanly good.

"Excellent chicken, Albert, did you Google that recipe too?"

"As a matter of fact, Jack, I did. Would you care for a short discourse on that subject?"

"I would, Albert. Everything you say usually scores a 10 on the interest meter.

"Why, thank you, Jack. The first codified preparation of fowl . . .

"But, if you could 'discourse' on the beings who lived here uh . . . in this . . ." I had interrupted Albert with my mouth full.

"Certainly, Jack. I can understand why that would eclipse your interest in avian cuisine."

A large semi-transparent screen appeared. On it was the embodiment of a Bre-eie-ee. The viewpoint slowly panned, revealing the most alien-looking creature I have ever seen. It was insectoid, as Albert had said, and looked like a cross between an ant and a centaur. There was the main body, about 4-5 feet in length, which was composed of four segmented legs, each ending with sharp pointy hooks. At the posterior were two barbed appendages, pincers. And between the front legs was what appeared to be a stinger. Many interlocking dark plates overlaid the exterior areas, with tufts of reddish-brown hair bristling in places underneath. Like a centaur, the thorax, the frontal part, projected upwards. Two multi-jointed arms extended from the shoulders, terminating with three fingers and an opposing thumb. Thus, satisfying one of Albert's rules for sentient life – the ability to manipulate objects.

I saved the best part for last – the V-shaped head. In the front bulged two very large compound eyes. Being closely spaced, most likely, they afforded the being with binocular vision. There was nothing resembling a nose and towards the base of the triangular face was a group of beak-like mouthparts. I chose not to envision the entity's culinary activities. For facial skin, it, too, was covered by hard segmented armor. From the front section of the skull projected two antennae, multi-articulated and about three feet in length. Oh, did I forget to mention the wings? They were small for their size, semi-transparent, veined, and folded back. Probably quite useful in an area of low gravity. Like here.

That was my first view of a First-Born. A member of the 2.37-billion-year-old Continuum of civilizations responsible for building Albert and millions more like him. I had to ask myself – is this what a god looks like? And, as I looked around – is this heaven? The display vanished, and I was glad.

"You asked, Jack. And I was not prohibited from disclosing the image." Surely Albert had discerned my astonishment. "Would you rather we talk about chicken recipes?"

"No . . . uh . . . do you have any footage on how . . . how they lived, like day-to-day?" My curiosity would someday result in my undoing.

The screen reappeared and displayed a cluster of stars within a galaxy. The picture zoomed in to a solar system. The star in the center was a red giant, a dying star that had lost its war with fusion and gravity. Fusion won. We sped past a few enormous gaseous planets and several cold naked asteroids. We stopped at a crimson planet. It was marbled with orange and coupled to a dismal and lesser version of itself. Its only moon. Our descent continued as we swung around to the light side. It was bathed in a dim ruddy glow.

Albert began his oration, "This scene depicts their homeworld as it once was. The Bre-eie-ee are a collective species with group intelligence. There is no individuality among them. Survival of the group has always been their primary concern, superseding all else – reproduction, longevity, even comfort. Eventually, they learned the tenets of science and used that knowledge to escape the impending doom of their homeworld. A commendable feat."

Our perspective changed as we entered the atmosphere. A swarm of what looked like immense flying spiders cruised by. "And they built starships, Jack. Not the kind you see in the movies, to use one of your favorite references." They had a rounded dome-like central structure surrounded by ten or twelve legs. No, tentacles would be a better word; their curvature was continuous, and they moved independently. The domes themselves glowed a mottled red, in contrast to the appendages, which were dark except for the tips, some of which emitted a dull yellow luminosity.

The picture on the screen continued to plunge downward, eventually closing in on a group of mounds bridged by a muddle of shapeless, intersecting connections. The air was alive with masses of . . . flying beings? Devices? Entities? The ground was also a living lacework of crawling things, armies of them streaming forth, coming from God knows where. *Strike the God reference.* And swarms of every manner of nightmare were flying in and out of irregular, dark apertures.

"The Bre-eie-ee chose the organic path to technical advancement, as opposed to the inorganic. They elected to build with living materials, unlike most races. And, as such, they have mastered the development of self-replicating molecules."

"What do you mean, 'they build with living materials'?"

"When possible, they prefer to grow instead of build, though they manufacture by ordinary means as well, with inanimate materials. For example, those flying craft you saw as we approached are alive, sentient, and part of the hive, part of the group mind, if you will. Shall we take a peek underground? That is where the majority of their activity takes place."

"Thanks, but no thanks, Albert. Just what was that chicken recipe you said you used?" I had had enough – of the Bre-eie-ee, not the chicken.

Albert actually began to deliberate on the domestication of fowl. He should have known that that was the last thing I wanted to talk about.

The Universe is a strange place. A truth I learned from our non-terrestrial picnic. How wonderful everything would be, could be, if we learned the secrets. But where were we? In a habitat that once represented the home of the Bre-eie-ee, a super-advanced race of immortals, members of a very exclusive club – the First-Born. The landscape was hellish, and frankly, so were the beings. The Pra'at, their fantastic cities, and saucer-shaped starships better represented the utopia of my dreams. Only one problem; they needed human guinea pigs to rack up their quest for immortality. But I had to admit, building with living tissue, now that was something impressive. I inquired further on this subject.

"Yes, Jack, that is their preferred mode of synthesis, especially if one chooses to . . . build-in intelligence. Indeed, many of the components of myself, this structure you call the Ship, have been organically . . . propagated. For example, my hull was gradually accreted in a process that resembles growth."

"Were you, yourself, grown, Albert?" The question was impertinent for sure, but I had to ask.

"Yes, Jack, 'grown' would be a semi-accurate summarization of the processes that created the animate object you call Albert." *Again, the clarity of lead-plate.* "However, my intelligence is collective. That is the advantage of organic technology."

Throughout all this, I had quaffed a couple of glasses of wine; three pieces of chicken – dark meat; a reasonably large portion of potato salad, with parsley, no dill; and a good-sized chunk of cheese. I was sated gastronomically and intellectually. I was overloaded intellectually, truth be told. It was a picnic I'd have no trouble remembering.

It had been a long day. My last day. And I was sad to leave. Albert had succeeded in one of his goals – making me feel at home here.

"Albert, I'm a little nervous about flying 'my conveyance' back to Earth tomorrow. Do you have any last-minute pointers?"

"You should have no difficulty, Jack. You have demonstrated an adequate level of operational proficiency. Once outside, just fly past the Moon and when you see the Earth, steer towards it. Next, engage the cruise control and then sit back and enjoy the view. The conveyance will constantly accelerate. At a distance of 2000 miles, slow down to 500 mph, and accordingly, enter the Earth's atmosphere."

"That's all?"

"That is all, Jack. Just don't forget to use the brakes. As you know, this version of your device incorporates that feature."

"No parachute?"

"You won't need one."

"I think I'd feel more secure if I had one. I mean, cars have spare tires, don't they?"

"Then you shall have one, Jack." Albert placated my irrational insecurities.

At this point, we both took some much-needed breathing space and finished off the delectable cuisine still left on our plates. Although Albert did most of the talking, he chowed down a respectable share of the feast. The picnic was thoroughly delightful. Though 'delightful' may not be the best word to describe the Bre-eie-ee and their homeworld. When the outing was over, and as we were packing up, a stream of white crab-like creatures streamed from a nearby fissure. Each about the size of a small pizza. Their legs were moving like crazy while their mouthparts desperately gnawed at our enclosure. Soon the entire zone around us was covered in a white writhing mass of nightmarish lice-like insects.

Albert commented on this, "We allow some indigenous species to co-exist as part of the ecological balance. They are a component of the habitat here, similar to the sparrows in yours."

They were pretty freaking far from being sparrows.

We entered the gray tunnel. It was no longer semi-transparent. Albert had correctly deduced my surfeited intellectual condition. We said our goodbyes as Albert delivered me to my habitat . . . my home. I felt privileged to have one. The Sun was setting, the Moon was rising, the stars shimmered, and my rusty old lawn chair awaited the implantation of my posterior. I readily obliged. Day three had come and gone. Time was hard to compute in this place. So much happened, so fast. Let's see, day one – spaghetti dinner, day two – lasagna dinner, and today the picnic. And what else did we do today? Oh yeah, we had lunch with the Pra'at and then evicted them - from the Solar System. Did we save humanity? Who knows? But we did eat well. I'll probably pay for it with "accelerated senescence."

And the picnic was nice. All right, so it was in Hell, but we were protected. My delusion of the First-Born being these wonderful heavenly beings . . . turned out to be just that . . . a delusion. The fact that the Bre-eie-ee were only one of several thousand species, collectively termed the First-Born, did mitigate the shock, though.

I was to go home. Frankly, I was ambivalent about that. If it wasn't for Janey . . . for certain, I'd stay a while longer. Though events were in motion, swirling around faster and faster, or so Albert had said. All I could do was – go with the flow, and you know . . . try not to get flushed.

The scratchy clicks of the cicadas pierced the night, accompanied by the sporadic chirrups of a cricket. Every once in a while, the evening quietude was punctured by the call of a night bird. It was time for the solace of sleep. I went inside, tramped up the rickety old stairs, stripped down, and hit the mattress. But not before watching some TV. Funny, it worked.

Interlude 4: It Turned

It is said that information cannot be destroyed. Stating an absolute in a tricky Universe is, for sure, asking for trouble. But assume the statement is generally true. What does it mean? It means that one event triggers another, which makes something else happen, and then something else again – ad infinitum. Basically, for every action, there is a reaction. Something Newton codified centuries ago. A butterfly flaps its wings, the air currents change the course of a mold spore. It lands in a Petri dish and is observed by Dr. Fleming, who invents penicillin. Humans live longer and venture forth into the Cosmos. Everything affects everything else. That is called information. It spreads and cannot be stopped. And, given enough data, the chain can be backtracked – back to the butterfly. Theoretically.

An interesting corollary concerns energy. It cannot be created or destroyed in a closed system. And the Universe is a closed system. This is another absolute that one should be cautious of. Technically, everything that was initially part of the Big Bang is still here, somewhere. And don't forget – matter and energy are equivalent. We know this thanks to Albert Einstein, the original one.

The third factor which must be brought forth for the purposes of our discussion is entropy. What is entropy? Answer: it's the second law of thermodynamics. And basically, it states that energy equalizes; it tends to spread out. A glass of cold water in a warm room will eventually warm, and the room will cool a little. That's due to entropy, and it's just the way the Universe works.

What's my point? The point is, events happen and, as a consequence, those happenings create reactions which, in due course, spread out – further and further. The big question is – where does this chain reaction end? Answer: at the edge of the Cosmos, where else? The Great Barrier. All information stops there and leaves its imprint. A record of all that has transpired, every flutter of our butterfly's wings is recorded there.

Until now. There was no trace left of the perfidy perpetrated by the "Others." The punching of 1.27 billion tunnels in the Progenitor's Outer Husk. For what purpose was this malevolent deed perpetrated? This was the logical question that had to be asked. Answer: to change its critical density via the injection of large quantities of various forms of energy. But there was no record of the deed. No traces, no clues. Though this was, in itself, evidence of what we were dealing with – an entity indigenous to the Aether with the power to destroy information and the power to destroy Universes as well. This was a wake-up call for all those living in Pleasantville, the locus of the First-Born.

Among the First-Born, there are thousands of different species. But someone had to come first, the first of the First-Born. The Eldest were the Ang, and it was, at this time, a collective consciousness. It commanded, "Define the results."

"Closure of the tunnel points is 72.3 percent complete. No new breaches have been detected." This answer was provided by the First Observer, the one who made the initial discoveries. His standing had risen; indeed, the entity had even acquired a certain celebrity status.

"Specify damage extent."

"Dark Energy accretion has expanded by a factor of 19.32 $x10^{-33}$ percent. Confinement shall continue as scheduled; insignificant damage will result. However, . . . the energy is degenerative."

"At what rate does it degenerate?"

"The rate is exponential."

This confirmed malicious intent. The First-Born had divined a plan for the Cosmos. Promote expansion to a certain point, then slow it down to a nice steady state for eternity. It was a good plan. How it was divined, that's another story. And somebody just threw a monkey wrench in it. The forced influx of these particular types of dark energy, if unchecked, would result in a universal decrease in density. As a consequence, the Macrocosm would expand at an ever-increasing rate until it ripped itself apart. Every last atom. Also, false vacuums would form.

Another voice emanated. Younger and brighter, with a deep penetrating penumbra, "Why does this Entity seek to destroy our Progenitor?"

The First One replied, "Unknown; this we must discern."

And the fibrils of the Old Ones were extended. The Younger Ones, the Observers, and the Implementers entered their ships and ventured forth. A new design, "Orbs," as they were called. And they journeyed far, farther than ever before. Mapping the Manifolds, the clouds of elemental materials, setting up monitoring beacons, and early warning systems. Nothing discernible would be able to sneak past again. After a while, they noticed something. A Manifold had turned, and it turned towards . . . Pleasantville.

Chapter 24: The Federal Penitentiary – Danbury – *Janey*

I was put in a real cell this time. No more comfy and humane detention for me. Though I must admit, I'm no expert on detention. I've never even had the after-school kind. However, I pissed off Ms. Civil, Special Assistant to the President, and exercising the full might and authority of the most powerful office in the world, she had me transferred to a genuine federal prison. They took away my things and made me wear a jumpsuit. It was orange. My least favorite color. In most of the prison TV shows I've seen the convicts usually wear orange. Maybe for some psycho-crap reason. Though it's likely, the shrinks just want to ratchet up the punishment. But if the prison authorities really wanted to make someone suffer – they'd make them wear pink and orange, say – stripes. Yeesh! But any judge would deem that cruel and unusual punishment, and it would probably violate the Geneva Convention as well. Though, as an interesting sidenote, I heard of this Sheriff in Arizona who makes his convicts wear pink panties. Grown men. Now that's sick. I tend to go with the white myself.

I guess it's a typical cell – six feet by ten, concrete block walls, a stainless-steel, toilet-sink combo. The darn thing was genuinely ingenious and easy to figure out. There was a bunk and a shelf and no window. The walls were painted dark green on the bottom, light green on top, with the ceiling some shade of off-white. Next to the toilet-sink combo was a small steel table and chair – no cushion. On it, they left a yellow pad and a pen. You'll never guess what I'm doing. Boredom is the ultimate enemy and motivator.

At least I was close to home, here in Danbury, CT. My parents could easily come and visit. Maybe even move nearby since the Feds probably took their farm. Yes, we would be one big happy family.

After the big "Pow Wow," Robert and Jamal brought me back to my room at Homeland Security. We were all rather disconcerted by what had transpired up there. I'm sure Robert was thinking about where to apply for a new job and Jamal . . . his forthcoming court-martial. We talked about everything except what happened . . . the weather, their favorite vacation spots – Robert liked the Jersey Shore, Jamal liked the casinos. There's a couple of them upstate. I never figured Jamal for a gambler. This oblique conversation served the purpose of pleasantly passing the time since we all assumed the van was bugged.

Later that afternoon, the boys came back and escorted me to the "Federal Correctional Institution – Danbury." That was the official name of my new home sweet home. There was nothing "sweet" about it. After we arrived, we all, most regretfully, said our goodbyes. I gave them both a hug. Not being members of the State Prison Employees Union, they could no longer attend to my "requirements." Though Robert said I was technically still his case and that he would check in on me often. Having the boys' friendship made me feel a bit better. It was nice to have friends. And I was forced to face a new reality . . . my life had radically changed. My old friends, gone. My job, gone. Even my parents were gone, maybe, though certainly not happy. But not Jack, he was coming. That was the one remaining constant. Still, my life would never be the same. I could not go back. I thought these thoughts as I entered a federal prison.

I had another friend in this new life – Winston "Sandy" Erhart the Third, and before I had even settled in, he paid me a visit. Sure, he had an agenda. Who doesn't? I do. I want to get out, the same as most cons. How quickly one's viewpoint changes; I was already thinking like a "con."

The visitors' section was rather civilized. No glass windows and telephones, like in the movies. Just a room full of tables and chairs. Winston stood when he saw me, waved, and pulled out a chair. On the table was a notepad and a laptop computer – open. A video from the "Pow-Wow" was playing.

As soon as I sat, he motioned to the video, "Well, that could have gone better." It was interesting; there was no small talk. We got right to it.

"At least I found out about Jack, and that was my goal."

"But what, specifically, did you learn, Jane? That he's comfortably sipping coffee up at his barn in Litchfield? We both know that's not real. And what about his phone call? It was untraceable, impossible to triangulate. And who's his new best friend . . . Albert? No, Janey, we did not learn anything about Jack. And now, we have more questions than when we started." Throughout his little speech, true to form, Winston was smiling. And it wasn't phony. He was a nice and likable guy.

"I found out what I wanted to know – that Jack's alive and well. 'Reports of my demise are a little premature.'" We both laughed at my imitation of Jack. I continued, "Wherever, or however he's alive, I don't care. And you'll get what you want too, Winston. He's coming in . . . tomorrow, and he's going to give you 'something you'll really want to see.'"

"Something tells me it's not going to be all that easy, Jane – there's a little voice warning that trouble's brewing." Winston waxed poetic.

"Well, Jack's 'little voice' said he's coming in, and that's good enough for me. Strike that! It wasn't some 'little voice' whispering in my ear. It was the Halleluiah Choir singing from the mountain top."

After a short pause, "I envy you, Jane, for having found your true love."

"I wasn't looking, Winston, we were neighbors, and it just happened."

"Sometimes I think the Universe steps in and plays with the odds. Nudging events to come together, collide and even . . . overlap in strange ways . . . for a higher purpose. Forgive me; I tend to muse at times."

"No forgiveness is necessary. In a way, you remind me of Jack – talking about the big picture – the Universe and how everything fits together."

"You mean like . . . 4,3?

Now it was my turn to pause. My parting words, "you don't deserve 4,3", lingered in my mind and . . . I should never have said them. That was a judgment call that was not mine to make. It was Jack's. He came up with 4,3. Yes, I was there, but still, it was something that clicked in his brain, not mine. Sure, Mr. McEvey and I were there to talk it out, the theory that is. Plus, we worked out the math. And I know that what we learned barely scratched the surface . . . of the big picture. The pause had become a hiatus. The smile on Winston's face relaxed, his eyebrows elevated, and his head canted in concern.

"Thinking whether to tell me the secret?"

"I should never have said those words, '4,3' . . . back there. It wasn't my call to make. It was Jack's, or maybe ours. But not mine."

"Not even a hint?"

"From what I heard you say before, you shouldn't need any more 'hints,' Sandy."

Sandy thought hard, assessing, and collating the details of what was just said: "Think big . . . and 4,3. I thank you, Jane. You have narrowed the search considerably." Now it was his turn to pause, "You just called me 'Sandy' . . ."

"Dualism . . . everything is dualistic. That was one of Mr. M's mantras. And you, Sir, are both Winston and Sandy. I called you Sandy before because . . . I felt you were . . . Sandy then."

"And you, too, are dualistic Miss Riley. Sometimes you're Janey, and sometimes you're Jane."

I laughed and said, "As long as you don't call me Esther!"

There was another pause, which grew awkward, "When this thing we're going through is over, and someday soon it will be, I was hoping that I could see you, as a friend? Do you think that would be possible, Jane?"

"4,3 tells us that anything's possible, Sandy." The silence grew awkward. Winston's smile dissipated, but not his eyes. Like gravity, they pulled me in. His hand inched closer to mine.

A guard motioned to us. Our time was up. We hastily and a little embarrassed, said our goodbyes after a quick little hug. It just happened – *first contact.* Then the guard took me back to my cell.

On the way back, we passed a few dormitory areas occupied by diverse, hard people. Why do I rate jeers and catcalls, I wondered? They must know I'm new and were giving the 'fish' a hard time. Hey, I'm doing "hard time." I secretly gave thanks for the luxury of a private cell. My keepers, no doubt, did not want me to get "messed up." Was I beginning to learn the lingo, perhaps by osmosis? For Christ's sake, it's only been a couple of hours. But my private cell sure seemed more and more like the sanctuary of home. Just the thought imparted *a warm feeling inside.* Einstein was right. It's all relative.

Unfortunately for me, the peace was not to last. I had another visitor. This time it was Alysha Civil, Special Assistant to the blah, blah. I suppose it did make me feel important. Lil' ole me being visited by a presidential advisor. The visitor's room was empty. They must have cleared the place for such an esteemed personage. And there she was, standing by a table with her entourage. Essentially, they consisted of two types; the security people who wore suits and sunglasses, and the aides – the young pups with rolled-up sleeves and "eager to please" attitudes.

Alysha wore a phony, sugary-sweet smile, betrayed by her cold, dark eyes. I responded to the thrust of her demeanor with a blast from Blank Jane, quarter-smile, elevated brows, and mindless eyes. Though alone, I felt her equal.

"Miss Riley," she extended both arms as if to give me a hug. I maintained an appropriate distance. Her hug morphed into a gesture towards a seat. She was smooth, very smooth, "Please have a seat." She actually pulled one out for me. I sat in it, thinking it would be awkward as hell if I were the only one sitting. But Ms. Civil joined me and sat in the opposite chair. Everyone else remained standing.

“I think we may have gotten off on the wrong foot earlier. But dramatic events can do that. Please permit me . . . to go about . . . starting anew.” Once a pauser, always a pauser.

I nodded and gestured for her to continue.

“The National Security Council has tasked me with . . . discovery. Finding out what you and Mr. Neufield . . . may I call him Jack?” I nodded. “What you and Jack built up there in your barn. Our satellites recorded 'the thing' going straight up, with no heat signature. And it did not come back.”

“How can you be so sure it didn’t come back? You were there when Jack called, and you saw where he called from.”

“Yes, the Neufield Anomaly is most assuredly, an anomaly, something unusual or unexpected. And the definition of ‘unexpected’ keeps expanding.” She motioned to an aide, and he set up a laptop. It displayed a recording of Jack’s phone call, the whole scene. I looked embarrassingly bad, face a mess, all red and swollen. And then I saw myself say, “Jack, it looks like you’re back at the Barn.” Jack responded by scanning his surroundings and saying, rather cryptically, I then realized, “It sure looks that way.”

“We both know that Jack was not at the barn, in the barn . . . or anywhere near that goddamn barn . . .” Her pauses were quite effective in heightening the emphasis; of course, blasphemy always helps.

“But it sure looked like he was.” It was fun dancing around the dragon.

"Yes, indeed. However, I'm not here to discuss the unknowns. I'm here to consider the 'knowns' – specifically what you know. And we know . . . that you know . . . everything."

Our little tete-a-tete was devolving.

"Can't you wait for Jack? He said he was coming in, tomorrow or the next day."

"We would like both of you to co-operate, for the good of the nation . . . for the greater good of all mankind!"

"Did you bring that piece of paper I requested? The one absolving Jack and me of all crimes – the Cobalt 60 theft and so forth . . . signed by the President?" I threw in that last part, 'signed by the President', for good measure. "And Alysha – may I call you Alysha?" She did not nod. "Our new start, from here – a Federal Prison, is not exactly the kind of 'start' I would like to, er . . . start from."

My statement must have flustered and annoyed Alysha in that her sweet mask turned a slight shade of red.

A considerable interlude elapsed. I thought I saw radiant heat waves emanating, but she managed to regain control.

"An executive pardon is being drafted, and your accommodations . . . I'm sure will improve . . . if you co-operate."

The devolution of our amity was, at this point, in free fall. Gravity, the downward kind, had taken hold. Next stop – Hell.

It occurred to me that any pardon could be un-pardoned. Is there such a word? Can the President undo something he did? Who's to say no? A judge somewhere, and what's he going to do – put the Prez in a cell somewhere? The one next to mine is empty.

I continued, "When Jack comes, let's meet again. He said he'd bring 'something you'd really want to see.' Then, we will enthusiastically share what we have learned if you bring that piece of paper. And be sure to include something in there saying you won't take our farms." I had to include both mine and Jack's in the deal.

"If Jack comes in, and all happens as you say . . . you will be released from custody. If not . . . well then . . . 'fun time' will begin." With that, she stood. An aid scrambled to stow the notebook. And, without another word, Alysha Civil, Special Assistant to the President for whatever, and her entourage left.

A guard escorted me back to my cell, past the jeers and leers of my fellow convicts.

Chapter 25: Earthbound – *Jack*

I slept well. Maybe it's the air, or maybe it's the water? Could it be by design? Add a pinch of this, perhaps a dash of that? Something to keep the natives in line, so they'll feel *"more at home here"*? No way. Albert said he's incapable of deception. And I believe him. Still, I did sleep well.

I was going home. It seemed like events had lined up like dominoes and were cascading, one at a time. Whether due to the pure random drift of chaos or not, I do not know. But things were in motion, and for me, the next stop was – Earth. Case closed. I got up, quickly dressed, made some coffee, and wolfed down a bowl of cereal. Then stepped outside, took a deep breath, and plunked back down on a lawn chair, swinging one leg over the armrest. I was partial to the light blue one. Some paint had valiantly resisted the onslaught of entropy. It was comfortable, almost unnaturally so. I'm sure the original intent was to match the natural contours of the human shape. Over the decades, it had sagged and bent to perfection, an excellent example of the settling down of the Universe.

Albert wasted no time. His familiar form jauntily stepped and caned his way down the lane. He had dressed for the occasion – dark checkered blazer, light brown pants and vest, winged collar, and a blue cravat. A straw hat crowned his head, and for shoes, he wore the orange and white two-toned lace-ups. The height of casual elegance, I'm sure. And for the coup de grâce, his cane matched his shoes – orange staff, bone handle. He was the epitome of dapper – circa 1910.

"You'll have to give me the name of your tailor, Albert, and I hope we're not having a going away party."

"No party, Jack, but I did dress for the send-off."

I felt like a real jerk, wearing the same clothes for the second day – a Tesla tee-shirt, jeans, and sneakers. My bureau was full. I had other options. I read somewhere that Einstein always wore the same clothes, claiming: "That way I have more time to think about more important things." I tended to concur.

"Is there anything you want to bring with you?"

I remembered Thutmosis's statue. I ran inside, up the stairs, and there it was, on the bureau. It reminded me of Janey. Suddenly, I felt like going home again, too bad I didn't have one, most likely. As I flew down the stairs, I paused for one last look around. Sitting on the shelf were Mr. McEvey's gizmos. There were many bizarre rigs. The one I liked best had antennas configured around a gyroscopic figure-eight coil. And there were others – the objective was to extract energy from the Aether. We know it's there, from the Casimir effect, the Lamb shift, and the background hum of the Big Bang itself. And Albert had confirmed the concept. He called it Fifth Level Technology. Was that a nudge? That last glance reminded me that I had promises to keep . . . to Mr. M, to Janey . . . to Albert? Those were my last thoughts as I walked out the door. Then.

Albert was sitting in my blue chair outside. He stood and said, "Are you ready to depart?" I noticed some rust on the back of his pants. He looked, reached around, and brushed it off.

Whoever invented the word ambivalent must have had me in mind. I gazed across the field; the morning mist was gently rising in the first rays of the rising sun. The sparrows were cheeping, and a hawk lazily soared. It was too early for the butterflies. "Lead on kemosabe."

"That word, 'kemosabe'? It is unknown to me Jack . . . would you care to explain?"

"In the early days of television, there was a western series titled 'The Lone Ranger.' He was a lawman who wore a mask. His Indian sidekick, Tonto, called him 'kemosabe.' It meant 'friend' in his native language." As we stepped into the tube, I took one last look. The hawk dipped a wing and twirled. Albert cracked a slight smile but kept on walking.

"Friendship is a concept . . . an attribute of humankind that I have been able to assimilate to a limited extent, thanks to you, Jack. However, I do not wear a mask."

"Why, thank you, Albert. I consider you to be a friend as well . . . if that's what you meant. But are you as you present yourself?"

"I am what you see."

The mask was off our tube as well. It was transparent again. I guess for one last look-see. My eyes devoured the view. There was so much to explore, so much to learn, and no more time.

Albert carried on a monologue of do's and don'ts, make sure's and don't forget's: ". . . you won't need any maps, just steer towards the Earth . . . and remember; with the auto-stabilization, attitude and orientation will be no problem and . . . use your rear-view mirror." At that time, I did not understand the rear-view mirror admonition. But basically, what it all amounted to was – step on the gas and steer towards Earth. It should be easier than driving a car.

We arrived at the hangar. The endless rows of black spheres, all sizes, all kinds. And then there were the clear ones, many glowed with a light blue radiance inside. The fleet. How I wanted to take one out, do a little globetrotting. Yes, globetrotting, i.e., hopping from globe to globe. *After all, 'most everything in the Universe is round.* We walked some distance, then came to my thing, our thing. In reality, truth be told – little of it was mine, or ours, or anybody else's. It was Albert's. And it was chock full of alien technology. What about our little prohibition: no tampering with the aborigines? I kept my mouth shut on that score. Again.

Anyway, there it was. And I was to be in it and on my own.

Albert opened the door for me. I just stood there. He had been explaining how to traverse the hull: "Do nothing, the Ship will take you through. And remember, before you enter the Earth's atmosphere, slow down. Maximum speed – 500 mph. Use the brakes, Jack."

Albert extended his hand, and we shook, then he clasped his other hand over mine and said, "Jack, I shall also be leaving."

"What! What do you mean – 'you shall also be leaving'?" We unclasped our hands.

"I have been called away on another . . . undertaking."

Will it never end, the discombobulation? "You've been here for some 270 million years, and now you've been called away? And just as Earth is about to transition to the Fourth Level?" I was totally flabbergasted, even more so than usual.

"Please allow me to reiterate. The First-Born have collectively assumed certain responsibilities. To nurture the

'Children' – those who came after; and to care for the 'Parent' – that which came before."

"Who's the 'Parent' . . . their 'Parent'?" My interruption was evidence of my loss of control.

"That which came before, 'the Parent,' is the Progenitor, our Universe. The entity from which all indigenous life springs, and of which, we all are part."

"The Universe? You speak of it as though it was some kind of a living presence."

"We are living, Jack, or at least, you are. And there are those who profess that the Universe cannot be less than the sum of its parts . . . also alive, but a different kind of conscious awareness."

There was a long pause. I checked my pockets: wallet, phone, Thutmosis's statue. It was time to move on. I just asked, "Where will you be going, Albert?"

"To repair damage to the Great Barrier, the outer husk of the Progenitor. All assets, such as myself have been marshaled for this massive endeavor."

"What the Hell can damage the Universe?"

"Your question is a very large unknown, Jack. But you and all we know will cease to be if our remediation efforts fail."

Of all the concepts and ideas that Albert had said or shown me, this one beat them all. My mind was totally and completely blown. I could have stood there and talked about this for a couple of lifetimes, but I didn't. All I said was, "Then, I guess it doesn't matter whether I come back or not. You won't be here."

"As per usual, Jack, the answer is not a simple yes or no. For those incipient races, like you humans and the Pra'at, smaller facsimiles of our original configurations shall remain. The First-Born have not abandoned you, Jack. Not entirely."

Another opaque statement. But despite the zillion questions I wanted to ask, I just looked deep into Albert's eyes. The twinkle was gone. I sensed sorrow. Perhaps it was only a reflection of my own crushing sadness. I would miss Albert – bad. Then he bowed to me, and I felt a stream of moisture creep from my eyes. I entered the craft.

"You are the key, Jack, the nexus around which, the future of your world and more, swirls. Be well." Albert closed the door, turned, and walked away. Inside, on the passenger seat, was a parachute. Albert had kept his word.

It took a few moments to compose myself. I turned the key and heard the slight whirr of the Cobalt 60 revving within the magnetic flux. The 'conveyance' rose a few inches. I depressed the 'gas pedal' and slowly maneuvered down the aisles and into the Hull. True to Albert's word, the Ship took over. I watched the blackness tinged with traces of color flow past. I was stupefied, stunned, and maybe even in a state of shock. I had hit the wall internally and was actually within the wall externally.

Medically speaking there are two types of shock. The circulatory kind; characterized by low blood profusion to the tissues, a life-threatening condition. I was not experiencing that kind. Mine was the psychological kind, arising from a terrifying or traumatic event. Signs and symptoms? Emotional detachment, numbness, and derealization. What's derealization? Psychobabble, yes, we all know that. But its medical definition is – "an alteration in the perception of the exterior world such that it no longer feels real." Perhaps I wasn't in shock because I knew that the past few days were real. And so was my current situation. I was traveling through the quarter-mile thick hull of a God knows what . . . alone. It was the "alone" part, I think, that affected me the most; because Albert, my friend, was gone. And also, I guess . . . it was all finally just catching up with me. This was the beginning of day four. I did not have the will to recall the prior three.

I exited the Hull. I was a solitary speck in the cold, endless emptiness of Space. The moon was a small globe off in the distance. Albert must have positioned the Ship several thousand miles beyond. I looked back and saw the empty blackness, flecked with thousands of points of light. The Ship was cloaked, but nothing could hide its overpowering presence.

Off in the distance was a blue and white marble. About the size of a golf ball held at arm's length. My homeworld. And the Sun was there too, my home star, but it was filtered, dimmed down considerably. I fully depressed the pedal and engaged the cruise control. There was no sense of motion. No acceleration or deceleration. That was the thing about these gravitational vehicles, so Albert had said, and so I had experienced. But the Moon veered a little to the left. I lined up the Earth in the center of my view. It would have been nice to have had the map with the blue and red arrows again. After a while, the Moon grew larger. It was half in shadow. I fantasized about seeing one of the Pra'at saucer ships rising, packed with terrestrial life forms. Presumably, they knew about Albert's new mission. In that light, would they obey the eviction notice? The circumstances had changed. Reality got a makeover. Were they experiencing derealization as well, I wondered? Had their perceptions of their reality changed? The answer was yes, big time. But it no longer mattered to me. That page had turned. I was moving on.

The Moon slowly expanded in size. The Earth had drifted off-center. I corrected. That was all I had to do, make a few course corrections, now and then. After all, the Earth was moving. A smart person would compensate for that. I didn't.

I sat back and blankly looked around. Assessing and reassessing my current situation, or perhaps plight, would be a better word, as I floated far above my homeworld. *Home, no matter where always kindles* . . . Not anymore. My homeworld had become alien to me. And, from what I saw at Janey's big meeting, the whole country was desperately looking for me and wanting to know what I knew – and was probably willing to do bad things to get it. Should I give them the "thing"? And if so, how?

I still had time, not much, but some. I reached over and turned on the radio. A song unfamiliar to me started to play. It was an odd female voice, a little bland but soothing. Funny, it was about the return of a space-faring prodigal lover.

The blue, blue, planet,

So far away,

Floating in the deep.

I had been with the gods; were they still with me? I learned that they cared about me, about us, about all. What about Albert? Was he a god? He has "the power of a small star" – his words. And he called himself an angel. The song continued; it had a forlorn feel and was wistful, like me. The singer was longing for where she'd been and what was gone.

It circles a light,

in the endless night

I remembered, back on the Moon, Albert had said, I could not crash because he was with me. Was he still with me? Albert had revealed, at the last possible moment, that he was going away. Going on some bizarre and inexplicable mission. Was I cast out? I could not return.

Do you know I'm coming?

Can you hear my song?

The knowledge of Albert's departure made my mission clear. I would give them the "thing." End of story. The decision was made. That left only one question – how? The Moon drifted by on my left. Large and half-lit, the dark plains hiding their color, the jagged mounts standing untouched, defying the heavens.

My blue, blue planet

Singing songs in the night,

Past a moon that gleams,

To the place of my dreams.

The cadence of the song took hold. I sat frozen, listening to the radio, hoping it would never end. That laconic voice was smoothing the way.

Should I fly down to wherever the hell the Feds jailed Janey and say, “here I am”? No. No leverage in that. What's to stop them from grabbing me and what I have? Nothing. They make the rules. They have the guns. The Moon slipped by. I looked up and stared in the rearview mirror. I would not be coming back.

Or should I call them, make a deal. I have my phone, it's in my pocket. And it works due to some strange-assed technology. “First, let Janey go, then I'll give you what I have.” Sure, they'll let her go, get what they want, then put the cuffs on – both of us, and die laughing while doing it.

Through the realms of Space,

Where angels frolic and gods embrace.

The glow of home is where I’m bound.

The glow of home soon to be found.

The only thing I can do is . . . give it to the Earth. As publicly as possible. Like, in New York City, maybe at Time's Square. First, I'll fly around a few times, real slow. Get their attention. Then gradually settle down, right in the little square they have there. The news media would go wild. And the video would sweep across the world.

And the Feds, they'd have no place to run, no place to hide. Because everyone would know. Millions would see me smiling and waving. Then I’ll open the door, step out and climb on top. The cops will surround me, hundreds of them, to keep the gawkers away. I'd motion for silence and say, "My partner Janey Riley and I, give you . . . the secrets of the Universe! Then the crowd would explode with screams of joy.

You will be King, and I the Queen,

"And forever again, we will be my love.

Two celestial spheres in the endless night,

Two gods, my love, in the heavens above.

Janey and I would be celebrities. They couldn't jail us, not after we gave the world "The Law of Connections." The key to the stars.

Forever we'll roam mid the heavens and stars,

And live in a place that we can call ours,

And dream in a place where life is ideal,

The words that I bring, the songs that I sing,

When I come, my love, we'll make all this real.

That was the answer. That's what I'll do. We would be . . . the saviors of the world!

I turned off the radio. The Earth was larger, the Moon smaller.

Chapter 26: Cruising – *Jack*

After a while, I turned the radio back on. The "radio." More alien tech. It was tuned, not to a station broadcasting ordinary electromagnetic waves. It was tuned to me, what I wanted to hear, or needed to hear? But that last song; where did that come from? Not my brain. And what about my phone – what with the gravitons? And the radar absorption, and the automatic attitude control, and the whole gravitic modulation thing that I was supposed to know all about? What's with all this, I wondered? Sure as shit, it's not – non-interference.

I needed to hear something soothing, meditative. A violin Concerto came on. It could have been Bach. Perfect for that endless metronome that was Space. The gently rising arpeggios massaged my troubled brain. Had I been with the gods? And then left – voluntarily? Did I have a choice? The answer is no. I had to go back and free Janey somehow; after all, her "circumstances" were all my fault. Did Albert have a choice? He said he did, and he chose the middle way – I was free to go back, in my own craft. The one that I presumably built. Ha! That was a laugh. And then he was called away. (?) I guess he had no choice either. *At the end of the day, we all just have to do what has to be done.*

As I gradually emerged from my stunned state of catatonia, the Earth slowly emerged as well, getting larger and larger, until it completely dominated my forward view. My homeworld, all blue except for the swirling white clouds and patches of green and tan. Looming so massive, I could feel its mass. And the overwhelming pull of 8 billion people. The continents were recognizable, the ones visible below. Gradually I applied the brakes and slowed the conveyance, not to 500 mph, but to zero, a complete stop. I gazed upon my world and felt like an invading alien.

It was time to answer the big question. What should I do? At the very least, cruise around a little before I got down to business. See some sights, enjoy the thing. Especially since the device was invisible to radar, so why not? The Serengeti Plains with all those animals, now that was worth seeing, or perhaps a quick flyby, past the Pyramids. Check out the Pra'at's handiwork. Better yet, how about a buzz along Venice beach – give the sun worshipers a real eye-full, and me too. And if I'm seen, so what, I'm just some newfangled drone. They're all over the place these days. Yes, I could have some serious fun with this thing –just a little. I figured I deserved that much.

That was my thought process as I cautiously pushed the wheel forward and began the descent. I looked at the speedometer. It read 480. No problem; that's slower than a commercial jet. It just so happened that North America was beneath me, so that's where I went. The altimeter, which used to be the tach, slowly rotated counterclockwise. At 500 miles, the Earth was still a large globe, like looking at a beach ball, pretty close up. Both North and South America were visible, covered with patches of swirly clouds. Curious, as I descended, there was no sense of falling. The Earth just got bigger.

At 300 miles, my home planet loomed larger than my field of view; the tip of South America was cut off. I pushed the steering wheel further down and dived straight in. Going 500 mph, you won't heat up and turn yellowish orange like the Space Shuttle. It's much too slow. They say skydivers fall at 220 mph, I was doing double that, and it still felt rather leisurely. No way was I going to speed up, though. It was time to steer. I headed for the middle of North

America for no particular reason. At 50 miles up, I was definitely in the blue sky – not space anymore, so I leveled off a little and generally headed west. I realized I didn't know where they were holding Janey. Maybe I should give her a call. I thought it strange that she still had her phone, back when I called. 25, 10, 5 miles. I had just traveled a quarter-million miles. The clear enclosure, the cockpit, being alien tech, did not transmit sound. Therefore, I could not hear the whoosh of air as I descended. Nor did I feel the deceleration. That took some of the fun out of it. But there was still plenty leftover. Fun, that is. And it was a real smooth ride.

At two, three miles up, I looked around for pursuit. And saw nothing. Not in the rear-view mirror, either. No trails of jet exhaust, no missiles, no laser beams. Laser beams? I heard they had them – ground-based laser defenses. Presumably, Albert was right; I was invisible to radar. But it's always wise to double-check. Down below were the Rocky Mountains. A jagged outgrowth that divided the Continent. And off to the South were a series of deep ravines. The Grand Canyon. A place I always wanted to see. So that's where I went, being the mega-tourist that I am. Though it would have been nice to have a tour guide. One with a proven ability to astound.

I must comment on my transportation device. It was a dream machine – truly. Like driving a car in mid-air. A fast car. One that always stays nice and level, though it did bank around corners, as one would want. Plus, it had a really good radio. And I had to admit; almost all of this was due to Albert's rebuild: the addition of brakes, life-support, and so on. Not exactly "of the Earth," except for my contribution – 4,3. And here's the best part, all these things probably could be reverse-engineered. (Maybe not the radio.) Given a little time, contrivances like this one might become commonplace.

And that's what I intended to give the Earth. But after I had some fun first. Just a small amount.

The Grand Canyon is a mile deep, 18 miles wide, and 277 miles long. Formed over the past ten, fifteen million years by the spillover from an ancient lake and the ceaseless carving of the Colorado River. I was still pretty high – about two miles up. The mountains loomed large below with the big canyon to the south. One would think that some form of navigation, like a compass, would come standard equipment on this thing. What would I do at night? Follow the highways, follow the lights? Or should I download a compass app for my phone? Hmm.

I continued to descend carefully around the clouds, constantly scanning for other flying vehicles, helicopters, airplanes, balloons, drones? Some kind of radar warning feature would have been nice. Also, there was a little wind buffeting. A modest amount of shudder and shake, nothing serious. I made some mental notes in the unlikely event that I'd be working on future models. There was a rear-view mirror, though. Kudos to Albert for thinking of that.

It was still early September, though it felt like I'd been gone a year. I was amazed at the amount of snow that lingered on the mountaintops. They looked somewhat bleak even in the late afternoon sun. Though, the stands of blue-green forest, with yellow alpine meadows, warmed the scene considerably. I headed south and took her down to a couple of hundred feet. Well below the air traffic, except for the helicopter tours. My impromptu plan was to enter the Canyon from the south, then leisurely cruise through it northbound. Afterward, I'd prowl around the Rocky Mountains; get a bird's eye view. All this was supposedly on my way east – to Times Square. Yes, that was still my plan . . . then.

The Great Rift yawned before me, and I dipped further down and entered. Here the river had carved a deep channel with steep jagged escarpments on both sides. And from where I was, it flowed from east to west. The sun was at my back, bathing the spectacle before me with strong yellow light. I was somewhat amazed by the reddish hue of the different types of rock layers. And all the stripes. Bands of light and dark red, intermixed with tans, and even some dull green in places. At the bottom snaked a brownish-green river – the Colorado.

I kept it slow and took it all in. The grand panorama that filled my view was my inner most fantasy come true. The motivation that kept me going; kept me striving through all the long hours as I built the thing, the dream machine. Sure, there was the quest for the unknown, and the greater good, and all that. But deep down, I just wanted to fly. Not like a bat out of hell straight to the Moon, but quiet and smooth, like a bird going here and there, looking, and wondering. That dream had come true.

I observed the splotches of green that dotted the vertical rock face. Small shrubs and perennials that clung to life in every possible niche. The tenacity of the living was on display. Not like the Moon; this was different. This was my homeworld. A rarity in the Universe; a place of life.

To test the machine's precision control and my piloting skills, I landed the thing. And not just anywhere, but rather, on the kind of place I always dreamed of going. The top of a butte. One of those tall, impossibly steep projections that simply jut straight up out of nowhere. I came to one doing just that, standing tall and vertical, with a small horizontal area on top. I landed there nice and gentle, right on top, and beheld the majesty of the Earth. The greenish river wending its way through a jumble of tumbledown ruddy-red crags. I wondered how many rock-jocks have climbed this piece of geology. Surely some have. And the view would have been worth the effort. I pulled out my phone and took a picture, just for posterity. Then I cracked open the door. The internal air hissed out, and I smelled the sweet, spicy scent of desert. The wind rustled, and I heard the distant thunder of an airliner. That reminded me of danger, my danger. Were they looking for me? Suddenly, I felt like an alien again, "a stranger in a strange land."

I closed the door, elevated the craft a few feet, and stepped on the gas. I shot forward like a Star Wars pilot. I was back, shooting the rilles of the . . . no, not the Moon, but rather the Earth. In reality, my speed was at most 50 mph, but I was low, skimming the river at about 50 feet. It was the thrill of a lifetime, and it felt like I was doing the speed of light, better make that the speed of sound. Up ahead and coming down the river were a couple of pontoon boats, chock full of tourists. Who else? They saw me coming. Many ducked, holding their heads. I waved as I went by. One kid up front, wearing a bulbous yellow life preserver, waved back. Upon further reflection, it may have been a one-finger salute. I pressed on, having the time of my life, zigzagging through the gorges.

As I traveled north, the ravine expanded, widening into a vast space. The setting sun painted the cascading cliffs a fiery orange. Above, the cloud cover had transmuted the sky to a puffy purple. It was glorious. I wondered how one small river could sculpt such a boundless expanse. Time, a lot can happen, given the time.

The water changed color to a greenish blue. Minerals, presumably. A waterfall passed by on my right. A spout of white water streaming right out of the rock face and pouring into a turquoise pool. The idea occurred to me to take a quick dip, but then I saw more rafters coming and nixed that idea. It must have been one of the last runs of the day. It was still the tourist season. I continued racing up the river. Up ahead was a tall outcropping, with a scenic overlook on top and a viewing area with handrails on the rim. And it was occupied by 40 or 50 people, onlookers, and they were all on-looking at me. Unfortunately, most of them had cameras, which were also pointed at me. I got a bad feeling about that, so I pulled up and exited the scene fast. For sure, I was made.

It was at that point in time when the error of my previous thought processes became apparent. Sure, people wouldn't freak out when they saw me; I'm just some guy in a crazy-assed drone. But they'd take pictures. And these days, everyone's got a phone with a camera, even me. And then they'd send those pictures to Facebook, Instagram, their friends, family, and to the authorities – local, state, and federal. And the Feds were looking for me, big time. Janey's big meeting with all those stern faces came to mind. They looked desperate. Desperate enough to do bad shit.

My new analysis began with the question; how soon till the Feds had the pictures? Assumption; 5 minutes. Figure another 10 for identification, then 5 more to scramble the F-16's. Where's the nearest base? Unknown. Best guesstimate; at a minimum, another 10 minutes. That's 30 minutes for the jets to arrive. No problem. The error in their thought process was the presumption that I would stick around. I got the hell out of there fast.

I took her up to 5- 600 feet and stepped on it. I was doing maybe 400 mph, heading north. The intent was to leave the Grand Canyon a few hundred miles behind. It was a nice place to visit; too bad I couldn't linger. But I was home free, being radar invisible. Albert doesn't lie.

After a while, I calmed down and started nosing around the mountains again. I was stalling for time. There were at least two, three hours left till nightfall. Surely motels were scattered around. I could get a room. No way, for a thousand reasons, not the least of which was the fact that the sum-total of my worldly wealth was in my wallet – $42.00. I left the change on the dresser . . . back home. Oh yeah, I had no home. Albert went away.

But the night was my friend. The conveyance would be invisible to cameras and eyes. There was one big drawback, though – no way to navigate, i.e., know where east was. I could take her up, say 500 miles and see the East Coast and then just drop in. And Times Square is always well lit, especially at night. However, with all this worrying, my joyride was not being particularly, uh, joyful. I was determined to rectify that with one last little look around.

The mountains were gorgeous this time of year. Lofty and dignified. Thrust upwards by titanic collisions within the Earth's crust. And, at 500 feet, the sights were awesome. Only one trouble, the mountains were a whole lot taller. No problem, this thing handled better than my old Yamaha, and I was a really good rider. I snaked down lower, down into the valleys where the trees were just turning yellow. And many of the meadows were golden as well, yet the ridges remained cloaked in blankets of evergreen – blue green and yellow, a nice combination, the colors of the lower Rockies in late summer. Up above, some of the summits were white, others colorless and bleak, the color of hard gray rock.

And I was not alone. Groups of caribou grazed in hidden glens, partaking in the culinary delights. One last binge before the long cold winter. Was it the rutting season yet? No, too early. Higher up, the slopes were occupied by goats, and I swear I saw a big brown grizzly rooting around in a purple and yellow field. I also flew over the occasional alpine lake, shining with the most beautiful blues I've ever seen. One lake I explored a little closer, swooping down and circling. I saw a hawk sitting on the top of a dead tree, no doubt, looking for his evening meal. That reminded me of my need for nourishment. Maybe I could find a restaurant, park out back and . . .

I pulled it back up to the mountain peaks, still heading north. I found that I was strangely attracted to the pinnacles. So were mountain climbers. They were compelled to clamber up – just because they were there. Well, I was there too, and without all that clambering. The view was nice but, in my opinion, not worth a climb. As I was musing on this and examining a particularly jagged pinnacle, I was violently rocked and spun about. Out of nowhere, a couple of fighter jets screamed by overhead, almost giving me a buzzcut. It was a pure "what the fuck" moment. My first thought was – how the hell did they find me? I regained control and saw that they had broken off and were circling back. I pushed the wheel forward all the way and stepped on the gas. The thing shot straight down like a bullet.

I went from 0 to 400 in about three seconds. Good thing for the zero-momentum feature; otherwise, I'd be a red smear on the canopy. But, despite the rapid drop, the thing was still rather sluggish, not like the first time I drove it back on the Moon. There, the problem was controlling too much speed. But then, too, it had a fusion generator.

I took her down to the treetops and raced along a dry riverbed. How the hell did they find me? That question dominated my rear brain. My forebrain was completely consumed with driving. Twisting through the tight valleys, circling the base of a crag, and then changing direction. I thought maybe I could lose them. No such luck. I saw them dropping down straight at me. A mountain ridge was coming up fast. The new plan was to fly over, almost scraping the crest, then to drop fast and double back. The thing may lack speed, but no way could the jets match my maneuverability. As I was approaching the steep rocky precipice, in my rearview mirror, I saw that the planes were gaining, and then one launched a missile! They launched a freaking missile at me! It was clearly visible. I saw it leap off the wing; the nose, the tail, and the orange-yellow exhaust. An inner voice screamed inside my brain. JUMP! JUMP NOW! I opened the door and did, but not before I grabbed the parachute, which was still sitting there on the passenger seat.

Sometimes, there's no time for thought. You just have to act. And I thank the heavens above that I did. Because a few seconds later; my thing, the conveyance, the dream machine – was a yellow ball of fire smeared on the face of a rock cliff. And if that wasn't enough, a second fireball erupted – the same place, a split second later. The missile had found its mark, a little late.

What happened to me? The jets pulled up, but their exhaust jostled the hell out of me. I was thoroughly disoriented but had the presence of mind to hook one arm through the harness and pull the orange cord. The chute unfurled, caught air, and almost yanked my arm off. I held on and, a few seconds later, landed on the ground, bruised but unbroken. And the ground happened to be a grassy slope, not a treetop, nor a rocky outcrop. Lucky me.

Why did I insist on having a parachute? Unknown. Maybe my intimate experience with Murphy's Law, "what can go wrong, will." Or perhaps it was my cub scout training, "always be prepared." Whatever it was, at that moment, I was very glad that I did. But real sad for many other reasons.

Chapter 27: My Homeworld – *Jack*

I was home, or strictly speaking . . . on my homeworld. The air was crisp and good to breathe, the gravity was normal, the temperature, call it 65. All the parameters an earthling would want. And *Home, no matter where always kindles a warm . . .* Too bad the welcoming committee didn't quite agree with that truism. They greeted me with an air-to-air missile. Although, upon further reflection, the warm part certainly applied. They melted half a mountain for me.

The big question – why, was bouncing around in my head. If they desperately wanted the flying machine, which surely, they did, then why shoot it down? And totally annihilate the thing by doing so? Was it factions again, like on the Moon with the Pra'at? One faction didn't want the other to get it. Those thoughts were fleeting since I did not, at that moment, have the luxury of quiet reflection. They knew where I was, and factions or no, the Army, the Air Force, and every other goddamn branch of the Armed Services would soon be looking for me. Rather intently.

Up ahead, on the face of a naked precipice, clouds of black smoke billowed. The fighter jets were, no doubt, pulling a U-turn and coming back to finish the job. They had to have seen the parachute. I mean, it was red and white striped, quite decorative really, and made to be seen. And it stood out like a neon sign against the green and yellow slope. I was a sitting duck. I gathered it up and ran for a clump of trees about a quarter mile away. Downhill.

And just as I made the trees, the air boys streaked past, coming in pretty low, from the other side of the mountain. They probably didn't see me. No matter, the place would be swarming with searchers soon. But I could afford a few minutes to take stock. I didn't have much. Stock that is.

One can assume that the Feds took my barn, the farm, and the whole shebang. That's just what they do, take the assets of the perpetrator; drug dealers, money launderers, cobalt 60 thieves, and so on. Spoils of war. And, as a result, my parents will likely disown me – legally. Will I have to change my name? I can't be a Neufield anymore? And because of my doings, my girlfriend's in jail, most likely a federal prison. Christ, on the phone, Janey looked like she'd been put through the wringer a few times. And let's see, my old best friend died from bone cancer, and my new best friend, well let's just say . . . he went away. Can't forget about my worldly wealth. I pulled out my wallet and counted; $20, 40, 41, 42 . . . 43 dollars! I thought I only had $42. Eureka! A real windfall. Hey, that's funny – the guy who discovered '4,3' has only $43. What are the odds of that?

But I wasn't finished; I had more. I emptied my pockets. There was Thutmosis's statue. It was very sexy and provocative. They must be getting a little bored with the native variety; of females, that is. It was an odd pose. A nude female (human) with long hair seated and examining . . . a ring on her big toe. Kind of strange. But then again, where was it coming from? In any event, it was a genuine alien artifact, though no one would believe me. It was probably worth mega millions.

Continuing with my personal inventory, the last but not least thing was my phone. Would it work? I pressed a button on the side. It did. Halleluiah was my first thought. And there's a cell phone signal. My second thought was – shit, now they know where I am. I quickly removed the battery. The phone can't work without a battery, right? Even if it's crammed full of alien tech.

Let's see, the final tally; phone, wallet – $43, statue, no friends or family, my girlfriend's in jail because of me, and I'm homeless and stranded in the middle of nowhere. Could I get any lower? Yes, I could be in jail too. Oh, I forgot one thing. The parachute. I could use that to keep warm. The Rocky Mountains must get pretty cold at night. And there was still one more thing; my American Express Card – "don't leave home without it" – I didn't. I checked my wallet to see if it was still there. Hey, maybe there was a restaurant over the next hill. But they'd track that instantly, just like the phone. Then I found, right on top – Bill Cambell's card. It was the last thing I put in. The scene back there in the "human section" replayed in my mind. He looked and walked like he'd just come off the rack. I took his elbow and walked him to the main aisle. He saw the huge laboratory arrays, the chimpanzee room, and all the Pra'at walking around.

"You'll be riding in a real spaceship back to Earth, Bill. Maybe you can tell me about it sometime?"

Bill gave me his card and said, "Look me up, man . . . I mean, Jack. If you do, then I'll know all this . . . wasn't something I smoked."

I put the battery back in; hell, they already knew my location and called Bill. No answer, his voice mail picked up.

"Bill Cambell UFOlogist. 'Aliens Are Us.' Sorry, we missed your call. Please leave a message."

I did. "Hi, Bill. This is Jack, uh, Jack Neufield? We met, um, you know where. You asked me to look you up, so you'd . . . know that, ah, it was all, er . . . real. Please give me a call." Then I left my number. It sounded like an answering machine. He probably didn't get back yet if he ever would. Still, I left the battery in.

As I was folding the parachute, my phone rang. It was from Bill – eureka!

"Bill, thank God you called."

"Is this really you, man, I mean, Jack? I only just got back; a couple of hours ago."

"So did I, Bill. We have a lot to talk about. But not over the phone. You uh . . . understand?"

There was silence then, "Yeah man, I'm cool with . . . that. Where are you? Can we get together?"

"Well, Bill, you see, that's the thing. I don't know exactly where I am. In the Rockies somewhere."

There was more silence, "You have GPS on your phone?"

I checked the apps and saw one titled 'Free GPS' and told Bill.

"I got the same one, man. All you have to do is . . ." And he told me what to do. Eventually, I came up with the GPS coordinates: longitude and latitude. I was about an hour away from Bill's house.

"Can you come and get me, Bill? I'm in deep shit here."

"Anything for you, Jack. You saved my ass. You saved us all, and maybe even . . . the whole world. I heard what you said up there; you 'terminated their operation.'"

"Well, that wasn't exactly all my doing, but I sure could use a lift." We worked out the logistics in code. I was to walk two or three miles east till I hit a road. Then wait for his car; he began to tell me the make and model, but I stopped him. No point in making it easy for the eavesdroppers.

"Thanks a lot, Bill. I really appreciate it."

"Sure thing, Jack. I just hope I have enough gas. But answer me one question, will you? Who are you, Jack Neufield?"

"I'm just some guy who likes to pick up a screwdriver, Bill; Joe Six-Pack, only I don't like beer all that much."

"I'll be there, Jack. You can count on me. Give me an hour."

I thanked Bill. Things were looking up. I could add hope to my inventory of assets. Only one thing bothered me. Bill's qualifying statement: "I just hope I have enough gas."

If the Feds were listening, they didn't need high IQs to figure out where I was and where I was going. A road east, two, three miles. I remember reading somewhere that the government stored everyone's phone calls, emails, and texts for five years up in Utah somewhere. And that's all the stuff they're not interested in. Were they interested in me? Yes, enough to shoot a missile at. And missiles ain't cheap.

I proceeded to fold the parachute and stow my gear: phone, statue, worldly wealth when the thought hit me. Why bother? Why should I even care anymore? "My conveyance" was no more, Janey was in jail, and Albert was gone. Why shouldn't I just sit down and wait for them to come and finish the job? Or better yet, why shouldn't I climb a mountain and, when I reached the top, take an extra step. The answer did not require much contemplation . . . the answer was . . . Janey. Her presence was always with me, and also, her absence. I just wanted to see her one more time. Even if it was .

. . for the last time. I'd even settle for a peek at her out in the exercise yard. And maybe, best-case scenario, to be incarcerated in the same prison with her. Do they have co-ed prisons? Why not? They have co-ed bathrooms. So, I folded the chute and then commenced to place one foot in front of the other – east.

The going was easy. No brambles or dense brush. Just the occasional downed tree, and of course, fallen branches everywhere. Plus, it was all downhill. Two, three miles, that's not very far. Ordinarily, it would have been a nice trek through a mountain forest. Probably something I would have wanted to do if I had the opportunity.

And the views were nice too, though I didn't see them. My eyes were focused on the terrain. Every step had to be mapped out. Over logs, around boulders, I even followed a creek bed for a while, hopscotching on the rocks. Another factor that diminished the aesthetic appeal was the fact that I was prey, the quarry and on the run. Being the hunted gives one a whole different mindset. A few times, I heard airframes in the distance; planes, helicopters. But no dogs. Dogs were bad news. There's no escape from dogs.

I made the two, three miles in less than an hour, hurrying through the partial clearings, outright avoiding the meadows. Why were there meadows sprinkled among the patches of forest anyway? Avalanches? Water table? It was an interesting question. Eventually, I came to the road.

It was a small country road, two lanes, faded white dashes down the middle. No traffic, nor did it look like it had much. I found a good vantage point behind a clump of bushes and began my vigil – waiting and hoping for Bill.

My thoughts drifted to Albert: "Others believe it to be something else entirely, a different kind of conscious awareness." I pondered his puzzling words. The Universe. It possessed a strange quality. A mysterious harmony that defied the dictates of causality. And it was some kind of living awareness. I mused these thoughts as I assessed my situation. The guy I had saved up there was now, about to save me down here. Curious. Albert also said, “events have begun to swirl and overlap.” Was this an example? Down the road came a small gray car. It was an old Dodge Neon, banged up on the driver's side. I had one once, a decade ago. It sure as hell was not something the Feds would drive. I saw the dark bushy hair and round, fleshy face, then stepped out and waved. He pulled over. I got in.

"Holy shit, Jack. It's really you."

"Yeah, Bill. It's really me."

"What the . . . how the freak did you get here, man?"

"I'm here because the sons' of bitches shot me down. Oh . . . you better pull the battery from your phone."

He looked at me funny, then complied, “Shot down? How the freak did you survive that?"

"Parachute," I motioned to the thing, “Look, Bill, they're probably looking for me . . . er, us now. Big time. You know any back roads?"

"Yeah. Up ahead is the Ruitt Forest. This road ends, but not really. It continues on, into the woods."

"Any big cities nearby?"

"Denver's not too far."

"Do you mind taking me there? To the bus terminal?"

"You got it, Jack. Anything for you, man. We'll go through the Ruitt. There's a service road that cuts across. It follows the Soda Creek."

We did not lack for conversation as we traveled. Not many people had in common what Bill and I had – history of the Pra'at. But first, I had to tell Bill the bad news.

"Bill, the Feds are looking for me. And most regrettably, after our phone call, they'll be looking for you too. And they're going to come down on you like a ton of bricks. I'm sorry, man, for doing this to you. For some reason, they want me dead. I'm desperate, man. Again, I'm sorry."

Although we had a great deal to discuss, a considerable period of silence ensued. Finally, Bill said, "My phone is prepaid. I don't think they can trace it. And I knew the score when I went into this line of work. This stuff just comes with the territory. The government doesn't want anyone to know. About the aliens, that is. And that's my job description – to tell the people. Besides, I owe you, Jack. I talked with a few 'abductees' on the way back. They were like zombies – not all there anymore. You saved me, Jack. You saved us all."

That's when I started to like Bill a lot. In return for his sacrifice, I told him about the Pra'at. Everything I knew. How long they've been here; the Pyramids, the Maya. Why they were here, their quest for longevity. Bill was all ears, and when my oration concluded, he had a zillion questions.

I answered when possible, within the confines imposed on a quasi-provisional uh, member. I don't know why. And Bill detected my evasion, which tantalized the hell out of him.

We turned off on a dirt road, and the driving became quite treacherous. Bill was constantly evading deep ruts, twice we stopped to remove large branches, and the hills were steep, both going up and down. The road, being rarely used, was a real workout for Bill's poor little car. I asked about the gas, seeing only a quarter tank on the gauge.

"No problem, man, we should have enough to get there. This thing is really good on gas."

"Well, how are you going to get back?"

"Resort to plan B." It was Bill's turn to be mysterious.

"What's plan B?"

"Well, you see, Jack, the UFOlogy business hasn't been exactly booming lately. I write the occasional article, talk to a group now and then. But to get by, I help out my brother. He's a landscaper. . . I borrowed his debit card." He paused to rub his hand over his face. "He'll be pissed, but I'll work it off . . . probably double."

Hearing that made me feel terrible. Especially since I knew I needed bus fare too.

"Jack, tell me this. There's a whole lot of . . . everything, going on out there, right?" He motioned upward.

"The answer is yes, Bill. The Universe is an awesome, mind-blowing puzzle, and it's more fantastic than you could possibly imagine."

"How'd you get there, Jack? To the base on the far side?"

"I learned a little piece of that puzzle, Bill. And built a 'conveyance' that defied gravity, countered it, actually, with my partner, Janey. And it worked better than expected. But I got caught stealing some Cobalt 60. Now the Feds have Janey. I have to go back and free her somehow."

All Bill said was, "Holy Shit. And that's where you're going?"

"Yeah, New York City. I figure she's in prison in New York or Connecticut. And here's the thing, Bill. I'll need bus fare too, but I have 43 dollars."

"Shit, man. My brother's really going to be pissed. I hope he's got enough in there."

The going was slow, and after a while, we came to a paved street. Employing the back-road strategy, Bill guaranteed he'd get me to Denver as a free man. I talked about Janey, how great she was, and I showed off her picture. Bill commented on how nice she looked and then talked about some recent liaisons he's had. Though, he was currently unattached. Eventually, we made it to the bus terminal as free men.

Chapter: 28 – The Sedgewick Manor

Pleasantville, New York is aptly named. Population – 7,123, median income – $87,000, crime – zero. It consists primarily of estates, corporate headquarters, a polo club, and a cute little village center. Anyone would be pleasantly happy there, even if they abstained from polo. But they were not happy at the Sedgewick Manor. Not on the day in question – a beautiful, late summer morning. The parking lot and lawns were full of late-model vehicles, many of them limos. And men in suits loitered about everywhere.

The Sedgewick Manor was representative of your typical, everyday CIA safe house. It was not the Cape Cod down the street sitting on an eighth acre. It was a vast sprawling estate with a huge Tudor-type, stone, and stucco, mansion. And, of course, the accompanying pools, tennis courts, and park-like grounds. And it blended in perfectly with the neighborhood – a necessary requirement. Also, it was extraordinarily fun to be at. But not this day. It had become ground zero for the Neufield Anomaly.

The glass snake table was filled to capacity. Indeed, so was the entire boardroom; there was barely room to walk. The two 80" LCD screens were set up, one filled with bitter faces – the remote attendees, the other displayed the Neufield barn. A cacophony of subdued human voices, anxious and irate, filled the room. Alysha Civil, Special Advisor to the President for National Security, stood with her back to the table, staring out the windows. The spires of a city were visible in the distance. It was a delightful morning, three days since the previous meeting. Like always, her hair was pulled tightly back, and she was dressed in a severe, dark gray suit, matching her cold, marble countenance perfectly. She turned to face the collective visage of anger. The seething room did not quiet. She pounded a dark walnut gavel on a matching wood base.

This garnered the attention of the room. The Uniforms and Suits self-segregated into clumps, with the faces on the screen in the middle. There was no preamble, no thank you for coming. She got right to it: "As you all know, the Neufield Anomaly was shot down." Raw meat to the wolves.

Cries of rage erupted, all communicating variations of the same thought: “How the fuck did that happen?” Yes, the f-word was used.

"Please, can we, at least, try to maintain some decorum?" She banged the gavel, this time more timidly, "We cannot make any progress . . . without some civility." She paused to wait for the anger to subside. Then persisted, "The Military . . .”

Immediately she was shouted down by the Uniforms. "Don't try and pin this on the military!"

From a clump of military types, an arm pointed, "You said the bogey was gone and not coming back!"

"No more lies . . . no more tricks!" Variations of this thought bounced around as well.

Alysha tried to assert the power of the Presidency: "Let me remind you that the Commander in Chief has the . . .”

More voices shouted, "Show the pictures! Yeah, show the pictures! We want to see the pictures!"

Alysha nodded to an aide, and a slide show appeared on the screen. Pictures of Jack waving and smiling as he cruised the

Colorado River, followed by a group of short video clips depicting similar scenes. Somebody yelled, "Freeze that!" with such authority that Alysha's aide did. It showed the rear view of 'the conveyance' ascending. A dark-gray metal hoop about 20' in diameter, with spokes fastened to a clear pod in the center. Jack's shocked face was turned around and looking toward the camera. The clip resumed, and the craft zoomed up and away in the blink of an eye.

"That sure as shit don't look like an 'amusement park ride' to me!" Many acknowledgments and voices of agreement accompanied the statement.

"Do you want to show us the receipts again?" This crack referred to her previous claims. Ms. Civil began to shrivel.

General Taylor, from Sarasota Springs Air Force Base, rose. His presence commanded respectful silence, "My colleagues and I have studied this video, and we conclude . . . that this vehicle 'was,' the most sophisticated flying machine we've ever seen. It was quiet, emitted zero exhaust, and accelerated faster than anything known. Madame, this was not built from discarded amusement park rides."

"Something must have happened to it while it was gone." This weak response from Ms. Civil only served to infuriate the crowd more.

Many phrases emanated anonymously from the periphery:

"She's full of shit like her boss."

"They're up to something, again."

Then, like a life preserver thrown to a drowning person, someone said: "Show the video from the pilot cam."

"Yeah, show the pilot cam video!" The call was repeated.

Alysha nodded to the aide. On the screen, the donut-shaped device was seen speeding towards a mountain ridge. For a few seconds, the contrail of a missile was visible, then a huge fireball erupted, quickly followed by a second explosion as the craft crashed into the sheer face of a cliff. Towards the bottom of the image, a red and white parachute became visible. The view shifted to the open sky as the jets flew past the billowing orange cloud.

Not many in the room had seen this footage. A large portion of the room was stunned silent. This gave Ms. Civil a chance to interject, "Next, I'd like to show you some excerpts from the debriefing of the two pilots. This may redirect your blame and perhaps establish some clarity as well. Roll it."

More shouts from the pack: "What about the parachute?"

"Was that Neufield?"

"Did you get him?"

The picture on the screen portrayed two men in flight suits seated before a panel of several high-ranking military personnel. The centermost officer asked the questions:

"Captain Bradley, please tell us, in your own words, what happened up there?"

"Late this afternoon, Captain Hiller and I were scrambled. Once airborne, we were given the coordinates of an unidentified bogey near Blacktail Mountain."

"And for the record, what base were you operating from?"

"Buckley Air Force Base, in Denver, Colorado, Sir."

"Thank you, Captain, please proceed."

"Apparently, the object we pursued was invisible to radar, but satellites were tracking its radioactive discharge, gamma rays, and relaying its position. Our orders were to make visual identification; then to follow, observe, and photograph only."

"And did you achieve visual contact, Captain?"

"Yes, Sir, we did. Near the Blacktail Mountain Group. Upon seeing us, the object initiated evasive maneuvers."

"Captain Bradley, did you engage in hot pursuit?"

"No, Sir, we laid back, slow and high, just maintaining eye contact. When the order came to lock on and launch, I did so immediately."

"Thank you, Captain." Then questions were addressed to the second pilot: "Captain Hiller, do you have anything to add to your wing mate's account?"

"Only that I found the order to fire inconceivable, Sir, since it entirely countermanded our previous orders, which were unambiguous. To follow and observe only. That was why I hesitated, Sir."

"And who gave the order to fire, Captain?"

"I assumed it came from Colonel Brittenham, Sir. He was in command. And it came over the designated com channel."

"And you both heard it?" repeated the officer.

"Yes, Sir." This was said in unison. Then the clip ended.

Ms. Civil elaborated, "This story does not end here. In the Flight Operations Center at the Buckley Air Force Base, no order was given to fire. All activity is recorded on video and audio, and there was no record of the order. All the personnel were interviewed and polygraphed, including Colonel Brittenham. Let me repeat: no order was given to shoot down the anomaly."

"Then where did it come from?"

"We don't know. But it definitely came from outside. The hack could have come from anywhere. We simply do not know who and how. But they penetrated our encryption."

"Well, did you pick up Neufield, at least? We saw his parachute."

"Umm . . . not exactly." Summoning her strength, "Frankly, the answer is no. He got away."

"Another colossal fuck-up by this Commander in Chief!" This voice arose from the military section of the room.

"Don't blame us," she responded, "The military; you were in charge at this stage of the incident!" Alysha had found some gumption. "Plus, he had help . . . an accomplice. Play the phone call."

Both the initial message and the phone conversation between Jack and Bill resounded through the room.

Alysha interrupted the playback, "Stop the tape; play that part again."

"Anything for you, Jack. You saved my ass. You saved all of us, and maybe even the whole world. I heard what you said up there; you 'terminated their operation.'"

Alysha added, "There's something very strange going on here. Jack went somewhere, did something, and then got outside help. That's obvious from this." She paused, then threw the pack another piece of meat, "And we've got the accomplice."

"Is he here?"

"Get his ass in here!"

Alysha complied, "Yes, he's here." Then to an aid, "Bring in Bill Cambell . . . and while you're at it, bring in the girlfriend, the Riley woman too. Maybe seeing Mr. Cambell will make her, mm . . . more compliant."

The murmurings and rustle in the room elevated.

Chapter 29: Prisoner #11357-042 – *Janey*

The Federal Correctional Institution – Danbury is primarily a men's prison. But it has an adjacent satellite prison "camp" for women. And adjacent to the women's camp is another "satellite camp" for special inmates. That's where I am. And from what I can observe, I'm the only one special enough to be in the "special, adjacent, satellite camp."

But it was no camp. I've camped out in the woods as a kid, went away once to summer camp, and even spent a few nights in a trailer camp. My parents rented an R.V. once to vacation in Maine. That was great, like traveling in your living room. This was not like any of those. No tents, no cabins, no R.V.'s. From what I could see, I was in a plain ordinary concrete building next to other plain ordinary concrete buildings. But I guess the Feds can call it whatever they want. *They make the rules. They have the guns.* They could call it "Camp Shangri-La" if they wanted. Only one problem – it would still be a group of plain ordinary concrete buildings, with bars on the windows.

I've been here one night and one day. A matron, that's what they call the female guards, escorts me everywhere. The dining room, the walking track, the showers (?). Her name is Stella Wjud - something - ski. She was a large woman, short light hair, moon face, squinty eyes. Her scrutiny usually ranged from low to high, rarely terminating in eye contact. She told me they called this place "Camp Cupcake." Presumably, she was referring to the women's section.

She wore a greenish gray uniform with numerous badges, emblems, buttons, and bling. From her thick black waist belt jangled keys, handcuffs, a walkie-talkie, and in lieu of a gun, a short thick baton. Her persuader. I read somewhere that 90 percent of employees dislike their jobs. Stella did not belong to that group. She seemed quite favorably disposed towards hers. Maybe she had become institutionalized. That's what happens after about 10 years of habitation in an institution. One grows to like it because, well, it's all you know. One feels at home there, *and home no matter where always kindles . . .* It was odd how that thought just popped into my head. Anyway, *institutionalization*, is this something I should look forward to?

Stella was special. Her job was to guard special prisoners in the special "camp." It was a cush job, earned by her many years of service, or so she said. However, it served my purposes. She was a font of information. I learned the history of the place, famous prisoners, the fire of '77, and notorious guards. Again, she avoided eye contact during the notorious guard dissertation. And she was well versed in the prison's amenities: baseball, tennis courts, and the exercise room. Minimum security means "easy time." I guess it's all relative.

Part of my special incarceration (I like that word – incarceration, though not the actual act of being incarcerated) was to attend "special" sessions. They took place in a special place, aka an interrogation room. It was fairly large. They could interrogate an entire girl scout troop in there. I am a girl scout – once a scout, always a scout. Our motto is – "to help people at all times." I try to live by that. Anyway, getting back to the interrogation room, for such a large room, it had very little furniture: just a gray steel table and matching chairs – very harmonious, non-eclectic. And of course, the requisite mirror on the wall, cameras stuck in the corners, and a small peep window embedded in the door. In my short life, I have acquired some considerable experience with interrogation rooms. Oh, and lest I forget, there was a drain in the floor. And my interrogators were obvious graduates of good ole Inquisition U.

One was my old pal Izzy. That would be Israel Santiago. This time, instead of a gray suit, he was swimming in a dark one. Dark suit for dark deeds. And he wore his brown shades perched on his head, the room not being particularly well lit, except for the table area. And this time, his partner was someone more his size – a diminutive Latin lady also dressed in a dark suit with a white blouse twice unbuttoned on top. A hint as to their dynamic, a piece to the puzzle. She introduced herself as Special Agent Angel Rodriguez. I always thought "Angel" was a boy's name. I guess there can be girl "Angels" too, at least in name.

I said I was pleased to meet her. Then I explained how a "presidential pardon" was being written for both myself and Jack. I motioned to the room, explaining how all this was superfluous. That was the test. Did they know that word – superfluous? Angel did. Izzy looked away and scratched his hairline. He didn't. I knew then who had the smarts in this duo. Angel wore the pants and Israel, well, once a beta, always a beta, but his big gun still bulged . . . under his jacket.

Angel explained how all this, she mimicked my gesture, was strictly a formality. She almost rolled her eyes, along with her r's. And explained further that "they had their orders." The session lasted maybe half an hour. She asked basic stuff like: "How long I knew Jack?", "Did I like nursing?" and, "Did I own a dog?" That one caught me by surprise. No doubt, something she learned at Inq. U. – people who own dogs are more likely to . . . fill in the blank. Steal Cobalt 60? Izzy was content to let the angel take the lead. I think he liked that in a woman – her taking the lead. He was not being the crazed Chihuahua like before, trying to impress the alpha dog. I wondered about Special Agent McCluskie. Did he unleash the Chihuahua; tell him to go play on the highway?

They gave me some forms to fill out, pure nonsense. Then they left, but not without cordial goodbyes. Hey, why not keep it nice? I liked being nice. I was a naturally born nice person. Everyone said so. Afterward, Matron Stella Wjud-something escorted me back to my room. There I faced the enemy – boredom.

And boredom was a new enemy. I lived on a horse farm, and my father owned a hardware store. If my mom ever noticed me wasting time, I'd be mucking out a stall in two seconds flat. And that was not an activity high on my list of likable things to do. Primarily because of the smell, not the work. Clean smells appeal more to me. Cut wood, cardboard, cleaning fluids. That's why I chose to work at the store, not the farm. And everything there was so darn interesting too. Ever wonder what a flange is? I know. How about an adze? We sold them both. And it was a great source for "flying machine" supplies.

But here, the beast lurking in the dark was – boredom, aka, ennui, languor, dullness . . . ad nauseam. I looked at the pad and pen on the desk. The pad was your standard yellow legal style. But the pen was exceptional. A modern-day miracle. It smoothly slid over the page, emitting a beautiful bold blackness. Glossy at first, then drying to a crisp darkness. And it possessed a secret magic – it made one want to write. I proceeded to do so, though I fully intended to destroy the end-product, flush it, rip it to shreds, or sneak it out in my pants. Anything, but give it to them. They weren't being nice.

It was my second afternoon in prison. What do the other inmates do with their free time? Hey, that's funny. The one thing everyone here has, in abundance, is free time. On the outside, where one is supposedly free, one has little. I had the free time to ponder that. Overall, I considered myself fortunate in not having a cellmate. "Hey, what are you in for?" I could do without that. Was this what they called solitary confinement? And I was not fraternizing, either. Not in the dining hall, the exercise room, or the recreation areas outside. No contact with the regulars. But Stella did fraternize somewhat while walking me around the track. It was pleasant, tree-lined, and with scenic mountains in the distance. I wondered if Jack was up there watching.

And Stella tried to make conversation, I'll give her that. Though she had to maintain an air of domination. An interesting dynamic and a unique experience – being a "newbie." She told me that's what they called the new prisoners. Also, newbies were the only ones privileged to wear orange. I told her that technically I was not a prisoner, not having been charged, tried, or sentenced.

"If you have a number, you're a prisoner." End of conversation. I accepted that reality. They owned me.

The prison was a big part of Stella's life. As we strolled by the baseball field, I inquired about its use. On that subject, Stella lit up like a beer sign in a bar window. She was the captain of the prison's softball team and a big hitter. Her hand involuntarily stroked her baton.

I told her I played on the nurses' team at Yale-New Haven. She looked at me, again from down to up, this time assessing my athletic abilities.

"You any good?"

"Softball is my sport. My parents encouraged me, thinking it might get me a scholarship. It didn't. No matter, I just like the game."

"What position do you play?"

"Pitcher and second base. We played fastpitch."

"Maybe I'll get a chance to see what you can do." She said this with a penetrating look, "eye to eye." It was very uncharacteristic. My general level of anxiety elevated.

Late that afternoon, I had another visitor, actually, the same one as the day before and the day before that – Winston Erhart III. The Visitors Center was hopping; late afternoon must be a busy time. Stella escorted me over to his table. He was smiling as usual but wore a different outfit; jeans, red and green madras jacket, blue shades hanging half out the top pocket, white shirt, and matching white bucks. He was still a real trip.

"Janey," was all he said, shaking his head, as he pulled out a chair.

"Prisoner #11357 - 042. That's what I'm called here."

"This whole thing is a travesty! You haven't been tried in a court of law or charged with a crime. You don't even have a lawyer!"

"Who's going to stop them, Sandy, you?"

"Yes, Jane, I am. And I'm working on it – working hard."

"Well, thank you, Winston. But there's no need. Jack's coming with 'it' any time now. Then they'll be happy, really happy and, at the very least, will set me free." For a moment, I fantasized about riding around in an R.V. with a big screen TV, going to speaking engagements before my adoring fans.

"That's why I'm here, Janey. To tell you that . . . that's not going to happen. They shot Jack down over the Rockies." Seeing the horror on my face, he quickly added: "But he's OK. Jack parachuted just in time. I saw the flight cam footage."

"Why? And he's OK . . . Did they pick him up?"

"He landed safely and somehow eluded capture. A thousand searchers combed the area. They used planes, satellites, dogs, everything. The Feds say he called someone, then disappeared."

Winston played the footage on his phone. I saw the flying “thing” zooming in the distance, heading towards a mountain. The viewpoint followed, zigging and zagging. Suddenly, a missile streaked towards it, front and center, and then a double explosion erupted on a rocky cliff. A red and white parachute could be seen drifting downward.

I was completely astonished, rubbing my brow while processing these new facts. Lunacy would be a better word for it. Everything had changed.

"Janey, I must ask you one thing. Please don't let on that you know any of this. 'The Incident,' as it's being called, is ultra-top secret. Naturally, they want to cover their asses. And I want to be kept in the loop."

"Why are you telling me this, Sandy?"

"For many reasons: first, because you're getting a raw deal. That's a fact. This Administration is doing the exact opposite of everything they should be doing. Their treatment of you, their treatment of Jack." Winston paused a moment to think while he tucked away his phone. "And because I like you, Jane . . . humans tend to form irrational attachments for no apparent reasons. But I have some." He flushed an almost imperceptible tinge as he said this.

Christ! He was coming on to me! Like I didn't have enough to deal with. The thing was shot down, Jack had parachuted safely, and then he strangely disappears. And now . . . Sandy's "coming on to me"! My mind was racing at the speed of light. I don't know why, but all I said was, "What reasons?"

"Because you're perfect." He dipped his chin slightly, and his blue eyes penetrated me. It was time to change the subject. But I knew that Winston Erhart III had likely become a powerful ally.

"Why would they shoot Jack down? When they desperately wanted the thing."

"That's the big mystery. Somebody hacked into the pilot's radio and gave the order to shoot, somehow evading the encryption. The air force heard it in the control tower. Everything was recorded. And one of the pilots obeyed the order before it could be aborted."

I just shook my head and said, "Maybe it was the Russians?"

"Who knows? But the Military is angry, and everyone else is all freaked out. They're having another big meeting tomorrow afternoon, and I got you an invite."

I put my hand on top of his and thanked Winston. I certainly wanted to be there, to be in on this. It was my party, but I had nothing to wear, except for basic orange. Sandy read my thoughts.

"What size are you?" I told him my dress size, 8. Then he asked, "And your shoe size?" I said, 7 1/2.

"I'll get you the kind of outfit you deserve. And when you walk in that room again, everyone will know who and what you are . . . a superior being, the key to unlocking the secrets of the . . . stars!" His hand swept above.

It was almost a relief when the buzzer buzzed, and the guard announced the end of visiting hours. Sandy and I stood and shook hands, I felt some electricity, and then he gave me another chaste little hug. He told me he'd be back for me tomorrow.

I had a great deal to contemplate.

Chapter 30: The Second Big Pow-Wow – *Janey*

I found myself in a bedroom on the third floor of the Sedgewick Manor. The estate was crawling with suits and functionaries. Winston whisked me through, flashing a badge. Robert also flipped his frequently, and Jamal, well, he wore his. He and Robert stood guard outside the door.

The room was sumptuous, done in the Victorian style like most of the house. A canopied bed, a divan – *is that what they call a couch with only one arm?* A makeup desk fully equipped, a free-standing mirror, and last but certainly not least, a marble bathroom. Winston said I had time, so what the hell? I drew a bath. The bathtub was, in reality, a small pool. There were two steps up, head and armrests, and a big window overlooking the grounds. This was definitely something I could get used to. The exact opposite of what I had – a toilet-sink combo.

There were electronic controls unobtrusively embedded within the marble near the faucet. It was set for 103°. I pressed the fill button, and water entered. I assumed it would automatically stop when filled. This type of luxury was entirely new to me and eminently worthy of going a little gaga over, which I did for a short period of time. Then I returned to the bedroom.

All the stuff Winston bought me was laid out on the bed. The boxes, the bags, and the suit on a hanger wrapped in clear plastic garnished with the name – Giorgio Armani. All, also worthy of gaga, which I engaged in, for another short period of time.

Earlier that day, Winston and the boys came for me after breakfast. I was isolated from gen-pop (prison-speak), so I ate after everyone else. Stella was my escort and bodyguard. Though she could not shelter me from all the eyes. Always staring like a hundred lasers. I was special. Special Convict Riley and the only one emblazoned in orange.

My entourage awaited me in the visitor's lounge. After cordial greetings and a few simulated hugs, we walked right out the front door, badge flipping all the way. Once in Winston's town car, we were free to talk. I expressed my amazement as to the boys' continued employment. Robert chin-pointed to Winston, explaining how "Word came down to leave us alone." Jamal nodded, which seconded the validation.

Sandy self-effacingly replied, "I know a guy who knew a guy."

Robert suggested we stop for breakfast, saying: "You can't have too many."

When Winston acceded, Robert directed us to a nice diner, classic styling, clad in lots of flashy metal. We sat in a booth, and it was great, like we were on vacation. Or maybe a field trip. Things had clicked between us four. We were all pals, and there are no secrets among pals. The boys had big breakfasts: "It's the most important meal." I had eggs and Winston – just coffee. Prison food was mostly filler, empty calories, and I was a protein person.

Winston described the crash site. He had stopped there, in Colorado, on his way East, "There was nothing left," he said. "Just a black smudge on a mountain and a few pieces of slag."

"How did they find it? I thought it went up, up, and away."

"Gamma rays, trace amounts. Satellites detected it coming back." Sandy looked at me real funny after he said that. "Then they tracked those emissions on Earth. Jack took a little cruise up the Grand Canyon. Want to see?"

"Yes." That was the biggest three-letter word I ever said.

Sandy pulled out his phone and showed us pictures and video: "It appears that Jack was having a good time."

I was stunned. My only thought was that was not what Jack and I built!

The boys suspended their culinary activity and observed intently. Robert asked, "You and Jack built that?"

Jamal only said one word, "Cool."

Winston read my incredulity and leaned forward to hear my answer. I remained quiet.

Then Winston said, "We think he had help. Jack went someplace. Do you remember the name he said, during his call . . . 'Albert'? Do you know anyone named Albert, Jane?"

I was still quite thrown by the video clip, so I answered the question straight out and truthfully, "No . . . no one, and I'm sure Jack doesn't either."

"There is a great deal of mystery associated with the Neufield Anomaly," Winston observed.

"Maybe that’s why they’re calling it an an-o-ma-ly,” said Robert, the word being a recent addition to his vocabulary.

I mentioned to Winston that his list of clues was growing.

"Yes, Janey, and the action has begun to quicken."

I turned my attention back to the goodies strewn on the bed. First, I removed the pants suit from the plastic. The tag read, "Giorgio Armani – cashmere-silk blend. Dry clean only". Good to know if I was allowed to keep it. The fabric was soft and somewhat shimmery. Expensive and way out of my jeans and T-shirt league. The color was a dark cream or very light beige. In perfect sync with my medium brown hair. The jacket had no collar, was tailored at the waist, and fastened, magically, by a single hidden button. The pants were longish, with straight legs, no belt loops, and the zipper was on the side. They say that what you wear is a statement. This suit stated – "perfect elegance, no further embellishment needed." I couldn't wait to try it on.

In a Neiman Marcus bag was a box with a silvery gray blouse, no collar, rounded neckline. The label said Thai Silk. It was unusually shimmery. Shoes were in another box, low heels; a soft, supple leather. An exact match to the suit. And for a splash of color, I found a short silk scarf with a swirly strawberry-red pattern. A stunning accent. I liked Sandy's style and vision. What did he call me? How could I forget – "a superior being." I would be that in this outfit . . . if it fits. I was sure to be the talk of the table.

I stuck my head out the door. The hallway was like a parlor. Wing chairs, potted ferns, tasseled lamps. Robert and Jamal were lounging in a couple of chairs, leafing through magazines. It was mid-afternoon.

"How much time do I have?" I asked.

"Take your time. Winston said it would be a while. They're waiting for more honchos."

So, I did. I needed time to expunge the scent of prison. And it wasn't just the smell. But there was that. The powerful cleaning fluids mixed with a tang of fear – human fear. It was also the essence of captivity, the taste of enslavement, the awareness of domination. I needed time to wash that away too. An hour would be nice.

White marble, gold fixtures. That was the bathroom. Though the word bathroom is completely inadequate. Bathing Palace, or maybe Suite of Ablutions? As expected, the pool had filled to the proper level at the proper temperature, 103°. I stepped in, and the warm water enveloped me. I thought this must be how heaven feels. I leaned back and let the liquid of life renew me. For certain, renewal was a desperate need. Could I get any lower? Broke and in prison. I did have $1,723 in my savings account. Would I have access to that, or did they expropriate that too? Not that the commissary was available to me.

What else did I have? Friends. Robert and Jamal were my new friends. They cared about me, and I about them. And that was a very valuable treasure. And who is Winston Erhart III? An ally at a minimum, though one with an agenda. But I think I'll count him as another piece of gold to be carefully guarded in my treasury of friends. And I had Jack. My life-mate. OK, so he's half-responsible for my current state of affairs, i.e., incarceration. But, most assuredly, Jack is coming. He'll make everything right. This fact was written on every strand of my DNA. With that thought, I laid back and drifted into a state of total relaxation as the stains of prison slowly dissolved.

I awoke about 45 minutes later. My relaxation went a little too deep. Utilizing the gold handholds, I pulled myself out and stepped into the shower. But not before viewing myself from several angles. There were mirrors everywhere, even on the ceiling. The reflections revealed a body that worked out three times a week. I thought I could use a bit more on top, a bit less below. But the image was a better sight than the tomboy I used to be.

There were space-age controls in the shower, too. I set the spray on medium, the temperature to 78°, and pressed the button. It was like Goldilocks - not too warm, not too cold. Just enough to wake me up. Afterward, I spent some time at the make-up desk. The girls in my UCONN sorority taught me about cosmetics. Though I was not in the attraction business, being with Jack and all. But I knew the basics, lipstick, blush, eyeliner. Then I dressed. Sandy had thought of everything; stockings – beige; underwear – nude. And hidden in the bottom of a bag was a small black velvet box. I opened it. A pair of 24 karat gold studs sparkled within. The perfect touch. An understatement that overstated the elegance. If the girls on my cellblock could see me now. Strike that. The prison in me was gone. Prison Jane was no more.

Everything fit perfectly. "Because you are perfect." Sandy's words replayed in my mind. But everything should not have fit perfectly. The odds were against that. Sure, I gave Winston my sizes, but still – it was strange. There seemed to be an underlying synchronicity in play. A coming-together.

I peeked my head out the door. Winston was pacing. Robert gave me the hurry-up sign, so I stepped out. Winston stopped and stared. Jamal's mouth gaped. And Robert dropped his magazine. All were speechless.

Sandy came over and took my two hands in his and said, "You are truly a superior being . . . an angel of beauty."

That complement left me speechless. I simply said, "Thank you . . . Sandy." From his pocket, he presented another black velvet box. He opened it and displayed – a gold brooch. It was a configuration of the numerals 4,3. The four was arranged, decoratively, above the three.

"Four, three." That was all I could say as I looked quizzically into his eyes.

Sandy carefully arranged my scarf, then pinned it in place, above my heart, and said, "She comes from beyond, bearing the keys to the doors of heaven."

Then, he took a step back and bowed. Next, Robert stood, and he and Jamal awkwardly bowed as well.

I was astonished at the effect my presence had. A trace of moisture settled on my cheek. And at that moment, I felt otherworldly, distinct, a different kind of being. And it was all because of what I knew. My knowledge was the source of my beauty.

Winston broke the spell, "We'd better hurry. The meeting is about to start." As I walked down the stairway, I felt the attention of a hundred eyes. I kept my chin level, brows slightly elevated, and mouth imperceptibly upturned. Their stares were futile.

Winston dropped the boys and me off at the library again while he went off to the Pow-wow. I assumed they'd come for me whenever. The room was fairly well occupied with suits, both the male and female varieties. A few uniforms were sprinkled about as well, huddled in small groups. All were sneaking peeks at me. We staked out some space by a bay window. Jamal stood by my side, guarding me against them, not them from me. I liked that. Robert went off in search of coffee.

There was a scruffy-looking guy who was not sneaking peeks but rather was staring intently at me. It was extremely awkward. And he stood out in that he was not dressed appropriately. He wore a UFO tee shirt, cut-off black jeans, and high-top sneakers with floppy socks. I tried to look away and ignore him, but he kept staring. Then he walked over, directly to me. Jamal stepped forward, his hand on his weapon. Not that he needed a weapon with this guy. He was rather soft and fleshy, face and body. Obviously harmless.

"Are you . . . Janey?" he asked.

My eyes opened wide, and my mouth dropped half-open. How could this guy possibly know me, I thought? But I said nothing.

"Jack showed me your picture. You were dressed like a nurse."

The word “what” screamed inside my brain, echoing around for a few short moments. Jack carried that picture in his wallet: "How do you know Jack?"

"Man . . . this is going to sound a little crazy, but you know all those shows about aliens, you know 'Ancient Aliens' and . . ."

"When did you last see Jack?" I had to interrupt.

"Two days ago. He called me up and asked me for a ride. The dude got shot down over Black Tail Mountain."

My mind was a whirlpool of questions. I grabbed his arm and ushered him to a quiet corner, and spoke in a lowered voice, "How do you know Jack?" I repeated.

"I'm trying to tell you. Everything you thought might be true about the aliens, you know . . . the Grays, is true. I got abducted, and Jack saved me. And there were lots of us. He saved us all."

"Where were you when Jack saved you?" *Can this guy possibly be for real?*

"Well, you see, this is the crazy part. The Pra'at, that's their real name, have this huge base on the other side of the Moon." He stopped to check my reaction.

"Go on," I said.

"They're experimenting on humans, and chimps and lots more. Jack and his friend showed me around . . ."

"Who's his friend?"

"Jack was with a few of the aliens too, I don't remember their names, but that dude looked familiar like I'd seen him before. His name was Albert."

Again, that name, Albert! My brain convulsed. Suddenly, everything this guy said had to be true. He saw my picture, knew Jack had been shot down, and now he mentions the mystery name – Albert. I asked, "What's your name?"

"Bill Cambell, I'm a UFOlogist." From a bulging wallet, he gave me a card.

"You're from Colorado. That's where Jack was shot down. And you gave him a ride?"

"I'd do anything for Jack. I was there when he told everyone, 'We have terminated this operation, and you will be returned to your homes very soon.' And I was. And do you want to know what he said when I picked him up?"

"Yes." I felt like grabbing him by the shirt and screaming the word in his face but didn't.

"He said he was sorry because he knew the Feds would come down on me 'like a ton of bricks.' But he said he had to do it . . . to get back to you."

I was so choked up I could hardly talk. I pulled a Winston and took both his hands in mine and croaked out, "Thank you, Bill Cambell."

He looked like he'd been touched by an angel and said, "I'd do anything for Jack . . . and you too."

We continued to chat in low tones. Jamal, being in range, overheard. What he was thinking, I cannot say, but his eyes were maximally opened. Bill relayed the history of the Pra'at, what Jack had told him. I asked if he ever mentioned the numbers – 4,3. Bill said no. Jack was not blabbing around our little theory. Therefore, I wouldn't either, and I was glad that I hadn't so far. But Winston had clues, and he was no dummy.

Robert returned with three coffees. He eyeballed Bill sideways. Jamal said, "He's OK." I gave my coffee to Bill. He looked like he needed something, anything. Robert gave me his, then left again to fetch more. He proudly announced that he found the kitchen. And Jamal continued to guard, for me, not against me.

I asked Bill why the 'Pra'at' were experimenting on us.

"Because we live longer than them. And they want to find out why. That's what Jack said." That made perfect sense to me, though I didn't think we humans lived all that long. Eventually, Robert returned with more coffee and some cheese-filled pastry. Bill dug into that, and Robert joined him. Presently, the attendants came for us. Alysha's young pups.

Chapter 31: The Rumble – *Janey*

As we entered the boardroom, we were accosted by a hundred faces. They revealed an interesting mix of anger and curiosity. The curiosity won out, and the raucous cacophony diminished. All eyes turned to Bill and then to me. In that order. I guess one could say we were polar opposites.

But the greatest attention was paid by Alysha. That would be Ms. Civil – Special Assistant to the President. And her usual cold, hard countenance changed: her pupils constricted, her eyes narrowed, and her top lip curled upward slightly, on one side, into an involuntary sneer. She could not hide her outrage and anger. She had been seriously upstaged.

I was ushered to a seat adjacent to Ms. Civil. Bill was to remain standing. He was exhibit A.

"Ladies and gentlemen, this is . . . I'll let him introduce himself. Please state your name for the record, young man."

"Bill Cambell, I'm a professional UFOlogist." Groans were heard from several areas in the room, accompanied by hands raised to brows.

"Christ, here we go." This phrase emanated anonymously from somewhere.

"Could you please explain to us what you did on the afternoon of September first?"

Bill looked at his watch, "Today's the third, so that was two days ago. I suppose you want to know about me picking up Jack?"

"Yes, that is correct. And let me remind you that I will be the one asking the questions here, and you are a criminal facing 21 Federal charges, which include," she picked up a paper and read: "Aiding and abetting a known terrorist, impersonation with the intent to commit larceny, and identity theft, to name just a few. Please proceed."

"My brother said he wouldn't press charges." Bill tried to defend himself.

"That doesn't matter; we are. These are "Patriot Act" offenses. You no longer have any rights. Now tell us what you did."

"Jack called and asked me for a ride. I took him to the bus station. I didn't know that was a Federal Crime."

"You stole money, transported a terrorist, and purchased a bus ticket under false pretenses. Those are all Federal Crimes."

General Taylor partially stood, "You expect us to believe that this is Jack's accomplice? That this is the special help he received?"

Alysha ignored the comment and asked, "Mr. Cambell, please tell us how you are connected to Jack Neufield?"

"I met him on the far side of the Moon. The aliens have this big base over there."

More groans and cries of outrage. Several phrases bounced around:

"This guy's a UFO nut!"

"You expect us to believe this?"

"Next, he's going to say he was abducted."

"Yeah, and they shoved tubes up his ass." Many laughed at this crack, except Alysha and me. Winston shot me an inquiring look, rotating his palms upward skeptically. I answered with a subtle nod, a telepathic contact that verified Bill's veracity. Sandy's eyes inflated.

But Alysha did not face the onslaught alone. She had her young pups and a few old dogs as well. Essentially, the assemblage had separated into two camps, the Suits, and the Uniforms. The Administration and the Military. Constitutionally, the President and her team should have been in charge. But here, the lines of authority had blurred, maybe separated would be a better word. There was too much at stake. With the conveyance and the theory behind it, we're talking about the potential for world dominion here. One would think the two camps would have worked together on such a profound matter. Not so. A few of the Suits sidled closer to Ms. Civil protectively.

Ms. Civil banged her gavel in a futile attempt to bring order to the meeting. She succeeded in toning down the rancor to a low, irate grumbling: "There may be some truth in what this . . . uh, UFOlogist has to say. You heard the phone call. Jack knew this guy and sought him out."

Alysha turned her attention back to Bill, "Let's say we believe you, Mr. Cambell when you say you met Jack somewhere." Guffaws and hoots followed this statement, "What was Mr. Neufield doing when you saw him 'up there'?" She actually mimed a quote sign while rolling her eyes.

"He was saving the Earth from 'them,'" he gestured to his shirt. "And you know them as Grays, but they call themselves – the

'Pra'at.' They've been here for thousands of years, experimenting, and doing who knows what. I heard Jack say, (here Bill mimicked Alysha's quote gesture, which only served to infuriate her more) 'We have terminated their operations here, and you will all be returned to your homes as soon as possible.' Man, I only just got back, and then he calls. And do you want to know what else he said?"

Someone shouted, "Yeah, tell us what else."

"He said . . ." He pointed around the table. "That you'd come down on me like a ton of bricks. And guess what, you have. But I'd do it again a hundred times, for Jack. He saved our asses up there, and probably yours down here too." He paused to think, and so did the room, "And man, do you want to know what the really funny part is?"

"Yes, Bill, tell us the 'really' funny part." Ms. Civil growled her response.

"Your asses ain't worth saving, but he did it anyway."

Inwardly, I was cheering Bill on. He had just turned the tables on his adversaries, all of them. But the one thing he didn't do was curb the level of animus. It swirled around the room like a viscous specter.

"Get that lunatic out of here!" screamed Alysha. And the room erupted again in a chorus of objectionable comments.

"We didn't come here to listen to this shit!"

"He's up to his ears in bullshit, like you are!"

Ms. Civil's exhibit A had failed. Bill came across like a real UFO nut. I didn't envy him. But if what he said was true – and the likelihood of that was high, then it was probably a good thing nobody believed him. Things were loony enough. Then a couple of goons grabbed Bill by the elbows. He fought back like a crazy man. However, he did display some martial arts training. He elbowed one guy in the face and kneed the other in the groin. What did he hope to accomplish, I wondered? Four or five of Alysha's retinue promptly wrestled poor Bill to the ground then dragged him out, kicking and screaming. He was particularly fond of the vernacularism – "You mother fuckers!" which he repeated loudly and often as he swung and kicked. I have to give him credit, though; he went down swinging. Maybe they'll put him in Danbury, next door in the men's annex. I could wave to him through the fence.

After all that commotion, Alysha turned her attention to exhibit B, which was me.

"Ms. Riley. At our last meeting, we established that your 'boyfriend' was alive and well. Now we know he's back, and more than alive and well, he's having the time of his life." To an assistant, she said, "Show a little of Jack on the river." A clip of Jack flying up the Grand Canyon, smiling and waving, played on the screen. I was happy for him. And, in general, glad to see Jack being happy.

"And, at our last meeting, Ms. Riley, may I call you Jane?" I remained silent. She went on, "Anyway, at our last meeting, you left us with some interesting words. Forgive me, they weren't words, they were numbers, in particular – '4,3'. Would you care to elaborate on their meaning?"

As I was thinking how to respond, she changed tactics, "And if I may say, I expected to see you wearing orange, accented with some steel-gray, as in handcuffs. The typical garb of a Federal prisoner, especially the terrorist kind. You must have a benefactor."

She shot Winston a dirty look, "Would you care to stand and give us all a treat?"

I thought about this. Ms. Civil had given sway to her petty and base emotions. She was jealous, and this was good. She had revealed herself. So, I would reveal myself as well. Slowly, I edged my seat back, placed my hands on the table, and stood gracefully and straight. My chin was set at the perfect level, not too high, not too low. My mouth was vaguely upturned; my eyes slightly narrowed, acute with discernment, sensing, and perceiving. The room quieted as my gaze slowly explored them, one by one, lingering on Sandy and ending with Ms. Civil. They felt my Presence, and Alysha shriveled as her light first dimmed, then snuffed out. She was defeated. Victorious, I gracefully sat, and the room went strangely quiet.

An aid pulled out his phone, spoke a few words, and then handed it to Ms. Civil: "You're going to want to take this. It's Jack Neufield."

The room heard this and freaked. A collective mental paroxysm would be a better phrase. Murmurings sprung forth. Someone shouted, "Put it on the screen!" This was taken up by a few more similar demands. Alysha nodded to her aides, who frantically tapped their tablets. Jack's image appeared on one of the big-screen TVs.

He looked the same. Same T-shirt – the Tesla one, same unkempt hair, and the same smiling face. My heart fluttered, and I involuntarily quivered.

"This is Jack Neufield still holding for the President." He didn't realize his FaceTime app was on. When he did, he stared into the phone, "Hey, this is the same place that I saw before."

"Yes, Jack, it is. My name is Alysha Civil, Special Assistant to the President. I'm in charge of your, uh, little incident, its National Security aspects. Care to say 'hello' to your girlfriend, Janey?" She panned the room, pointing the phone at me.

"Janey, you look like a million dollars!"

"Not really, Jack. They've got me in a Federal Prison."

"That's why I'm calling . . ."

Alysha interrupted, "Where are you, Jack? We'll send a car. Let's talk. We can work out a deal. I'm holding a Presidential Pardon in my hand." She waved a paper in front of the phone.

"What prison have they got you in, Jane?"

Alysha answered for me, "The Federal Correctional Institute – Danbury. You come in, Jack, and we'll let her go. Then we can talk."

"You'll let her go?"

"Sure, Jack. She's almost free right now. See how she's dressed?"

"Don't believe her, Jack," I said.

"I don't, Janey. But what else can I do? And there are a hundred witnesses in the room who just heard her say – there's a Presidential Pardon, and that they'll be letting you go if I come in. Those are the reasons why she'll keep her word. I'm coming in, Janey. I've got what they want, and they'll have to play nice to get it." The screen went blank.

Immediately, Alysha turned to her aides, "Did you get that?"

"Yes, ma'am. He's in New York City, Penn Station, the bus terminal."

"Call New York, get someone over there now." Her aides frantically pulled out their devices and talked and typed.

Winston Erhart III stood, "Is that really a presidential pardon you showed Jack?"

"Get real, Mr. Erhart. There'll be no pardons, not for these two terrorists. We own them and plan to milk them dry of everything they know. It's in the national interest; it's a question of national security."

"But you just said . . ." At this point, Sandy realized he'd been duped.

"Mr. Erhart, in case you and your DARPA buddies haven't noticed . . . many unexplainable incidents have happened of late. Such as, who gave the order to shoot down the anomaly? And where did Jack call from that just happened to look exactly like his barn? *And who is Albert?* Until we know the answer to these questions . . . and everything else, nobody's going free. There's too much at stake here."

From his seat, Winston continued: "We are all very aware of the many unknowns associated with this . . . event. What I question, and I'm not alone in this, is this Administration's methods for dealing with these enigmas. We would prefer the carrot to the stick. The luxury suite to the interrogation room. What you are doing, and intend to do, is wrong . . . just plain wrong." Sandy wound up pounding the table. He had just proved his sincerity and loyalty to me.

This prompted another chorus of anonymous shouting.

"Everything this Administration has done for the past 7 years is wrong. Why stop now?"

"And they're a pack of liars!"

Attempting to quell the revolt, Alysha responded, "Let me remind you that we have a civilian Commander in Chief . . ." She banged the gavel as the intensity of discord rose. "Duly elected by the . . ."

"We know you rigged the election!"

Thoroughly outraged, Ms. Civil threatened, "How dare you . . . I'll have your jobs . . ." screaming and banging the gavel, "You'll all be wearing orange instead of your fancy soldier-boy costumes!"

Red-faced and apoplectic, a highly decorated Uniform rose, pointed his finger, and roared, "How dare you, you fucking . . . bitch!"

The Suit next to him pushed him in the chest, "Don't you call her that . . . you piece of shit!" Things had been heating up, but that was the spark that lit the tinder. A conflagration ensued. Shoving matches proceeded to break out across the room, which quickly led to a full-fledged brawl. A wholesale, big-time, rumble, like "West Side Story" – only, it wasn't the Sharks and the Jets. This time, it was the Suits and the Uniforms.

I had never seen a genuine rumble before. Oh, the occasional fistfight, out in the schoolyard. But nobody got hurt there. And boxing matches, of course, and all kinds of violence on TV. But what I saw that day was the real thing. And the difference between reality and TV is the intensity. When one gets punched in the face, it's a very big deal. One does not get back up and act as if nothing much happened. A new reality sets in. A new way of looking at things – through a thick veil of pain and disbelief. Didn't Mike Tyson have something to say about this?

Fists flew, legs kicked, elbows swung, and heads butted. The headbutt is probably one of the most effective techniques, though generally under-utilized. Applied correctly, for example, upon a nose, it will draw copious quantities of blood, completely stunning the victim. I observed this in more than one instance. How do I know this? I took karate for two years in high school. Though they did not teach the headbutt. Too dangerous. It's like getting hit in the face with a bowling ball.

What was particularly noteworthy about this battle – and that is the proper term for it, was the cacophony of the rage. The volume of the roars, the bellowing, and the non-verbal communications of pure aggression mixed in with grimaces, sneers, and bared teeth. (Though I didn't see any actual biting, I'll give them that.) Furthermore, it served a purpose; to release all the animosities, resentments, jealousies, and hatreds that had been building. And hatred always begs to be released.

Also, it occurred in the best possible way – in close quarters. Combatants were writhing on the floor, grappling, pulling hair, kicking, and punching. On top of the table, one Suit had a Uniform in a scissors lock across his stomach, sporadically reaching in and punched him about the face. A similar hold to the scissors is the headlock. Here the arms are employed instead of the legs to apply leverage to an opponent's head until it turns purple. Occasionally one arm can be freed to punch the exposed skull as well. I noticed one older Uniform employing this strategy to a rather youngish Suit, whose arms flailed uselessly. It looked quite effective but painful to the employed fist. Another highly decorated Uniform was a master of the chokehold, executing it upon one Suit after another, leaving a trail of limp bodies in his wake. A very valuable team player. But there were no guns pulled. At least, not while I was there. And though I write this rather dispassionately, at the time, I was in a state of shock – like I too had been punched in the face.

I felt a pair of arms lift me. It was Sandy and Jamal. They whisked me quickly away. Robert used his bulk to clear a path.

Out in the hallway and on the stairs, people were running around wildly, generally towards the Board Room. We extricated ourselves from this tide of lunacy, made our way out to Winston's town car, and drove out the front gate. I had escaped, with a little help from my new best friends.

The boys wanted to talk about the 'Big Fight,' as it was dubbed. The Big Fight at the big Pow-wow. Who, they noticed, doing what.

"Did you see the crew cut guy in the gray suit elbow that fat General? He hit him so hard his teeth went flying." A recollection by Robert.

"I guess his Poligrip didn't make it," Jamal elaborated.

I think that's just what guys do after a fight – count coup. Though my presence must have been a restraining influence. Plus, Winston changed the subject, focusing our attention back on the situation at hand. Were we all fugitives? Or just me? Did Jamal leave his post of duty, i.e., did he desert? Or was he just A.W.O.L.? We all agreed Robert was fired, especially after the previous incident. And the big question was – what do we do now?

Winston offered a very creative resolution, another field trip. Only this time to Santa Monica, California. To his Institute – The Erhart Institute for Advanced Gravitic Research. He said we could be there in six hours. All we had to do was hop on his plane, which was parked down the road at Westchester Airport, about five minutes away. None of us were truly aware of this side of Winston. He was just one of us – Sandy, till now. He had never played the billionaire card.

Then he offered me the Sun and the Moon. In particular, a job with him at the Institute. One that he said guaranteed protection, immunity, a Presidential Pardon . . . whatever it took, to keep me free. And a lavish salary, with luxurious accommodations thrown in as well. It was certainly worthy of some serious thought. We drove in silence for a few minutes.

Robert broke that silence when he asked, "Do you think you could use a Homeland Security liaison? You know, to help coordinate with the . . ."

"Plenty of room at the Institute for a good man like you, Robert." Jamal was also deep in thought, weighing his options as well.

A short time later, after not too much thought, I declined Sandy's offer and asked to be taken back to the prison. That's where Jack was going; ergo, that's where I had to be. Winston remained impassive and inscrutable. I knew he hadn't given up; nonetheless, he stoically turned, and we headed back to Danbury. After a while, Robert asked if we could stop at a diner.

Chapter 32: Checking In – *Jack*

We pulled up right in front of the prison, the Federal Correctional Institute – Danbury. Kind of an odd name for a prison. At least put the "Danbury" first. The front entrance looked more like a corporate headquarters than a prison – tall windows with brushed stainless-steel trim and fancy glass doors. The prisoners probably won't feel so bad entering here. On second thought, they'd likely arrive around back, surrounded by raw concrete and razor wire. Let them know this isn't going to be summer camp. The front is for the administrators only.

The bus ride from Denver was uneventful. Only one hitch. I was late getting back to the terminal in Omaha, so I took the next bus. Late from paying $12 for two $2 hamburgers. No matter, my hunger was sated, and it only cost me a couple of hours. They let me, or rather, Mat Cambell (Bill's brother, I was impersonating him) on the next bus, and maybe that threw off my pursuers. I made it to New York a free man.

A big unknown was – where's Janey? With the appropriate resources, computer, phone, etc., I could deduce the answer. I mean, how many women's prisons are there near New York? But I had no resources since I kept the battery separate from my phone. What to do? Call someone from a payphone. Who? Well, that was the question. Answer: begin at the top and work down. It's like looking for a parking space, start close, work back. I called the White House. They put me on hold for quite some time – good thing I had a few quarters. But my strategy worked. I found out where Janey was.

Outside the bus station, all kinds of cars were lined up, not just taxis. I approached one – a black Toyota SUV. Not knowing the proper etiquette, I knocked on the window and asked for a ride. The driver was reading something. The air was on. He lowered the window and said, "Where ya headed, Bub?" It seemed he didn't know the proper etiquette either.

"Danbury, Connecticut," I replied.

He pulled out a tablet, pecked on it, and said, "That'll cost you $53.40." I told him I only had $47. Bill had withdrawn an extra $150. The bus fare was $109, plus he gave me an extra twenty. It probably wiped-out his brother's reserves.

The driver looked at me hard, then said, "All right, get in, I'll take you."

I hopped in the front seat, it smelled like dog, and there was Uber stuff plastered around.

"Hope you like dogs. I'm a dog guy, trainer, and groomer, and walker. Check out the sign." He motioned to a magnetic sign on the back seat. It read 'The Boomer Groomer – Canine Services.' "I just drive to supplement my income."

He was an older guy, gray hair on the sides, bushy gray mustache, double frown lines, and inquiring gray eyes. And they were inquiring about me.

"Where you going in Danbury?"

"Uh . . . the Federal Correctional Institution." This elicited a short period of silence.

"Are you checking in?" He said this in jest. We laughed a little.

"Nah, I'm going to visit my girlfriend."

"Oh yeah? What's she in for . . .? I'm just kidding, Bub, if you don't want to tell me . . ."

"No, it's all right. She's a terrorist."

He busted out laughing – loudly. "That's a good one, pal." He kept on laughing, and I joined him . . . for a while.

Then I added, "But do you want to know the not so funny part?" I didn't wait for an answer. "It's true."

This time he didn't laugh but looked at me sideways for an excessively long time. An oncoming car honked. He corrected.

"Sorry about that, Bub. But like I said – it's none of my business. By the way, my name is Mike Mullens, but everyone calls me 'Moon.'" He handed me his card, and we shook hands.

"Pleased to meet you. My name is John Neufield, but everyone calls me Jack."

"I'm supposed to get paid upfront, Jack."

"I gave him what I had and said, "I guess I won't be needing this anymore; money, that is. You were right before . . . I am checking in."

"One thing I like about driving is, I meet all kinds of people. And Jack, it sounds like you're going to be way up there on the list."

Talking about turning myself in brought home the reality. They could be nice, or they could be bad. I heard Janey say, 'Don't trust them, Jack.' That tilted the scale to the bad side. Probably for both of us. But that's where Janey was, so that was my destination:

"The blue, blue, planet,

So far away,

Floating in the deep."

"You all right, Bub?"

I had just drifted off to another place, and Moon noticed, "Yeah . . . well, I guess not." Time to change the subject, looking at his card, I asked, "The Boomer Groomer?"

"Yeah, you like it? I'm going for the boomer crowd. You know, baby boomers? A lot of us out here have dogs."

Mr. Mullens went on talking about his business, all the dogs there are in New York City. While he rambled on, I thought about my dilemma. It was the same old problem. How do I get Janey out? Should I tell? To be totally honest, I did not want to lose my quasi-provisional status. That was a very special club. Membership restricted to one – me. I pictured the rows of black spheres, all kinds; big, small, and clear, *"They are limited to short interstellar distances, Jack."* Albert said that with such equanimity. Too bad he's gone. But he also said, *"The First-Born would not abandon you."* Whatever that means.

"You ever have a dog, Jack?" Moon was really into dogs.

"When I was a kid, my parents had one, Duchess. She was part beagle, part something else. They didn't let her in the house."

"What did you have . . . a dog line set up?"

I pictured a dog tethered to a clothesline: "No, she was just free. There was a doghouse out back, and I let her sleep in the barn on cold nights."

He looked at me, completely flabbergasted. This was beyond the Boomer Groomer's comprehension; he being a city person.

I explained, "We lived in the country."

"Well . . . who shampooed her?"

It was my turn to be flabbergasted. "She liked to jump in the river, every once in a while." Our concept of the canine subculture was wholly opposite. And that's why we had an interesting conversation. Also, my new 'Bub,' Moon, sensed my troubled soul and sought to keep me sidetracked. He was a nice guy.

After a while, we pulled up in front of the Prison. I wished Moon success with his business. Told him if I ever got a dog, I'd look him up.

"I don't think they allow dogs . . . in there." He head-pointed. It was a bad joke. "I know you're bothered big time, Jack, but hang in there. Remember, after the darkness, always comes the dawn." With that, Moon Mullens, The Boomer Groomer, waved and drove off into the night. I had arrived at my new habitat – a federal prison.

Home, no matter where always kindles a warm. . . Not this time, and not this place, though it was to be my new home. The front doors were locked. Standard practice for a prison, I suppose. I knocked, then banged. Finally, a couple of burly guards came and told me to go away.

"Visiting hours are over at seven."

"I'm not visiting. I'm checking in."

"What are you, some kind of a frigen wise-guy?" This was a bad beginning.

"They're waiting for me; my name is Jack Neufield."

One guard picked up a phone, said a few words. His eyes bulged. In a panic, they scrambled to unlock the door, fumbling with the mechanism. The wide guard grabbed me by the arm, the tall one spoke on the phone: "Yeah, we got him."

They lead me thru several locked doors, some electric, some keyed. The deeper we went, the bleaker it got. I kept my mouth shut, not wanting to be a "wise-guy," especially not the "frigen" kind, which I basically was.

They brought me to a spacious room with counters and various paraphernalia cluttered around the periphery. Forms came first, medical history, mainly allergies, etc. Next came the "de-inventory." Is that a word? They took all my stuff. Wallet, phone, Thutmosis's statue; with that, the tall guard gave me a funny look like I was some kind of pervert, and last, the parachute. Yes, I still had that damn thing. Carried it all the way from Denver in a black plastic bag. It made for a good pillow. And it elicited a wise-guy type comment from the wide guard.

"What are you doing with a parachute? Plan on jumping off a tower?" They both laughed at the magnitude of his wit. I just smiled, still trying not to be . . . wise.

The guards wore black uniforms decorated with badges and doodads. And big black belts, from which hung numerous pouches and packets, though it mainly served to hold up the wide guard's stomach, which projected beyond a good 3-4 inches. Projected with pride, I noticed. By this time, both guards had donned rubber gloves and kept their distance. Also, our conversation centered on the concept of spit masks. Beginning with the question:

"Do you know what a spit mask is?" asked the wide one.

I replied in the negative. He continued, "If you try any funny business," he cocked his head and looked at me sideways, "you'll find out." I pictured the guy in the movie – 'The Iron Mask.' I didn't want to do my time wearing a spit mask.

Next, they made me take my socks and sneakers off, gave me a pair of slip-ons to wear, and made me stand with arms extended while they searched me. In my estimation, the guard, the expansive one, patted me down excessively. I mean, what's the point? They planned on taking my clothes. Which they did next, in front of several members of their profession, one of whom looked to be a female. Still standing, arms wide, I opened my mouth, stuck my tongue out while they looked in there with a flashlight. Then I had to bend over, shake out my hair, and cough. They probably employed the flashlight back there also. The humiliation was total, and so was the domination. I think the domination was worse. The knowledge that some ominous authority had absolute control over me, inside and out.

The shower had warm water. It was then that I began to notice the little positives in life, like warm water and a shower in general. It had been three days, and it really did kindle a warm feeling. For shampoo, they handed me a gallon jug of “Liceall.” On the side, it said, “Kills all Lice.” My guard engaged in further conversation, "You've got to keep this shit on your head for three minutes." Then he stood and watched as I did so. Who knows? Maybe I had picked up something . . . on the Moon.

Subsequently, I was given my new clothes. An orange jumpsuit, prison shoes – matching orange slip-ons; and underwear – pink. Go figure. Finally, after I was all decked out and de-loused, they fingerprinted me and took my picture. I tried to smile a little, though I was not happy. I didn't want to look like a thug for my “mug” picture. And they took a DNA swab from my inner cheek. Man, they knew me better than I knew myself. My guard, the wide one, whose nametag read – J. Archer, told me I was lucky . . . the blood girl had gone for the day. Another one of life's little blessings. They were beginning to add up. For the piéce de résistance, I was given a number: 63702-043. I had been reborn.

Chapter 33: Prisoner # 63702-043 – *Jack*

The purpose of a "Correctional Institution" is to correct. Correct an inmate's propensity to commit errant behavior, as the name would imply. Did they sincerely care about me and want me to mend my ways? Were they saying, "Tisk tisk – mustn't do that anymore?" No. I was there to be interrogated. Plain and simple. The authorities wanted to know what I knew. In other words – extract my knowledge. And the ends justified the means. After all, it was for the greater good.

What about the pardon they waved at me while we were on the phone? "Come on in, Jack, we'll make a deal." Or "Of course we'll let Janey go, see how she's dressed? She's already free." And "Can I see her?" "Of course, Jack. We'll send a car for you." What about all that? It was all bullshit. I was taken straight to a cell after being processed as prisoner #63702-043. Again, with the 4,3. It was strange.

I guess it's a typical cell; six feet by ten, concrete block walls, a stainless-steel, toilet-sink combo (the thing was, design-wise, quite ingenious), a bunk, a small steel table, and chair (bolted down). No redecorating allowed. They gave me a day to stew before the interrogations began. I know that's what they do from the movies. I was supposed to freak out, holler and scream, trash my bunk. Then the guards would come and . . . restrain me. Put on the riot gear, get all jacked up and . . . have some fun. Teach "the frigen-wise-guy" a lesson. I was determined not to be one – a wise guy, frigen, or otherwise.

There was a pad and pen on the table. A devilish ploy. A correctional facility corrects through the application of negative conditioning. I remember Mr. McEvey once talked about a guy who rang a bell every time he fed his dog. Maybe that's the wrong kind of conditioning. Here, the bell is always ringing. It's called boredom. Also known as sensory deprivation. And the devilish thing is . . . the guards, the warden, et al., need do nothing to achieve correction. No rack, no thumbscrews, and no bamboo shoots under the nails. All they have to do . . . is leave a pad and pen on the table and let time do the work. And it worked on me. I recalled Albert's statement: "Go ahead, tell the world. Nobody will believe a word you say." So, I started writing.

After being booked, the walk to my cell was quite the tour. Most regrettably, I was not a tourist. Nor was J. Archer an astounding tour guide. There were no oohs and ahhh's. Strike that, there were plenty. Only they were directed at me by the other inmates. Catcalls, gestures, and phrases; "gonna miss your mommy tonight?" and other unmentionables. I later found out that only the newbies wear orange, so my fellow inmates would know who to "give the business" to.

We passed through several cellblocks and recreational areas, both inside and out. Along the way, I asked my guard, J. Archer, what the J. stood for. He frowned and said, "J. is for J." Presumably, J. meant Jay. Case closed; the conversation was over. Probably, a non-fraternization policy was in force. I deduced that information would be hard to extract. And conversely, I had decided, at that point, to make information hard to extract as well. Not to talk. They weren't being nice, so neither would I. They didn't deserve 4,3.

I have been here a few days now, and the highlights have been the interrogation sessions. And the room J. brought me to was larger than it needed to be. The only thing in there was a table, a hand full of chairs and a big mirror on the wall. In case an emergency coiffure adjustment was needed. So far, the routine has been one session in the morning and another in the afternoon. And they were actually amusing. Good cop, bad cop – that sort of thing. No rough stuff. Who were my interrogators? There were many participants.

Let me start with the two guards. Sorry, "correction officers." I was corrected on that point and had mended my ways. They were the same two I encountered when I checked in. The wide one – J. Archer, and the tall one – I never got his name. They were ominous looking, standing around in the background wearing black uniforms, heavy boots, and thick belts loaded with accouterments: cuffs, clubs, canisters, and yes . . . stun guns. Plus, to top it off, metal baseball-type helmets, but the freaky part was, they also wore masks. Why? Were they reverse spit masks? A prophylactic against the possibility of airborne saliva. And what could be their purpose; to conceal their identity in case "the participants" did some really bad stuff? If so, they failed. Of course, I recognized J.'s midriff protrusion. It was projected over his belt with pride. Maybe the outfit was standard correction officer riot gear. If not, it would make a passable Darth Vader costume if one threw in a cape.

My main inquisitors were a Latin duo, both diminutive suit wearers and obviously three-lettered, like CIA or FBI. They were competent, proficient, and maybe even professionally trained in their field of endeavor – interrogation. But ignorant of the big picture. They weren't in the loop, being too low in the pecking order. How do I know? Easy. One can always tell when someone is reciting. Like when they get some vacuous movie star to narrate a science documentary. Like we're not going to know, right? But the couple put on a good show. And they "obviously" liked working together – fraternizing.

Their names were Special Agents Santiago and Angel, something or other. Angel (I always thought that was a boy's name) usually took the lead. I deduced that the little guy liked to be led, especially by her. They would ask questions like, what is 4,3? First, how did they even know about that? Probably from my notes. I must have scribbled something down somewhere, back at the barn. But my questioners had no idea what they were talking about.

I told them that the "3" stood for the number of dimensions that humans can perceive. They looked at each other, and Special Agent Santiago jotted that down. They lapped it up like a couple of puppy dogs. When they asked about the "4," I replied, "Time is the fourth dimension." Then I proceeded to give a short discourse on String Theory. How there are tiny, infinitesimal strings connected to other dimensions. Different types of space. They bought that like a dozen roses on Mother's Day. Man, I could sell them the Brooklyn Bridge. Though, the funny thing is, that's the kind of stuff Mr. McEvey, Janey, and I often talked about and even joked about. Like the threads of space-time. And Albert once said, Space and Time were comprised of discrete components. That they had structure. Anyway, it kept my inquisitive twosome happy. They probably even got a pat on the head and maybe, were thrown a couple of bones.

And that was my job. To stall, evade, and deflect. I'm not sure why. Maybe just to forestall the nasty stuff. Nasty for me. I couldn't help but notice the drain in the floor. And all the electrical outlets; some even 220.

The controlling authority, the big enchilada, was someone I had met twice before, albeit only on the phone. Ms. Alysha Civil, Special Assistant to the President for something. She was the person “in charge of my, uh, little incident.” And she was very civil, as one would expect.

"I'm pleased to finally meet you." We shook hands – hell, why not keep it pleasant, "There have been . . . so many misunderstandings. I hope we can finally clear everything up."

"I thought the pardon cleared everything up."

"Well . . . you did commit a Federal crime, Jack. May I call you, Jack? The theft of radiological materials is a serious matter. When the investigation is completed . . . and it will be soon, I'm sure the “pardon” will be forthcoming."

"There's a hundred witnesses who saw you wave that pardon around."

"So, what, Jack. Those people only care about what's best for the country. And that should be your main interest as well. You stumbled upon something up there in your barn. And we want to know what that is. Think about the greater good, Jack."

"Let me see Janey first, then maybe I'll talk." I played the Janey card. That was my *raison d'être*, my primary motivation.

"Oh, you'll be seeing Janey soon enough. Then you'll talk."

Ms. Civil, Special Ass – to something, left me with those words.

Then the underlings took over. The interesting thing was, they all wore headsets. Wire headbands with an earpiece and a tiny wrap-around mic. Flesh-colored and very unobtrusive. Were they telepathic translators? And what, they didn't think I'd notice? I did, and it revealed that Ms. Alysha was the man behind the curtain. She was calling the shots, directing the investigation. And, with the several cameras in the room, hundreds, make that – innumerable people could be watching from all over the country. I'd better comb my hair. Good thing they have a mirror.

There's something about September that's different from all the other months. Of course, all months are different from each other. But September is even more so. It signals the end of summer. There are hints of orange in the greenery. And the birds, tired from manic mating, pause for a few weeks to enjoy Mother Nature's bounty.

And to me, September was a deep breath before the start of a new year. That hiatus between an ending and a beginning. And not because of school. I never really went to school. Mr. M. and Miss McCarthy were always around. Coming and going. Funny, we never called her Miss M. Eventually, she got married and went off. Broke my heart, almost. But all in all, September was a cusp, an inflection point between the best of what was and what will be.

And I experienced those particular aspects of the ninth month here at the prison as well. Officer J. took me for a walk once a day, around the walking track. It was good to get out. Experience the blue sky and the green hills. I scanned for Janey constantly. Just a glimpse, that's all I wanted. Then they can do to me what they wanted, and I'll suffer in peace.

On the fourth morning of my captivity . . . *Had I been free with Albert? We planned our days together – the driving lesson, the tour of the base, the picnic. I wanted to do all those things. Could I have said, "No, Albert, I think I'll just hang around the barn today?" Yes, I think I could have said that . . . with Albert. Ergo, I was free.*

On the morning of the fourth day, Correction Officer J. came for me as usual. And he was "non-fraternizing," as always. But this time, he brought me to the room behind the mirror. It was well-appointed, comfortable chairs, even a couch. Beneath the mirror was what looked like the control panel of a starship. No, make that a recording studio. A big console with sliders and knobs, and to the sides were racks of equipment, with speakers all over. At the controls sat Alysha. One thing though, she was no phony, like the Wizard of Oz. She was the real deal.

"Welcome to my world, Jack," said Alysha.

I was speechless. All this, just for little ole me? No, I reasoned. This was just what they do here. There were a few others in the room. The tall and wide guards, doing their best to imitate Darth Vader, and pretty much failing miserably. And a couple of others, suit jackets off, sleeves rolled up. Alysha's eager young suck-ups.

"Here, take a seat." She motioned to a chair next to her. It was not comfortable like the others. Gray steel, straight-backed, small armrests, "I want you to have a good view, Jack." Alysha looked excited, psyched up. A bad sign.

I was thrust rather roughly into the chair. Handcuffs were quickly applied, connecting my wrists to the armrests, and my ankles were shackled to the floor. Guards, Wide and Tall, were good at this like they'd done it before. Probably went to school for it. In any event, I didn't resist. I was still trying not to be a “frigen-wise-guy.” And to not do my time in a spit mask. But I was a little bit confused. “Hey, you've got me on the wrong side of the mirror!” I wanted to shout this loudly but didn't. No matter, the shit was about to fly.

"You might find this glass interesting, Jack; you being scientifically inclined and all. When I press this button, a current is sent to the pane, and it becomes transparent. On this side only. It's still mirrored on the other side, and of course – it’s soundproof." She motioned to the headsets. Her hand hovered over the button, eyes wide, face bright with anticipation, "Shall I?" she asked. She pressed the button, and my most fervent desire came true. I saw Janey. She was strapped on a gurney, head tilted upside down with a washcloth over her face. And she was about to get water boarded.

"Just tell us about 4,3, Jack, and they'll stop. It's very simple." Then into her headset, she said, "Proceed."

Chapter 34: Fun Time – *Janey*

Stella took me out to the softball field. She had a pitching machine setup. It looked like a good one. Fancy, light blue, it stood on a tripod with a control panel attached to one side. She wanted to see what I could do. No problem, softball was my game. Plus, I needed the diversion.

The interrogation sessions had become tedious. I mean, how many different ways can you ask, "what's 4,3?" Though, it was entirely my fault. I had to open my big mouth as they dragged me from the first big "Pow-wow." But it also revealed their collective level of intelligence. They couldn't add two plus two. Everyone knew what the thing looked like – a donut with a pod in the center. A cursory deduction would conclude that something had to occur inside the outer ring. Add the Cobalt 60 and all that electric power, and any high school physics student would know that the weak force and electromagnetism were involved. And guess what – as a result, the thing went up. Whooo! Wheee! We're all geniuses. But no. They had to hassle the hell out of me, and probably Jack too. He had to have come in by now.

So, I told them the "three" stood for the atomic number of lithium. You know, what's used in lithium batteries. I elaborated, "That's what you line the outer ring with. It's very important. And if you take me to Jack, I'll tell you the next part – what the four stands for. Angel said she'd pass along my request. Izzy was frantically scribbling on his pad, and the ceiling cameras all had red lights glowing.

They seemed to buy that for a while. Then Izzy asked, "Are you connected to any organizations?"

"No," I answered, "We were only connected to Mr. McEvey, but he passed on."

"Oh, really, where to?" Izzy asked, revealing the breadth of his English idiom. Angel actually chuckled while subtly shaking her head.

"I wish I knew," I replied.

Angel resumed her leadership, "And, uh . . . how did you come up with the idea for this, mm, project of yours?" She didn't even know what we built. Didn't they show her the pictures?

I told her the truth, "In the bathtub." They both smiled and gave each other "a look." Evidently, they had shared some "bathtub time" as well. "But it was really Jack's idea." Angel again exchanged knowing looks with Izzy.

Although Izzy and Angel were easy to fool, I'm sure the eyes behind the cameras weren't. All I could do was delay, stall, and bend in the wind.

And speaking of bending in the wind, that's what the softball was doing as it sped towards me. Stella had set the machine to throw a curve. That was my pitch – a curveball over the outside corner. I smacked a hard line drive over second base, almost hitting the machine. Stella stood to one side with a remote control. I wore my orange jumpsuit along with the standard-issue orange slippers. But I still connected in my usual manner – hitting the ball straight up the middle. Which, inevitably, proved to be my undoing once the opposing team figured that out.

Be that as it may, Stella was impressed – in a big way. With her remote, she was changing each pitch; slow, fast, curve, slider. I didn't care, you put it over, I'll hit it, except on the inside. I don't like inside pitches. Those I let pass.

The wheels were turning inside Stella's baseball hat. I could tell she was formulating big plans for me.

"Practice is on Mondays and Thursdays," she explained. "Games are usually on the weekends, except for the playoffs. Fall-ball is coming up. You'll be just in time."

"Do you think they'll let me play? I mean, it seems like I'm in some kind of special category. Not being convicted of a crime and all." I had to throw that last part in, twist it a little.

She looked at me funny again and said, "I'll see what I can do." The wheels kept on turning.

That evening, we talked softball at dinner. What else? We ate alone after normal dining hours. I inquired about the teams. Stella expounded, "The first thing you need to understand, Jane, is that softball is big up here." She called me Jane. That's better than #11357 - 042. "Everybody's got a team. Both the correctional officers and the prisoners, in two divisions – men's and women's. And we play local civilian teams too." I was somewhat dismayed to realize I was no longer a civilian. "The nurses from Danbury Hospital, the Daughters of the American Revolution . . . don't laugh, they're good. And sometimes," and here she winked, "we combine the men and the women into an All-Star Team."

Stella planned on my being around for quite some time. I thought to myself – it could be worse. I was wrong. That evening, Stella left me with some distressing words, "Jane, if things get rough," she looked me straight in the eye this time, readying me for a telepathic blast, "Take a deep breath and hold it." I got the message, all of it. Then she left.

It's funny how the jailers know all the tricks. When you're tied to the stake: "inhale the smoke fast and deep. You'll pass out first." I heard that somewhere. And they could slip you a potion, a powerful painkiller, before they led you to the cross. Anodynes have been around for millennia. There are tricks about everything. That's just how the Universe works. It's a tricky place. It lays down its laws but gives you ways to get around them. All you need is a good scientist, a good lawyer, or a sympathetic jailer, as the case may be.

And telepathy is like that as well. How many have said, "you can't talk with your mind." That's nonsense. It's done all the time: to control prosthetics, to diminish depression, it's even used in jet fighters with special helmets. And we all have cell phones; some of us even wear them on our heads, or at least on our ears. It's simply electromagnetic radiation. And soon, anti-gravity will be no big deal either. Our cars will fly around in the air. And the stars? No problem. Interstellar travel will become routine. But they won't learn the tricks from me. Torturers don't deserve to know.

I was going to be water boarded. That was the message. Why? I thought we were all getting along so well. Izzy and Angel and me. But not Alysha. I stole the scene, and it was her show. Also, "the eyes behind the cameras" weren't buying my little act either. Maybe if I had tried out for the school play instead of softball . . . they were going to ratchet it up, take it to the next level. All I could do was . . . "take a deep breath and hold it." But Jack was out there, and for that reason, I knew I could get through this. My dreams of softball stardom faded.

For breakfast the next morning, I had coffee only. Stella nodded in approval, though we talked softball. Particularly my fielding abilities. She knew I could hit. And since we were pals, I told her one of my deepest, darkest, secrets . . . I was afraid of the ball. I caught a bad hop to the lip once, and it swelled up like a plum. Same color too. Stella was very sympathetic, "I wouldn't want to see that pretty face of yours get all messed up." I thanked her for her concern, and she took me to the interrogation room.

There were a few extra people in the room this time. Angel and Izzy stood to one side, presumably preoccupied with paperwork. They avoided eye contact and pretended not to notice me. A strange-looking guy in a white smock stood by a cart loaded with medical gear, monitors and machines, and wires dangling everywhere. I begged the Universe, “Please don't let it be electricity.” But one doesn't hold one's breath for shocks. Breathing stops automatically. Did Stella fake me out? My thoughts raced.

The strange guy had a stethoscope hanging from his neck. That told me he was old-school. He had white hair brushed straight back and a goatee, well-manicured. Affixed to his almandine eyes were a pair of no-rim glasses, slightly tinted. Probably the kind that darkened in sunlight. Expensive. His face was tight, with a couple of vertical lines on each cheek framing a thin, no-nonsense mouth. Doctor Strangelove with a little Foo Man Choo thrown in. No doubt a real character, and apparently, my attending physician. I wondered if he was an inmate. A doctor who'd gone bad and now was being put to some good use.

And there were a couple of beefcakes. Hunks. The kind of guys who belonged on a “Playgirl” centerfold. *Whatever happened to “Playgirl” anyway?* They were dressed in tight, camouflaged T-shirts and cargo pants. Were they trying to hide, conceal themselves? They'd blend right in . . . to a jungle. The scary part was – they were wearing masks. Why? So, I wouldn't recognize them out on the ball field? The studs stood next to a rolling stretcher. It looked very antiseptic, all stainless steel with a big wheel, midway, on each side, presumably for tilting. It was locked in the upright position. On the floor, nearby, was a garden hose and a couple of watering cans. And I must admit to being somewhat relieved. It was not going to be electricity. Not with all that water. *Thank you.*

As to my mental condition, I was barely keeping it together. Should I resist? Pull a Bill Cambell and go down swinging? No, that was not my style. Blank Jane. Should I do a Blank Jane? I didn't know. I just tried to maintain some dignity.

As I stood there, surveilling, trying to take it all in, I was greeted by a voice. It was omnipresent and filled the room. A voice I knew and did not like. It was Alysha Civil's. She was behind the mirror.

"Welcome to my party, Miss Riley. And whether you like it or not, I'm going to call you Ester. Not Janey. Janey's too cute. And you will soon learn . . . that cute is not an appropriate word . . . for what we do here. Oh, you didn't get an invitation to the party? Maybe that's because . . ." she tried not to laugh, "you are the party." She switched off her laughter. Then resumed, "Strap her in, boys." There were no red lights on the cameras. Another bad sign.

The Playgirl boys hastened to buckle me up. *"Seat belts save lives."* My inner thoughts sometimes even amaze me. They rolled the platform over and fastened the belts to my ankles, chest, wrists, and even one around my forehead. *"Mustn't move. We wouldn't want you to get hurt."* This, the boys thought, and almost said. I remained blank. My eyebrows were not elevated, nor was my mouth slightly upturned. Next, they wheeled me over to Dr. Strangelove, who proceeded to tape many electrodes on me. He actually said, "I won't let them go too far." Gee, thanks doc, that's good to know. I feel better already. The preceding thought, I also rejected and did not say.

I had mentally prepared myself for the ordeal. Intellectualized the situation and put to good use my medical training. Stella was right to advise, "hold your breath." The sinus cavity has no outlet. Once it fills, there's no place for the water to go unless I breathe. Then it will fill the lungs, and that's called drowning. How long can I hold my breath? I saw this magician on Oprah hold his for a good 15 minutes. First, he inhaled pure oxygen for several minutes, and then he entered this big transparent water tank. If I hadn't seen it, I wouldn't believe it. And if he could do 15 minutes, I could do, say, 30 seconds. The key fact is – don't breathe. It will only make matters worse, 10 times worse. Heck, when I swim, water goes up my nose all the time, especially doing the backstroke. And I hate it a whole lot.

They had me all strapped in and hooked up. Angel and Izzy finally walked over and summoned the nerve to face me. I gave them a *"you must be fucking crazy for doing this"* look. They both turned away, ashamed.

"Just tell them you'll talk, then they'll stop." Angel imparted this sage advice.

And Alysha seconded it: "Ms. Rodriguez has given you some valuable counsel, 'Ester.' Just agree to tell us all you know, and we'll stop. Ooops, here comes the guest of honor. You'll have to excuse me."

Jack! They've got Jack behind the mirror! It's not me they want to break. It's him! And I'm the pawn, and pawns are expendable. Don't talk, Jack . . . don't talk. That was my only thought, and I broadcasted it powerfully.

A washcloth was placed over my face, I heard the microphone click on, and Alysha said, "Proceed."

In the background, I heard Jack shout, "You fucking moth . . ." Then the mic went dead, and so did I. I forgot to hold my breath. The washcloth quickly saturated, and water went up my nose, down my throat, into my lungs, stomach, and everywhere else. So much for the best-laid plans. The pain and agony were pure hell, the worst thing I ever felt, as I tried to breathe, snort, vomit, and cough, all at the same time. One instinctively, desperately wants to inhale, but only water comes in via the mouth and nose. It was indescribably awful. They stopped after a few seconds and rotated me back up. As they toweled me off, I gagged, snorted, and puked. When I had recomposed myself, as much as could be expected, that hateful, ubiquitous voice sounded again.

"Is there anything you'd like to tell us, 'Ester'?" I heard Jack in the background. He sounded muffled like he was gagged.

I did have something to say, "Don't talk, Jack. The evil bastards don't deserve it." My voice was hoarse.

Ms. Alysha Civil, special bitch to the President, uttered her favorite word, again, "Proceed."

This time I was ready. I took a couple of deep breaths, then held the last one as the Playgirl boys poured. They took turns. I wondered why as my sinuses filled. They were probably just playing fair. It wasn't so bad this time. And . . . I was angry, ultra pissed-off.

And anger, as I learned, is the best antidote for panic. I wonder if that's in some shrink's tome somewhere, or did I just discover a profound, psychological principle. All those people going around having panic attacks – just slap them around a little, get them really pissed-off, or pour water up their noses, and they'll snap right out of it. I discovered another interesting principle – one can snort when not breathing – in short bursts. It's useless, of course, in that it only delays the inevitable – the filling of the sinuses. But it helps to pass the time. And every second counts when you're being water boarded. After 7-10 seconds, they stopped again. Then, wheeled me upright and cleaned me up. I snorted and wheezed, but there was no retching this time. At that moment, I vowed to never go swimming again, and I said a silent prayer of thanks for Stella.

I looked at Angel. She was suffering more than me. Her eyes were puffy, red, teary, and reflecting the horror in her soul, "Please, Janey, talk. Just say you'll . . . talk." She was pleading with both me and Alysha.

The voice spoke again, "An excellent suggestion, again from our little Angel girl. She, too, has learned the price of failure this morning."

"Don't talk, Jack. I can take this. All-day long. Just don't talk." I was lying, of course. One more time and I would have broke for sure, sang like a canary in a coal mine. But I didn't get the chance. The stupid shit fell for my bluff.

"You little bitch. We'll see what happens when the shoe's on the other foot. Bring Jack in there," she commanded.

When you wish upon a star, sometimes that wish comes true. And mine just did. I saw Jack. They carried him in gagged and chained to a chair. Our eyes locked, and in that instant, a blizzard of thoughts and emotions were exchanged. We were together again, bound to our respective torture devices but nonetheless, together again. And I felt oddly relieved. Jack had come, and I knew deep down that somehow, everything would change.

And, indeed, everything did change. Angel wasn't anguished anymore. A beatific glow radiated from her. Izzy was strangely quiescent, at peace with himself. Doctor Strangelove detached my electrodes and declared me – in perfect health. As if I just got a physical exam. One of the Playgirl boys was unbuckling me; the other was toweling me down, even adjusting my hair a little. Jack's guards were undergoing a similar transformation. Unlocking his chains and removing the towel, which was stuffed in his mouth. Once free, Jack and I flew together and hugged hard. United again, at last. Though, frankly, we'd only been apart for a couple of weeks. But so much had happened.

Through the little window in the door, I saw a high-ranking military officer talking to Alysha. He wore a tan uniform with numerous decorations on the pockets and three stars on each shoulder. He looked like a General.

Then Alysha opened the door and walked in. Her hair was the same, pulled straight back, and she sported her trademarked, severe, dark-gray suit. Her demeanor, though, expressed a strangely detached look. She blithely announced, "There has been a singularly major mix-up. We sincerely regret any inconveniences that may have occurred."

Any inconveniences? Like being thrown in prison and tortured?

Alysha went on, "You are being transferred to the Military immediately and are to go with this gentleman."

The General backed into the room. He was still signing papers as presented by Alysha's aides. Then he turned. Oddly, he had a cane hooked on one arm and an unlit pipe in his mouth. Longish, unruly hair protruded from beneath his hat. And his eyes twinkled a little. I felt Jack go slack in my arms and gasp, "Albert."

That name again. It bounced around in my brain, firing axons and activating synapses. Memories and references were triggered. Jack straightened, looked me dead in the eye, and said, "Everything's going to be OK. We're getting out of here."

All I could think to say was, *"Who is Albert?"*

Interlude 5: "Let the Progenitor die!"

Neurons in the brain exchange electrical information fast, up to a thousand times per second. And there are billions of nerve cells. But most of these signals are just raw data; sensory perception, breathing, digestion, and so forth. On occasion, the signals are repeated and reinforced, following old and familiar pathways. That's called memory. Sometimes new patterns are formed, triggering different sequences. These are called thoughts. And all these electrons swirling around in the brain are occasionally relayed to the larynx. There, with the appropriate modulation of air, the thoughts are voiced. And as is always the case with flows of electrons, they emit fields, which radiate outwards. Ripples of pulsating magnetic charge, directly analogous to those thought patterns. The key to all this lies in the patterns. They are non-random and organized into a code of some sort. And as such, information is communicated.

An interesting question is – where do these new patterns, these thoughts come from? A caveman looks up at the Sun and thinks: "That ball of fire in the sky is a god." Where did that thought come from? In days of old, leaders were believed to be in direct contact with supreme beings. It's interesting how almost every culture and civilization held to this belief. The ancient Chinese had their "Mandate from Heaven," European monarchies had their "Divine Right of Kings," and so on, down to the shaman dancing around the fire in a village clearing. And how does one communicate with a god? Were the recipients decoding electromagnetic waves that, as a consequence, triggered thought patterns? Maybe, maybe not. But if so, then thoughts are a means of communication, both for sending and or receiving information. Prayers can be sent, and answers received. But how does one truly know if one's thoughts go to, or come from, a god?

By definition, non-terrestrial beings must be denoted as aliens, whether they be supreme or otherwise. The question must be asked – why were most civilizations so sure their thoughts came from . . . aliens? They could have come from other powerful, thought transmitting humans. Or even other indigenous species – say whales. Therefore, it was in everyone's interest to ascertain where said thoughts came from, even among the First-Born. And a grand search was initiated.

It was assumed that non-random electromagnetic waves would carry the information. What else is there? There is more, a great deal more, but again I digress. On Earth, SETI (The Search for Extraterrestrial Intelligence) has been looking for patterns in the sky for many decades. Regrettably, the results have been inconclusive, though some interesting patterns have been observed. My fellow humans on Earth were looking in the wrong places but in the right medium – electromagnetic waves.

And the First-Born looked for patterns as well. Of course, they were well aware of any and all sentient life as it arose in their Cosmos. But they searched for more, a larger awareness – patterns of thought from the Progenitor itself. There were those among The First to Arise who were curious and posed the question, "Is our Universe an aware presence?" Which led to a larger question, one that, in some civilizations, spawned religions. Can the whole be less than the sum of its parts? Can something be less than what it is made of? A wheel is part of a car. Therefore, cars have wheels – ipso facto. Intelligent beings are part of the Universe; therefore, the Universe is intelligent – ipso facto. This was the reasoning behind the quest undertaken by the First-Born. And they discovered the answer.

It lay in the Gamma-ray bursts – the concentrated explosive output of supermassive stars. The radiation was non-random. Hence it contained information, which was decoded. Then, the First Ones communicated with their parent and learned many things.

Thoughts, somewhat akin to panic, emanated in Pleasantville, the Locus of the First-Born:

"You mindlessly screamed like non-sentients and were heard." This came from a particularly powerful, older Presence, "You drew attention to ourselves and awakened something."

"And it comes for us now!" This piece of information was contributed by the First Observer. An entity that no longer enjoyed celebrity status, being the bearer of very bad news.

Several Manifolds had turned and were heading towards the Enclave. Pernicious clouds of anti-stuff, anti-quarks, anti-time, dark actualities, and more. The barbarians were at the gates, and Pleasantville was not very pleasant anymore. The threat was mortal, and they faced annihilation. Many Presences left or were leaving. But where to go was the question. Their home Universe was under siege, and now their blissful little Locus was in the process of being destroyed.

"We must venture outward, travel far, find another Locus, and then build a new home." This was the analysis of many. The Aether was large; they proposed nomadism; to wander for eternity.

"To be perpetually hunted. This is your proposal? We will never be safe." The statement – "never be safe" – to an immortal being, who valued safety above all else, was anathema. Yet it was said.

"No, we must stay and resist! We are powerful. We can overcome!" The younger Presences proposed this course of action.

"We cannot overcome. We are nothing compared to what is out there, that which can move and control the Manifolds . . . and destroy Universes. That which seeks our death." The First-Born would have screamed at the formulation of this thought, but they had learned the value of silence.

"Negotiate!" This logic infused outward from the Oldest One, the first of the First-Born."

And so, another Great Quest was initiated. They looked for patterns in the Aether itself, patterns which would convey information – sentient thought. They sought communication with the Others so as to arrange an accommodation.

"We can find a third way, give them what they want, and in turn, obtain what we need." A perfectly reasonable proposition.

"But they want to kill the Progenitor!" There's always one in every crowd – the killjoy.

After some considerable silence, a singular but powerful voice was heard, “Then let it have the Progenitor. Let the Progenitor die!"

This concludes **Book One – the Neufield Anomaly**.

The Fourth Level Series, the saga of Earth's rise to the Fourth Level, continues on the next page with the first chapter of ***Book Two – The Emergence***. Our homeworld begins to emerge. Please enjoy and . . . transcend.

The Fourth Level Series:

Book 2:

The Emergence

By Mariner Pezza

Creative consultant – Cheryl E. Kemeny

The Fourth Level Series: Book 2

THE

EMERGENCE

The Earth is ready.

MARINER PEZZA

with CHERYL KEMENY

Table of Contents

Chapter

Page

Chapter 1: The Getaway – *Janey*

They say the first few days in prison are the worst. I can attest to the truth of that. One must undergo the transition from freedom to subjugation. Learn to submit. And forcing the newbs to wear orange has a role to play. It gives the other convicts a target. Someone to hurl their invective at. But the walk through the prison was different this time. There were no jeers, catcalls, or obscene gestures, though Jack and I were wearing that horrible color. Oh sure, they all still stared as their hands clasped the bars. But their eyes were vacant, and their gaze came from empty faces – like they belonged to a cult. One inmate even flipped us a peace sign. It was strange.

Even stranger was the behavior of our escort – Ms. Alysha Civil, Special Assistant to the President for whatever. She was *Chatty Cathy*. Pull the string and watch her talk – non-stop. And she wasn't talking to Jack, and she wasn't talking to me. Her incessant blather was addressed to Albert. *Who is Albert?* That question rather thoroughly permeated my brain. I seriously doubted that he was a General.

He was dressed in an army general's uniform. Though he didn't play the part very well. High-ranking officers expect their orders to be abjectly obeyed. And their comportment reflects this. They exude an air of authority. Albert did not display this. His "air" was more like . . . reserved amusement. Like he was enjoying the diversion. His uniform was light tan, probably the summer style, and not all that cluttered with badges and bling. But the shine off the three stars on each shoulder caught the eye. Overall, it looked quite authentic. However, some oddities stood out. For example, from under his hat peeked several strands of longish hair, and, in one hand, he sported a cane, obviously for show. In no way did he appear impaired. Also, there was something about him that seemed familiar. But I just couldn't place it. Jauntily, our little party strolled through the cellblocks.

Alysha's chatter was pure ingratiation. She was a natural-born brown-nose, "I can't tell you how thankful I am that the Military is removing this . . . lunatic affair from my portfolio." A strategic pauser, she was always careful with her words. "My responsibility is National Security. I can't be dealing with oddball anomalies . . . UFO's, and such. You have a division that deals with this, don't you, General?"

"Oh, yes. These kinds of incidents are of special interest to us." The alleged General's eyes revealed the slight glint of a sparkle. Like he was enjoying himself.

I walked close to Jack because we were close. He was my life partner, my significant other. We grew up together, being neighbors. I lived on the horse farm down the road and hung out at Jack's place, the barn specifically. They were always doing such seriously interesting stuff there. And that's where we built the "thing" – with Mr. McEvey, of course.

"Everything's going to be OK." Jack said after he almost fainted upon seeing Albert enter the picture. And what was the picture? Well, I had just undergone two water-boarding sessions, and Jack was slated to be next. We were at some special annex at the Federal Correctional Institution – Danbury. *Why don't they put the name "Danbury" first?* Our nemesis was Alysha Civil – chief torturer extraordinaire. And she enjoyed her work.

Alysha was on the fast track coming from a parentage of government functionaries. She looked like an ancient statue excavated from an archeological dig in Athens or Rome. Her features were classically perfect; eyes and nose flawlessly sculpted, but her mouth was a bit thin with the upper right lip often up turned, revealing the temperament that usually accompanies a sneer. And it's hard to carve hair in stone unless it's pulled tightly back, which hers typically was. She wore her standard dark-gray suit that matched her countenance – dark and severe. Only one thing was different, she had changed. She was *Chatty Cathy*.

Ms. Civil cackled all the way to the front doors. Relating her life's story, how great she was – to Albert, always to Albert. She whisked us through the many checkpoints and locked doors, smiling and small talking the guards. They smiled and small-talked back. In due course, we exited the front doors.

The General's vehicle was parked out front. It was a Humvee done up in desert camo. That was it. No driver, no entourage, just the Humvee. I thought Generals were supposed to be the real deal; make a big splash wherever they went. But then again, I knew that Albert wasn't a General. We said our goodbyes, waved, and Alysha quipped, "Now I don't wan'a see you-all coming back here." A pure W.T.F. statement.

Albert drove, Jack rode shotgun, and I hopped in the back, though there was enough room for a whole army upfront. We did not engage in personal conversation during our little stroll through the prison for two reasons. First, *Chatty Cathy* didn't give us a chance. And second, because there was some very strange shit going on, and I kind of assumed Albert was breaking us out. But normal conversation resumed once we drove past the front gate. Though "normal" may not be the most accurate word.

"Albert, I thought you went away. How come you're . . . here?" Jack was the first to speak.

"If you will recall, Jack, I did specify that a smaller facsimile of my original configuration would remain. I am as such." Albert's response was about as weird as anything I could think of. And it only got worse.

"But you're here, on Earth. What about . . . you know, non-interference?"

"My strictures prohibit me from allowing a member, even a quasi-provisional one such as yourself, from being harmed. Especially by a nascent civilization." Albert's voice was perfectly modulated. Spoken without hesitation or any indications of an emotional state. There was a power there that did not fit the man. Though it was an exact fit for the complete bizarreness of the content.

"Albert, allow me to introduce Janey Riley." Jack half-turned with one arm up and looked at me, smiling. I sensed he was enjoying my total befuddlement.

"I am very pleased to make your acquaintance, Jane . . . finally." He reached over the seat, and we shook hands as he continued to drive.

"Janey, this is Albert . . . uh, Einstein. But he's not really Albert Einstein."

Why didn't I notice the resemblance sooner? Jack continued, "I know we have a lot of explaining to do."

It was then that I heard the sirens in the distance.

Jack asked, "Albert, are those sirens for us?"

"Yes, Jack. I am quite certain they are."

"What did you do . . . steal this vehicle?"

"Yes, but that is probably not the reason for their employment at this time." We turned onto a two-lane, semi-major road. A couple of yellow lines ran down the middle, with many trees and smallish ranch-type houses spotted here and there. Albert floored it, and the Humvee leaped forward, "Please allow me a quick explanation. At the prison, we reorganized the electromagnetic thought patterns of those individuals in our immediate vicinity. The purpose was to render them amenable to our departure. Implementations of those procedures are no longer in effect. Hence the sirens."

Jack responded to this gobbledygook. "So, they came to their senses and freaked!"

"That would be an accurate assessment, Jack. I suggest you apply the seat restraining mechanisms. They probably will be needed." We did.

More sirens added their voices to the chorus. It was at least a quartette, and they were singing our song, though the scream of a cop car is not on my list of all-time favorites. The windows were open, and the strains entered from all sides. But within my head, an old tune blared a little louder – *Who is Albert*, and now it was coupled with – *What is Albert?*

Jack commented, “Maybe we should avoid the main roads. There’ll likely be roadblocks. We're dealing with the Feds here, and they have unlimited resources." We were, at this point, strategizing on how to avoid capture. More sounds joined the chorus, and Jack looked up, "Shit! It's a helicopter. How did they get one up there so fast?" After some more upward gawking, "Albert, where are we going?"

I could see the speedometer. We were doing about 60. A dangerous speed for curvy back roads. Albert traced a rectangle in midair halfway across the front seat. A semi-transparent display of a street map appeared. I think it was a holograph. I saw something like that in an "Iron Man" movie once.

The streets and towns were labeled. Our prison was located in the lower right corner, and from it, a red line emanated. Presumably, it represented our distance traveled. In the upper left corner was a big blue X. Our destination.

"They've got us pegged. For sure, they'll set up roadblocks."

"I suggest you consult the map, Jack, and deduce probable locations for said 'roadblocks.'" Jack slid over and studied the map. Albert's driving bordered on the reckless, passing every car we met. I hung on for dear life to the overhead handles.

"We're coming up on New Fairfield." A cluster of colonial-style buildings came to view. A post office, a supermarket, and a red brick village center. Albert slowed, and we negotiated our way through the town, generally heading north, "We've got to get off this main road. Turn left here on 39, then we'll take Bigelow north to Pine Hill." Albert heeded Jack's advice.

It was midmorning in mid-September, not much traffic, and we were on another country road; two lanes, maybe a bit more residential. And there were trees, lots of trees. Albert was driving crazy again, using the whole road, swaying from lane to lane, even around blind corners. It was extremely distressing. But we were making progress, and the red line on the map lengthened.

"Albert, what's our destination?" Jack and his buddy, the General, worked well together like they had a history of doing so.

"An old rock quarry no longer in use. I parked a . . . vehicle there, in an equipment warehouse. That is our objective."

I wanted to question the term "vehicle." Like get a definition, but I didn't. There was no time for explanations.

Albert nailed it on the straightaways. These Humvees can really go, and corner too. Also, they stick to the road like glue, maybe because they're seven feet wide. The whoop-whoop sounds got louder. Jack's head exited the window and looked up, "Shit, now there are two helicopters! And one's right on top of us!"

That's when the shooting began. I took a quick look. A soldier was hanging out the door with a rifle. Bullets began ricocheting off the roof, and the hood and I cringed with each impact, "Albert! They're shooting at us!" Jack felt the need to state the obvious, "Why are they shooting at us?" We quickly rolled up the windows.

Albert began zigzag-ing in a random manner. I hung on as though my life depended on it and tightened the seat belt.

"They know this vehicle is bullet-proof; the metal, the glass, and even the tires are solid rubber. Therefore, I assume their objective is to induce panic, force us to make a mistake, and possibly, drive off the road."

Jack resumed studying the map, "If we can only get to Bigelow Road, then we'll have a chance of making it all the way." The automatic fire resumed. The impacts sounded and felt like cannonballs. And we didn't make it to Bigelow Road. A couple of minutes later, we hit a roadblock. A ribbon of spikes had been laid across the road, and a patrol car was parked to one side. A police officer was crouched next to it, weapon drawn.

First, they must not have been aware that our tires were solid, and second, the police cars must carry that spiky stuff standard equipment. But in New Fairfield, Connecticut? They'll use it, what . . . once in fifty years? I figured we'd just drive right over it as we waved goodbye to the cop. Albert went around.

There was a stonewall perpendicular to the road. It was about three feet tall and two feet thick. Pretty substantial. The thing about this part of the state is, there are rocks everywhere. The glaciers deposited them, or so the geologists say. But what's interesting is – the rocks were mostly medium-sized. Pickup-able by one or two strong guys. So, what did our forebears do? They cleared the fields and cleverly fit the stones into rock fences. They were all over my parent's farm. Strike that. It's probably not their farm anymore. Anyway, they were everywhere, and one was right in front of us. Albert veered left, missing the spikes, and crashed through the stonewall doing about 70. Rocks and boulders flew like pins on a bowling lane. The cop was so stunned, she did not fire her weapon. And we did not wave goodbye. But she got in her car, turned on the siren, and floored it. Now we had a tail. Make that three tails, two in the sky, one on the road.

We continued driving crazily up the road as Jack inquired, "Why didn't you just drive over the spikes? The tires are solid rubber."

"The strip would have entangled in our wheels and impeded our forward progress." Albert's answer was a good one, in my opinion.

The helicopters seemed to have pulled back and were firing less frequently, even though the area was becoming more rural. Jack was studying the map again, "They'll probably be setting up a major barricade, up ahead somewhere. One we can't go around. There's Bigelow Road." He pointed to a street up ahead. "Turn left there." We did.

Bigelow Road was narrower and curvier. It seemed to be located on the top of a ridge with a major drop-off to our right. Albert slowed down a little. Jack continued, "In about a quarter-mile, we'll hit Route 37 again. Turn left there, go about a hundred feet, then turn right on Pine Hill. About a quarter mile up is the Quarry. We're close." He resumed studying, the choppers resumed firing, and Albert resumed zigzagging. "If I were them, I'd put the roadblock here." He pointed to the short stretch on Route 37. We were close, and Jack was right.

This time the blockade was substantial. They used cop cars. Four of them doubled up across the road. Behind them, a small army was deployed with guns drawn. Mostly handguns but a few rifles as well. We stopped about a hundred feet away. One cop with a bullhorn stood and bellowed, "Exit the vehicle and put your hands on the hood – now!" Albert touched the map, and it changed to an aerial view. *What, did he have a satellite up there?*

"We have to go off-road, Jack. Pick a route."

Jack intensely examined the picture and said, "Go left down that dirt road. It's a business of some sort."

It was a construction company's yard with several buildings and large excavating equipment scattered about. Jack guided us through, over lawns, down paths, and then into a clearing near a wooded area. The sirens started again, like the howling of wolves, or maybe hyenas, "Keep heading north. If we can make it past these trees, there are fields up ahead." He pointed to the patch of forest before us.

We had bypassed the roadblock. But from the sound of the sirens, a whole battalion of cops followed us, and off-road too. We entered the forest. It was young in that the trees were smallish – some only 3 to 4 inches in diameter. Maples mostly, a few were just turning color – yellow and orange. We mowed them down flat. Bulldozed a road right over the smaller saplings while detouring around the larger trees. These Humvees can take one hell of a beating. And so did we inside. Albert was a good driver, though. He never lost his cool, and we made it to the fields.

They were cornfields, ready for harvesting. We initiated the reaping process a little early, as we ripped across that field doing about 60, leaving a cloud of corn and dust in our wake. I saw the farmer off to one side, standing by a tractor near a silo. He just stood there, gaping. Again, we didn't wave.

In the distance and past some trees, I could see the road. It was about a quarter mile away. Several cop cars were there maintaining a parallel course. Behind us, three or four police vehicles broke out of the woods and started plowing through the corn also. In their wake, a huge cloud of dust billowed. There would be no need for a harvester this year. And the farmer no longer stood and stared. He was jumping around like a crazy man.

Jack was still intently studying the map, and Albert stole a glance once in a while as well. They agreed on an easterly course towards a more heavily wooded area, but generally, in the direction, we needed to go. The cops were still on our tail, and the choppers were closing in as well. We entered the forest, barreling through bushes and thickets, swerving around the big trees and flattening the smaller ones. Then we slid down a small ravine and splashed through a stream, bouncing, and crashing over the rocks. It felt as though our guts were being ripped out – both the vehicle and ours. The good thing was the little river stopped the cops. And the thick foliage above stopped the gunfire.

After traveling a short distance, we stopped and took a few moments to catch our collective breaths. Jack was the first to speak as he studied the aerial layout, “Why are we stopping? The rock quarry should be right up ahead." We all stared at the map. We were almost on top of the big blue X. But we had to cross the road.

"We should rest here for a minute or two, allow our pursuers to gain some distance beyond our objective." Albert pointed, “We can emerge back onto the road at this point, travel this short stretch, and then enter the Quarry here."

"Sounds like a plan, Albert. Just like old times. Tearing up the backside of the Moon. Shooting the rilles, cruising the caves." I surmised that they had had some work history. *But on the Moon?*

"But if I may remind you, Jack, you were driving then. And, as per my non-interference directives, we tore up nothing and caused zero damage. Nonetheless, they were good times. I think we can proceed now. Sufficient time has elapsed."

Slowly we resumed our forward progress. Picking our way around the impenetrable areas, plowing through bushes, skidding down a small gulley, and finally, up and onto the road. Albert's plan worked. No one was in sight until a helicopter dropped down a short distance away. It hovered a few feet off the ground, kicking up a hurricane of dust as the trees violently gyrated.

It was a standoff. We both maintained our position, just staring and testing each other's will. In a way, the scene was reminiscent of gunfighters in a spaghetti western. We were the Good, they were the Bad, and the Uglies had driven up the road. Who would draw first, that was the question? The only thing missing was the music. All we heard was the loud throbbing of the airframe before us. Then the helicopter guys blinked. I guess they just couldn't stand the suspense. The guy with the rifle hung out and began firing again. Loud pings erupted on our front grille, the tires, and the windshield. It was time to have a little faith in our vehicle's armor.

Jack did not diminish my anxiety when he inquired, "What if they shoot a missile at us? Like in Colorado?" I hated to admit it, but he brought forth a good point.

All Albert said was, "Open the sunroof, Jack."

"What the freak for . . . to let the bullets in?" Another good point was raised by my significant partner.

"Hear me out, Jack. Once the sunroof is open, stand up and point the cane at them." He handed Jack his cane. It was a standard cane, orangey wood, nicely polished with a carved bone handle and a rubber cap on the base.

"What?" Jack reiterated his incredulity.

"With the cane, you will control them. Just drag and drop them away, so we can pass."

There were no more questions from Jack. He obeyed. That's not to say I didn't have about a zillion.

"And do it quickly, Jack. We don't want to get shot or blown up."

Meanwhile, we were still under rifle fire. Not so much at the cab. More like the tires; I think they were trying to shred them.

Jack unlatched the sunroof, hastily stood up, pointed the cane at the chopper, and with a quick wrist motion, flicked the base of the cane upwards and away. The helicopter also went – upwards and away – immediately and fast. I had a hard time believing my eyes. Upon looking twice and scanning the sky, I saw in the distance a black speck. I had to assume it was our prior adversary.

Jack re-entered the cab and gently returned the cane to its place beside Albert, who commented, "I should have instructed you to perform the cane-action slowly. No matter, they survived. Now we can proceed."

My assessment of Albert was expanding. He was no longer some kind of magic mapmaker. He was considerably more.

We proceeded down the road, accelerating rapidly and then decelerating just as fast. Traveling from point A to point B as rapidly as possible. Not a word was said, though I'm sure whole encyclopedias were thought. We came to a dirt side road. “No Trespassing” and “Violators Will Be Prosecuted” signs decorated the trees near the entrance. They were old and partially rusted. This was our destination. Journey's end. But our travail was not over. The other helicopter flew by.

"Did he see us?" I asked.

Jack looked up and said: "Can't tell."

"We have arrived. They can no longer impede our departure." Albert said this in a matter-of-fact manner but seemed relieved. We turned in and immediately encountered a chain-link fence, padlocked with multiple chains and locks. Albert handed Jack a wad of keys and pointed to the barrier. Jack got out, fumbled around for what seemed like forever, then opened the gate. After we drove through, he closed and locked it again. Why can't they impede us now, I wondered? What's in the quarry that's going to solve all our problems? *What kind of vehicle?*

We drove a considerable distance down the dirt road. Weeds had taken root, certainly a sign of disuse. A spacious clearing eventually came to view. It was a huge excavation pit surrounded by grayish-white cliffs. To my eye, the stone was granite. What else? That's what Connecticut's made of. It terraced down in steps to a small blue lake and then scaled back up on the other side. Huge semi-rectangular blocks of stone haphazardly littered the horizontal surfaces, joined by the occasional piece of rusting mining equipment. Everything looked frozen in time. As though one day, the word was given to shut down, and everyone just dropped their tools and left. They probably hit water, most likely underground springs, and the fight just wasn't worth the effort anymore. Hence the big pool of water.

My parents, when they remodeled the kitchen, chose granite countertops. It was a similar color, a composite of gray and white.

Very pleasant and unobtrusive, unlike some colors – like orange. Maybe they came from this place, though the quarry appeared long abandoned. I wondered when the "No Swimming" signs were set up. There were several positioned next to the swimming hole. Anyone would know that almost all teenagers would interpret this as an invitation. It's called the Law of Opposites, as any shrink would confirm. But it applies only to teenagers. I know. I was one once, and not too long ago, if I may add. And I also know that I could have been one of those kids down there enjoying one of the last good days of summer. Though I'm quite sure I would have worn a bathing suit.

They had rigged up a rope swing on a decrepit derrick that hung out over the water. One young man saw us and put on a show. He ran with the rope, swung out, grabbed his knees in a cannonball position, and splashed into the water. The level of difficulty was low, but the fun factor seemed high. Obviously, they did not fear us. Humvees are driven on the street quite routinely these days. Though ours must have looked quite beat, with bullet pockmarks all over, plus it was making odd noises and left a trail of smoke. For certain, we did not look like the local constabulary. We could have passed for fellow fun lovers. I rolled down the window and waved. A couple of the kids waved back. I seriously wanted to join them, take a quick dip. Then I remembered. I was wearing orange. *Everyone knows who wears orange.* I didn't want to scare them away. But the distant gunfire did. And if that didn't, the helicopter swooping in clinched it. The kids took off, without dressing first, probably to watch the scene surreptitiously from the woods.

The chopper was hovering not too far in the distance, no doubt engaged in a running commentary about our activities. Directing the cavalry to our position. It must have been the cops we heard before, probably shooting the locks off the gate. We kept on driving, winding our way around mountains of rock, past piles of indecipherable equipment, and past various buildings and sheds. The sirens resumed in the near distance, and they sounded like they were coming fast. Our course pretty much traversed the entire mining complex. In the back was a rusty old warehouse with large sliding doors. We parked in front. This was it. The spot that the big blue X marked. Now what? I almost didn't care, having just been severely rattled. *Was I suffering from posttraumatic stress syndrome?* I understand that doctors prescribe marijuana to treat that condition these days. If I had a joint, I would have lit it. You can bet on that.

Albert got out first, then Jack, who ran around and opened my door. I was fumbling with the seat belt. If the vehicle had caught fire, I would have fried. Jack unfastened the mechanism and helped me out. We walked over and stood by Albert. He seemed unfazed by the screams of the rapidly approaching authorities and the steady drone of the copter.

It was difficult to hear what he said, "Jane, have you ever wondered about 4,3?"

Jack flung his hands in the air and underwent a few small conniptions. Then he turned and, with a pleading gesture, said, "Now?"

"Yes, Jack. The question is of extreme importance. You know that, and you know why."

I was flabbergasted. In about two minutes, we would be surrounded by a brigade of angry cops. And what does Albert do – he asks me if I've ever wondered about 4,3? It was totally and completely out of this world. But apropos, I guess, considering the present company.

"Ok, ok. Jane, just answer the question and answer it quickly." Jack looked back the way we came expecting to see the enemy rounding the corner.

I did as I was told: "Yes, I have Albert."

Jack interrupted, "Just tell him what it is!"

Which prompted Albert to warn, "Don't tell her, Jack."

So, I told him, "The three fundamentals of the Universe, Space, Time, and Matter, in different combinations, comprise the four forces. Then I began to elaborate: "Space and Time make gravity, and the weak force is . . ."

"Thank you, Jane. You have answered the question satisfactorily. I must inform you that you have the option to come with us or not. But if you do, there are certain strictures . . ."

Jack interrupted again, "She's coming!"

To which I added, "Where Jack goes, I go."

"Then, so it shall be." Albert turned his attention back to the situation at hand, "Jack, will you please help me with this door?" Albert had concluded the conversation, much to my relief. The boys cracked open the door a couple of feet. *I wondered how old Albert was. He looked to be in his early forties.* Then we slipped in without a second to spare. The Cavalry had arrived, and that was pretty much the last I saw of them.

Before us floated a big black sphere. *Floated?* It was about the size of a garage, maybe 20 something feet in diameter. And it was black. The blackest black I've ever seen. And no light seemed to reflect off it either – no glint, no sheen, nothing. It just hung there a few inches off the ground, seemingly absorbing – everything. Though, upon further inspection, the darkness within was moving like it was alive. Various gradations of darkness looked to be boiling. It was stranger than strange. An opening appeared, and a stairway extended. It, too, was black. Evidently, this was to be our ride. *Somehow, I knew it would not be Uber.*

Albert stood to one side, swept his arm in a gesture towards the entryway, and almost bowed. Like a perfect host, he said, "Shall we leave all this behind for a while?" I could hear the bullhorns bellowing outside, something about us coming out with our hands on our heads. I felt like taking a quick peak but didn't. We boarded the vehicle and did, most definitely, *leave all this behind*.

Glossary:

#2 – The Black Sphere assigned to guide the Pra'at as they rise through the various Continuum membership stages.

1.48 thousand years – The interval of adjustment between the discovery of 4,3 on Ta-ea and Caretaker contact.

4,3 – An extension of Einstein's General Theory, which posits that Space + Time = Gravity. The theory that connects the four forces and three fundamentals: Time + Matter = Weak Force; Matter + Space = Electromagnetism; and Space + Time + Matter = Strong Force. It is also known as the "Law of Connections" and is the basic requirement for induction into the "Continuum."

49,000 years – The age of the Pra'at Civilization.

Aether, the – A rarefied, ethereal substance, which fills the interstices of Space, Time, and Matter and imparts the "charge" in matter. It was long sought after by the alchemists of old and modern physicists as well. They seek to derive energy from it. So-called zero-point energy.

Aitken Basin – An impact crater on the Far side of the Moon, one of the largest in the Solar System, being 1600 miles wide and 8 miles deep. It is located towards the Lunar South Pole and can be partially seen from Earth. It is the location of the "Crystal Gardens of the Moon."

Albert – An Albert Einstein simulacrum (avatar) designed to induce Jack to "feel more at home." One of the millions of Black Spheres built by the "First-Born" and left behind to tend to those nascent civilizations, their younger siblings, whom they refused to abandon. They are also tasked with tending to the needs of their parent, the Progenitor.

Albert Einstein – A physicist known for his General and Special Theories on Relativity. The identity Albert took to interface with the humans, primarily Jack.

Aldabra Giant Tortoise, The – A species of tortoise common to the Seychelles with a lifespan of 250 years or more. They do not die from old age, but rather from shell confinement.

Alpha Particles – Are particles identical to the Helium 4 nucleus, consisting of two protons and two neutrons bound together. Produced during the process of radioactive decay, they carry little kinetic energy and have a low penetration depth. A piece of paper will stop an alpha particle.

Alysha Civil – Special Assistant to the President for National Security. "She was dark, her hair pulled tightly back, with features handsome and classical, like an ancient marble."

Ang et Setem, the – The first of the First-Born, angelic god-like humanoids.

Angel Rodriquez – A female Homeland Security Agent assigned to interrogating Janey at the Prison.

Apollo 11 – Mankind's first trip to the Moon, which occurred on July 16, 1969. Landfall lasted 2 hours and 44 minutes, and the astronauts returned with soil and rock samples.

Ay – A Pra'at honorific meaning "very respected."

Bakenkhonsu, Ay – A high Pra'at leader and Chief of the Life Sciences section at Qa'a re.

Beta Rays – High-speed electrons ejected from an unstable nucleus during the process of nuclear decay. They have moderate penetrating power and can be stopped by a sheet of aluminum.

Bethlehem Elementary School – The elementary school in Litchfield, Connecticut, where Jack was asked to leave, half involuntarily, half voluntarily, during the third grade.

Bill Cambell – An abducted UFOlogist whom Jack rescued. Bill subsequently rescued Jack after his crash.

Bose-Einstein Condensate – Also known as the Fifth State of Matter, a super-liquid. What the hull of a Black Sphere is composed of; various layers and varieties, interlaced with a ligature of degenerate matter. The substance was once popular, it being both impenetrable and permeable.

Bre-eie-ee, the – A First-Born Species that evolved in a dying solar system under hellish conditions. They look like a cross between an ant and a centaur.

Burke, Mr. – A college professor who taught Jack Algebra II. A dapper bow-tie dresser who spiced his lectures with humor, the kind that usually bombed. He was likable, good-natured, and generally popular in a respected sort of way.

C.A.R.R.S. – Cargo Advanced Automated Radiography Systems. The Homeland Security department responsible for radiation detection at the ports of entry.

Candy Land – An Ang et Setem habitat maintained within Albert as part of his basic configuration. A sky loomed above, ranging from dark gray to cream on the horizon with a scattering of pink swirling clouds. Located amidst a field of pink wheat was a fantastic, towering city, situated next to a barren, dark-red, alien terrain.

Caretaker – The generally accepted term used to designate the Black Spheres left behind by the First Born.

Cartouche – small, open-carriage-type conveyance, used for short distances at the Moon Base.

Cobalt-60 – a synthetic radioactive isotope with a half-life of 5.27 years produced artificially in nuclear reactors. A high gamma-ray emitter, used for medical equipment sterilization and radiotherapy. Also, a power source for "Neufield" type anomalies.

Continuum of Species – That select group of civilizations who have independently acquired the Theory of 4,3.; and thereby gained membership. Their purpose – to guide the younger races once they have been inducted. One problem, though, they all left our Cosmos.

Crystal Gardens of the Moon, the – Huge zircons and amethysts that grow within certain underground lunar magma domes. One of the premier tourist attractions of the Solar System.

D.N.D.O. – Domestic Nuclear Detection Office. A Homeland Security Department that manages the response to radiological and nuclear threats.

D.S.S.I.H.E.I. – Department of Standards and Specifications for the Implementation of Humane Enhanced Interrogations. A division of good ole Interrogation U.

Dark Energy – a rather ubiquitous instrumentality, believed to be accelerating the expansion of the Universe.

DNA methylation – The process whereby epigenetic or environmental factors diminish a gene's effectiveness and even to switch off. A genetic feedback mechanism that operates contrary to random natural selection.

E.I.A.G.R. – The Erhart Institute for Advanced Gravitic Research. The institute, founded by Winston Erhart III to unravel the secrets of gravity.

Edgar Rice Burroughs – A very prolific early 20th Century author of adventure and science fantasy, best known for Tarzan.

Ernesto Cavalierro – A debonair, well-tailored, Italian style, FBI agent. He transported Janie to the Bridgeport Homeland Security Office.

Ester Jane Riley – "The girl next door, really. She lives on the farm down the road. Awesomely typical, she doesn't need unnatural embellishment. Brown hair, brown eyes, 5'-7", healthy face and body." She is a registered nurse at Yale-New Haven Hospital, their Nuclear Medicine Division, and life-partner to Jack.

Ester Riley – Janey's mother. Owns and operates a horse farm in Litchfield, CT, down the road from the Neufield farm.

Fifth Level Technology – The science that deals with the extraction of energy from the Aether. Only one drawback, it weakens the surrounding fabric of Space-Time.

First-Born, the – A term that refers to members of the Continuum. Originally, the phrase was applied to those first civilizations to arise in the Universe. The oldest is the Ang et Setem at 2.37 billion years. Currently, there are several thousand species that qualify as members.

First Observer, the – A lower-level First-Born whose proclivity it was to monitor. A collective Presence originally of the Tan Teen race, and the first to observe the breaches in the Progenitor's outer husk.

Fox-O gene – known as the immortality gene. Regulates metabolism, stress tolerance, cell maintenance, and possibly lifespan.

Freeman, Private, J. – a tall, dark guard, "a real mean mutha' assigned to guard Janey. Carried a large side-arm and dressed in camos.

Frieda Gunther – head nurse on Janey's floor at Yale-New Haven Hospital. A nurse with bad knees, "there's nothing worse."

Gamma Rays – Electromagnetic radiation emitted during radioactive decay. They consist of high-speed photons and are shielded by large quantities of mass, except in the case of graphene, a lightweight form of graphite, which converts the energy to current where it is stored in its crystalline structure. Used on 4,3 type conveyances.

Gray Conduits – The vessels that interconnect locations within the space edifice that is Albert. They are usually cloaked internally with a gray effluvium. Their purpose is to provide life-support and to shield the internal pedestrians from an otherwise disconcerting view. Within these passages, Space is compressed, such that "one walks slow but moves fast."

Hall of Immortality, the – A section of Qa'a Re, the Moon Base, specializing in life extension.

Hubert Riley – Janey's father who owned and operated the local hardware store in Litchfield, CT. "A real one-man operation."

Hull, the – Usually refers to the exterior shell of a Black Sphere. Composed of a Bose-Einstein Condensate, an unusually deep, dark blackness, seemingly absorbent of all light and energy. Upon closer examination, the blackness writhes with movement, displaying the occasional streak of color. Albert's hull is 1198′ thick.

Hydra, the – A small aquatic animal that "looks like an octopus on a stick." Due to their genetic make-up, particularly the Fox-O gene, the organism simply does not age.

Israel Santiago, Special Agent – A Homeland Security Agent, 5'-5 or 6, Latin looking, olive complexioned, dark curly hair, neatly groomed, who tends to wear oversized suits.

J.T.T.F.T.R.C. – Joint Terrorist Task Force Threat Response Center. A partnership between various Federal, State, and Local law enforcement agencies working against terrorism.

Jack Neufield – The discoverer of the theory – "4,3", and the builder of the "Neufield Anomaly," with a little help from his friends. "A generous 5'-9", fair complexion and hair, normal build, and not handsome, not ugly – somewhere in between. "The big sculptor in the sky had a dull chisel when he made me."

J. Archer – Jack's "wide" guard at the Prison. The J. stands for Jay.

Jimmy Dolan – "Donut Dolan," a hospital security guard with a proclivity for rotund pastry. Friend to Janey.

John Taylor, General – Stationed at the Saratoga Springs Air Force Base in New York State. He was one of the first to track the "Neufield Anomaly" as it passed through the Earth's atmosphere.

Kaiu – A Ta-ean form of coffee.

Khayu – A long-limbed primate from the Ta-ean equatorial regions.

Kheperkheprure, Ay – An esteemed Pra'at leader on the Qa'a Re base. One of the initial greeters of Jack and Albert.

Ky – Pra'at honorific meaning – noted artist.

Litchfield, Connecticut – "A small town in a small state." Located in the Northwest corner of the state, known for its picturesque hills. Litchfield has a permanent population of 1232 and a temporary population (the summer people) of 8,466. It is one of the oldest towns in Connecticut, incorporated in 1719. Called the Beverly Hills of the East, famous people such as Marilyn Monroe once lived there, and of course, Jack Neufield.

Mike (Moon) Mullens – "The Boomer Groomer." The Uber driver who gave Jack a ride to Prison. He also conducts a dog grooming business on the side.

Milky Way Galaxy – Our home galaxy, 13.789 billion years old, and one of 363.239 billion others in our Universe.

Miss Murphy – Jack's home-school liberal arts tutor, and former second-grade teacher. "Short, 5'-1 or 2, cute round face, bright dark eyes, brunette hair flipped at the shoulders."

Moon, the – A small planetoid orbiting the Earth at a distance of 240,000 miles on average. Its orbital period is 27 days and is tidally locked, in that the same surface is always facing the Earth. It is the location of the Pra'at's largest extra-terrestrial base.

Mother, the – An omniscient Presence within the Aether, directing the Manifolds, and causing the genesis of Universes. She maintains communications through the threads of Space-Time, which the First-Born learned to tap.

Mr. McEvey – A physics teacher at the local college, hired to tutor Jack in science and math. "50 something, thin, 5-10ish, and dressed in blah clothes, except for his two-toned saddle shoes. Also, the simulacrum that was assumed by #2.

Neufield Anomaly, the – What the Military calls the anti-gravity conveyance that Jack and company built.

Nicolo Tesla – An early experimenter with electromagnetism. Invented the electric motor, wireless communication, and popularized alternating current.

O.B.I.M. – Office of Biometric Identity Management. Homeland Security Department that stores fingerprints, facial recognition, watch lists, etc.

Oliver Johansen – a hefty, rather bumbling, hospital security guard. One half of the duo known as Laurel and Hardy.

Olympus Mons – a mountain on Mars believed to be the tallest in the Solar System.

Others, the – A malevolent entity or awareness responsible for the attempt to destroy all life in our Universe; by drilling 1.27 x 10^7 tunnels in the Great Barrier and injecting Dark and Phantom Energy.

Paul Tanaka, Major – Air Force Major in charge of the aftermath and the removal of the contents of the Neufield farm.

Phantom Energy – a pernicious form of dark energy that causes a decrease in the Universal density, thereby accelerating the cosmic expansion. Eventually, the injection of this "substance" will result in "The Big Rip," the situation whereby every atom is eventually ripped apart.

Pra'at – inhabitants of Ta-ea comprising three separate species; the Qe'ma u, the Sek hem're, and the Rams'su.

Prisoner # 11357-042 – Janey's official designation at the Correctional Institute.

Prisoner # 63702-043 – Jack's official number at The Correctional Institute – Danbury.

Progenitor, the – Our home Universe, the parent of us all. It was reasoned that; since the whole cannot be less than the sum of its parts, our Universe is a sentient and aware being. One whom the First-Born learned to communicate with.

Qa'a Re – Huge underground Pra'at complex, comprised of many levels and several million square feet. It's located on the Far side of the Moon and has been there for over 3000 years.

Qe'ma u – The smallest of the Pra'at, 4' tall. They are the worker caste.

Ra – The yellow star that Ta-ea orbits. Somewhat larger than our Sun and 1271 light-years away.

Rams'su – The tallest and most humanesque of the Pra'at. The thinker cast. They always wear green robes embellished with yellow designs.

Robert Smolanski – A Homeland Security Agent. "Plump, with a round face, transparent hair, and a bushy mustache. A member of Janey's inner circle.

Ruitt Forest – A forest near Black Tale Mountain in Colorado.

S.A.V.E.R. – System for Assessments and Validation for Emerging Responders Program. A Homeland Security Program to assist emergency responders in making procurement decisions. Robert Smolanski's former workplace, but he didn't save the taxpayers any money, "What are they going to do, doc my pay $200 million."

Sek hem're – The mid-sized Pra'at caste. They are the enablers and implement the thoughts and policies of the Rams'su.

Sekhem Shedwast – a dish served in Pra'at restaurants that "tastes like chicken".

Space – One of the three fundamental entities comprising the Universe. Composed of many different units called spaceons, which interact with the chronomes of time.

Springz – A lightweight, z-shaped spring-shoe employing novel front and rear springs designed to capture, store, and release the user's impact energy, while emulating the three basic foot movements; heel impact, roll-over, and metatarsal thrust. They were Jack's main source of remuneration. See US Patent # 5701685A.

Stan Livingston – tall, somewhat vacuous, hospital security guard who was once a classmate of Jane's. The other half of the Laurel and Hardy duo.

Stella Wjud-something-ski – a matron at the Correctional institute – Danbury. Janey's special jailer.

Ta-ea – Homeworld of the Pra'at, 1271 lights years away, but on the same spiral arm as the Sun. The fourth planet from Ra, cloudy, larger than Earth with three moons – one red, two gray.

The Sedgewick Manor – A Tudor mansion compound that served as a CIA safe house in Pleasantville N.Y. Site of the Neufield Anomaly "Big Pow Wows."

Thutmosis, Ky – A high Pra'at leader, a Legate of the Arts. Also, a noted sculptor, specializing in the human, female form.

Time – A specific entity with structure, created at the birth of a Universe. It flows with the expansion of Space, though at unequal rates in different places, and is composed of many discrete integrals called chronomes, which primarily interact with Space to cause gravity.

Turriilopsis Dohrnii – Also known as the immortal jellyfish. In times of adversity, it reverse-ages to the polyp stage and then plants itself back on the seabed.

Victor McCluskie, Special Agent in Charge – "A tough hombre who probably doted big time on his granddaughter." One of the initial interrogators of Jane Riley.

Winston Erhart III, Sandy – Blond hair, parted in the middle, forty-ish, craggy face with cleft cheeks, and generally handsome. An ex-surfer on a spiritual quest to define gravity. The founder of E.I.A.G.R. – the Erhart Institute for Advanced Gravitic Research.

Yale New Haven Hospital – A hospital located in New Haven, Connecticut, and considered one of the best in the country. Workplace of Janey.

Zhukoysky Crater – A crater on the Far side of the Moon 721 miles from the Aitken Basin.

Appendix: The Law of Connections: Mathematical Proof

Symbols: U = Universe, S = Space, T = Time, M = Matter

WF = weak force, EM = electromagnetism, G = gravity, SF = strong force

Given: The Universe is comprised of Space, Time, and Matter. (What has been detected, not theorized.) *Note: Matter = Energy; as per Einstein

$$U = S+T+M$$

Given: $S + T = G$ Einstein's General Theory

$S + M = EM$ (electrons traversing through Space)

$T + M = WF$ (particles released periodically)

$S + T + M = SF$ (all three make the strongest force)

$3! = 4$ (Factorial definition; 3! Yields 6 permutations and 4 combinations of the integers: 1, 2, and 3.)

$3 \bullet 2 \bullet 1 \rightarrow 4$ combinations

And $1 + 1 + 1 + 1 = 4$ combinations

$\therefore 3 \bullet 2 \bullet 1 \rightarrow (1,2) + (1,3) + (2,3) + (1,2,3)$

By substitution $\therefore$ $STM \rightarrow SF+WF+EM+G$

Or: $SF + WF + EM + G = STM$

$[SF + WF + EM + G] \div M = [STM] \div M$ (divide both sides by M)

$MST/M + MT/M + SM/M + ST/M = STM/M$

$\therefore \cancel{M}ST/\cancel{M} + \cancel{M}T/\cancel{M} + S\cancel{M}/\cancel{M} + ST/M = ST\cancel{M}/\cancel{M}$ (M cancels where possible)

$ST + T + S + ST/M = ST$

$S + T + [TS - ST] = -ST/M$ rearranging and since TS – ST = 0

Multiplying both sides by M:

$S (M) + T (M) = (-ST/\cancel{M)}\ (\cancel{M)}$

$SM + TM = -ST$

$\downarrow \quad \downarrow \quad \downarrow$

$\therefore \quad EM + WF = -G$

Therefore, electromagnetism plus the weak force equals negative gravity.

We sincerely hope you enjoyed this, the first book of the **"Fourth Level Series."** Currently, book two – **"The Emergence"** and book three – **"First Contact"** are available at the author's website – marinerpezza.com. Please join us on our journey to the Fourth Level, spread the word, and take part in the transition!

Thanks, most cordially, your humble servants,

Mariner Pezza and Cheryl E. Kemeny

Made in the USA
Middletown, DE
04 April 2022

63566628R00255